FOOL'S GAME

It's his game. His rules. Are you ready to begin?

STEPHANIE MAY

Fool's Game

© Stephanie May 2022

Cover design by Nada Backovic

Photographs by Arcangel Images and iStock

Internal design by Impressum, Newcastle NSW

www.impressum.com.au

A catalogue record for this book is available from the National Library of Australia

National Library of Australia Cataloguing-in-Publication entry

Author: May, Stephanie

Title: Fools Game / Stephanie May

ISBN: 978-1-922588-21-0 (print)

978-1-922588-22-7 (ebook)

IMPRESSUM

Dedicated to Edward Raymond May.

My father.

It was all for you.

PROLOGUE

THERE ARE SOME THINGS in life a man never forgets. His first kiss, his first car, the first time he fucks, the birth of his first child ... experiences indelibly etched into a guy's mind.

I don't know whether (even in my present condition) I believe in fate. I never used to, but in a way fate releases me from the guilt and sense of failure I feel. God, for instance, is a ubiquitous symbol resembling the good in life, and Satan is who we blame for every fucked-up thing that goes wrong.

But what happens when you're a good person who constantly gets crapped on? What happens when you're a narcissistic arsehole who, in a drunken stupor, finds a lotto ticket on the ground and hits the jackpot? What or who the hell do you chalk it up to?

That's why I would like to believe in fate – the idea of it, at least. Fate is Switzerland in the war of life: neither good nor bad – it just is what it fucking is. Fate cannot be blamed for tipping the justice scales in one direction or the other. It's without prejudice.

Some dates are predetermined whether you like it or not. Our birth date, the day we die. They're already chiselled next to our names; I know that for a fact.

So, it is with precise clarity I can tell you the exact day, location, and what I was consuming at the time my life was turned upside down and inside out, or as I like to call it: the day that sparked the beginning of the end. Although at the time I could never have foreseen how this chapter of my life would unfold, had I known, I would never have picked up the goddamn telephone.

CHAPTER ONE

MY SERVING OF French toast sat floating in a pool of maple syrup and melted vanilla ice cream. Like I gave a damn about calories; my weight and health were no longer a concern to me. Living the simple life was all I had on my mind. Mostly.

My wife had made us breakfast before ducking out the sliding glass door to attend to a day's worth of gardening. She'd left me in 'peace' to read *The Sunday Telegraph*. But as I turned the front page, I spied an article about a middle-aged man who was on trial for the brutal murder of a young boy. In the dead of night, high on drugs, he had 'allegedly' snatched the young boy from a campsite in Lithgow and taken him to a nearby creek. He had 'allegedly' sodomised the boy before strangling him, then weighed the body down with a flat tyre some campers had discarded. I closed my eyes, nostrils flaring. Abbie … I took a deep, cleansing breath and opened my eyes, gritting my teeth.

My eyes settled on the date of the newspaper: 2nd December 1984. It was approaching her anniversary—

'You're never going to enjoy retirement if you're still on the job.'

I glanced up as Ava peered at the newspaper article. So engrossed in painful memories, I hadn't heard the glass door leading to the backyard open, nor smelled the fresh earth lingering on her gloves. My German shepherd, Bogart, stood at the door, peering in and sniffing as if to gauge my mood.

Folding the paper in half and placing it on the table, I pushed back my chair and pulled my wife onto my lap. 'How long you been standing there?'

She smiled in the same lopsided way she had ever since the day I'd met her in Gardenia Café in Toongabbie decades ago. Her brown hair, now laced with strips of silver, spilled out under her white sun hat. Her hazel eyes penetrated mine to see what was really going on. We'd been together longer than a murderer's prison stretch; I knew her well enough to know what she was thinking. Or so I thought at the time.

'Long enough to know you're never going to enjoy your well-deserved retirement if you keep reading about how bad the world really is.'

As I leaned up to kiss her, the phone rang. An inch away from my lips, her head turned to our wall phone near the kitchen archway.

'I'll get it.' She climbed off my lap, her blue gardening dress swaying as she moved to answer the call. 'Probably Hayley,' she said, removing her dirty gloves.

How I wish it had been our daughter.

'Hello?' Ava's sweet voice hadn't lost its flavour over the years. 'Mm-hmm.' She fingered the cord attached to the earpiece as her eyes darted to mine. Worry lines marred her forehead, as if she was contemplating telling me who was on the phone.

Ava turned her back to me and whispered something into the receiver. Her back expanded on a deep sigh. She turned to me, hand outstretched, offering the phone.

'Who is it?' I pushed my chair away using the backs of my legs and stood up. Ava's right eyebrow shot north, as if I was supposed to know who it was.

Frowning, I held the receiver to my ear. 'Hello?'

'Eddy!' Mitchell O'Brien's voice boomed from the other end. Now my wife's apprehension at giving me the phone was as clear as water.

My mouth creased into a smile. 'O'Brien, it's good to hear your voice, mate. What can I do for you on this fine Sunday morning?'

'How does retirement suit ya, pal?' Mitchell O'Brien was not that much younger than me, but he showed no signs of slowing down. Retirement to a guy like O'Brien would be death disguised as TV guides and bingo nights.

'About as agreeable as a cat in the bathtub.'

Ava walked away, adjusting her hat before exiting the glass door and slamming it shut. I watched her shove her gloves back on as she trod across the luscious lawn, Bogart at her heels.

O'Brien chuckled; a kind of chuckle so clearly forced it sounded like a choked-up kookaburra.

'Listen ... I hate to bother you like this, but there's been an incident.'

If I told you my heart didn't kick up a notch at O'Brien's enticing words, I'd be a fucking liar.

I looked through the wide double doors as Ava, trowel in hand, walked towards the flowering azaleas she'd planted. Pink, yellow and purple shrubs dominated our backyard, emitting sweet perfumes.

'What kind of incident?'

'It's a head-scratcher, and we could use a man of your expertise – if you're not too busy?'

On her knees, Ava set to work in the garden. The sun hammered down even though it hadn't yet reached eight in the morning. The cloudless sky promised a brilliant day – little did I know it was a scene of deceptive bliss.

'What happened, O'Brien?'

'It's like a mystifying puzzle.'

Inhaling, I closed my eyes, picturing sirens blazing, police tape, cameras flashing, scribbling ideas on notepads. Being a cop gives a certain thrill you cannot obtain even on the best theme park ride. 'I'm retired, O'Brien. Remember?'

He scoffed. 'Yeah … it's been, what – six – seven months now, right?'

'Something like that.' I knew damn well it had been one hundred and ninety-seven days since I'd handed in my badge. One doesn't forget saying goodbye to their most treasured possession.

'Can you honestly tell me you don't miss it?'

I opened my eyes and glanced outside once more. My focus brightened as the haze surrounding my mind dissipated, and the excitement racing through my aged body dwindled when I pictured my wife's reaction. 'What about Ava?'

'What about her?'

'About how she'd feel if I took on another case.'

'That's just it, my friend. You're retired now, which means no official investigating, pal. If Davies finds out … All I am asking for is some insight. No guns, no licence, no badge – nothing to tie you to us, got it? You'll be like a fart in the aisle of a supermarket: we'll know you're there, but we can't see you. It needs to be this way. C'mon, you know the deal better than anyone.'

Of course, I knew the ramifications if my fingerprints were discovered all over this. Inadmissible evidence. The equivalent of going into a suspect's house without a search warrant. No badge meant no authority. May as well send Ava in there asking questions and expect it to hold up in court. The defence would tear our investigative process apart. We'd be labelled a laughing-stock.

'And how the hell will you explain my presence?'

'I'll give you all the clearance you'll need. It's a Barnum and Bailey Circus around here, anyway, so I doubt anyone will recognise you or ask questions.'

I continued looking at Ava's backside wiggle up and down as she dug into the soil.

'Edward?!' No-one ever called me Edward, unless I was being naughty.

I pinched the bridge of my nose. 'Sorry, yeah, I'm still here.'

'Well? Yes or no? I promise – just take a squiz at the crime scene and give me your opinion. That's all you'll have to do. Scout's honour.'

How could I resist? If Ava was my wife, then the job was my mistress. Being a homicide detective was not something that stopped once you handed in your gun and badge. It stayed with you like a shadow under the midday sun. Unseen but present, all the same. And that was something they never taught you how to deal with once you signed on for the job. It wasn't a fucking job, it was a lifestyle. Retirement was someone telling you not to be you; telling you not to breathe. I'd heard stories of cops offing themselves after retiring. The job was a drug, and once you knew your addiction would never be fed again, you sometimes saw no way out. Especially true for those who had given up on the notion of marriage and kids during their time on the force. Luckily for me, I had a family. But my addiction – my craving – had gnawed at my insides ever since I'd stepped away from who I really was. The taste of it always seemed to linger on the tip of my tongue, just enough to tease me. Every day I sat in my usual chair at the dining table and read whatever I could in the newspapers to stave off that hunger. It was about as useful as a vampire switching to a tofu diet. But it was a fix. A lousy one, but a fix, nonetheless. This phone call was like receiving news from my dealer that some grade-A shit had been delivered. And like a junkie, I told myself 'One more hit'. That would be okay, right? Just one more hit and everything would be fine ...

Stephanie May

CHAPTER TWO

'SULTANS OF SWING' by Dire Straits played over Air FM 100.7 as I pulled in behind a peacock-blue Ford Falcon on the bustling Winston Road – a place not too far from my house. I hopped out of my car as Jeremy Retmeyer (the rookie) and Mitchell O'Brien (the supervisor) came bounding over. We shook hands in a familiar manner.

'You still driving that Statesman, Matthews?' O'Brien said. 'I thought you'd trade her in for a younger model.'

Grinning, I glanced at his Fairlane. 'As opposed to that – what, aren't they payin' you enough?'

We shared a chuckle, just like old times. It was surreal to be back again, even as a one-off. Looking at the expressions on the cops' familiar faces as they walked around set my juices flowing like a wet dream.

'Wait a minute ...' O'Brien said, handing us blue shoe covers and gloves. We donned the typical crime scene attire and started up the gravel drive towards a two-storey, red-brick house plonked on an enormous property at 114 Winston Road, Emu Plains. Our soles churned the gravel driveway, which was chock-full with CSU and emergency vehicles. The sound produced a sense of guilt in me, for I had lied to Ava about what I was doing. I understood the real danger and implications of me being here. Retired detective or not, I had as much right to be here as a paedophile priest preaching the good word from a pulpit. I had given poor Ava a cock-and-bull story about going out for coffee with O'Brien, but I never had been a good liar. Especially not to her.

Our victim's front yard was straight out of a *Better Homes & Gardens* magazine, from the budding deep-red rose hedges to the manicured lawn. The officers littering the front yard stole focus away from the serenity it offered. Most appeared to be sleuthing with one another, swapping theories. Others stood in silence and sipped from Styrofoam cups of steaming coffee, looking serious as hell, while a CSU photographer took photos of the house's exterior. Best of all, no-one looked over as I walked up the stoop of the house and onto the porch.

Whoever lived here wasn't short of a quid, so the immediate thought of money being the motive trumped the top of my list as soon as we passed through the stained-glass front door.

'You haven't told me much, O'Brien,' I said as the three of us waltzed up a sweeping carpeted staircase, which led to a brightly lit hallway with an Oriental runner along the centre and spectacular works of art lining the walls by painters I wouldn't even try to pronounce. Members from the CSU were dusting for prints on a blue-and-white Ming vase, picking at the carpet with tweezers before placing fibres into small baggies. The fierce summer sun poured through from the east as it rose ever higher, illuminating the red-and-gold-patterned carpet so well it highlighted every nose hair shed by those who'd come before.

'Brace yourself,' Jeremy said, as though I had never seen a crime scene in all my years as a homicide detective.

We continued down the hallway until he stopped in front of a doorway on the left. Then, with a deep breath, Jeremy entered.

CHAPTER THREE

THE VICTIM LAY on a king-size bed against the wall directly in front of us. An invader had entered and ended this man's life in the comfort of his own home. The first thing that struck me as odd was the positioning of the corpse. The naked body of a robust man who appeared to be in his mid-forties was lying upside down: head towards us, his feet resting on the fluffy pillows. A duvet cover lay rumpled by his head, his shrivelled penis nestled amid dark, wiry pubic hair, exposed for all to see. As I moved towards the body, each step on the carpet produced a squelching sound. When I gazed down, I realised the carpet was sopping wet, as though it had rained inside the bedroom. Little air bubbles gathered around the soles of my protected shoes.

I turned to Jeremy and O'Brien, who both wore blank expressions. I focused once more on John Doe, gazing into the lifeless eyes of a dead man – as though two gemstones were deposited in his eye sockets. His face a permanent mask of terror. The throat had been slit, a circular shape of flesh carved out of his forehead, and a triangular shape sliced from his hairy chest. Missing flesh ... perhaps a trophy for the killer? But why the two different shapes? The slicing and peeling of flesh had been done post-mortem, obvious to me because of the lack of blood around the wounds.

The coup de grâce had been the slit throat, the arterial blood splatter consistent with him being alive when the killer struck. An arc of dried blood splatter adorned the wall behind the bed.

Looking over his body, I spoke to the two gentlemen behind me. 'The body positioning and cuts were made post-mortem. They're symbols of something our killer wants us to piece together, or the reason why he offed this man.'

'A trophy for the killer?' Jeremy said.

My eyes roamed over the body. His flesh was marbled purple and rigour mortis apparent; my guess was it had sped up due to the hot temperature. He could have been killed as recently as last night. 'But why the different shapes?' I mumbled, reflecting. 'Usually, a keepsake is a lock of hair or something the victim owned, like a wedding ring.'

'Ed Gein used to take trophies from his victims' bodies,' O'Brien said.

'But why a circle and a triangle? Why that specifically? And why two? Why not just take one piece of flesh? These certainly didn't cause his death; it happened after he stopped breathing.'

'When it was called in,' Jeremy began, 'his mother told Constable Jay Jacobs she found her son lying on the bed and the sink taps were turned on.'

Turning to the en suite on the right-hand side of the bedroom, I tiptoed across the soaking carpet and stood in the doorway. There lay the bare essentials of a bachelor: blue toothbrush, a half-used tube of Macleans toothpaste, Brylcreem, shampoo and conditioner, a cake of Cussons Imperial Leather soap with a short, curly black hair stuck to it, and a blue hand towel. A thin layer of dust was settled on the bottom of the bathtub; it hadn't been used for some time. Everything this man used or needed was either in the shower or on the sink.

Nothing here seemed out of the ordinary, but why would the killer have turned on the taps and walked away? Had he washed his hands to get rid of the blood and left it running without realising? Had he been interrupted halfway through washing his hands and left in a hurry? If so, who or what would have disturbed him? Drawing a mental profile in my mind told me the perpetrator seemed methodical. No broken windows or doors and so far, no witnesses. How were Hair and Fibre coming along? I had a hard time believing our perp hadn't wiped over everything after he left; I had that sense about him already. He didn't appear a sloppy, half-arsed kind of guy. O'Brien had informed me while walking up the stairs that the phone cord had also been cut. Delving into any killer's psyche was like foreplay with a virgin: you had to take your sweet time. This was only the beginning.

'Everything been photographed and dusted?' I asked, eyeing black finger-print powder on the silver knobs of the sink tap handles.

'Yep,' O'Brien confirmed. 'Even swabbed the sink drain pipe for blood. Natural for him to want to wash his bloodied hands.'

Inhaling, I looked around the en suite, trying to gauge why he'd left the water running. Or had John Doe been brushing his teeth, or shaving before the murderer struck from behind? Somehow, I didn't think so. Especially since the blue toothbrush was in a holder, and his razor placed inside the shower on a hanging wall caddy.

'Norman Colbert,' O'Brien began, 'was one wealthy son of a bitch. Bought this place in the late seventies and added extensions and artificial surroundings over the years. Owns a vineyard in the Barossa Valley, but spends his time here pissing everyone off, according to neighbours.'

I looked back at O'Brien, who held a small notepad. 'What do you mean?'

'Well,' Jeremy took over, 'if you want a list of suspects, then put aside a few hundred man-hours to interview all of them.'

'The list is as long as John Holmes's dick,' O'Brien added.

'Married?' Not that I thought so. Nothing screamed out feminine in this room, and no wedding pictures were about the house or on the nightstand. I'd already spied his bare ring finger, where a faint discolouring of skin showed where a band used to reside.

'Divorced,' O'Brien said, consulting his notepad. 'One son, a kid named Danny who lives with his mother, Catherine, née Blankley. Those two moved out of Penrith after the divorce.'

O'Brien strummed a thumb over his five o'clock shadow as I stepped back into the room, eyeing off what I could while I still had the chance. A mahogany chest of drawers stood to the left of the bed, a floor-to-ceiling window with blinds drawn took up the left side of the room, and a red cedar double-door closet, partially open, exposed pressed slacks and business suits. Feet sloshing on the carpet, I made my way over to the chest of drawers – usually a magnet for bits and bobs – and peered at the contents. Perched on the top were a couple of gold rings, a bottle of expensive cologne, even a wad of crumpled fifty-dollar notes. A hardened Kleenex, a tube of hand cream and a jar of Vaseline.

I looked back at Norman's mottled face. 'This was not motivated by money.'

However, that didn't narrow it down. My immediate thought was this was not an attack by someone who knew the victim; this was not someone Norman Colbert had fucked over with a business deal gone sour. The killer was a man with a purpose. People who had been rear-ended through hefty business deals didn't take their pound of flesh. They burned bodies, they drowned them in a river, they set houses on fire. They certainly didn't leave sink taps running.

Which meant there'd be little to no paper trails or evidence left behind to connect the dots. But I never ruled anything out. Rule number one of being a homicide detective: You just never fucking know.

If my assertions that this was not motivated by greed or revenge were correct, then what sick son of a bitch would have done this, and why?

CHAPTER FOUR

I CAME HOME THAT evening to find our daughter, Hayley, and her husband, David Warner, in the living room with their daughter, Lucy. Ava bounced the little cherub on her knee.

My granddaughter was a sight I couldn't get enough of. Having a child is the most fulfilling thing in a man's life, but when your baby (no matter how old they are, they will always be your baby) has a kid of their own ... it's like you can die peacefully, knowing you did something worthwhile during your time here on earth.

I went to peck Ava's cheek, but she turned away just as my lips connected with her flesh. Smiling for everyone's benefit, I brushed my fingers over Lucy's head, the softness of her fine hair tickling my coarse flesh.

Hayley enveloped me with a hug, and I then shook hands with David, exchanging pleasantries all the while. 'It's been too long!' and another favourite: 'How's this weather, ey?' The sort of crap no-one gives a toss about.

Lucy gave me a gummy smile and blinked several times as Ava kept bouncing her. In marriage, it's as much about telepathy as it is communication. Ava knew I'd lied. Of course she would; the only person in the world who knew me better than I knew myself was Ava. Swallowing past the knot in my throat, I also couldn't deny the fact that going back out on the field today was the first bit of genuine excitement I'd had in months. One hundred and ninety-seven days to be exact. I dared not tell Ava that, who'd practically dragged me out of the headquarters the day I retired – already planning our trip to Aruba as I put the car into gear and rolled away, watching the building behind me grow smaller and smaller in my rear-view mirror, my heart shrinking with it.

Ava had not disguised the fact that she was more than elated at having me around the house more often. In the months leading up to turning in my badge, I had cut back on work, sort of like a trial run. But it was like trying to quit cigarettes. Even if you went from twenty to ten, you spent the rest of the day thinking about the other ten. Redundant. Cold turkey was the only way.

'How's work, pumpkin?' I directed towards Hayley as I sat in my comfy recliner, leaning forward. From a father's point of view, her red dress was a little too revealing – but hey, I suppose all guys want to see their daughters in a potato sack around men (husband or no). Her brown hair cascaded down her shoulders and back. Any admirer of hers always commented on her hair. The length and sheen sure as hell didn't come from me. By now I had what Ava diplomatically called salt-and-pepper, although it was more how I like my steaks: heavier on the salt.

Hayley swept aside hair from her ear and cleared her throat. 'We've picked up a few new clients as the months have grown hotter, which is great – isn't it, Dave?'

David, dressed casually in a white polo shirt and dark jeans, ran a hand over his black hair – hair as neat as a colonel. David Warner was a horticulturist, and at only thirty, he owned his own house and business. Hayley had joined in on the admin side of things, to cut back costs on employees. Business admin was her passion, and it gave her freedom to be a full-time mother while working from home. As David waffled on about dahlias, I kept looking at Hayley as she rummaged through her handbag – pulling out bits of paper, baby wipes and a diary, until she located her lip balm. How had we created something so beautiful?

Dinner that night was grand: fettuccine lemon chicken and asparagus, and I licked the bowl afterwards, much to Ava's chagrin.

We sat around the eight-seater glass dining table and spoke about general topics that circulated in the news and everyday life. We continued shooting the breeze until Ava left to prepare dessert. At that, I took Lucy into my arms and sat back in my chair, pressing my nose into her soft-as-silk skin to breathe in that baby scent.

'Mum's pissed off, Dad,' Hayley whispered. All three of our heads turned to the direction of the kitchen where banging pots and pans ensued.

I nodded before kissing Lucy's rosy cheeks. They were as soft as an angel's kiss.

'You lied to her. Hasn't she had enough of you being out, working?'

I looked into my daughter's eyes. 'I won't do it again; I was just helping out O'Brien.'

Ava emerged from the kitchen with two bowls. She handed one to David, then to Hayley.

'Thanks!' David said, grabbing a silver spoon from the table, digging in before I'd received my bowl. Warmed pecan pie and homemade vanilla ice cream. My favourite.

Ava returned to the kitchen to collect our bowls.

Hayley leaned forward again as we watched David eat like a prisoner having his last meal. 'What happened?'

I didn't need to be asked twice, so I bent my head forward, too. 'Some rich guy was murdered in his house last night. He had chunks of flesh carved out of his body, and his throat was slit from ear-to-ear.' I did the motion with my thumb, a straight line across my throat.

David peered up from his bowl, cheeks puffed out like a chipmunk, face whiter than the ice cream dripping from his bottom lip.

Hayley picked up her spoon and cut off the tip of her pie. She was used to these dinner banters when Ava wasn't around. My wife disapproved of any such talk around the dinner table, even as the kids grew older.

'You want me to take Lucy now?' Hayley said, shovelling a spoonful of gooey pie into her mouth.

Shaking my head, I caught sight of Lucy's stroller. Hayley had parked it in the corner near our Christmas tree. On the handle was a mobile that emitted the musical equivalent of chloroform once switched to ON. Dangling from the mobile were various colourful geometric shapes, including a circle and a triangle.

'Nah, I'm not hungry for dessert tonight, darlin', ' I said, staring at the shapes.

CHAPTER FIVE

THAT NIGHT WAS hotter than John McEnroe's temper, despite the ceiling fan rotating full speed. Staring at the blades was hypnotising, giving me licence to think about Norman Colbert. Catching criminals had been all I'd known for decades. A murder would happen, and I'd solve it. I'd put the bad guys behind bars and move on, feeling like I'd made a difference in the world. It wasn't about being perceived as a hero, it was about being the best man I could be, and making sure my kids had a safe upbringing.

As Ava's snores resonated like some distant steam engine, I formed a plan – a scenario in my mind about Norman.

Robbery was out of the question: too many expensive items – not to mention the wad of cash and jewellery – left untouched. The gold rings and oil paintings. Nope. Wrong way, turn around, pal.

This wasn't a passionate murder, either, nor was it sexual. They usually go hand-in-hand, but not for Mr Colbert.

The ex-wife, Catherine, was most certainly not a suspect, despite no signs of forced entry at any doorway; same went for the windows around the perimeter. The detectives were, however, as per protocol states, following up Catherine's alibi.

It is a well-known fact most victims know their murderer. *Most*. However, I strongly doubted Mr Colbert knew his attacker, therefore it must have been a whoppin' doozy our killer told him to convince Norman to let him enter the house.

Furthermore, why flood the room? What was the significance of that? Turning my face away from the fan blades, opting to stare out of the window instead, I made a mental list of what water represented. In the Bible (not that I knew too much about it – after the things I'd seen, how could I possibly believe in God?) I knew water symbolises purification of the soul. On the other hand, it can also be seen as destructive. Noah's Ark, for example – everyone knows that story.

Perhaps the shapes held some religious significance? I would consult my books in the morning to see if I could find something useful about geometric shapes.

Sickos liked to retain something personal of their victims as a keepsake. A wedding ring, an item of clothing, a driver's licence or jewellery are typical. But then, others scrapbook clippings of newspaper articles about their crimes. Why? Because it helps them prolong, even nourish, their fantasy of their victims. Some wackos go back to the scene of the crime, reliving the incident in their mind as they stand there with a hard-on. But sometimes they can't go back. In that case, procuring a trophy is more than a requirement – it is almost a necessity to do so. Maybe to sit back in their recliner and whack off to Mrs Johnson's pantyhose as they relive their crime. Sometimes they'll gift a victim's jewellery to a girlfriend or wife, so they can see it around her neck and fantasise about the victim they'd raped or murdered. Their own little secret. That sick son of a bitch Ed Gein, who'd died earlier in the year, kept face masks from his victims, and crafted lampshades out of human flesh, going so far as eating some of his victims. Was that a possibility here? Was this a late-night crispy snack of human flesh and sea salt in front of the TV for our killer? Maybe we had an Ed Gein copycat killer on our hands?

One clear thought I had, though, was that this was a staged murder scene, as though the bedroom were the stage and we, the police, were the audience, witnessing a sort of act. Maybe the guy thought of himself as a modern-day artist?

Ava rolled over to face me, interrupting my line of thought. Glad for the distraction, I placed my arm around her waist and kissed her damp forehead. She was always my tonic, even when she didn't know it. She had deigned to speak to me during the evening while Hayley and David were still here, but it had not been nearly as light-hearted as the night before when, both tipsy on red wine, we'd passed out on the couch while watching *Casablanca* – something we hadn't done in years.

Ava resumed snoring, and after another sleepless hour passed, I slipped out of bed to retrieve my joggers and an old sweatsuit I used for lazing about the house. I pulled the bedroom door closed just enough so it touched the jamb, and tiptoed downstairs. That was the easy part; the hard part would be suppressing the excited yelps from Bogart once he saw his blue leash dangling from my hand. I kept it on a key hook next to the back door that led onto the patio.

I'd built Bogart a massive kennel years back, and in the moon's silvery hue, I could see his muzzle sticking out of the arched entrance. I'd named his shack 'Rick's', and had painted the name over the archway. (If you don't know what 'Rick's' refers to, then you need to watch more classic black-and-white movies.) As soon as I unlatched the back door, his head raised sharply. I had to do this in a hurry, so he knew it was me before he sprinted out. I'd had a complaint from the neighbours once before about Bogart's barking. It was said light-heartedly, but I knew better than to piss off my neighbours – especially the old battle-axe next door, Mrs Murphy, who had a face like a dropped meat pie. I'd seen a few homicides result from neighbourly disputes. It always started off small – maybe the hedges growing over someone's precious fence – next minute I'd be called to a scene where some poor bastard had a meat cleaver protruding from his neck. Oh yeah, always watch out for Johnny-Boy next door. That's rule number two.

Bogart and I ended up walking for over an hour, without even realising until we walked through the front door and I saw the green neon light on the microwave read 04:58.

Of course, theories about the Norman Colbert case kept swirling in my mind. I hadn't conjured any more theories on the walk, but from what I remember, it was a pleasant night. Humid, but there was something peaceful about strolling around while everyone else slept. Walking in and out of the shadows of streetlamps, having the pavements to ourselves. Bogart sure loved it; he watered every post we came across.

However, as I crept up the carpeted staircase, it struck me that I couldn't go back to sleep now – not because it was too hot, but because a part of me had awoken again. As bad as it sounded, I could come home from spending hours with a mangled corpse, and then sleep as soon as my head hit the pillow. My brain was like a flashlight: either full beam or not at all; it was a switch I could usually turn on and off. As a homicide detective I had to, otherwise it would've sent me gaga. But being on the scene again, seeing the familiar faces and being thrust back into the action had been like a shot of pure adrenaline.

And foolishly, I told myself that was that; I would conduct research on religious symbols in the morning and then pass on what I found to Jeremy Retmeyer and Mitchell O'Brien. Afterwards, I'd make a day of it with my sweetheart. Pack a picnic, perhaps. The opportunities were endless, but it'd put me back into her good books. Yeah ... I reckoned that was a pretty neat idea. Climbing back into bed as stealthily as a diamond thief, I held Ava. It felt good holding the one I loved – even after thirty-eight years of marriage. She was all I reached for during stressful times, but even in her sleep, Ava turned away from me.

Stephanie May

CHAPTER SIX

NOT LONG AFTER sunrise, I heard Ava call up to me from below: 'Breakfast is ready!'

My eyelids flickered; my nostrils were like a bloodhound for food, especially when it was as fine as Ava's cooking. I rolled onto my back, feeling the warm sunlight infiltrating the windows before I'd even opened my eyes. The air, redolent of crispy bacon and eggs, wafted up the staircase before consciousness had fully tackled me. Smiling, I thought about things I could pack into our family picnic basket, and where we could venture to on this fine summer's day. Bogart would enjoy the change of scenery, too.

A retired man has no need to change clothes before going to breakfast. Ava couldn't stand eating in her pyjamas, though.

Yawning, I descended the stairs to see Bogart's black nose pressed against the door, tail wagging.

'Morning,' I said to Ava, clamping my hands on her shoulders from behind before kissing the back of her head.

'Morning, sleepyhead.' She threw me a lopsided smile over her shoulder before taking my plate over to the table. A glass of freshly squeezed orange juice waited for me – no doubt the Valencia oranges came from our backyard (Ava's idea to plant them, of course). *The Daily Telegraph* beckoned me beside my knife and fork.

'Now eat,' she said.

Grabbing a piece of buttered toast, I glanced at the empty table. 'Not joining me?'

'I have errands to run.'

A wave of disappointment washed over me. 'How long are you going out for?'

'Mmm, not too long. I'm meeting Hayley for a coffee at Café Olé, and then I'll pick up prescription medication.'

'But you'll be back within about two hours?'

She emerged from the archway, eyeing me. 'Why do you ask? Planning to invite a harem of women over while I'm gone?'

'Little lady, my knees wouldn't be able to keep up with their demands.' She gave a close-lipped grin while shaking her head. 'I won't be doing much except maybe reading a book.'

'That sounds nice; I'm still reading *The Woman in Black*. Jeepers, that's giving me nightmares.'

Laughing, I grabbed the salt shaker. I always did prefer more salt than pepper. 'Well, dear, as long as you're back in a few hours ...'

'Why?'

'Just do as I say and no-one will get hurt.'

She wiped down the stove with a wet cloth and mumbled something as I picked up today's newspaper. Our killer had received instant overnight fame. Would he be poring over this exact segment I was reading at this very moment?

When Ava deliberately coughed beside me, I lowered the paper and peered into her disapproving eyes. 'I'm sorry, love – what did you say?'

Ava sighed and looked from the paper back to me. She turned around, shaking her head.

Rising fast, I almost tipped over my chair. 'No, tell me – what did you say?'

She turned to me as I reached her at the bottom of our staircase. 'I said, would you like to do something today – is that why you're asking about when I'll be back?'

I grabbed her hands. 'Don't be mad.'

She gazed into my eyes, her mouth downturned. 'I'm still waiting for Aruba.'

'I know. Soon.'

Her eyebrows furrowed. 'I'm still waiting to spend quality time with the man I married – the one who is now retired.'

'I still kept the handcuffs, little lady; *don't* make me use 'em.'

She grinned. 'Wouldn't be the first time.'

I smacked her on the rear and she ducked away, giggling as she walked up the stairs. No, it certainly would not have been the first time. And as I recall, she'd rather enjoyed it. Especially the role play, which began all those decades ago when I had my police uniform. God, she used to go crazy over that uniform, but once I was promoted, my days on the beat or doing highway patrol came to an end. Before long, Ava was ironing out my black pants to go with my black jacket and matching tie. It also meant less time at home, and certainly less time for role play. But by God, I still have those memories stored.

As she entered our bedroom, I pictured us as the teenage lovebirds who'd met at Gardenia Café back in the '30s, rather than a pair of old fuddy-duddies now in their sixties.

By the time Ava had got ready and now stood in her summer dress at the front door, I'd devoured my breakfast and read most of the newspaper. I walked over and kissed Ava's cheek before she left.

As Ava reversed out of the driveway, I hurried to the back door and let Bogart in. 'Don't tell Mum,' I warned him as he bounded through the door, almost knocking over a lamp on a table beside the couch. Peering up at the Windex-blue sky, I shook my head and closed the door. Then I walked to the refrigerator and swung the door open, inspecting its innards: a punnet of strawberries, a packet of Don ham, Coon cheese slices, Hellman's mayonnaise, butter, and English mustard. I yanked open the fruit-and-veggie drawer and retrieved a bunch of vine-ripened tomatoes. This was a no-brainer: I'd make us a stack of ham, cheese and tomato sandwiches, and bring the punnet of straw-berries. I also grabbed a block of Cadbury's hazelnut chocolate that lay at the back, unopened. Just as I turned it over to check the expiry date, the telephone rang. Before the refrigerator door had closed, I'd scooted over to the phone.

'Hello, this is the Matthews' residence.'

'Eddy, it's me.' Why do people bloody say that?

Frowning, I tried to place the male caller. Then it dawned: Retmeyer.

'Jeremy?'

'Yeah. Mitch asked me to call you.' My heartbeat hastened at his flat tone. He'd never once called me at my house. 'There's been another one. And he thinks you might want to see this ...'

CHAPTER SEVEN

IAN MCLAUGHLIN LIVED in a block of units in Kingswood, facing the Great Western Highway. The entire apartment complex emitted a sickly smell of greasy takeout, and was the kind of place that made you want to get a tetanus shot after leaving. Colourful graffiti adorned the brown-brick exterior, and the garbage bins overflowed with sanitary pads, soiled nappies and rotting garden vegetation. The flies were having a field day. It was obvious to anyone with logic that no-one involved in politics or any sort of socially upstanding position would emerge from this area. Harsh? Yes. True? Also, yes.

As I entered the victim's bedroom, the first thing that struck me was a dead dog – its throat slit – as was the upside-down body of Ian, which lay beside Fido on a flimsy mattress, his cloudy eyes peering upward in eternal prayer. His identification had been verified against the photo on his NSW driver's licence, found in his faded black leather wallet on his cluttered nightstand.

Blowflies serenaded the bloated bodies. As far as I could see, Ian didn't have any ligature marks on his wrists. A sense of dread crept deep into my ageing bones: the killer was one and the same. And that's why I had been called again. This was another staged crime scene, and there'd be more clues, more pieces of the puzzle waiting to be found. As I approached the bed, I stared at the red feather placed on Ian's pale forehead.

Jeremy and O'Brien stood by my side and informed me that Ian's girlfriend, Candice, had found him like this when she'd arrived home from work in the early morning hours. An exotic dancer at the Foxy Girls Bar in eastern Sydney, she'd told the police she had no clue who would or *could* have done this, let alone why.

According to O'Brien's summary, they were both immigrants who'd moved from Clara, Ireland, a few years prior. O'Brien said Candice, or 'Candy', was now at the Penrith Police Station in a formal interview, but this was the intel they had initially gathered.

The click of a camera caught my attention, so I turned to see an old buddy of mine, Harold Lucado, the crime scene photographer. Dressed in a navy-blue suit, he looked every inch the professional.

Harold glanced up from his camera and walked over with a smile, showcasing crooked bottom teeth. I didn't shake his gloved hand, but we had a quick, meaningless conversation about retired life. Not that he was close to my age. Far from it.

O'Brien pulled me away from Harold to whisper in my ear. 'By the way, Norman Colbert's ex-wife, Catherine … her alibi checked out.'

I could have saved them the trouble of wasting those resources. I'd've been less surprised if someone told me Elvis was alive and well, living it up on a tropical island.

'The coroner's doing the prep for Colbert's body today.'

'Something's not right,' I said.

He scoffed. 'That's a no-brainer, I mean …' He swept an arm towards Ian.

I shook my head. 'No, with Candy – or Candice – whatever. If they lived together, why is the body so far advanced that it's bloated? The decomp looks earlier than Norman Colbert's.'

'Candy admitted they'd had a fight and she'd been gone for over a week. She'd been staying at a guy's house – the guy they had a fight over – and came home for the first time this morning because she couldn't stand being away any longer. Said the guy she shacked up with is a homosexual, but Ian wouldn't believe her. Got all jealous about their friendship and kicked her out.'

I walked around the bedroom but couldn't detect any other obvious clues. I searched for anything that would explain the perfectly placed red feather. A pillow. A duvet. An outrageous feather jacket, even. There was nothing. Moreover, the carpet was not damp; there were no taps left on, and no geometric-shaped pieces of flesh removed from the corpse. Yet something tickled the back of my mind. And O'Brien had obviously sensed it, too, as he was staring at me expectantly.

There was one thing that stood out in parallel with Norman Colbert's murder scene (apart from the phone cord being cut). Again, even though this placed screamed 'junkie', as I surveyed the room, I inventoried a few items worth taking, for anyone looking for a quick buck. A Sony Walkman, a Casio c-380 calculator watch, a Polaroid 660 camera, an authenticated, signed photo of Sylvester Stallone from *Rocky* ... and a gun. O'Brien explained he'd found that hidden in a sock drawer. It was already in an evidence bag. On first sight, I told the lads it looked like a Colt Cobra .38 Special – a double-action, snub-nosed revolver. With gloved hands, I opened the bag and pulled it out to check the cylinder, but six empty chambers stared back. I handed it to Jeremy to place in the bag again as I resumed inspecting. O'Brien had found an '83 Ford XE downstairs in a designated garage – the keys to it lay on the bedside table. Ian owned a Philips TV, and on top of the living room cabinet was a Milo tin full of cash. Nothing seemed to be missing. The lads would have to get Candice to come back and verify that, though.

'Any ideas, Eddy?' Jeremy said.

'Yeah, I have an idea.'

Jeremy looked up from his notepad, giving me his full attention. So did O'Brien.

'Your killer is really starting to taunt us.'

CHAPTER EIGHT

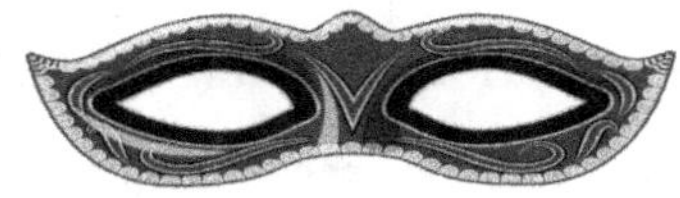

'LET'S GO OVER this again,' O'Brien said as the three of us sat in his study at his house over in Parramatta. Various photos hung about the peach-coloured walls – family portraits, his deceased schnauzer, his grandchildren. Distractions from reality. It were as though they were supposed to protect us; to watch over us as we debriefed (like we usually did) when some nutcase was goading us. All cops needed a sanctuary, and this was his.

'Eddy, no offence, but I think you've been off the job for too long,' Jeremy said. He turned to his superior, who sat behind his desk, facing us. 'Mitch, surely even you agree that to say it's the same work as our guy seems like a stretch?'

As I stared at Jeremy, I clasped my hand around a coffee mug bearing a picture of a droopy-eyed alien saying: Close Encounter of the Blurred Kind.

Jeremy Retmeyer and I had worked together for about nine months before my retirement. This pipsqueak bothered me somewhat, in the way his arrogance weighed him down. Yet, sometimes he eyed me like I was a deity he worshipped. That pissed me off, too. I never wanted to be paraded around the station like

I was J. Edgar Hoover. To me, being a homicide detective was as natural as someone serving coffee, or digging graves.

O'Brien's wife, Janice, re-entered the study with a plate of homemade chocolate chip biscuits, the aroma reminding me of my childhood. Homely cooking did that for me. Biscuits, roast dinners, meat loaf and mashed potatoes triggered happy thoughts of my childhood in Guildford.

My parents were long gone, but not a day went by when I didn't think of them and wonder if they were looking down with pride. I think any man will always miss his mother, no matter how old he gets – not that I have an Oedipus complex or anything. I'm just saying …

Taking a warm and gooey biscuit off the plate, I nodded my appreciation to Janice.

She clapped me on the shoulder. 'It's good to have you on the force again.'

I shot O'Brien an amused look.

O'Brien jerked forward, chair creaking. 'Ah, honey, he hasn't come back to the force, remember? He's helping us out this one time, then he'll slip back into the coma he's been in, right?' He completed this with a stupid grin.

'Oh. Sorry.' Janice winked at me before offering Jeremy a biscuit.

'Thank you, ma'am.'

Seeing Janice only deepened my guilt at skipping out on my picnic with Ava – not that she'd known about my plan to do so – but she'd suspected something was up. I'd felt like a real wet fart when I'd written a note, telling her I had to 'duck out for a while'. I'd stuck it on the fridge before shooing Bogart out the back again. I'd be a lying arsehole if I told you Jeremy's phone call hadn't excited me. Guilt aside, if this was our same guy, then it would mean more pieces to the puzzle, and from there we could get a clearer picture. The more times he committed an offence, the more likely it was he'd fuck up. They say no crime is a perfect crime, and that is true. There is always *something*. Even in the case of Jack the Ripper, or the Black Dahlia, there were *clues*. But clues don't always lead to an arrest, much less a conviction. If this was our guy, then we'd find the links. All we needed was time to find his errors. Rule number three: There's always *something*.

After Janice left, O'Brien continued. 'I still don't know if it is our same guy, but it seems too coincidental. That's why I brought you in, Eddy, to see what you think. Are you being serious here?'

Pushing aside the notion of taking Ava out for a romantic dinner, I looked up. 'I am deadly serious; as serious as a heart attack.'

Finishing his cup of java, O'Brien leaned forward and placed his mug on the oakwood desk. 'Why do you think there's any correlation between Norman's murder and Ian's? First guy had flesh removed from the body; Ian had a red feather – oh, and the dog.'

'I'll tell you why, because even if there had been flesh removed from Ian, it wouldn't have been the cause of death, like it isn't for Colbert – who was already dead when the cuts were made.'

O'Brien's shoulders jerked. 'But what's the connection?'

'He's putting on a performance.'

O'Brien's face scrunched up. 'A performance?'

Jeremy chewed on a biscuit as his light-brown eyes darted back and forth between us.

'He's acting something out; he's showcasing the body. The slitting of the throats isn't significant. It's not the killing that is the rush he desires, that's why you don't see any apparent enjoyment in it. No, what our killer takes pleasure from is making a *statement*. He's making an example, or a mockery, of his victims. He doesn't stab them in a fit of rage, or strangle them with his bare hands. In fact, it's the opposite. It's almost like he's calm while doing it. That's the scary part, like he's a mortician dressing up the dead for a viewing

– completely natural.'

'But again, what makes you think they're linked? There must be something.'

My eyes locked with O'Brien's. 'You must have thought so, too; otherwise, you wouldn't have had Jeremy call me.' He nodded, but knowing Mitch, he wanted me to lay my cards down. 'Three reasons – no, maybe four ...' I held up my fingers to count off. 'First, lack of motive. Robbery is ruled out, and so is passion: Norman wasn't killed by his ex; Ian wasn't killed by his girlfriend. Second, the closeness of the dates. How often do we have two bizarre murders within days of each other? Third parallel is the foreheads.'

Jeremy swallowed the remainder of his biscuit. 'Colbert had a circle cut out of his forehead, and Ian had a red feather placed over his – if it was placed at all – and you think there's a connection?'

'I do,' I said. 'And last, the upside-down bodies.'

Now that I was retired, I wasn't warming to Jeremy any more than I had during our nine months of working together. Don't get me wrong; he was a nice enough bloke, but you could tell he came from a well-to-do family, and now that I had retired, it was O'Brien getting the rim job. Jeremy was only in his late twenties, but he was as serious as Malcolm Fraser. I'd never heard him crack so much as a fart joke, and the clothes he wore were so tight-fitting it looked like he shopped at Queers R Us. I had no idea if he even had a girlfriend – or boyfriend – because he was so stiff while at work. Everything was head down, bum up, 'I've got something to prove'. Still, he was good enough to get the job done, I suppose.

My expression did not change as I turned to Jeremy. 'Did you see any feather boas in the unit?'

'His girlfriend's a stripper,' O'Brien said. 'She probably has them lying around the place. Could have them stuffed up her whatsit for all we know.'

'There is a distinction between removing flesh and placing a red feather on the forehead,' Jeremy added. 'It's like going from grievous bodily harm to a slap on the wrist.'

I held Jeremy's gaze. 'All right, Sherlock, let's go with your theory: that the feather came from Candy. Seeing as it was found on Ian's forehead *after* he died, we must then presume she was present to at least oversee the murder. And why would that be?'

'We are checking out her story,' Jeremy said.

I placed my cup on the oakwood desk, holding his gaze. 'And the dead dog? I suppose Candy did that, too?' They looked at each other, communicating silent thoughts through glances. 'Candy didn't kill their dog, nor did a red feather magically land on Ian's head.'

O'Brien stuck a pinkie in his ear and wiggled it around. 'Let's assume our guy is still on the loose, prowling. Presuming it is a male.'

'I'd say it is.'

'Right; what other connections do we have? And don't mention their foreheads.'

'Two Caucasian males. Both alone at the time of death. Both had the phone cord cut. Both with their throat slit, eyes wide open.'

'The eyes?' Jeremy said.

I turned to him. There were still some things this young blood needed to learn.

'The windows to the soul. Their eyes were open at the time of death. For all we know, the killer's face was the last thing they saw before lights out. The image of their killer burned into their retinas.'

'Any chance the killer might be gay?' O'Brien said. 'Two males, alone in the house with no forced entry ...'

'I wouldn't think so. But maybe this guy likes to work to a pattern. Most killers do. If we work out his pattern, then we'll solve it. We will pick up on his clues.'

O'Brien scratched the back of his neck and sucked in a deep breath. 'And you still think the circle and triangle mean something?'

'Possibly. Or I'm completely wrong and he's just good at fucking with us.'

CHAPTER NINE

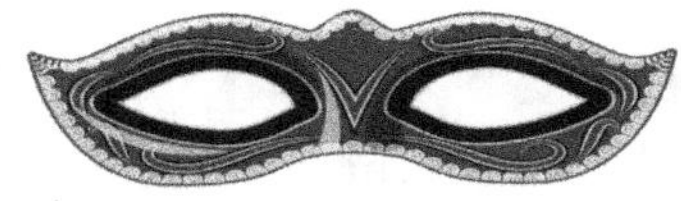

I ARRIVED HOME at around three in the afternoon, the creases in Ava's forehead like a corrugated tin roof. I tried to smooth it over by offering a kiss, but she turned away, focusing on her book.

'Where have you been?'

'Running errands, and—'

'You're a liar.' She chucked the book beside her on the couch, but it cartwheeled to the floor. When she hopped up and stormed off, I began the chase, catching her by the shoulders and turning her around.

'Get your hands off me!'

The lump in my throat became more jagged with each swallow, so I released her. The wounded look in her eyes made my heart constrict like a fist, because I was the one responsible for it. *I* was the one who'd promised to make her happy. 'I've been working on a case.'

Her eyes closed as she inhaled. 'I already know; I just wanted you to tell me yourself.' She opened her eyes, for which I was thankful, even if she glared at me.

'I'm sorry. I didn't want to upset you—'

'So, you'd rather lie to me than be straight?'

'I didn't think it'd be that big of a deal – the case, I mean – but we've got a live one on our hands.'

'This is exactly what you said with Abi—' She cupped her mouth, refraining from slipping up.

Turning away while ignoring the stab of pain, I said, 'Can we not talk about her?'

'It's coming up to the—'

'Can we drop it?' I cleared my throat and looked at her. 'This case is worse than I thought.'

Her crinkled brow smoothed out. '*I'm* your partner now – not them. They had you for the better part of your life, now it's my turn. *I'm* supposed to be by your side, to be your confidante—'

'You're my *every*thing, and you know this. I'm sorry I lied.' Wrapping my arms around her, I held her tight. 'Can you forgive me for being an arse?'

Her chuckle made me smile. 'I've been doing it all my life, haven't I?'

Pulling back, I looked at her. The years of being cooped up in the *Mad House* as we called it, had given her premature lines around her hazel eyes. Her skin was no longer the perky, spotless mask of youth; it was a showcase of the many tough years she'd gone through being married to a detective who was gone all hours of the day and night.

'Love you,' I whispered.

'Me too,' she said before kissing me. Her lips still tasted as sweet as our first kiss after our third date. I'd taken her to the drive-in to see *The Adventures of Robin Hood* and kissed her during the opening scene. We'd kissed all the way to the end credits. I think it was a good movie. I couldn't really say.

'What time is Heath coming over?' I asked. Our thirty-four-year-old son popped over about once every few months. He'd long since left the *Mad House* and had a family of his own – well, technically a partner who had a child to somebody else.

'I told him to be here at six o'clock.'

'Good.' Taking her hand, I led her up the staircase. 'I wonder if he still has the job he had last time we saw him.'

CHAPTER TEN

DINNER THAT EVENING was roast leg of lamb with mint jelly, mashed potatoes, cinnamon carrots, and a creamy cauliflower bake. God, wasn't I the luckiest man on earth?

My son had black carrier bags under his eyes, and he smelled like a footballer in a locker-room after a game. He was on his third beer of the night, and we hadn't even finished dinner. At one point, Ava and I sat back and witnessed Heath murder his meal, slicing and dicing meat, cramming it into his mouth then washing it down with beer. Ava's face over the course of dinner had turned paper-pale, and I was stumped for words, watching this imposter at my table.

'Are you sure you're not hiding anything from us, honey?' Ava asked Heath, reaching out a hand towards his. His oily hair practically screamed 'Wash me!' and remnants of tomato sauce stained his blue singlet.

'Mum! Don't ask me again!'

Ava retreated her hand and glanced at me with misty eyes.

Sitting forward, I said, 'Hey, we won't pry, son, but you know our house is always open, right?'

Heath nodded, staring at his meal, and shovelled a spoonful of mash into his gob. He washed it down with the remainder of his Tooheys Old, and went back to dicing his lamb so hard the knife screeched on the chinaware. I looked towards Ava and gave a smile that translated to *Everything will be okay*. Her return smile didn't reach her drooping eyes.

Dinner was a fairly silent affair after that. Ava, of course, made dessert: apple crumble and homemade custard, and after Heath and I had talked about cricket, the Bathurst 1000 car race, and our own opinions about the nail-biting NRL grand final between the Bulldogs and Eels back in September, conversation headed south. It became an awkward silence, the type you pray to God for an interruption. It hurt, because I would have loved to have seen my kids every day of the week, as their visits now were becoming few and far between. But having gone through it myself, leaving the nest was the passage of becoming an adult. Now I knew firsthand how my parents had felt. I understood why Mum had cried her heart out, blotting her eyes with a hanky as Dad draped a loving arm around her slumped shoulders when I sped off towards the start of my new life. That shit *hurts*.

Ava was uncharacteristically quiet after Heath's outburst, and looking back now it makes me wish I had said something more. Hell, looking back, I would have changed a helluva lot more than just saying something to Heath.

When Heath said goodbye, he actually smiled, like he'd genuinely had a good time sitting in awkward silence with the occasional Hmm and head nod from me.

When we closed the door after waving him off from the driveway, Ava rushed inside and ran upstairs. I followed and gave two knuckle-knocks on our bedroom door. 'May I come in?'

Sniffles rang out, and because she didn't say 'no', I turned the knob and opened the door to see Ava sitting on the bed with a crumpled wad of tissues in hand.

'Don't cry, love, he's a grown man—'

She shook her head. 'I-I saw needle marks on his ... his ...'

My eyes widened as she bent her head and sobbed into the tissues. Hearing those words was like a knife to the gut. I blinked in stunned silence, my thoughts and mental images trying to find a proper landing strip. Needle marks? My own son shooting up? How the hell did I oversee that? I gritted my teeth over the rising guilt. Because my mind had been otherwise occupied, that's how.

'God, no,' I whispered, walking over to hold her. 'Are you sure?'

During this decade, there had been a spike in needle use. Don't ask me why, but it seemed every decade had a defining drug trend. The sixties was marijuana; the seventies was pills, and the eighties, so far, were cocaine and needles. To be frank, a flurry of emotions arrested my heart and stomach, but mainly I felt rage. Rage that he would or *could* think of doing that to himself, but there was also an element of guilt – as in we, his parents, were to blame. Had we not been strict enough? Had the time I'd spent away from the family affected him more than I had thought possible? What had happened in my son's life that he felt he had no other option but to turn to drugs? Knowing that his father worked as a detective, too. Pretty effing ballsy, I tell you.

Ava wept into my arms. 'I d-don't ... under*stand*. Did I mollycoddle him too much? Did I—'

'Hey, hey, hey, stop that.' I rocked her back and forth, which was quite a feat considering I was full of emotion, too. To use drugs, then come here and snap at his mother. To not even have the decency to try and hide the physical evidence from us; put us through this agony. But then again, maybe he wanted us to cotton on. Of course: tonight was a cry for help. Acting like a starved POW, looking as dishevelled as a vagabond, snapping at his own mother.

'Neither one of us is to blame. He's old enough and ugly enough to take care of himself, but right now, something's going on. I promise you, little lady, I'll get to the bottom of it. I *promise*.'

CHAPTER ELEVEN

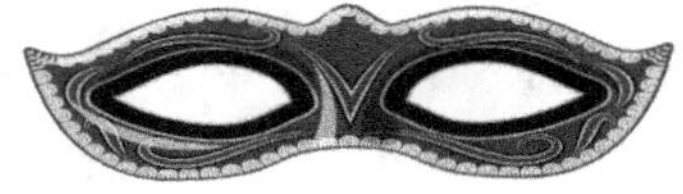

AS I MADE MY way downstairs, a sense of dread weighed on my shoulders like a steel blanket. A feeling of helplessness I was not used to. It was like seeing a drowning man and being unable to throw him a buoy to keep afloat. I could console the family of a murder victim, but I could not console my own wife. I could not protect my son. I'd had a shocking night's sleep. Judging by Ava's tossing and turning, I dare say we both did. I vowed to speak to Heath; I just did not know when. I felt like I needed to prepare myself, plus I was still livid. Saddened, yes, but also peeved. Mainly at myself. How could a parent not point the finger at themselves when their son started using needles, and God only knew what else? People don't start off injecting without ever having touched anything prior. It's going from playing with water pistols to using a semi-automatic. There are always steps beforehand. Weed is considered the gateway drug. That I could have handled more. That I could have accepted. But needles? Christ, I had no idea where he'd even get that shit; I knew some of his friends and Hayley's, too, but I couldn't pinpoint any mate of his who I would pick as a heroin dealer. I would find out, though.

Mark my words.

Bogart stood at the back door, tail wagging.

Despite my queasiness and anxiety, I could still appreciate the fact it was a marvellous summer's day. The perfect day for a picnic. I walked into the kitchen to find Ava whisking eggs in a pan of melted butter, and I kissed her temple.

'Morning,' she mumbled.

'Morning, little lady. Smells good.' I stared at the pan as she whisked away. Two slices of toast popped up to say hello. 'I'll butter.'

'No, it's fine. Please sit. The paper is on the table.'

I glanced at the dining room table where a folded paper lay next to my cutlery. I bypassed it; I didn't feel like reading just yet. I had homework to do, anyway. But before that, I walked to the back door to greet Bogart. I stepped onto the patio before venturing out, warm grass between my toes.

'Where's your ball?' I asked him, the sun heating my head.

His big brown eyes gazed up at me, his jowls pulled into a grin, and he sprinted to grab his favourite tennis ball. When he brought it back, it looked worse for wear in his slobbering mouth. I struggled with him to retrieve it, prying it from his jaws, and pegged it across the yard. While he bolted, my gaze turned to the cloudless sky. God was holding up a rich blue colour sample, saying 'What about this one?'

Looking back now, it was one of the last days where everything in my life seemed almost normal. It was one of the last days where the sun really shone for me. I wish I had taken more time to absorb it. But how was I to know? None of us can foresee what lies ahead. A simple murder had started the pull of the thread. I had been on the scene of many horrific crimes. Never had there been a time where I actually threw up, but by God, I had come close. A few occasions spring to mind. People always used to ask how could I possibly look at dead bodies for a living. 'Isn't that sick?' I gave them the old spiel I told everyone who asked: I'm the good guy, helping to put the bad guys behind bars. Someone has to do it. Someone has to stand up for society.

However, it was more than that. If I am to be completely blunt, there's a certain fascination that goes with the territory. I have always been interested in murder and serial killers, and not because I harbour sick fascinations with dead bodies, but it's the psychology of it. To me, killing for pleasure is inconceivable. But the interesting part is how some people out there think it *is* completely normal. How can someone crave plunging a knife into an innocent person's beating heart? That's what reels me in. Working out why people do this, and then sometimes, go home to their wife and kids. How can a man cut the throat of a little girl, rape her, dump her in a lake, and then go home to play Mr Family Man?

It's a concept I will never get my head around. Sometimes it plays on my mind and I see visions in my sleep of past victims I came across. I wouldn't call them nightmares as such; *visions* seems a more appropriate word. These visions sometimes weigh me down. It never leaves you, this job. Never. That's why they provide retiring officers counselling. That's why officers of the law have a high suicide rate. Every case you attend sticks with you, like burrs on a dog's coat. But some are harder to forget.

'Breakfast is ready,' Ava called through the open door.

'Thank you. I'll be in in a minute.' I hadn't realised Bogart was already beside me, waiting. I grappled with the slimy, furry tennis ball once more and threw it again before making my way back to the house, pushing the memory of Abigail from my reverie.

After demolishing the scrambled eggs on toast and fried tomatoes, I made my way to the study. I told Ava to give me an hour tops, then I'd be taking her somewhere.

I leaned against the closed door for a moment. This was my favourite room in the house. My private sanctuary: a place to gather my thoughts and find peace. Some guys have man caves with basketball hoops, a mini bar fridge, a stack of porno mags and a bottle of hand lotion. But for me, this was it. Two studded leather chairs faced a cherrywood veneer desk. On the wall behind the desk hung accolades I had accumulated during my time on the force. I never displayed them around the house. Not because Ava had told me not to (she wouldn't have) but because they belonged in my private haven. They were not to boast; rather, they were to remind me that good prevails over evil. That hard work and dedication will bring you things in life. Rewards. Recognition. Respect.

To my immediate left stood an oakwood bookcase large enough to hold hundreds of titles that I'd collected since I was a young boy. They no longer held Batman comics; instead, this was my library of the macabre. Every book written pertaining to crimes could pretty much be found on the shelves. A filing cabinet and fax machine stood against the right-hand-side corner wall, beside a large, low window that looked onto our backyard. Sometimes Bogart pressed his nose against the glass – even now there were smudge marks from his wet schnoz. Fax machines were hellish expensive, but well worth it when sending and receiving vital information that could close a case.

On the wall opposite, a corkboard faced my desk. Here I used the old-school method of pinning up pictures and crime scene photos, connecting them with thumbtacks and red string to help piece together clues. I'd kept photos of previous victims, so they faced me when I sat at my desk. A little weird, perhaps, but it was my way of never forgetting them. Their killers may have taken their lives, but these victims would not be forgotten. They would not be erased from the history books that easily. Sometimes, their pictures gave me hope. Well, they used to. I hadn't really ventured in here since my retirement – the drooping houseplant was proof of that. But now, being in here stole most of my breath and left me aching inside. It brought back a lot of memories. There is a sense of power and seniority that comes with being a detective. Hell yeah, I'll admit that. It makes a man feel worthwhile. Always useful and needed, as long as he's working on a case. I'd never felt so important in all my life.

My bookshelf loomed above me as I scanned the dusty spines, one by one. I couldn't recall any cases where geometric shapes were involved. Sometimes arseholes liked to fuck with us, leaving letters and calling cards, and cryptic messages we were meant to decipher. But actual shapes cut out of a person's body? I'd never had a case like it. Proof that there's a first time for everything, even in retirement.

My eyes rested on a book with a black jacket. White writing on the spine said *The Geometry of Art and Life*. I picked it out of its hidey-hole and blew on the cover, revealing the author's name: Matila Ghyka – second edition published in 1977 by Dover Publications. *Great, so that's step one. Next is the occult.* This was a bit far-fetched, but that's what you do at the beginning of any mystery. Cast a wide net and see what it brings back. It was better to overestimate than underachieve, especially since I had no idea what we were dealing with. Were two killings his fill? Was there another one waiting for us right now? It was semi-frustrating not being able to go into the station. All of what I heard came after a delay; however, Jeremy and Mitch promised to keep me in the loop and pass on photocopies of everything.

I took a few more steps and stopped in front of what I was looking for. The spine needed repair; I had consulted this book a time or two back in the day when I had dealt with weird sacrificial murders. I once apprehended a man who thought he was a descendant of Count Dracula, carrying on the bloodline. Again, what fascinates me is how people think this is normal. His followers would offer him their blood, then once the Drinking of Blood ceremony finished, they had one giant orgy around a pit of fire, smearing blood on people's flesh as men and women fucked each other in every hole, claiming it was all in the name of Satan.

My fingers caressed *The Satanic Bible* by Anton LaVey. Published in 1969, this book outlines the core principles of the Church of Satan. It delves into the occult, rituals, Satanism, and Satan worship. I hadn't a clue if this would help me, but it was a start. This was what casting the net was all about, and I couldn't wait to see what I hauled in.

CHAPTER TWELVE

'THE TOXICOLOGY REPORT came back,' O'Brien told me on the kitchen wall phone just before midday on the Friday. 'Nothing unusual in Norman's system, but Ian's had traces of LSD.'

The Daily Telegraph was splayed before me on the kitchen bench; I'd finished reading it after breakfast. Bogart stood beside me, wagging his tail as he looked at the fridge in anticipation. Ava was out grocery shopping before dropping into Hayley's for a cuppa.

'Eddy?'

'Yeah, I'm still here; I just don't know how significant LSD is.'

'Candy's story checked out as well. She'd been staying with a guy called Sapien, and Ian's neighbours verified the fact they hadn't seen Candy the week leading up to her boyfriend's death.'

'Was Candy banging this bloke – Sapien?'

'That's the thing, Eddy, he's gay. But that's why Ian and Candy had been arguing! Ian thought she was cheating on him, but turns out Sapien is in fact bent.'

My mind went walkabout: Two males alone in the house. Both with slit throats. The attention to their foreheads prominent in both situations. I'd found a few things in both the books I'd been reading, but they were somewhat contradictory. Water is symbolic of life, a building block we cannot survive without. It was meant to be paradoxical; was that it? Our killer having a laugh?

I hadn't found out much about red feathers. In fact, I now felt more confused than a bird who'd flown into a window. My research had left me with more questions than answers. Circles also mean life. Yet this circle was on a dead person. I wasn't giving up on the occult theory. Not yet.

'I'll call you if anything else comes up,' O'Brien said. 'I also have copies of files – as promised.'

'Cheers – take it easy.'

After hanging up, I took a moment to register the information. I still had that strange feeling that the killing part wasn't this guy's aphrodisiac. It was what he did *afterwards*. I'd read about some rapists who couldn't get hard unless the person they wanted to screw was dead. They quickly got that part out of the way, bumping off their victim so they could then really get their rocks off.

That's not what was going on here. No signs of anal penetration or seminal fluid, I'd been told after O'Brien spoke with the coroner. Not surprising; I did not believe our man was a homosexual who liked necrophilia. What were the goddamn signs pointing to?

I ascended the staircase, thinking about how I had promised Ava I'd try calling at Heath's place again while she was out. Before the afternoon picnic with Ava on the Tuesday, I had tried to catch him by surprise. But he wasn't home. We'd finished our day by catching a late-night movie. Personally, I don't enjoy going to the cinemas. Too much talking and mucking about nowadays. Give me back the drive-in any day of the week. But her wish was my command, so we ended up seeing *The Terminator*, and I have to admit, I thoroughly enjoyed it – despite the yelling and carrying on by teenagers around us.

This gave me the idea of an opportunity to speak to Heath by asking him to see the same movie with me. He'd be suspicious; not once had we ever done this as adults. When the kids were younger, of course we did things as a family. Ice skating (well, they did; I sat back and watched), ten-pin bowling, trips to Taronga Zoo, and we certainly took them to the movies. But when they got older, they preferred to go with their friends instead of being embarrassed by us old farts, and I have to admit I was okay with that. So, I'd never once asked my son or daughter if they wanted to go to the movies alone with me. They would think it was weird. But I would do it now. I was going to reconnect with my son, no matter what.

I found casual clothes, put on my shoes and left the house, yelling out goodbye to Bogart as I closed the door.

'In the Air Tonight' by Phil Collins played over Air FM as I backed out of our driveway. River Road boasted the usual sights of people out jogging or walking their dogs alongside the Nepean River. I was always slow taking off down the road; I had tended to the victim of a car and bike accident a time or two here over the years.

Heath's place wasn't too far away, about twenty minutes. He lived in Bidwill, over near Mount Druitt with his girlfriend, Lorraine 'Loz' Stein. They'd been together for the better part of three years, and she had a five-year-old son, Aaron. Her Mexican ex-boyfriend sounded like an utter prick. Didn't see his son or anything. I didn't mind that Heath had shacked up with her. He was thirty-four and knew what he wanted out of life. Or at least I thought he did. I didn't mind Lorraine, either, although I got the sense that my daughter wasn't a huge fan of her. Lorraine was a looker, and I think Hayley had caught David giving her the eye a time or two when we all got together. Ava had also commented that she wished Lorraine would dress more conservatively when she came around for dinner, but I had the sense that overall 'Loz' was a good woman. A few years younger than Heath – I think she was twenty-seven – but she seemed to have her head screwed on. And hey, all we want for our kids is to be happy and healthy, agreed?

I cut the engine, silencing Prince halfway through 'When Doves Cry'. I always parked outside their apartment complex on Albert Street.

Placing my Ray-Bans in the V of my polo shirt, I glanced around. Vigilance was second nature to me. Children cavorted on the street, barefoot, playing hopscotch. Kids were out in full swing, taking advantage of the midday sunshine. I waited for a father-and-son duo on their pushbikes to pass me before I crossed the road.

Heath's and Lorraine's cars weren't anywhere in sight, but I pressed on, hoping today would bring me luck.

I *tap-tap-tapped* on the door of Unit 14 with my index knuckle and waited. When I heard movement inside, my heart kicked up a notch. Then I heard shuffling sounds inside, like someone tidying up; paper rustling, a plastic bag moving. I rapped again, louder this time.

A minute later, Lorraine answered the door, shielding her breasts with a blanket. Her eyes widened upon seeing me and I turned away, staring at the gritty floor.

'Shit! Eddy ...' She chuckled nervously.

'Sorry to disturb you, I just wanted to know if Heath was in.'

'Oh.' She gave a giddy laugh, a little too falsetto for my taste. 'Um, no, he's not.'

I turned back to her. 'He's not?'

The rosy colour in her cheeks spread like an ink stain on fabric as she shook her head, her eyes conveying a hidden message, but what? 'No, he's helping a mate with his car.'

More movement in the background. Why the blanket around the naked body? Midday seemed an odd time to be taking a nap, and her hair was messy, but not wrapped in a towel.

She licked her bottom lip and scraped her teeth over it as she looked past me, wishing me to bugger off. Stuff it, if she chose to answer the door half-naked, then let *her* be embarrassed about it.

'When is he due back?'

She swayed from foot to foot. 'Ahh, dunno. Sorry.'

'Right. Is Aaron here? Mind if I give him a kiss from Poppy?' Aaron was not my flesh and blood, but that did not matter. Ever since Aaron met us, I had been 'Poppy' and Ava had been 'Nanny'. It was quite touching. I appreciated it more than I ever let on.

She scratched her temple with her free hand. 'Jeez, ah, he's with my mother at the moment.'

Lorraine shielded the door pretty well from me; all I could see in the background was part of the kitchen to the left. There wasn't any sign of redness in her eyes, nor could I smell smoke – weed or cigarette.

Resigning to defeat, I said, 'Well, tell Heath when you see him – ask him if he'd like to see the new *Terminator* movie with me, yeah?'

She nodded a little too enthusiastically. 'Sure, you betcha.'

I smiled once more, peering into her blue eyes. 'Great. Don't be a stranger, you hear? You should all come around to our place again soon. It's been too long.'

'Yeah, I miss Ava's cooking.'

While my brain worked a mile a minute, I laughed convincingly. I retrieved my sunnies, held onto the bridge, then flicked them out so the temples straightened. 'I'll tell her you said that.'

She chuckled.

'Okey-doke, well … I'll be seeing ya.'

Her smile expanded. 'Take care, Eddy; I'll pass on the message when Heath gets home.'

'You do that.' I put my sunnies back on. 'Bye for now.'

CHAPTER THIRTEEN

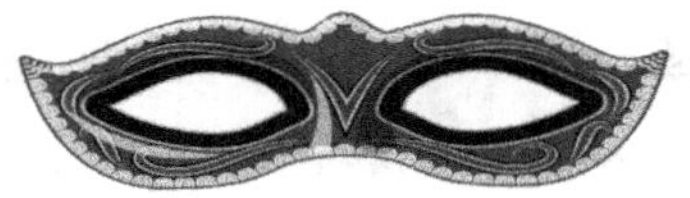

SITTING IN MY car, I ruminated on what I had seen (more accurately, what I *hadn't*). Maybe it was innocuous – maybe I'd caught Lorraine in the middle of shaving her legs or masturbating. Admittedly, I hadn't heard any other voices, but I was sure there had been movement. Someone else was in there, surely. Or was it the TV? God, my thoughts flew around like balls in a lottery machine, but instead of numbers, each had a name: Norman! Ian! Abbie! *Heath!* God, it didn't end, did it? Not even in retirement. At one point I'd decided to stay inside my Statesman to scope things out, but what good would that do? What if Loz and her 'visitor' were occupied for hours? I had a few things to tend to, anyway, like visit the lawnmower shop for one, and buy a lottery ticket, as well as visit my good mate Dan Murphy's. One car sat near the shoddy court near their block – a green Honda, paint peeling – I jotted down the licence number, just in case.

By the time I made it home, dinner was being served.

I kissed Ava on the cheek, murmuring my hello and resembling a lowland gorilla as shopping bags weighed down my arms.

'And how did Heath's go?'

I sucked in a deep breath. 'I'm sorry, little lady, but he wasn't home.'

She turned to look at me through a veil of steam rising from the potatoes she'd just poured into a colander. 'Then where have you been?'

I held up a bag from Dan Murphy's with my left arm. The beer bottles clinked together like wind chimes as I placed the bags on the bench. 'Plus, I needed that new alternator for the mower, remember?' I went to grab a beer from the fridge and restock with my new purchases.

She moved to the stove to collect the frying pan, which was a bubbling bouquet of creamy wine, herbs and garlic.

Peering into the pan, I breathed the aroma through flared nostrils. 'Smells great; what is it?'

'Veal marsala.'

'Oh, haven't had that in a while!'

She scooped half-cut potatoes onto a plate, followed by steamed veg. 'So, no luck with Heath again, huh? That's a shame.'

'Lorraine was home, though.'

Her eyes widened. 'Oh, what did she say? Was she dressed more conservatively, or does she only do that when she comes here for family dinner night?'

How could I not smirk? 'You jealous?'

She glared at me. 'Don't insult me.'

I placed my beer on the edge of the kitchen bench while she busied herself with heaping the sauce over the thin slices of veal already on the plate. 'Imagine if I'd rocked up to your parents' house wearing the things Lorraine does. Imagine your mother's face if my breasts were hanging out.'

As she wiped the plate with a cloth, making it look as presentable as possible, I wrapped my hands around her front.

'Eddy! I'm trying to serve dinner.'

'I know *I* wouldn't have cared if you'd rocked up to my parents' house with them hanging out.' I cupped her breasts. They didn't have the same perkiness as they'd once had, but hey, my plums sure as hell weren't as firm as tennis balls anymore, either.

The telephone rang.

'It had better not be those damned telemarketers again! Always at bloody dinnertime, too. Mongrels.' I walked to the wall phone as Ava carried our plates over to the dining room table. 'Matthews' residence!'

'Eddy …' O'Brien said. 'You haven't had dinner yet, have you?'

My pulse quickened at the urgency in his voice, pressing into my skin like prodding fingers. 'No, why?'

'There's been another one.'

My heart pumped faster as I straightened. 'What's dinner got to do with it?'

'Now there'll be nothing for you to throw up.'

I turned to Ava, who sat at the table, reaching for the pepper grinder. She glanced at me, expressionless. I smiled reassuringly before turning my back to her.

'Are you sure it's our guy? Do you really need me there?' God help me, I wanted him to say *yes*. I wanted him to tell me he couldn't do this without me.

'I'm not saying you *have* to come … But I just called to tell you.'

'How sure are you? What makes you think it's our same guy?'

'Perhaps you'd better see for yourself.' And that was good enough for me. I hadn't consulted Ava, but this was like following the pheromones of a seductive deity – one meant to be worshipped. My appetite for food was no longer existent – to me that was now as bland as decaffeinated tea, but this call was like flame-grilled meat dripping with juices as the fire roars, assaulting the senses and making me tingle all over.

'O'Brien, gimme the address.'

CHAPTER FOURTEEN

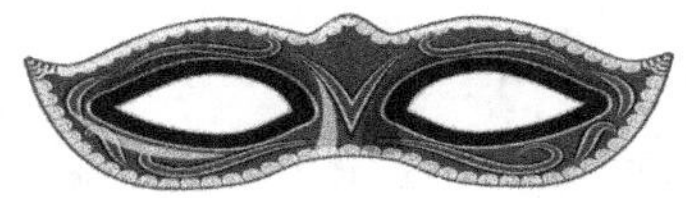

THE WOUNDED LOOK in Ava's eyes stayed with me like a flash of light remains visible long after you've closed your eyes. But what could I do after feeling that insatiable emotion I could not supplement or substitute? I didn't have to check the numbers on the house as I pulled alongside the kerb. A television crew milled about like buzzards, the driveway was cordoned off, an ambulance was parked in the driveway, and neighbours rubbernecked from every vantage point they could find. Some stood on bins to get a better view. Two white CSU vans were parked opposite where I'd pulled up. It was the scene of the latest murder: 37 Mullion Road, Kingswood.

Mitchell O'Brien hadn't relayed anything more to me over the phone, so I had no idea what I was stepping into. I paged O'Brien as soon as I opened the door to my Statesman.

Turning to my right, a tall blonde woman with a bob cut and a navy-blue two-piece suit rushed over, microphone in hand. A woman I knew well. Unfortunately.

'Eddy, can you shed some light on what has happened here tonight?'

Shit! I was supposed to be an invisible entity. I knew the ramifications of being caught. O'Brien hadn't said anything to me about there being a camera crew.

Blinding light shone in my eyes, and a video camera was poised about two inches away from my face.

'How many victims are there?'

'I'm not authorised to answer any questions at this point in time.' I shoved my palm up to the video recorder held by some beefy guy with two plump hands. 'Get that camera out of my face.'

As I sauntered off towards the latest crime scene, they followed. If it bleeds, it leads.

'Is it true drugs were involved? Was that a motive?'

'I'm not answering any questions; please stand back and let us do our job.'

Fuck. I'd used the word 'us'. I tried to quash my rising anger. I was used to these parasites by now, but this was different. I was officially retired. I could not go around throwing out words like 'our' and 'we' anymore. Everything had changed.

'Eddy!' Jeremy yelled. I looked over, squinting from the camera's light as Jeremy hurried down the driveway, past the ambulance.

When he grabbed my arm and pulled me from the mob, I felt like McCartney at a Beatles' concert.

'They've been here for about ten minutes, asking everyone they see all types of questions.'

'I'm not supposed to be seen.'

'Not much we can do now.' Jeremy led me up the front steps and into the house, slamming the door shut. Several CSU members looked at me indifferently, then went back to their job. Jeremy handed me blue booties and gloves.

'They've almost wrapped it up here.'

Snapping a glove against my wrist, I nodded once.

He led me down a hardwood hallway and to the third room on the right.

I turned through the door and faced the victim on the bed. Upside down, yet again, with his throat slit.

The medical examiner, Dr Michael Wong, conducted the preliminary exam on the body, while Mitchell O'Brien stood over him, squinting, as though searching for some miniscule thing.

O'Brien looked up and made his way over. 'Hey.'

I bobbed my head before looking at our latest unfortunate. 'What do we have?'

He took out his notepad. 'Mark Andrews. Thirty-eight years of age, married with two kids.'

'Where are they?' I asked, scanning the room. Alarm bells started tolling as I spied a wedding photo on the wall behind me, next to the door. She was pretty. Brunette with oval-shaped green eyes, standing next to a handsome man who now lay here as dead as a slab of butcher's meat.

'On vacation.'

'Who called it in, then?'

'A business associate of Mark's. Apparently, they were supposed to have a meeting, but Andrews never showed. Said he'd been calling Andrews for hours, with no response. Then he swung by. Said he heard Mark's dog barking ferociously behind the locked front door.'

'What's the guy's name?'

'The businessman?' When I nodded, he consulted his notepad. 'Eric Partridge. He's at the station giving his official statement now.' I kept glancing around as a queasy feeling settled in my stomach. 'Anyway, this guy, Eric, knocked on the neighbour's door and that's when he learned that no-one had seen Andrews in days.'

'Where's the dog?'

He squinted. 'Huh?' Then recognition. 'Oh, um, at the vet's getting looked over, I believe.'

That didn't add up to me; it didn't fit. 'What breed?'

O'Brien turned to Jeremy, who then answered.

'Um, a kelpie. Why?'

I closed my eyes as general chatter from outside filled the silence. 'They're known to be loyal.'

'Yeah …?' O'Brien's tone said he was waiting for me to elaborate.

I opened my eyes just as Michael Wong peered inside Mark's mouth. A few immediate standouts correlated with the first two victims. First, this was a white male, alone in the house. Second, the upside-down body, throat slit. Third, there was a red cloak draped at his feet near the pillows, which looked out of place, but that was just my opinion. It could very well have belonged to Mark, but this was the middle of summer in Australia – of all places. Extra layers, even at night, are about as welcome as an STD. And fourth – the obvious one – was a crown. Over Mark's head, a crown sat askew. Nothing fancy like Queen Elizabeth's, but a gold crown just the same. Another prop.

But again, no flesh taken. No trophies of the human body. Why? And the dog … I couldn't wrap my head around it.

'Why was the dog allowed to live?' I asked, facing O'Brien.

O'Brien scratched his jaw. 'Um, I guess maybe – shit, I don't know.'

'Ian's dog was killed, but it was much smaller – yes? A Maltese terrier, correct? Yet, we have a bigger dog – one more known to being loyal to his master – that is allowed to live.'

'You wanted the dog to die?'

I glared at Jeremy with a deadpan expression. 'No. But it doesn't fit. And that red cloak – another prop. What is this guy's angle? What is he trying to tell us when he's not being consistent?'

'Look at this,' Dr Wong said.

O'Brien crouched, knees cracking. 'Whaddaya got?'

We all gathered around the bed as Dr Wong lifted Mark's stiff right arm to show an engraving into the flesh. Thanks to my books, I recognised it as an ankh. The Egyptian symbol for life.

'I've seen that before,' Jeremy murmured.

'It's an ankh,' I whispered.

'That's correct,' Dr Wong said. 'The cut appears to have been made with a small carving knife. It's the sign of life and reproduction.' He looked up and spoke behind his mask. 'It's also a symbol of masculine virility. This was made post-mortem.'

'C.O.D.?' I asked, not that Blind Freddy couldn't see. But, you never know.

Dr Wong pointed to the slit throat. 'Severed trachea is my bet, but until we can get him on the slab, I cannot say for certain. There are no ligature marks. No redness around his feet or wrists, no discolouring to his lips that would indicate poison.'

'That red cloak' – I pointed to Mark's feet – 'was that over his body when it was discovered?'

Dr Wong nodded. 'I peeled it back after Forensics combed over the place. Hair and Fibre will collect it when I'm done here.'

So, he had been covered after he died. The killer had placed a crown over Mark's head, covered him with a red cloak, but allowed the dog to live. What was I not seeing?

I walked into the hallway, passing people as I went by, nodding my acknowledgement. Some I knew, most I didn't. After opening and closing the bathroom door, I crouched, inspecting. Nope.

I got up, left the room, and went to another bedroom – this one belonged to a girl. Soft-pink carpet, dog-eared poster pinned to a wardrobe of a shirtless Rob Lowe in tight jeans leaning against a jagged rock face, and friendship bracelets on a nightstand.

I repeated the same process. Crouched, and looked behind the door. Nope, not here, either.

'What are you doin' there, Eddy?' O'Brien asked.

'Tell you when I see it.' Not if, but when.

I opened another door, but was faced with linen sheets and bath towels. Definitely not this one. I travelled back up the hallway to the door before Mark Andrews' bedroom, opened and closed it. I bent down and discovered what I had been searching for; what I had known I would find.

When I opened the door again, Jeremy and O'Brien swapped frowns, then looked back at me. 'Here. He was kept in here.'

'What are you talking about?' O'Brien asked, walking inside the room, followed by Jeremy.

'This.' I crouched down as they did the same, pointing to the scratch marks on the door.

'Made by the dog – yes, so what?' Jeremy said.

'Our killer locked Fido in here while he took his time slicing and dicing.'

'That's not unusual, Eddy. C'mon, you know that.'

I turned to O'Brien. 'But why not the other dog? If you break into someone's house and you see two dogs: one chihuahua, and one German shepherd, which dog are you going to bump off first? Which one would be more of a threat?'

'The biggest one,' Jeremy said.

I snapped my fingers and pointed to his face. 'Right.'

'You can't compare a kelpie to a shepherd,' O'Brien said.

'No, but the principle is the same. You knock off your biggest contender.

Have Hair and Fibre comb this room down; maybe you'll find little bits of doggy treats on the floor. Maybe our killer lured Fido in here, shut the door, then went to have his fun without being distracted.'

'I'm still not following you,' Jeremy said.

We rose to our feet, knees cracking. I glanced around. A dark pinewood desk dominated the room. A filing cabinet, a stack of books and business magazines, and a paper shredder half-filled. Framed accolades hung about the walls.

'This is an office. Wouldn't you say it's odd to keep your dog locked up in here? Strange place, isn't it? I can guarantee you Mark Andrews did not keep his dog locked away in this nice, tidy office. Fido made these marks in recent days, but what puzzles me is why not kill this dog?'

'What would be the reason here, Eddy, then? You tell us,' O'Brien said.

Closing my eyes, I breathed in slowly. 'Because it wasn't in the script.' I breathed out before opening my eyes again.

O'Brien double-blinked, ruminating.

'Huh?' Jeremy said.

'Our guy – he's following a script or something. Maybe replicating another crime scene, doing everything by the book. He's sticking to what the director wants. Maybe there's two of them.'

O'Brien squinted while staring at the scratched panel. 'It has crossed our minds.'

That was the first I'd heard of it, but then again, I wasn't working alongside them in the office anymore. Information would be delayed, I understood that. But still …

Jeremy used a thumbnail to scratch his nose. 'Yes, we were discussing how it would explain why the victims are all males. It'd be easier with two. And I think we can rule out two females.'

'I never thought it could have been.'

Jeremy squinted. 'So he kills one dog, lets the other dog live, and instead of a red feather, it turns out to be a crown.'

'Is this a fucking Shakespeare production here, or what?' O'Brien said.

'I don't know,' I whispered. 'I don't bloody know. I'm assuming there was no forced entry?'

'You got it,' O'Brien said.

As we made our way into the bustling hallway in single file, Jeremy said, 'So, what's next?'

'You know what it means now, don't you?'

Jeremy's eyebrows knitted together. 'What?'

'It means you officially have a serial killer on your hands.'

CHAPTER FIFTEEN

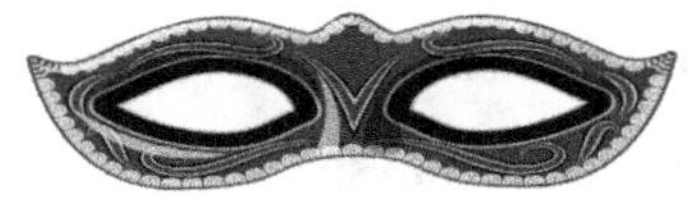

BY THE TIME I arrived home later that night, the television's blue glow shone through the vertical glass panel beside the front door. After closing and locking it, I approached Ava – fully aware I was acting like a teenager tiptoeing into my folks' place at 3 am after a night of drinking. Ava was watching a late-night movie: *The Howling*. She loved anything horror-related; perhaps that's why we got on so well.

'Hiya, little lady.' I placed my wallet and keys on the coffee table near her half-empty glass of white wine. Bogart stood at the back door, paw to the glass in a frozen high-five as the Christmas tree lights flashed an assortment of colours every two seconds.

Propped on her side, a thin blanket around her, she watched the images on the screen, eyes fixed on Dee Wallace. 'Hi.'

I sat at the other end of the couch. 'Please don't be mad.'

She shrugged and drew in a lazy breath. 'Why would I be mad? I'm used to this.'

'But you shouldn't have to be.'

She turned to me. 'Just answer me this: why did you retire if you're still working on cases?'

I steadied my breathing before answering. 'I'm just helping unofficially.'

She turned back to the TV.

I watched different shades of light play across her set expression as the movie continued. Bogart whimpered at the back door, demanding attention from me. I couldn't even keep my dog happy. Ava did not protest when I grabbed her foot from under the blanket.

I began massaging her heel. 'I'm sorry. I thought it was going to be just the one time. But it appears we have a serial killer on our hands.'

'And no-one else on the force can handle it? They cannot possibly manage without Macintosh Matthews, huh?'

It'd been my nickname during the start of the year when the computer came into production, so-called because I was fast, efficient, and got the job done. Macintosh Matthews. God, I hadn't heard that in a while.

My thumbs kneaded into the arc of her foot. 'Guess they thought I could pass on some wisdom.'

Her chest inflated as she continued watching the movie. 'Are you close to catching him?'

I turned to the TV. 'If I am honest, no.'

My heart rate slowed. If she was asking questions, then it meant I wasn't sleeping in the doghouse tonight.

'What makes you think it's the same person?'

'The staged scenes. Props are left behind. The bodies positioned upside down on the bed. All male. All white. All alone in the house.'

'Is this three so far?'

I continued watching the TV as an attractive dark-haired woman removed her clothing. 'Yes.'

She turned to me. 'Is this why we haven't organised Aruba?'

My neck cracked as I turned to her, shaking my head. 'No. How was I to know?'

'Maybe you were waiting for something like this to come along; to be called back to crime scenes. Maybe you miss it more than you let on.'

Before collecting the right words, I stopped massaging her. 'I will not lie to you, love. I do miss it. A helluva lot. It still feels strange after almost seven months, and I'm not even close to adjusting to normal life. Of not being where the action is. It was all I knew for decades of my life.'

She turned away, her jaw set.

'It's like with you. I've been with you so long that if you left, I wouldn't know what to do. I wouldn't even know where to begin, because you're part of me.'

'So is your job.'

'Yes,' I whispered. 'Yes, and I'm sorry to say, but it always will be. It's who I am.'

'So is being a husband and father.'

My body reacted before my brain played catch-up. Receiving that was like taking a sucker punch to the gut by Goliath. I looked back and forth between the TV to Ava's stoic face. 'I don't enjoy screwing up. And I remember there were important times I had to miss because of work. And I have apologised a thousand times for not always being able to go to our kids' recitals and school plays. Of missing out on swimming carnivals and, yes, sometimes birthdays.'

'And anniversaries ... family weddings ...'

Guilt swirling within me, I raked my fingers through my hair. 'Yes. Those too.'

'I put up with it for decades; I am used to this.' She grabbed her glass of wine. More than ever, I craved a beer. But I wouldn't indulge in one while Ava sat brooding. 'Also, your dinner is wrapped up in the fridge.'

'How can I make it up to you? You said you forgave me for those times I let you down; that you understood it was part of my job. Same as if I were a doctor, I'd be called off at all hours.'

She placed her empty glass back on the table and pulled the blanket higher about her shoulders. It was summer – not blanket weather. She was shielding herself from me.

'I can't tell you what to do.'

I turned back to the TV as werewolves howled. 'Can we at least not go to bed angry?'

She laughed. 'Oh, I am not angry.'

I glanced at her. 'Then what? Tell me what you're feeling.'

'Disappointment. I was looking forward to having my husband back – the man I married.'

I nodded once more, the Christmas lights flickering in the corner of my left eye. 'I will tell the guys tomorrow I won't work on this case anymore.' God help me, as soon as it left my mouth, I knew it was a lie. I didn't *want* to stop working on this enigmatic case, but Christ, I hated that wounded look in her eyes.

'I didn't tell you to do that.'

'But that's where this is headed.'

'I guess I had a different vision of what your retirement would bring to our marriage. And you running off and getting involved in cases again was not one of them. Stupid me for thinking that, once you handed in your badge and all.'

I stared at her profile as the TV's bright glow turned dark. 'That's a fair statement. And for what it's worth, I am sorry for being a disappointment to you. I don't want to see you hurt.'

She turned to me, tears glistening. 'Will you try harder with Heath, then? If you can put this much effort into dead people, surely you have it in you to look after your own son.'

My nostrils flared as I breathed in. 'Ava, I told you I've tried. He wasn't home.'

'Truly?'

'What, you think I'm lying?'

Her crinkled eyes smoothed out. 'I know you wouldn't; you're terrible at lying to me.'

'That's because I love you; I wouldn't want to lie to you.' Her facial features relaxed. 'Come here.' I outstretched my arms.

She hesitated, but moved over, climbing on top of my body as we fell back into the couch, where we remained snuggling, watching the movie. Well, I know Ava was. Her nails dug into my arm during the scary parts, her heartbeat resonating through my chest. I, however, was not watching the movie. Movies weren't scary for me. Real life was. Real life was a living nightmare.

Stephanie May

CHAPTER SIXTEEN

TWO DAYS LATER, I drove to Mitchell O'Brien's house in Parramatta for a debriefing. I had been stuck at home while Ava was out shopping with some mothers with whom she'd formed close bonds over the years when our kids had been at school. After reading *The Sunday Telegraph*, I took Bogart for a walk around the river, then showered and shaved. I'd received the call from O'Brien just as I headed to the study to read more on the occult. I still wasn't letting that angle go. Harmless research – nothing wrong with that. Ava would be gone for hours – you know how some women get once they start yapping; as long as the coffee keeps flowing, the talk could continue until the next full moon. Things between us were a little better, but not smooth sailing. I had a plan, though. And whenever I thought about it, I smiled at visualising my wife's reaction.

I cut off Bruce Springsteen halfway through 'Dancing in the Dark' as I killed the engine. Janice welcomed me with a kiss on the cheek and took me to Mitch's office, where Jeremy already waited.

'Have fun,' Janice said, a twinkle in her eye as the blokes rose from their chairs.

'Morning, boys.' I shook each hand that was thrust towards me, then took a seat in a chair next to Jeremy. He appeared clean and sharp as usual, in a white long-sleeved shirt and black pants.

'Morning. How's retired life?' O'Brien said with an undercurrent of amusement. I wasn't used to seeing him dressed in a blue polo shirt and denim jeans.

I folded my hands together in my lap as he sat back down behind his oakwood desk. 'Getting better as each day goes by.'

O'Brien grinned. 'We're not keeping you from Ava, are we?'

'No, why?'

'Janice said if I ever worked on another case after I retired, she'd cut my balls off.'

'No way she said that,' Jeremy said, eyes wide.

'She did. She can be bloody vicious when she wants to! See this scar here?' We both leaned in as he pointed to a small cut above his left eye. 'Well, Jeremy, when your wife tells you to take the garbage out ... son, believe me, take out the goddamn garbage.'

The flabbergasted look on Jeremy's face was hilarious. I'd been with Mitch when he acquired that scar during an arrest gone wrong. Some crazy immigrant had brandished a knife as soon as Mitch brandished a pair of handcuffs. Also, Janice didn't have a mouth on her – that was all bullshit; O'Brien liked to stir the pot. He was as deeply in love with Janice as I was with Ava. We came from a different era where we stuck things out. No matter how bad it seemed, no matter how dark it appeared, we were men who didn't give up. I respected that in Mitch, and he was a fine-looking man, even if he was greying around the temples. Women stared at him, but he paid them no mind. He was a good lad. He was my best mate.

'Let's not pull each other's dicks; let's get down to business,' O'Brien said, serious now. 'Eddy, we received the results from Hair and Fibre from the first two cases, and it's inconclusive. There are different strands of hair other than Norman Colbert, but that means diddly-squat. He had people coming in and out of the house all the time. Doing renovations and such, but we're following up a lead that he engaged the service of prostitutes.'

'Well, he *was* divorced and not all that good-looking, so that doesn't surprise me.'

'In truth, we don't have much to go on. Trace fibres on the soles of shoes are transported all the time. Fingerprints came back as inconclusive as well; there were multiple sources, but it's a fuckin' mixed bag.'

'And I'm guessing same goes for Ian?'

'Yep, canine fibres all over the place.' He looked skyward as he continued. 'Um, multiple hairs obtained, but again, these blokes had friends and acquaintances over all the time.'

'Anything from Ian's gun? Is this gang-related?'

'Nada! It *was* a .38, as you thought. The serial number was scratched off, and we took different prints – including Ian's. But it's untraceable; it doesn't appear to have ever been fired. We didn't find the bullets.'

'Dead end, then?'

'Afraid so; the gun was all for show.'

'What about footprints in or around the perimeter?'

'Nothing below any windows that were clear. Our killer either used the front door or the back. No signs of forced entry to any of the three properties.'

'Or they let him in.'

Jeremy raised a hand. 'What would be the story?'

'Your guess is as good as mine. Maybe the old broken-down car shtick, or maybe he's dressed in a uniform.'

'Still thinking it could be two guys?' O'Brien said.

'Yes; I think two,' Jeremy said.

My mind recalibrated, and I shook my head. 'I've thought more about that, and I think one.'

O'Brien cocked an eyebrow. 'Why?'

'Because it wouldn't mean as much to anyone else apart from our guy. If he had help, he couldn't share the sense of pleasure or glory. And two guys placing props on our victims? I don't see it.'

'None of our victims were scrawny dudes,' Jeremy said. 'Mark Andrews looked like he could have taken down a few guys at once – did you see his muscles?'

'I noticed. But these deaths are meaningful to one killer alone.'

O'Brien leaned forward. 'And the missing flesh?'

'This baffles me.' I paused, scratching my jaw with a thumbnail. 'Is it symbolic? You cannot fit a triangle into a circle – was he suggesting Norman was an outsider?'

'Maybe he's just a demented psychotic,' Jeremy said. 'Maybe it's nothing more than some guy off his mind on drugs. We're spending too much time wondering what a triangle means, which is probably what he wants.'

O'Brien looked at me.

I shrugged noncommittally. 'Look, we're all in the same boat. I can only speculate, but this guy seems methodical. I don't think he does something for the hell of it, just like the taps being left on in Norman's en suite. It wasn't an accident. These clues add up to something.'

O'Brien squinted. 'And when we work out what these symbols are supposed to mean, then what? How does that lead us to him? Or them?'

'We go with what we have. I still believe this could be ritualistic. I'll visit the Penrith Library and ask about books pertaining to the occult, and see if any have been checked out recently. I'll start compiling a list of names.'

O'Brien sat back in his chair. 'Okay, you do that; that's safe for you to do. Meanwhile' – he lifted up a copy of *The Sunday Telegraph* – 'what are we gonna do about this?'

My own face stared back at me in black and white, on page four.

Snatching it off him, I brought it to my face. 'What the hell?' My eyes roamed over the article:

QUESTIONS RAISED OVER EX-DETECTIVE 'MACINTOSH MATTHEWS' WORKING ON HOMICIDE CASE.

'You've got to be shitting me!' I glanced up. 'I didn't see this this morning.'

'Isn't that your ritual?' O'Brien asked. 'To have a cup of coffee and read the morning paper?'

My heart could have out-galloped a wild brumby. 'Exactly. I read it from front to back, same as I always do. I did not see this.'

'Maybe you skipped a page,' Jeremy said. 'Maybe they were stuck together.'

No way, stupid; what are the odds of that? This was not good news for a multitude of obvious reasons. While blood pounded in my ears, I continued reading.

The picture had been taken outside of Mark Andrews' house, and it was not a flattering one. My head was down, pronouncing my double chin – a scowl across my brow.

'Recent murders may be linked – a source tells Liz Fulton.' Her picture was next to the article; it was the blonde reporter with the bob cut. 'Even those parasites are linking this together,' I mumbled, reading on.

'Yeah, it's pretty clear now, even to those nitwits,' O'Brien said.

Sighing, I sat back. 'So, we have a serial killer in our midst. He leaves no clear fingerprints, no footprints – what about tyre marks? Any impressions?'

O'Brien shook his head. 'None, and it hasn't been raining. Besides, if our boy is as smart as we think he is, then he wouldn't park his car on their front lawn.'

'Maybe high vantage points – high fences, the book depository, or even the grassy knoll.'

Jeremy flashed me a look that had mysti-fucking-fied all over it. 'Book depository?'

O'Brien chuckled, a hand to his stomach. Age had to count for something, I guess.

'We need to check surrounding areas; no doubt the victims had been watched. They'd've been under surveillance for a while. It's no coincidence they were alone during the time of attack. Luck isn't dispensed to one person so easily.'

O'Brien nodded. 'Agreed. I think he knew their whereabouts and movements.'

'It wouldn't surprise me if he wiped down everything he touched, including all doorknobs.'

'Yeah, they brought back nothing,' Jeremy said. 'Only partials, not enough to go by.'

O'Brien's lips were pursed; he was ruminating. 'How's your research coming along, Eddy?'

I inhaled and shook my head, trying to push the article far from my dazed mind. 'I'm still reading up on a few things. It shits me because the signs are pointing to life: water, circles, the ankh, but he leaves them on dead people. The ankh is also a sign of protection.'

Janice interrupted our musings with a tray of piping hot coffee, milk, sugar and biscuits. She smiled, placing the tray on Mitchell's desk as he made room for it by pushing aside various books and papers. 'Help yourself,' she said before walking out.

We didn't need to be told twice.

'Surely door-to-door brought up something?' I said, dunking a Tim Tam into my mug of aromatic coffee.

O'Brien poured in a glug of milk, then stirred, his spoon tinkling against the ceramic. 'One elderly lady thought she saw a white van parked across the road where Norman Colbert lived.'

I cocked an eyebrow. 'That's it, a white van?'

He blew the steam away from his mug. 'Yep.' He took a tentative sip before blowing again, adding: 'We are continuing with the interviews, though.'

'Anything more from Michael Wong?'

Jeremy shook his head. 'None of the bodies showed signs of defensive wounds.'

'You mean, they stood there while the killer slit their throat? I highly doubt that. What would our guy use as a spiel to lure grown men into their own bedroom? We're missing something.' Ruminating, I took another sip. 'Anything unusual about the knives used?'

O'Brien used his tongue to dislodge a bit of Tim Tam from a molar before answering. 'According to the coroner, they're your standard carving knives. Nothing unique about them; sold in every bloody kitchenware store across the nation. No way in hell of tracing it back.'

I glanced at my picture in the paper again. 'Same weapon used to carve out Norman's flesh.'

'Yeah, and make an ankh incision on Mark.' O'Brien raised the mug to his lips and swallowed coffee before sitting back in his chair. 'This is one of the crazier ones, I tell you.'

'I couldn't agree more,' I said. 'Where to from here?'

'Tomorrow we have a meeting with Basil Humphries.'

'Tell that arsehole I send my warmest regards.'

O'Brien laughed, slapping the desk with a flat palm. I'd never liked Basil from the get-go; a pompous English prick, in my humble opinion. He was a forensic psychologist who'd worked on some of my bigger cases. Brought in to help give us detectives the scope of what we were dealing with. He was arrogant to buggery and spoke down to people, looking down his bulbous nose at anyone who dared ask him to repeat himself, or explain the jargon he dispensed whenever he could. Admittedly, Basil had helped us crack a few cases with the pointers he'd suggested, but his job wasn't an exact science; it was just textbook on prior serial killers. Helping us work out what ticks off a madman, and what gets his pecker hard.

'He's not so bad,' Jeremy said. That made sense; they were both on the arrogant side. Always had something to prove. Born with a silver spoon and all that jazz.

'We'll keep you in the loop, Eddy,' O'Brien said. 'And, ah, just keep reading up your books. And check your files to see if we have a copycat killer on our hands. Who knows, maybe this psycho *is* going off old crime scene photos, staging them in the exact same manner. Maybe even from an overseas case – try America, lots of fucked-up ones over there. I dunno what happened there during the seventies to produce such madmen; I can only hope Australia doesn't follow suit.'

'I'll look into it.' I retrieved a piece of paper from my pocket. 'By the way, I have a registration I'd like you to check out. Not related to this case, I assure you. For my personal use.'

'Righto, I'll get back to you when I've found out.' He took the paper off me, glanced at it, then turned to us. 'Let's finish up here, gentlemen.' O'Brien drained the last of his coffee, banging the mug on the desk. 'The sooner we catch this bastard, the sooner we can get a decent night's sleep.'

CHAPTER SEVENTEEN

AFTER LEAVING O'Brien's, I popped into Heath's on my way to the library. I was not surprised no-one answered my knocking yet again, but I was peeved my son had not called me. The thought of leaving a note under the door crossed my mind, but I believed Lorraine would have passed on my message; Heath obviously had other things on his mind. I had omitted telling Ava about Lorraine's strange behaviour, and the blanket around her naked body. Although my wife meant well, she sometimes gossiped, and she liked to pop in to Hayley's every other day, so I could not entirely trust Ava to keep it to herself.

I left the apartment building with a heavy heart and hopped back into my Statesman, scanning the area for that green Honda. With no luck on any front, I started the ignition and drove off with Penrith in my sights. The library was going to be a hard task – asking for logs of any books on the occult being checked out. I had no badge, but when your wife is good friends with a librarian, a lack of identification can be overlooked when trying to pull a few tricks.

Inside the brightly lit library, I made a beeline towards Olivia Hitchcock, who held a load of books in the crook of her skinny left arm, while scanning the MILITARY aisle. Her full-length red dress with white daisies swayed with every step, as did her short mousy hair.

I crept up behind her and said, 'Boo!'

She turned with a gasp. Upon recognition, she smiled. 'Oh, Eddy! You gave me a fright!'

Grinning, I brought my shoulders to my ears. 'Couldn't help myself, darlin'.'

'Fancy seeing you here. Bored at home, are you?'

'Actually, I'm conducting unofficial research.' Tapping my nose, I leaned down. 'You know, off the record.'

She frowned and faced me fully. 'Oh. Is there anything I can help you with?'

Tilting my head, I said, 'As a matter of fact, yes.' Her eyes danced with intrigue. 'I wonder how difficult it would be to obtain a list of all books that've been checked out in a certain genre.'

She glanced about the aisle, then held my gaze. 'How far back are we talking?'

'I don't really know.'

She twisted her lips. 'That might make things more difficult.'

Grinning, I bobbed my head. 'I suspect it would.'

Stepping closer, she said, 'What type of books?'

'Anything on the occult. Or religious sects.'

She frowned. 'Funny you ask.'

My spine straightened as my heart perked up. God, could this be so easy? 'Why is that?'

'I showed a man a book on such things not a month or two ago, and I remember it because we don't have a big calling for those types of genres. Religion, yes, due to school studies and whatnot, but books on Satanism and the occult are more your after-hours-type thing.'

'Do you remember the book? Or the guy's name?' Up ahead, a teenage boy with a Walkman and earphones trailed past, eyes red-rimmed with a dazed expression – probably stoned.

'I don't remember his name; I just showed him our selection, and he took the book up to the counter once he was done.'

'What was the name of the book?'

'I remember it well because it's said to be the Holy Grail pertaining to the lore of sorcery. It's called *None Dare Call It Witchcraft*.'

'I see. Is there any way you could retrieve his information?'

She looked around conspiratorially. 'I could. But you know I could get into trouble for this, right? I mean, you haven't even shown me a badge.'

I smirked. 'You know I've retired.'

'Exactly!' Her eyes softened. 'But far be it from me to not help my good friend's retired husband with unofficial duties.'

'I could kiss you, darlin'!'

She giggled. 'Please don't. I stopped kissing boys in libraries when I became an adult.'

I couldn't help but chuckle. 'I surely appreciate your help. How long, do you think?'

'Not too long. And it depends if it's even been brought back yet. In fact, let's check right now.'

She placed her pile of books on a two-step ladder at the end of the aisle. I followed her around to the other side of the library, where kids sat laughing and pointing at their books, swapping sweets and trying the aerodynamics of paper aeroplanes. A poster caught my eye: Whiskers the Cat – a large black feline with a book in its paws, and a speech bubble: 'Good books will satisfy your curiosity, too!' The lively ambience brought back memories of my own happy childhood and being at school with my buddies, causing me to wonder what the hell they were all up to now.

'Say, you're not related to Alfred, are you, Mrs Hitchcock?' I asked, touching the smooth, waxy leaf of an indoor plant as we strolled by.

She swivelled her head as she continued walking. 'If I had a dollar for every time someone asked me that.'

I laughed, scanning the surroundings until we stopped at the farthest aisle from the front desk. There was no second-guessing we were in the Forbidden Section – either that, or the make-out aisle.

'All the way back here, huh?'

She scanned the book spines. 'As I said, we really don't have a market for this type of material. We try to be as wide and varied as possible. It's not totally uncommon, but definitely in the lower echelon of the list of "most checked-out books" or "commonly asked-for books".'

I scanned the dusty book spines myself, catching faces of demons, inverted pentagrams, upside-down crosses—

The tiny hairs on the back of my neck stood up as though a skeletal finger had scraped the tip of my spine. Upside-down crosses. My days of reading about religion stated that inverted crosses were symbolic of Satanism. It was the antithesis of the cross on which Jesus had died, so an upside-down cross represented the Devil.

My stomach muscles clenched as my flesh tingled. How had I not seen it before? The bodies placed upside down on the bed in the same manner, representing evil. I grabbed two random books, my heart thumping so hard it drowned out the endless chatter and giggling around me. Could this be it? Would it all be so simple to correlate the murders to this man who'd checked out a book on the occult in this exact library? I grabbed more books before continuing on.

'Oh, here it is ...' Olivia Hitchcock stopped in front of a book. The black spine featured writing in red. 'This is the one he borrowed on a two-week loan.'

I walked up behind her and peered over her shoulder as she plucked it from its resting place.

None Dare Call It Witchcraft by Gary North. The front cover depicted the zodiac signs enclosed in a yellow circle, and up the top above the circle was the red, diabolical face of Satan. The word WITCHCRAFT was written in red block letters. My stomach churned as excitement raced through me.

'I want this one. And these, too.' I referred to the books under my left arm as I took the book from her.

'Do you have a library card?'

I shook my head, turning the book over and opening it to read inside the jacket: Published in 1976 by Arlington House.

Religion.

The occult.

Satanism.

Wait, what did a red feather have to do with Satanism? What did a crown have to do with it, or running water? The killing of Ian's dog indicated sacrifice, but why not Mark Andrews' dog? Rituals weren't usually performed in a bedroom with only one person watching. Let's say for argument's sake it was two men, or even three. My impression of that Dark Lord worship crap was people with eerily white faces wearing black cloaks, standing around a bonfire and throwing live animals into the flames, or even human babies.

My head ached from an influx of confusion. My senses told me I was on the right path, sure, but I still wasn't entirely certain as I was navigating unknown waters. I'd have to bury my head in these books over the next few days – as well as finish *The Satanic Bible*, which had yet to mention red feathers or red cloaks.

'Okey-dokey,' Olivia said. 'I'll let you use my card, as long as you promise to bring them back within the two weeks.'

I looked up from the book jacket. 'Have I ever lied to you?'

'Gee, I don't know you well enough to have been in that position. I think I recall seeing you about ten times in all over the past decade.'

'If this leads to where I hope it will, I'll be your best friend for the rest of your life.'

I went straight home after my trip to the library. Olivia Hitchcock had let me borrow the books on her staff card, and she promised she would get me information pertaining not just to the man she'd spoken of – but for any other similar books checked out over the past few months. Out of all my wife's friends, I now liked her the most.

Ava's Honda Accord sitting in the driveway surprised me; I'd assumed she'd still be out with the girls. I opened the front door to hear frantic banging emanating from the kitchen, cupboard doors slamming and drawers being yanked open. I placed the books on the foot of the staircase and followed the racket. Guilt pricked my gut – surely Olivia hadn't called about the books? Or maybe Ava had seen my photo in the *Telegraph*.

'Hello, little lady.' I propped myself against the archway, listening to the oven fan whirring.

Her flushed complexion put me off guard, and she held an empty baking tray. 'Hi.'

'What's wrong?'

Was Ava's dishevelled hair the result of her raking a hand through it a hundred times already?

'It completely slipped my mind that I'm hosting the Book Club at our place tonight.'

I inwardly cringed. 'Oh, really?'

She looked at me with apologetic eyes. 'I'm sorry. I thought it was next month for some silly reason. So now' – she pointed to the plastic bags of meat, vegetables and fruit on the kitchen bench – 'I have to prepare dinner for eight, instead of just us two.'

I ached to head to my study and begin reading, but Ava looked too frazzled, and I was too relieved I hadn't been caught out.

'Can I help in any way?'

Her spine went rigid as she looked at me. 'It's a matter of putting the pork in the oven, but I have to get the crackling just right. As soon as this' – she slapped a huge portion of meat that looked like it'd feed a small African village – 'goes into the oven, everything will be fine.'

'Surely I can do something?'

'Then it's a matter of peeling vegetables and making gravy. That's the easy part.' She turned around and grabbed the container of salt and a bottle of white vinegar.

'I love your crackling.'

'I know you do, but it takes time. The oven has to be hot enough, the skin has to be dry ...'

'Why didn't you plan something easier, love? Why not order a bunch of pizzas?'

She slammed her knife down and turned her head to me slowly. 'Ava Matthews ordering pizza for Women's Book Club night? You must be joking.'

Laughing, I made my way over, kissing her sweaty temple. 'I'm looking forward to it.'

She patted the pork dry with a paper towel. 'What did you get up to today?' She picked up the knife to score the pinkish rind in diagonal slits.

'I went to see Heath.'

She looked up, her eyes as wide as dinner plates.

Sucking my lips inwards, I shook my head.

'Oh,' she mouthed, turning back to the task at hand. 'I wonder why he's avoiding us.'

'Love, I don't think he's avoiding us; he's just busy.'

'I asked Hayley today to reach him, to give him a call. She said she would.'

I went to retrieve a beer from the fridge. A cool blast slapped me in the face, but it felt refreshing in this hot kitchen. 'I'll keep trying myself.'

'Mmm ...'

I turned to her, watching her process, noting how much care she took. 'Love?'

She began slicing diagonal cuts against the grain of the first ones.

'Did you see today's paper? I misplaced it.' Escaping gas hissed as I popped the cap off my beer bottle.

At first I thought she wasn't going to answer, she was that engrossed. 'Umm ... gee, I think I saw the paper lying around somewhere, but darned if I know where.' As I raised the bottle to my lips she added: 'Oh, I forgot to tell you: a letter came for you today. Found it on our doormat.'

Interesting. Where the hell is the paper? I thought as I took a swig. God, it tasted good; there is nothing finer than an ice-cold beer on a hot summer's day. Now that Ava had declined my help, I was dying to read those books and absorb everything I could on the occult. If we could *just* work out this guy's motive for the props, then maybe it would lead us to him. Staging still felt like the right path as well. It was as though he held a photo up in the air at each crime scene and then positioned the body and props just so. I did not want to sit around the table with a bunch of women over dinner. Granted, I always took off either to take Bogart for a walk, or to do menial things around the house, but I longed to lock myself away and not emerge until I solved this thing.

'I left the letter on the coffee table,' Ava said, interrupting my thoughts. 'Don't know who it's from. No return address.'

I kissed the back of her head as she began rubbing vinegar and salt into the scored cuts of pork rind. 'Thank you. I'll be in my study if you need me.' I walked away, but halted, turning my head. 'What time are they coming again?'

'It's always six-thirty.'

'Okay. Love you.'

'Uh-huh,' she murmured, but I smiled as I walked away. She always tried to please everyone; always tried to be the perfect hostess. It wasn't like her to be forgetful.

Bogart's nose pressed against the glass door, his top lip pushed up, baring his little teeth into a cheeky grin. I chuckled as I made my way over to him, glancing absent-mindedly at the letter on top of the coffee table. I raised the beer to my lips and then stopped, my hand frozen mid-air. The letter. Just looking at it gave me this sense of foreboding, like a storm cloud hovering above me. Bogart whimpered in the distance; it seemed he was miles away.

I took a tentative step towards the coffee table where a white envelope goaded me. I noticed two things: First, there was no stamp. Second, the black writing spelling my full name and address looked cautionary. I can't explain the damn thing any more elaborately than that, but it was menacing – written in black, probably with a Sharpie. Call it intuition, but a trickle of sweat trailed down my scalp, running behind my earlobe. I picked it up as though handling a ticking time bomb and held it against the light of the back door. It appeared to have a single piece of paper inside, nothing more. I turned it over and Ava was right: no return address. This feeling of drowning while in a straitjacket comes to mind when I think about what it was like to hold it. If I am honest – and haven't I already been? – I shuddered violently. A big, tough man on the force for decades, dealing with the worst kinds of people and their evil ways, but this dreaded letter …

After rushing over to retrieve my books from the staircase (and forgetting all about Bogart), I hurried back past the kitchen just as Ava popped the slab of pork into the piping hot oven. I opened and closed my study door as quickly and quietly as humanly possible, then plonked in the chair in front of my desk and grabbed my late father's silver letter opener with an ivory eagle head for a handle. I closed my eyes briefly as the last bit of resistance from the envelope gave way to my opener, the flick creating an arc in the air.

Exhaling, I pulled out the piece of paper and unfolded it:

Dear Edward Matthews,

May I call you that? Or shall I say ex-detective?

You don't know me. And from what I gather in the papers, you and your team of investigators aren't even close to finding out. But I know all about you, see, more than you probably think I do. I know, for instance, that you have an adorable wife. The smell of her cooking reminds me of my late mother's. I also know you like to walk that German shepherd of yours late at night. You really ought to be more careful; there are lots of weirdos around. But you know this already, don't you? Of course you do, from your time on the force. The highly decorated Macintosh Matthews, correct? But your record is not unblemished, is it? Does the name Abigail Jerkewitz mean anything to you? It does to me. Oh yes, I remember that case well. Shall I remind you? Six years old at the time in 1976. Raped, sodomised, and then tossed into a nearby lake. Her pink lunchbox was found floating in the dirty water, wasn't it? Her sandwiches and biscuits meant for her visit to grandma all soggy. Do you still think of her at night? Do you see her bloated face floating in the murky water whenever you close your eyes?

Fear not, I am not the man who took her innocence. Little girls do nothing for me. I like more of a challenge. I think you know this by now. But tell me, does it eat you alive that he was never caught? They say there's no such thing as a perfect crime. But shall I give you a list of examples?

The Black Dahlia

The Zodiac Killer

The Mad Butcher of Kingsbury Run

The Wanda Beach Murders

D. B. Cooper

Jack the Ripper

Shall I go on?

Do you still believe, detective, that perfection cannot be obtained? That is what I have set out to do: Obtain perfection. Three down. Many more to go. At this rate, you'll be six feet under before any of these are solved.

Have you worked out yet what the symbols mean? Do you understand my M.O. at this point in time? It vexes you, does it not, that I keep changing my pattern? You think you've got me all figured out. Three white males, all alone, and all facing upside down. Yet, not one crime scene duplicated.

Maybe, for your sake, I should shake things up a little? How would you like two this time? Yes, a double homicide sounds about as nice as your wife's cooking smells.

You take care of yourself in the meantime, won't you? It'd be a shame if anything were to happen. I do so much enjoy this cat-and-mouse game we have going, don't you, Edward? Or, Eddy ... That sounds better, doesn't it? It's what your close friends and family call you. Well, I feel close to you. I feel as close as a lover. I get your heart racing, don't I? You want to quit, but you won't, because I will pull you in every time. I am the apple in your Garden of Eden. Do you dare take a bite?

Keep your eyes and ears peeled at all times. I could be anyone. I could be anywhere. Even under your bed as you make love to your wife.

Ta-ta for now, old boy.

Yours sincerely,

Jerry.

CHAPTER EIGHTEEN

I SAT AT MY desk as rigid as a bowstring until Ava knocked on the door some hours later. I didn't respond, but she opened it a moment later, regardless.

Glancing up, I lowered the letter behind my stack of books. My knuckles throbbed from their dead-locked position. Only then did I register the sun had made its journey to the west, the last remnants of sunlight clinging on.

'Yes, love?' Jesus H. Christ, I did not recognise that voice.

Deep lines marred her brow. 'You okay? It looks like you've seen a ghost.'

God, how I tried to muster up my best acting skills. 'No, I'm fine.' I smiled. 'What's up?'

She licked her lips. 'If you insist. The girls will be here shortly. I wanted to see if you'd like a bath – to get cleaned up before they arrive?' She grinned. 'And don't worry, I'll save the biggest piece of crackling just for you.'

The aroma of dinner wafted through the door, but I was feeling too crook to appreciate it. I tried to swallow discreetly, but my throat clicked. 'You are undoubtedly the best.'

She stared at me, squinting for a moment, and then closed the door.

I leaned back in my chair and let out a gush of air I had been holding in, like someone letting go of a balloon the size of a beer keg. I was shaking. I was *livid*. I was also fucking scared.

Never in my time on the force had I been personally targeted. There were too many questions, a plethora of possibilities running through my bleary mind. Every emotion one can experience in a lifetime hit me at once. The protective part of me was furious. He'd mentioned Ava. He'd mentioned Bogart. He knew I walked around the streets. This fucking madman knew where I lived, and knew about my time on the force – even my nickname. And, he knew about Abigail.

Rising slowly, I walked to my fax machine on what felt like Aeroplane Jelly legs. Blowing dust off the fax buttons, I powered it up and sent a copy of the letter to O'Brien. I also sent it to Jeremy.

I closed my eyes and breathed through it all, consciously avoiding looking at Abigail's picture on the corkboard. I ran a quaking hand down over my parched mouth. God, I needed another fucking beer. Hell, I needed three fingers of whisky to quell these usurping emotions.

And soon I would have to play host to a bunch of itty-bitties talking about some book. Food was the last thing I needed, and I'd lost the will to make fake conversation. But I could not let Ava find out. That was paramount.

I waited until my faxes went through, then I folded the godforsaken letter and hid it inside the cover of *The Satanic Bible* – where it fucking belonged!

Sometime later, I was half-submerged in hot water. I hadn't said a word to Ava as I'd passed the kitchen. A to-do list ran through my mind: *Protection. Update our home security system. Make sure Bogart is safe* – perhaps Ava would let me keep him inside of a night? But how to get around that without telling her why. I couldn't tell her. And don't blame me for that. I didn't want her to worry; she already had too much on her mind – tonight's forgetfulness being testament to that. I didn't want her to hate me for taking on this case. It wasn't a matter of pride. It was not about having to listen to her say *I told you so!* It was about keeping her mental state in check. But I could do nothing more until I heard from O'Brien and Retmeyer.

The bathtub was usually my place for thinking (or chewing the fat, as my late grandmother used to say). The steam did nothing to help clear the growing panic assaulting my senses. I tried to convince my brain to tell the rest of my body this could be a hoax. That this could be some drongo who'd read the paper, saw my picture, knew where I lived, and decided to make a dummy threat. But somehow, I did not think I could be so lucky. He also mentioned a double homicide. Was this statement prophetic? I hoped to God it wasn't.

And 'Jerry'? Not his real name; anyone with half a brain knew that. At first, I wondered what it referred to; I even thought back to the people from my police academy days – even cold cases I'd led. Then it clicked: the mouse from *Tom and Jerry*. I was the cat to his mouse. The sick fuck wanted to play a game with me. Probably tossing his rocks at goading me. Taunting me. Well, if he wanted to play, I'd say let's dance. He'd obviously never been up against someone in my position before. And I swore, at that moment, as I was lying in the steaming water, that he would regret ever having addressed me so personally. I would live to see this guy behind bars, or at least I'd die trying. He'd stabbed me where it hurt most. Despite referencing Ava, despite Bogart, despite him telling me he knew my movements ... he'd mentioned Abigail. He knew my weak spot, and he'd gone for it. Twisting the blade where it nicked the bone. Retired or not, I vowed I would find this arsehole. I would bring this sick fucker to his knees before my time was done, so help me God.

Stephanie May

CHAPTER NINETEEN

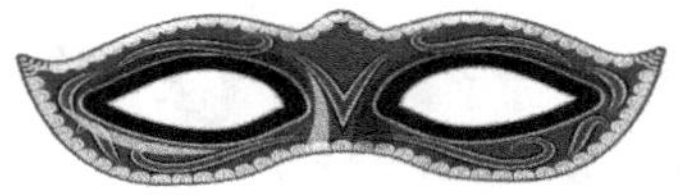

MEMBERS OF THE local Women's Book Club sat around our large dining table. Once a month they went to a member's residence and chatted over dinner and wine – or beer in Roberta's case. Luckily, I'd bought more from Dan Murphy's. I, too, sat with a beer in front of me as my stomach churned and I pushed bile to the back of my throat.

I never could remember their last names, but seated around the table were Roberta – the largest and sloppiest of the lot; always went for second helpings. Then there was Gracie-Ann, a primary school teacher; Jacqui, a Frenchwoman who loved reading erotica; Lyndell, a former flower child who claimed to have had sex with Jimi Hendrix at Woodstock in '69; Marilyn, who was the antithesis of Monroe in every way possible, and finally Agatha, a divorced mother with four boys, and a turn in her left eye.

The huge hunk of oven-roasted pork was the centrepiece, a bowl of broken pieces of salty crackling to the side, as well as an oval dish with buttered beans, a large pot of steaming mashed potato, a tray of roasted pumpkin, and homemade pepper gravy in a boat.

Roberta dug in first. As usual.

'Okay, ladies,' Ava began after finally sitting down. 'How did we fare with *Pet Sematary*?'

'I thoroughly enjoyed it!' Gracie-Ann said, reaching for the buttered beans once Roberta had moved her flabby arm out of the way.

'I didn't!' Roberta said, smothering her pork in so much gravy I couldn't see anything on her plate but a brown lake. 'That Stephen King just waffles on! And then, to kill off that poor little boy …'

'Yes,' Agatha said. 'As a mother of four boys, I found that truck scene hard to deal with.' I couldn't work out who she was actually talking to; one eye was on Lyndell, the other on Jacqui.

'I agree wiz Gracie-Ann,' Jacqui said, her heavy accent clinging to every word. 'It was 'arsh, *oui*, but powerful.'

I peered up over the neck of my beer as Ava eyed me.

'Are you going to eat?' she whispered, the tinkling of silverware erupting around us.

'Yes, just waiting for the ladies to help themselves.'

After I downed more beer, someone – I don't know who – dropped their knife or fork against the chinaware. The shot-like sound made me jolt, and I banged my knee on the underside of the table.

Ava glared at me, leaning forward. 'What *is* the matter with you?'

My heart pounded, pushing heat from my neck up to my cheeks. 'Sorry …'

'What did you think, Ava Gardner?' Marilyn said. That was their nick-name for my wife. By God, she was so much prettier than the actress, though. I thought it was an insult but, of course, they were trying to pass a compliment.

Ava turned to Marilyn. 'Well' – she licked her thumb that'd caught a spot of gravy – 'I really enjoyed this book. It was exciting, compelling, utterly horrifying. This guy, Stephen King, he is quite the master of the macabre. I believe we'll still be discussing his work decades from now.'

Roberta leaned forward, chewing. 'Don't bet your life on it! He's too descriptive!' She pointed the tip of her knife at Ava. 'You could easily cut a quarter out of his books and still get the point.' I held back the urge to gag as a piece of chewed something flew from her mouth and onto the table. 'Might save half the Amazonian Rainforest, too!' Roberta added for good measure.

Ava sliced into her pork with finesse. 'I don't mind that, though; I like his descriptiveness. It transports you into another world. That's the point of stories, is it not?'

'I agree with Ava,' Lyndell said, her mouth full of potato and green beans. 'I have been a fan of King's since *Carrie*. He is remarkably adept at creating fictitious worlds. His characterisation is tantamount to having the characters jump off the page to form some sort of 3-D vision in front of you.' She turned to Gracie-Ann. 'It was a good pick; thank you.'

Gracie-Ann beamed at the compliment. And that was when I finally helped myself to a small portion of food. Ava eyed my plate with overt frustration while the others continued discussing the book and its author.

Trying to push aside my thoughts about the letter would have been like trying to stop bubbles rising to the surface of a popped champagne bottle. The more you tell yourself not to think about something, the more your head laughs at you. My hand still had a slight quiver. My bowels were still liquified, the gurgling sounds I felt sure were audible over the clatter and chatter.

'I'm glad to see the back of it!' Roberta said, reaching for the salt shaker yet again. On each shake, her flabby arm wobbled. 'What is the next book? It's Ava's choice, yes? Pick something decent this time, for God's sake ...'

Ava raised a fist to her mouth and cleared her throat. 'I was thinking *Schindler's Ark*. This one was released two years ago, by Thomas Keneally.

He's Australian, plus it's won a few awards. Has anyone read it?' She glanced around the table.

Lyndell continued to shovel in food, while Jacqui sipped her West Coast Cooler and Marilyn dug something out of her mouth with a hooked finger.

Roberta gave a swift eye-roll and stole a deep breath. 'Not another Jewish book, please.' Her pudgy, greasy fingers clamped around her beer bottle. *My* beer bottle.

'Do you even know much about Schindler and the Holocaust, Roberta?' Gracie-Ann asked, blotting her mouth with a napkin. I suspected she was offended some people hadn't liked her Pick of the Month.

Roberta leaned forward, cheeks puffing out on a burp. 'Enough to know I don't want to read another thing about the plight of the Jews. I'm not agreeing with Hitler, but I think the topic is overdone now. People want to move on with their lives, not be sucked back by the past – it happened; let's move on.'

Ava's cheeks lost their colour, her mouth was downturned, her eyes drooped.

That's when I cleared my throat. 'I've heard nothing but good things about it.'

They all looked at me then; suddenly, the Invisible Man had reappeared. I hardly ever said much during their talks – tonight was no exception. I would typically (sensibly) stay with them during dinner, playing the part of loving husband and gracious host, and then disappear once they gathered about our living room with cups of coffee, plates of Pavlova, and the relevant book in hand. Swapping more ideas and theories, posing questions. It sometimes lasted for hours. The person whose turn it was to host the dinner chose the next book they were to read over the course of the following month. Fair's fair, and if my wife wanted to read this book, then I was on board.

'And have *you* read it?' Marilyn directed to me.

I gave a close-lipped smile. 'No. At the time of its release, I was probably out trying to protect the community. But I do read the paper and I did read its reviews.'

Ava stared at me, her expression unreadable, her hand frozen mid-air with a chunk of gravy-dipped pork on the tines, only inches from her parted lips.

'Oh yes, how is retirement going?' Lyndell asked. It was a good-natured question, but I thought *Christ, can we get back to Stephen King, please?*

'Retirement, ha!' Roberta said, slapping the table, causing the contents to rattle. 'I saw your picture in today's paper, *Macintosh* Matthews.'

Ava turned to me, tight-lipped, her hand still frozen mid-air.

Shaking my head, I chuckled. 'No-no, just helping out an old mate.'

'*Yes.*' Roberta sneered. 'Now that you have all this time on your hands, perhaps you'd like to become a member of our Book Club. *Then* you can have all the input you desire ...'

Boy she was really pissing me off, *and* she'd dirtied our tablecloth by slopping my wife's gravy over the sides of her plate. 'Well, Roberta, I would *like* to join the club, but unfortunately I don't have a cunt.'

Ava gasped and dropped her fork on her plate; in the stunned silence it could have been mistaken for a gunshot. Lyndell, who sat beside me, choked on her own laughter.

Roberta's mouth flung open, so did Marilyn's.

'Boy, someone 'as a sense of 'umour!' Jacqui said, breaking the awkward silence and raising the napkin to her mouth to contain her giggle. See? The French got crude humour.

Ava leaned forward to address Roberta. 'He was only joking ...' Her feeble laugh died on her lips. She then glared at me – a look as deadly as a woman saying 'I'm fine!'

Then, a saving grace came to pull me out of the shitter: the telephone rang. *I'll be damned.*

'I'll get it,' I said as everyone stared at the Martian who'd dropped in for supper. With a pounding heart, I pushed back my chair, grabbed my beer and raced to the telephone. God, you should have seen the look on Ava's flushed face. Anyone would think I'd slapped her.

My first thought as my fingers brushed the receiver: *Jerry*.

'Matthews' residence.'

'I just received your fax.' As usual, O'Brien was straight to the point, his tone giving nothing away.

I took another swig of beer, savouring the bubbles searing my aching throat. 'Well?'

He sighed heavily. Regretfully. 'I don't know what to say. What are you doing right now?'

'Oh, I'm just digging my way to China – how about you?'

'Quite frankly, shitting bricks. How the fuck did he find you?'

I moved further into the kitchen, away from the archway. 'I, ah, can't really say.'

He hesitated. 'Do you need me to come over?'

'The Book Club is here, spreading the joy.'

'If Ava's got friends over, can you come here?'

'Yeah, I'll come. Mind if I bring Bogart along?'

He hesitated again. 'All right, but only because Janice isn't here. And make sure he shits at home first!'

'I'll keep him in the backyard.' Wiping my sweat-slicked forehead on my arm, I swallowed another blessed mouthful.

'Deal.'

I downed the last of my beer as general chatter emerged from the dining room again. 'I'll be over in less than thirty.'

I cradled the receiver back in its place and exhaled as I headed to my study to retrieve *The Satanic Bible*. I then went upstairs without passing the ladies another glance, but they were busy again chatting up a storm, anyway. Thank God for that. I donned a jacket and hid the book, propping it against my left side as I descended the stairs again. After unlocking the front door, I peered around, satisfied. The night was still and silent, so I made my way to the dining room. Roberta glared at me, but it hadn't stopped her appetite – she was the first one finished, lips glistening with brown gravy. Ava sliced into her pork instead of looking at me.

'Ladies, it's been a pleasure.' I then locked eyes with Roberta the Porker. 'Excuse my French before, it was a tasteless joke.'

Roberta turned away from me, her expression as pompous as a British Royal. *Ah well, fuck her.*

'Don't worry, we know,' Lyndell said, smiling. She leaned forward and faced Roberta. 'Right?'

Roberta's mouth suggested she'd been sucking sour grapes.

'Nothing wrong wiz using French!' Jacqui said, winking at me.

'Yes, well, enjoy the rest of your night. See you all next time.' I bent down to Ava, gripping her shoulder. I could have gotten more warmth from the food in front of her. 'Love, I'm going to duck out for a while.'

She turned to me then, smiling for the benefit of others. 'You'd better not be working on the case.' She spoke through gritted teeth, low, yet deadly.

'No-no, little lady, I'm taking Bogart for a walk – away from here.'

Her shoulders relaxed a little. 'Fine.' She turned back to her food. I stood straighter and smiled as everyone stared while I walked past the table to retrieve Bogart's blue leash from the wall hook.

'Can you take him through the side gate, please?' Ava said as I opened the glass door. Bogart pranced from left to right, tongue flapping about, warm saliva splashing everywhere.

I turned the lock, closed the door behind me and left without another word.

CHAPTER TWENTY

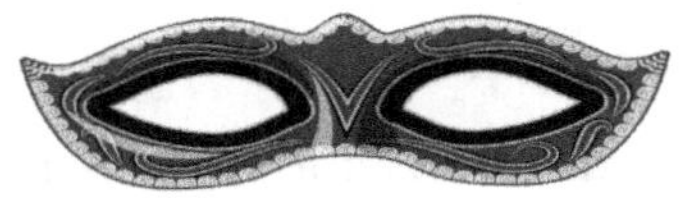

MITCHELL O'BRIEN HELD the fax in front of him as *The Satanic Bible* lay on his desk. I waited for him to read it again. I don't know how many times he'd re-read it. Hell, I didn't know how many times *I'd* read it, either.

On the drive over, I viewed every car I passed along River Road with suspicion. Paranoia already held me in a chokehold. I paid close attention to the headlights that crept up behind me for some time, too. Only allowing myself to breathe once the car veered off down another street. Already it was playing on my wayward mind.

Inside O'Brien's office, I held a tumbler of whisky in one hand as his squinted eyes darted across the page and back.

Finally, he lowered it, exhaling. 'It could be a hoax.'

I scoffed in a *cut-the-bullshit* way. 'Do you really believe that?'

O'Brien shook his head solemnly, his jowls drooping like a hound dog. He placed his hands over his face, resting his elbows on the edge of his desk. 'What now?'

'I need protection.'

His hands dropped like a stone. 'You know I am not authorised to hand out weapons. I have to sign and account for each one.'

'I will get it on my own, then.'

'You already have a gun, though,' he whispered as though there were wire-taps around the room. 'At least two that I know of.'

'True. But I need more. Another for home. One for the car. One that'll fit nicely into my back pocket when I'm out.'

O'Brien shook his head. 'Eddy, I don't want to know. I can't hear about this.'

'Understood. However, I need protection for the house. I don't even like the thought of Ava being there without me now.'

'She has friends over?'

'She has *people* over.'

He squinted. 'Same thing ...'

I gave a mirthless smile. 'Never mind. I want more security around the perimeter.'

'What do you have now?'

I took another nip of whisky. It burned my throat as it slid down, and I envisioned a river of fire destroying everything in its path. My insides were alive and singing 'Hail Mary', even though my heart was stone-cold. 'Just the front. We have high side gates, so we never bothered. Plus, our place – we thought – was fairly secure. There are always people around, so we didn't worry about it.'

'You know what the world is like, though.'

'Yes, but from what I am aware, there's never once been so much as a robbery on the street.'

O'Brien flat-palmed his desk. 'Times are changin', man. God, what is the world going to be like fifty years from now?' I stared without offering an answer. 'Anyway, we amp up the security. Extra locks on the doors, more cameras –

especially out the back. Where do you park your car at night?'

'In the driveway.'

'Never on the street?'

'No need to.'

'But not in the garage?'

I shook my head, raising the tumbler to my lips to swallow more fire and brimstone.

'That needs to change.'

I dipped my head. 'Agreed. I have stuff as storage in there, but that'll change tomorrow.' (It was always tomorrow, right?)

'Make sure you explain to Ava how serious it is that she parks in the garage from now on.'

Shifting in my seat, I said, 'I haven't told her about the letter.'

His lips twisted and he raked a hand over the back of his neck. 'I understand that.'

'Would you tell Janice?'

He mulled it over for a moment. 'No. No, I wouldn't.'

Just then, Bogart barked outside. Turning my head, I listened, but he'd stopped. My ears perked up, waiting. Probably a cat. Turning back to O'Brien, I said, 'So, it's agreed. More cameras, more deadbolts, thick padlocks on either of our side gates that lead to the backyard, and park in the garage at night.'

He leaned back in his leather chair, fingers strumming the oakwood desk. 'Windows?'

'I'll keep an eye on them.'

'You know, though, if this guy really wanted to ...'

By closing my eyes, I blocked out his worrisome expression. He didn't need to say it aloud. 'I'll have to give Ava something to protect herself with whenever she goes out.'

'How are you going to go about it?'

'I'll think of something.'

Moments later, a knock at the front door interrupted us, and I don't mind admitting I crapped myself, until O'Brien relieved my anxiousness.

'That'll be Jeremy.' He heaved himself to his feet using the edge of the desk. 'Hang on.'

As O'Brien left to answer the door, I rose to stretch my legs and looked towards the framed awards hanging on the walls. I heard the front door open, then close on a squeal, followed by voices, so I put my tumbler on the desk.

Jeremy came through the door first. 'Eddy, what a terrible thing to happen.'

We shook hands and took a seat, both silent as he stared at me. O'Brien returned a minute later and closed the door.

'Where'd you go?' I asked, craning my neck to look at him.

'To piss.' O'Brien approached his mini bar.

'Where's Janice?' Jeremy asked. Again, he was dressed like a seasoned professional. This kid would go a long way; he had the brains and balls for it. Never a stray hair out of place.

'Poker night at her sister's house.' O'Brien looked over from the row of liqueurs and spirits. 'Looks like I'll be your bartender tonight, son. What'll you have?'

Jeremy's lack of colour made me wonder whether *he* had also received a letter from the killer. 'Whatever … I don't mind; you pick.'

O'Brien pulled down a tumbler from his shelf, then grabbed the bottle of Chivas Regal.

Jeremy turned to me. 'Why does it say "Jerry" at the bottom of the letter? My nickname is Jerry; is he trying to frame *me*?'

I had to smirk. 'Ain't you ever watched cartoons as a kid?'

He frowned. 'Yes …?'

'You ever heard of *Tom and Jerry*?'

He stole a shallow breath. 'Of course. He references "cat and mouse". He wants you to be his Jerry – no, wait, sorry, his Tom. You're his *Tom*.'

'Precisely.'

'Here.' O'Brien handed a glass to Jeremy. 'This'll put hairs on your chest.'

The ice cubes clinked against the glass as Jeremy took it. 'Do you think this is legitimate?' He was seemingly unaware he held anything – he didn't even look close to taking a sip.

'I think we had better treat it as such.'

'Stupid question, but how are you feeling?'

I reached for my tumbler on the desk. 'Mostly, I am angry.'

Jeremy closed his eyes, going for a sip. He winced and pulled the glass back, looking at it as though it were poison. 'D-Do you think he'll come after us, too?'

Easing back into my chair, I shook my head. 'This is between me and him … for whatever reason.'

His body sagged upon hearing this, his frown smoothing out.

O'Brien took a seat behind his desk. 'How did you go at the library? Manage any research?'

'No, but I believe we should head down the path of this being tied in with religion – the very least, an occult of some sort.'

'What makes you say this?' Jeremy asked, a little more colour splotching his cheeks. 'I just don't see what a red feather has to do with Satan.'

'Do you know what an upside-down cross represents?'

His mouth twisted, then his eyes widened. 'The positioning of the bodies. The inverted cross is a symbol of evil; it denounces Jesus Christ!' He said this like it was a breakthrough he himself had discovered. I scratched my temple as he lifted his glass to take another sip.

'Exactly. I am certain the way the bodies are positioned is a sign of the Devil.'

O'Brien held up a finger: *Hold your horses.* 'We don't fully know that yet.'

'No, we don't,' I conceded. 'We are grasping at straws at this stage. I was planning on reading the books I'd borrowed from the library, but when I arrived home, I had that little gem waiting for me, didn't I?' I pointed to the letter on O'Brien's desk in a sealed bag.

'What about fingerprints? Is that the original?' Jeremy said, pointing to it as well.

O'Brien nodded. 'Yep. But I think we all know we won't find a match on here. Our boy is too smart for that.'

'True,' Jeremy said. 'If he can go to painstaking lengths to wipe away all traces of evidence from three households, he wouldn't be sloppy with a tiny piece of paper. No doubt gloves were worn.' Jeremy looked back and forth between us. 'I just still can't believe this has happened, Eddy.'

Maybe it was at that point I started warming to Jeremy more. Hell, maybe before my testicles had dropped, I'd come across as a bit of a stuck-up prick, too. Maybe to get ahead in life a bit of arrogance is required, because nice guys really *do* finish last.

'Give me a few days to do my research. There's a lady I know, Olivia, who works at the Penrith Library, and she's getting back to me with names of people who borrowed books relating to the occult and religion within the past few months.'

'I don't think you'll find too much from that,' O'Brien said. 'Our boy's more than likely been cutting off birds' heads in the name of Satan before he graduated from primary school. You know how this goes, Eddy.'

'Start 'em young, I know. But I cannot sit on my arse doing nothing; I need to be where the action is.'

'We do have others helping, you know,' Jeremy said. 'And the door-to-door is still ongoing, plus that white van is being followed up – the one across from

Norman's house.'

'He'd be less conspicuous than that,' I said, sucking an ice cube into my mouth, the crunch sending volts to my ears.

'It mentions a double homicide in the letter,' Jeremy said, leaning forward. 'Is it a bluff?'

'Let's goddamn hope so!' O'Brien said. 'All we can do is keep our chin up – and Eddy … do what this sicko says, and keep your eyes peeled. God, if it wasn't for me, you wouldn't be in this mess; I should never have called you.'

When we'd all had too much to drink, I called it a night. Janice was due to arrive home any minute, and I didn't want to be away from the house, or Ava, for too long.

I stretched my legs and walked through O'Brien's house to open the back door. 'Bogart?' I stepped out over the threshold as Jeremy and O'Brien said their goodbyes at the front door. Frowning, I looked from left to right. 'Bogart?'

When I saw no movement, my heart hammered. No rustling of grass or leaves, not even the whisper of wind. I raced all around the backyard, not that it was too big, but it was dark and I didn't want to yell out and wake the neighbours just yet.

'Bogart! Come here now!' Heart thumping, I ran to one side of the yard, then to the right-hand side, halting when I faced the wide-open gate.

Without thinking, I sprinted across the ground as fast as my old legs would carry me. I ran past the house, past the front porch where O'Brien and Jeremy shook hands under the dome of light.

'Eddy?' O'Brien said, somewhere in the distance.

'He's gone!' I yelled over my shoulder. My heavy footsteps pounded the cement as I ran to the end of the driveway, looking left, then right as images blurred across my vision. Only streetlamps and a few parked cars surrounded me.

'Huh?' O'Brien bounded down his steps.

'The fucking gate was wide open!'

'Buh-But you said you checked it! You checked it before we let him out there!'

I took off running, not knowing where I was going, nor caring who I woke. 'Bogart!'

'I'll drive around!' Jeremy yelled. I kept calling out as two car doors slammed shut, followed by an engine rumbling to life in the still of night.

'Bogart, come here now, boy!' Tears pricked my eyes, gooseflesh dotted my skin, my heart was on the verge of collapsing. My throat was so goddamn sore from the whisky and yelling, it ached to breathe.

Sticking my fingers in my mouth, I whistled while running. 'Bogart! Come on, boy, where are you?' My clapping hands sounded like thunderclaps in the night's silence.

A porch light sprung to life. Dogs barked in a domino effect. Someone came out on the stoop of their veranda – their front door clanging shut.

'You all right, mate?' a male neighbour asked me as I kept running. Jeremy's Gemini TG took off in the other direction.

'Please, Lord, no.' My teeth chattered as hot wind whipped my face. My eyes blurred worse as a sharp pain struck my chest.

I sprinted towards a man saying goodbye to his wife or girlfriend as she sat in an idling Holden Camira, peering up at him before they turned to me.

'Any of you see a German shepherd?'

The moustachioed man protruded his bottom lip. 'Nah, dude, sorry—'

Despite a stitch ripping my left side open, I kept running. 'Bogart! Come here!' Hot tears ran down my face, my fists clenching as sharp, quick breaths tore from my wheezing lungs. God, I was fucking scared. My boy. He was so innocent, so beautiful.

I whistled again, clapping as I wheeze-gasped my way out of passing out.

More dogs barked, one as deep as a trombone. Another porch light flicked on as I dashed past someone's front lawn, peering up the sides of the house. I crossed the street, searching through hedges, and as I turned back to the road I spied a blue leash dangling from a tree ahead. I clutched my aching chest while staring at it. It was on a low-lying branch reaching out like an arm towards the other side of the road. Bright pinpricks of light dotted my vision.

Standing there in the dark, I trembled while trying to drag air into my screaming lungs. My body shook with a murderous impulse as I dragged my feet towards the message waiting for me.

Religion was not my go-to, but in that moment, I prayed harder to God than I ever had before. *Please, not my boy. Lord, don't let it be his.* But I had bought that leash for him as soon as I'd picked him up from the animal shelter. Even in the moon's diluted hue, I recognised my boy's collar and leash waiting for me.

I lifted it off a small protruding stub and held it in my trembling hand. I closed my eyes, savouring the residual warmth on his leash. His unique scent impregnated the nylon fabric. My whole body shook as every sickening thought about my boy crossed my mind. 'I. Will. Fucking. Kill. You.' My teeth chattered like one of those wind-up toys we'd bought Heath years before when he'd wanted to open his own joke shop called Heath's Crack-Up.

A car approached from behind, the high beams flashing.

'Eddy!'

I turned on hearing O'Brien's inflated voice. And then Bogart's head popped out of the back window, his tongue protruded; I could tell he was wagging his tail by the way his body jiggled.

'The bugger was up near the Windsocks' place, sniffing around. Ha! We found him, mate!'

While trying to even my breathing, I rushed to the back door and fumbled with the silver handle. I jumped in beside Bogart, who began licking me all over. Joyous tears fell. But they were also laced with feelings of something far more aggressive than anger.

When I closed the car door, I grabbed Bogart, pressing my damp face into his warmth.

'You okay, Eddy?' Jeremy said, doing a U-turn. 'We found him, it's okay now.'

Sniffling, I took my time to catch my breath. 'He's fucking with me.'

'Whaddaya mean?' O'Brien said from the passenger seat, swivelling his head around.

'He left me his collar.' I held up the leash so O'Brien could see. 'That *cock-sucker* with brass balls went into your backyard while we were inside and led Bogart out the side gate.'

'What?' He took the collar from me as Jeremy rolled the car along – dogs still barking. Bogart's identification on an engraved silver, bone-shaped pendant swayed.

'I found his collar and leash on that tree just there.' I pointed behind us as Jeremy drove on.

'I don't believe it,' O'Brien whispered, incredulous. 'Shit on a stick, he's watching us all. Fuck! All from that article printed in the damn paper? This is bullshit!'

Jeremy turned to O'Brien. 'Oh no, this can't be happening. I still live with my parents!'

'Don't soil your trousers, son; he's just getting his kicks.'

'And I'll kick him right in the goddamn face when I catch him.' I patted Bogart's head. 'Go for a nice adventure, did you? Scaring the crap out of Dad ...' I scratched him under his chin as he panted.

'He looks to be okay, at least,' Jeremy said.

Nodding, I closed my eyes. 'Yeah. For now.' I loathed the thought of what could have happened. Of what this madman was capable of. If he could cut shapes out of human flesh, then what the hell could he have done to a dog? Most sickos started out with animals. They start off small, and then get bigger. Adult-size bigger. And, he'd already killed one dog.

'It's okay, boy,' I said, gazing out the window as Jeremy pulled into O'Brien's driveway. 'We're going home now.'

CHAPTER TWENTY-ONE

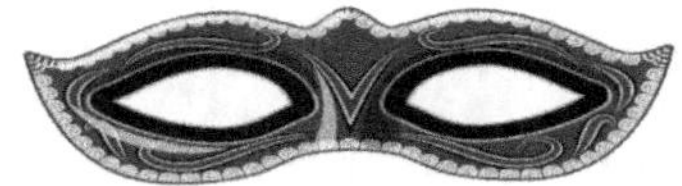

MY HAND GLIDED along the smooth banister as I crept up the staircase, the smell of roast pork lingering in the air. I'd taken Bogart out the back, and he had gone straight for the water bowl. After he'd piddled, I'd called him back inside. He would sleep inside tonight, and the next night, and all the nights until we caught 'Jerry'. Sleep would not come easily for me tonight.

Upon slowly opening the bedroom door, I saw Ava on her back, eyes on the ceiling.

Shit. This was not good.

She inhaled through her nostrils and in the silence, it sounded amplified, akin to a whirlwind. 'Where have you been?'

Closing the door behind me, I said, 'I took Bogart for a walk.'

Her head shot off the pillow. 'For five hours? You took your car, so you obviously went a lot farther than the river!'

I approached my side of the bed and sat; the mattress dipping and squeaking under my weight. 'I wanted to give you space with your friends. I didn't feel welcome.'

She sat up; the bed creaking. 'You insulted Roberta!'

God, how I wanted to argue the point. Instead, I lowered my head, for in marriage, sometimes you have to pick your battles. 'I know.'

'Since when do you use disgusting language like that? I hate that word. It's revolting!'

'It slipped out. I'm sorry.'

'You ruined my dinner, I hope you know. And you hardly touched your food. What *is* the matter with you?'

How could I face her and say: *Honey, a serial killer is on the loose, and guess what, baby? He knows where we live!*

'I guess I took offence to Roberta tonight. She was being dismissive of you, being disrespectful to you in your own house after you cooked a wonderful dinner.'

'How would you even know? You hardly touched it. And that's just Roberta, she is a domineering character. We can't all be as perfect as Edward Matthews.'

Shrugging, I said, 'What do you want me to say here? I'm agreeing I was out of line. What more can I do tonight?'

Her tongue clicked. 'You can sleep on the couch.'

I turned to her, the pale moonlight shining on her glistening cheeks. I didn't say another word as I rose, grabbed my pyjamas and left the room.

As bad as this sounds, I was glad she kicked me out, because now I could watch over the house. If any prick walked through the back door (or front), or climbed through the windows, then he was a goner. After what he'd done regarding Bogart, that was unforgivable. You never fuck with a man's best friend.

I had, of course, double-checked everything when Bogart was outside drinking water. I'd checked all the downstairs windows and made sure they were locked. After Bogart had finished pissing, I had made sure the back door was locked, too. Even as I passed the front door, I wiggled the knob again, just in case. I mean, I *knew* I had locked it, but I wanted to be *sure* I had.

Bogart sat up on the couch as soon as I stepped off the staircase.

'What did I tell you about the couch?' I whispered, shaking my head.

He wagged his tail, thumping it against the pillowy cushions.

I took the knife I'd taken out of the kitchen drawer and then hidden under the left sleeve of my jacket, and placed it on the lounge room coffee table, emitting a *ting!* as it collided with the glass. I removed my clothing until I was in my jocks, and climbed into my summer pyjamas – a red cotton set with short sleeves and short pants.

'Shove over,' I said to Bogart. He moved to the other side of the couch and stared at me. I lay down, resting my head so it faced the front section of the house.

It was eerily quiet. I could not sleep and my legs and lower back ached. I kept blinking – each time I glanced to a different section of the house, sinister shadows played pranks on me. I could make out body shapes and human faces of just about anything. It was like living in a real-life horror movie, one where Jason Voorhees would appear above me at any second. Shadows from cars passed the front door like ghostly apparitions, and someone's car horn blasting made me jump up. I looked again to make sure the knife was on the table and saw it glistening in the moonlight. It would have been too obvious if I'd grabbed the gun from the dresser drawer with Ava watching me, so a knife would have to suffice – if it came to it.

Inhaling, I placed my hands over my chest. 'You scared me tonight, boy,' I whispered into the darkness. He was already fidgeting near my feet. 'I never want to lose you.' I waited for a response, but Bogart was biting a flea, his teeth chafing together incessantly against his fur coat. 'And if anyone ever touches a single hair on your head—' I couldn't finish that sentence, couldn't think about what could have been. I said a silent prayer of thank you to my guardian angels – Mum and Dad, Grandma and Grandpa – and closed my eyes in vain. Every sound, every groan of the house and my eyes flung open. At one point, at around 3 am, I would guess, I grabbed my knife when the floorboards creaked. All five of my senses were primed and at the ready as I sat up. Deducing it was my overactive imagination playing tricks on me – which is exactly what 'Jerry' wanted – I settled down, heart rate decreasing as the seconds drew by.

So far there was a mark next to his name, while I had a big, fat, shiny zero in the shape of an arsehole.

'I'll even it up soon enough,' I whispered as the comforting warmth of Bogart at my feet helped me to drift off to sleep just as the sun peeked over the eastern horizon.

CHAPTER TWENTY-TWO

THE BLAZING SUN infiltrating the glass back door woke me. My scratchy eyes rebelled against the glare, and I sat up before I could register where I was: the couch. Bogart lay curled at my feet, sound asleep. The knife on the table. *Ava must still be in bed.*

I rubbed my eyes and stretched my back before standing with a yawn. Already a sheen of sweat covered my face, my underarms damp. I grabbed the knife and returned it to the kitchen drawer, then crept up the stairs to check on Ava. She had her back to me and didn't stir. The rise and fall of our bedsheet told me she was in a deep, comfortable sleep, so I closed the door and headed for the bathroom not too far down the hallway.

After taking a leak, I headed downstairs and peered out the glass panel beside our front door. Nothing screamed alarm. No letters waiting for me on the doormat, which read 'THE NEIGHBOURS HAVE BETTER STUFF'.

As I spied a young go-getter peddling past on his mountain bike, my mind went to work on how to smooth things over with Ava. I couldn't remember the last time she'd kicked me out of bed.

Shuffling to the kitchen, I opened the fridge as Bogart trotted over, snooping inside for himself, schnoz going berserk and pushing me out the way. I opened the packet of ham and chucked him a slice. He ran off with it, snorting huffs of appreciation. A few plates from last night's dinner were covered with cling wrap, taunting me, but I would have that for lunch. All of last night's adrenaline had worn off, and I was peckish this morning.

Spotting eggs and a packet of bacon, I thought, *Success*! I'd make Ava breakfast today for a change. Using my elbow to close the door, as my arms were full, I put the food on the bench and placed a pot of coffee on the stove. Our bedroom door upstairs opened.

Two separate pans sat on alternate hobs to fire them up, and I went to our bread tin.

'Shit!' I whispered, remembering, running over to collect Bogart before ushering him out of the house. 'Shh!' I said, finger to my lips as he looked at me as if to say *What'd I do, Dad?*

As I slid the door shut, I heard the toilet upstairs flushing, pipes groaning. Re-entering the kitchen, I placed a hand over the pans, testing if they were hot enough. I expected Ava down here at any moment, but I waited and waited.

As I cracked two eggs into the pan of melted butter, Ava descended the staircase.

'I'm going out,' she yelled. The handle of the front door squeaked as she turned it. I chucked the eggshells into the sizzling pan and hurried out of the kitchen.

'Wait!' The front door closed as I rushed over. I opened it and flew outside, but Ava was already in her car and had started the ignition. Keen early joggers sprinted along the path across the road, dogs on leashes, struggling to keep pace with their overzealous owners.

I knocked on her car window with my index knuckle. 'Stop!'

Her chest expanded, but she wound down her window as she focused on the steering wheel.

'Where are you going?'

'Out.'

'Yes, but where? I just put breakfast on.'

'It'll make up for the meal you skipped out on last night.'

I reached in the window to touch her cheek, but she leaned to the other side, like my fingers were poison ivy. Her eyelids had a slash of blue, her sweet perfume floated out the window.

'Where are you going?'

She turned to me, eyes narrowing. 'It is none of your business.'

Eyeing her pink lipstick, I frowned. 'It's a simple question, Ava. What are you hiding?'

She sucked back air. 'What am *I* hiding? What are *you* hiding? You've been acting funny!'

'Funny how?'

'Funny like when ...'

Don't say Abigail. Do not mention her name.

She shook her head and whispered, 'It doesn't matter.'

'When are you coming back? Maybe we can go to the movies?'

'We are not going to the movies. I will be back later.'

'Before dinner?'

'You can sort out dinner for yourself.'

'I didn't mean it like that – I was just asking. Christ, you're acting worse than some criminals I've brought in for questioning.'

She rolled up the window in a huff.

I palmed the window as she put it in gear. 'Wait, hang on!'

She reversed out of the driveway, and if I hadn't retracted my foot, she would have clipped it. She took off down the road and I shook my head in disbelief.

I turned and made my way back to the house, but if I'm honest again, I saw the advantage in organising the house while she was gone. I would install cameras out the back and arrange for deadbolts from whoever was free to come to my house today, and then I would head to the local hardware store to buy industrial-strength padlocks for our side gates.

While this was happening, I'd soak up the information inside the library rentals like a thirsty sponge.

Because I had a full day ahead of me, I barely thought much about where Ava was going at all.

CHAPTER TWENTY-THREE

BOGART LAY AT my feet inside the study. A barrel-chested man with a bald patch worked on the front door with an upscale deadbolt, a team from EYE SPY were installing cameras that faced out the back, and two facing the front. Every angle of the house was covered. I had to pay extra because I'd demanded it on such short notice, like I gave a toss. I couldn't put a price on the safety of my family.

A library rental was spread in front of me, a notepad and pen lay beside the book. I'd scribbled down a few key sentences, but nothing so far linked Satanism to a red feather, or a crown. Satan was the 'Prince of Darkness', but I felt that angle was as weak as piss.

As I flipped the page, I heard someone clear their throat at the open door – I hadn't closed it, in case the tradies needed something. I didn't want to be too far away from the action.

Seeing Ava's beetroot-coloured face made my stomach clench. 'Love?'

Her nostrils flared. 'What is going on? Have you gone mad?' She waved an arm behind her towards the front door. 'Who are all these men? When did you decide this? I couldn't even park in my own driveway because vans are blocking it.'

Holding up a placatory hand, I said, 'Don't be upset; I am adding more security to our house, that's all.'

From the corner of my eye, I saw Bogart's ear flick up, his head tilted. *Stay down, boy…*

She folded her arms over her heaving chest. 'But why?'

'It's not a bad thing, is it, love? One can never be too cautious.'

The corners of her eyes crinkled. 'Has something happened?'

Shaking my head, I said, 'I worry about you when I'm not here.'

She threw her head back and laughed. 'It never worried you a single bit while you were on the job. I can remember a lot of nights when I was here by myself. A lot.'

'So you keep reminding me. And I wasn't okay with it; I did fret.'

'Well, what's changed? Is this a way of compensating for you not working?'

'Maybe. I guess so.'

Her hands flew up. 'What is with you?!'

Bogart rushed out from under the desk and headed straight for her, jumping up.

Standing, I shouted, 'Down!'

He looked back at me with fear in his eyes, ears pulled back, body hunched.

She glared, waiting for an explanation.

'He's only in here because of the work; I can't risk having him run off.'

She closed her eyes, chin tilting as she breathed through her nostrils. 'I don't care about the dog being in the house. I am worried about *you*. I came home to take you up on your movie offer.'

My lips curled upwards. 'You did? We can still go, if you like?'

She laughed mockingly. 'How? With men walking in and out of our house?'

'They've been here for a while; they should be done soon.'

She wrapped her arms around herself. 'You planned all this and didn't tell me.'

'That's not true. I didn't make a single call until today.'

'Why?'

The boys outside started drilling a hole into the brick exterior. Bogart looked around for the source of the noise.

'Where did you go before, Ava?'

She cupped her forehead. 'I don't want to fight with you. I truly don't.'

I walked out from behind my desk. 'And you think I do?'

She peered up at me as Bogart stared at me, too. 'How about we finish this conversation after the movie?'

I wish I could say elation soared through me, but the more time I wasted cavorting, the more time our killer had to plot his next murder. Or murders, if he was to be believed. 'Done. You pick the movie, I'll find out how much longer the guys will be here for, okay?'

I went to hug her, but she pushed my chest. 'No getting out of this until we've spoken. But movie first.'

'Fair call.' Then the telephone rang.

Ava turned to the sound. 'I'll get it.' When she strolled off, I raced to my desk, closed the book, and shoved the notepad into the top drawer.

'Bogart, come here.' He came to me, wagging his tail. I ruffled him up about the jowls, watching his pink tongue wiggling about. 'I'm sorry I yelled at you, boy.'

When Ava returned a minute later, her cheeks resembled the red puce of old bricks.

'What happened?' Fear tapped against my sternum. 'Who was on the phone?'

She managed to pry her clenched jaws apart as she glared. 'Janice O'Brien.'

I pinched my brows together. 'And?'

'*And* she said you forgot a book at their place … last night.'

Oh shit!

She breathed hard, her glare said she was close to thwacking me on the side of the head. 'Took Bogart for a walk, huh?'

'Let me explain …'

She closed her eyes and held out a stop sign hand. 'I don't want to hear another lie.'

'Honey, it's not like I was with another woman—'

'Don't you *dare*. You *promised* me you would be off the case. Now your picture is in the papers. And now … you're still secretly working on this case.'

The pulse in my neck throbbed like a triphammer. I waited for an electric drill from inside the house to stop whirring before I spoke again. 'Yes.'

'You lied to me about it.'

Someone outside knocked on the wall with a hammer.

I kept my eye contact with her, waiting for a lull. 'I did.'

She took a moment before running a tongue along her lower lip, brushing aside her hair. 'I'm heading out, and I don't know when I'll be back.'

All I could do was sit back at my desk and wait for the front door to slam shut.

CHAPTER TWENTY-FOUR

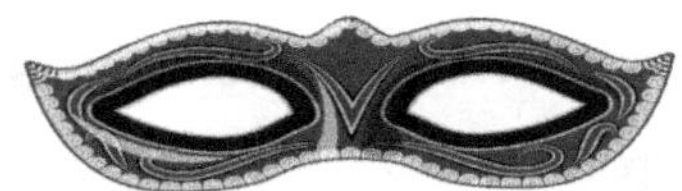

THINGS SEEMED TO be spiralling out of control faster than an unmanned hose on full blast. Once I was satisfied the house was more secure than Alcatraz, I grabbed a beer and sat on the couch with my feet on the coffee table. Bogart lay beside me, my arm draped around him. I kept seeing Ava's hurt expression in my mind's eye. Boy, I'd really fucked up. I guessed she'd gone over to Hayley's, but Ava was good in that she didn't gossip about our marital problems – or so I hoped. She wasn't the type of mother to trash her husband in front of her kids. She believed marital issues should stay between a husband and wife, and thank God for that; Lord knows I had given her plenty of material for an entire episode of a daytime talk show. I thought I could trust she wouldn't say a word to Hayley, but if she did, I couldn't blame her. Not one iota.

I was too down in the dumps to do much else apart from drink beer and stare into space. I kept looking at the wall phone, expecting it to ring. I wanted to hear Ava's voice; I'd rather have her yelling at me than nothing at all. I hated being alone, but now more than ever, I understood what I had put Ava through on those long nights when I was in the field, chasing someone down, organising busts and raids, and arrests on unsuspecting perps, while she had only herself for company.

The silence kills you. Silence so profound, it becomes claustrophobic. Just as I took another swig of beer, someone knocked on the front door. I looked over and then rose, Bogart at my heels.

Through the floor-to-ceiling glass panel beside the door, my brows shot north when I saw Heath. My heart rate increased as I opened the door. 'G'day, mate! What a lovely surprise.'

'Hey, Dad.'

He could have knocked me over with a feather. This was great. This was really something. 'Would you like to come in for a drink?'

Heath shrugged, mouth twisting.

'Your mother's gone out.'

Heath hesitated before nodding. 'Yeah ... yeah, I'll come in.' He followed me inside.

Despite the blazing sun, he wore a blood-red long-sleeved flannel shirt. 'Would ya like a beer?'

'Yeah ... yeah, a beer would be great.'

Something lingered in the air like pent-up kinetic energy, but I would not probe him yet. After opening the fridge, I grabbed two bottles of beer before closing the door.

Heath already sat on the couch, Bogart by his side, sniffing his clothing.

'Were you sitting here?' he asked.

Shaking my head, I said, 'Don't worry about it. Here.' I handed him the beer and watched as he took off the cap with one twist of a shirtsleeve.

'So,' I began, plonking in the armchair closest to him. 'How's things?'

He focused a little too hard on his beer label. He eventually took a swig as

I waited for him to begin. I didn't want to press a thing, no matter how much I wanted to bombard him with questions.

'Lorraine told me you popped by.' He stared at his beer, his knees bobbing up and down. 'You never pop by.'

'Maybe it's time I start.'

There was an elongated pause as I continued to observe his behaviour. His eyes weren't bloodshot; he seemed okay to me.

'Did you get extra security?'

'Today. A man can never be too careful.'

He squinted. 'Where's Ma?'

My free hand flew up in the air. 'I don't know. Just out.'

He nodded, avoiding my gaze. I kept watching him, trying to read any and all signs. What was this bugger hiding from me?

'Heath?' His knees kept bouncing, his agitation mounting. 'Anything you wanna tell your dad?'

He shook his head.

'Are you positive?'

He shook his head as tears gathered. My son was not emotional; I had rarely seen him cry. Not that he didn't express emotion, but he was used to keeping it under wraps. He was a chip off the old block. I had shed tears last night over thinking Bogart was ... but before that, Christ, it'd been years. Since 1976 to '77 to be precise. I didn't understand how women could cry over movies and gush over books. But of course, I was not immune to emotions. Last night had tipped me over the edge.

'Heath,' I whispered. 'Whatever it is, you can tell me.'

He shook his head, wiping his nose with his shirtsleeve. 'I *can't*.' There was turmoil in that word 'can't', an ocean's worth of meaning in that one syllable.

'Why can't you?' I spoke as softly as I could. This was his game. He could take the lead whenever he chose.

''Cause you're a cop.'

'I'm your *dad*. Above anything else, I am your father. Whatever it is, you can tell me.'

He closed his eyes as the tears descended. Breathing became a struggle for me. I had never seen Heath in so much pain, so much inner turmoil. What in the hell was going on here?

'I'm, ah, in some deep shit.' He half-opened his brown eyes.

My hand clamped around my beer; any tighter and I'd be wearing shards of glass for a glove. I took a minute, waiting for him to elaborate. 'Do you want to tell me from the beginning?'

He threw his head back, stretching his neck.

'Okay, let's try this, then. Is it gambling?'

His head fell forward; he was now gulping in air. 'Sorta.'

'Sort of. Okay. Is it drugs?'

He whimpered, nostrils expanding. I wanted to go to him, but I also knew while conducting interviews to get the truth, you never crowd a person. You let them believe they hold the reins. You sit back and let it unravel, inch by inch, no matter how long it takes. Heath was here because he needed to get this off his chest. He had wanted to talk but didn't know how.

'What drugs, Heath?'

He laughed, a crazy, maniacal laugh. 'Whatever you can fuckin' name, man.' He looked at me, his eyes bleeding with pain. It was gut-wrenching to be on this end of my son's own mayhem. I almost broke down just looking at him. Maybe I should thank Janice O'Brien for spilling the beans to Ava. He would not have opened up had my wife been here – not like this.

'How bad is it?'

'Preeeeetty bad ...' he said, laughing again, a mirthless laugh.

My eyes never left his, even when I took a long swig of beer. 'Are you in debt?'

'Yup!' Heath sniffled, wiping his eyes and nose again. I glanced at Bogart. His ears perked up, his eyes wide and confused.

'So you owe someone money?'

He blubbered, using the heel of his free hand to press into his closed eye.

'It's all right. It must have been difficult for you to come here. I don't want you to worry about the past. I'm your dad, which means you come first.'

'You know what, *Dad*?' His nose scrunched up, ready to spit venom. 'Pretty fuckin' rich of you to say this to me now. Where the hell were you when we needed you? Huh?!'

Inhaling, I tried to keep my breathing steady – that was another nickname of mine before Macintosh Matthews came about: Steady Eddy; self-explanatory, really. 'Heath, I have apologised for not being there when you needed me. I can't change the past.'

'I was probably better off without you, anyway.'

Shaking my head, ignoring the stab of guilt, I said, 'You don't mean that.'

'Oh yeah? Pretty fuckin' embarrassing when you look into the audience expecting to see your old man there, smiling like other proud dads, but not Edward Matthews, he's got better shit to do!'

Anger rose within me, arresting my better logic. 'So you're blaming this all on me – that it?'

He looked at his beer again, gasping for air. 'No.'

I pointed my finger at him, my mouth set in a thin horizontal line. 'Good, because you're better than that. I may not have been around as much as either of us would have liked, but Hayley is not out there making excuses. And let me tell you, you could have had it a helluva lot worse! I *know*, Heath; I was out there making sure you and your sister and mother could walk the streets safely at night! You didn't come home to witness me bashing your mother or raping your sister.' He gazed at me. Christ, I was trying to keep my cool, but internally, something had snapped. He'd hit a sore spot, all right. 'I got us a house by the river so you and Hayley could spend your weekends playing by the water, and hanging out with other kids. I paid for your private education, I paid for your first car; whatever you wanted I practically gave it! So yes, I may not have been around as much as the other dads, but don't you dare say that I am the sole person to blame for you picking up a bad habit.'

Bogart's brown eyes were wide as he stared at me.

'I'm not pinning this on you, Dad, okay?'

I settled back in my chair and took another swig. I sucked back a few purifying breaths before speaking again. 'How much in debt are you? And don't lie.'

He sighed, wiping his mouth. He stared hard at the carpet. 'Ten thousand.'

Inside my gut, Mount St. Helens erupted. I clamped my jaw as a gush of air tore through my nostrils, waiting for my anger to subside. 'What's that for?'

'For me taking drugs off tick, then gambling to try to pay off what I owed. It just got bigger and bigger.'

'Does Lorraine know?'

'Yeah, we've had some pretty big blues over it. She almost left me a few times.'

Tilting my head back as heat surged through my chest and neck, I asked, 'Are you clean?'

'Marijuana – but that's it. No-one will give me anything now; I've got a bad reputation.'

'Anyone threaten you?'

He nodded.

I ran a hardened tongue over my upper teeth, mouth closed, heart thwacking against my chest. 'By doing what?'

'Smashed my car rear windows yesterday.'

'How'd you get here?'

'Lorraine let me borrow her car.'

I gazed out through the glass door as a black-and-white willie wagtail glided an inch above the grass, dipping down, then up. No worries in the world apart from getting his next worm. Life was easy for some, not so for others. 'And is Lorraine doing anything to help?'

'She keeps giving me money, yeah.' He sniffed hard, then swallowed.

'Where is *she* getting it from?'

He shrugged, wiping his wet chin on his sleeve. 'Dunno. I ask her and she says her parents lend it to her, but I don't believe that because they're not too well-off with money, either.'

I sat back and pondered this; I had some hypotheses of my own.

His sorrowful eyes connected with mine. 'Can you help me, Dad?'

'How much do you have in the bank?'

He snorted. 'Practically nothing.'

Thirty-four years old and nothing in the bank account. What good did drugs ever do anybody?

'I can give you half. Is that fair?'

His face scrunched up like a piece of old parchment paper, tears streaming. 'I'm sorry.'

'You're not, because you kept doing it. It's like when someone cheats; they ain't sorry for it, they're sorry they got caught.'

'I didn't see it getting this far out of control.'

My body softened at his tone. 'I can believe that. But there were times when you could have quit. You chose not to. And that's why I am only going to give you five. But hear me now when I say: if you ever touch drugs again, then do not step foot back inside this house.'

He shook his head. 'I won't.'

'No – promise me. If I give you half tomorrow, then it's considered a deal.

Those are my terms, take it or leave it. I could ask for names, but I know you'd never give them to me.'

'Nah, I get it. I won't.'

'Promise me. And then shake on it like a man.'

He leaned forward, as did I.

'I don't want to have to bullshit to your mother about why you never come around anymore. Don't let this break up the family.'

His hand stilled mid-air. 'Are you gonna throw this back in my face again?'

I held his gaze. 'Once it's done, we move on. So, do we have a deal?'

He looked me square in the eye, grabbed my hand, and shook it. 'Deal.'

CHAPTER TWENTY-FIVE

AFTER HEATH LEFT, I received a call from O'Brien. I forewent telling him about the trouble Janice had caused; that was the least of my worries. Janice always had good intentions – how was she to know my wife would answer the phone? How was she to know I'd been lying to Ava? Besides, O'Brien had more pressing things to talk about.

'We just finished the meeting with Basil Humphries.'

I leaned against the kitchen archway. 'And?'

'And he said the same usual shit that every forensic psychologist throws out: white male, aged thirty-five or older. Probably lives by himself so he can move around without being noticed, or he has a job where he can be in and out at all hours without it deemed suspicious to a wife or girlfriend.' Paper rustled from his end as I listened intently. 'Um ... he's probably described by those who know him as a "nice guy" – would do anything to help others and seem like a good Samaritan.'

'Ted Bundy once saved a kid from drowning, *and* he used to work for a crisis hotline.'

'Exactly; it's always the ones you least expect. Anyway, Humphries went on to say our guy is an introvert, so he uses his crime like a stage to show off, where he fears no judgement from others. Um ... extremely intelligent – almost too intelligent for his own good – with a possible knowledge of criminology. Says these killings aren't sexual; it's about how damn good he is. He's trying to prove himself better than the rest. Reckons he could be impotent, actually. Doubts these are his first killings; probably started off by strangling the family cat ... you know the drill.'

At his end, fax machines whirred and telephones trilled over the endless chatter.

'But look, some good news. We have a lead on the white van that was seen parked across the street of Norman Colbert's.'

'Oh yeah?' I pressed the phone hard against my ear to drown out the refrigerator's hum.

'Yes, registered to a Mr Mustafa Akhmed, registered address ... Bondi.'

I frowned, ruminating. 'Bondi? What's he doing this far out west?'

'That's what Jeremy and I are about to find out. Now, here comes the interesting bit. We've dug deeper into the victims. So far, *all* of these guys were involved in shady dealings.'

Shifting my weight to the other leg, I said, 'Like what? Who?'

'*All* of them. None were saints. Norman Colbert – his employees say he was a narcissistic piece of lard. Apparently, he owed them money for overtime and all sorts of things. One employee – and I quote – "I am glad that he's dead. It is not surprising someone bumped him off". Unquote.'

'Did you check into *that* guy more closely?'

'She. A Miss Brittney Lake.'

'Okay, *she* ... What about Ian from Ireland?'

'Drugs, and you saw the snub-nosed .38.'

'And Mark Andrews?'

'Turns out his wife wasn't the only one warming his sheets.'

'Did she know – the wife?'

'Ahh, she does now! Mark kept nude photos and raunchy letters from his raven-haired mistress – Valerie Burnett.'

I shook my head. 'What is the connection to all three men? Did they know each other?'

'Highly unlikely. We've seen no evidence to support that, although we are trying to link it.'

'So we have a killer who is, what, a vigilante punishing the bad guys? Does he see himself as ridding the streets of sin?' The blanket of fog swirling around my mind suddenly cleared. 'Sin! They were all *sinful*.'

'Yeah, but, look, Eddy, aren't we all? I mean, if you dug far enough back into my history, my sheets wouldn't look as clean as a preacher's, okay? I'm sure for you, too.'

He could say that again. 'I guess. But this is too big to ignore.'

'Agreed, and it's pretty much all we have, except one other thing.'

'For God's sake, tell me ... stop with the suspense.'

He chuckled. 'One eyewitness came forward this morning. A homeless man by the name of Fuzzy. Says he was in his usual spot in an alleyway, near Ian's apartment block in Kingswood.'

'Yes ...?' My stronghold on the receiver could have snapped it in half.

'This guy reckons he woke up from a drug-fuelled haze to see a tall man in black exit the apartment building wearing a mask.'

'What kind of mask?'

'He said, and I quote, "like one of 'em Halloween masks", end quote.'

Squinting, I said, '*Halloween*? As in Michael Myers?'

'He didn't say which character, just that this guy was wearing a mask. Oh, and the nose was long. He saw that when the guy in the mask turned to the side.'

I scratched my head. Nose was long? 'When did he witness this?'

'That's just it. At the same time and day the coroner ruled Ian's death. But there's more.'

I waited, heart thumping.

'He said this masked guy turned right to look at him, paused, but then kept going!'

A wave of disappointment tugged on my stomach. 'Then it wasn't our guy. He wouldn't leave a witness alive to tell the tale.'

He hesitated. 'At the same time the coroner stated. Wearing a mask. Dressed in black.'

'You're right; it doesn't make sense otherwise. And Fuzzy is sure it was just *one* guy?'

'Yes, but how much can be believed? He'd just woken up from a noddy – he probably waved to Lucy in the Sky right afterwards.'

'Still, this is the first witness to come forward, is it not?'

'We've had neighbours of all three say all sorts. "At 1 am I heard a dog barking…" and "I saw a man in a hoodie walking down the street – it was very suspicious …" Another favourite: "I did see a car, but I don't know what make, model, or colour".'

'Same old, same old. No-one else reported seeing a white van at either Ian's or Mark's?'

'Nope, but we're following up Mustafa from Bondi today. Do you have anything?'

'Negative. I am still reading books and waiting for Olivia Hitchcock to get back to me on her compiled list of books taken out on loan.'

'Gotcha. Roger that. And by the by, I'm still trying to work out a way to present your letter to Davies or Humphries without getting either of us castrated.

Leave it with me. Thank God they haven't seen or mentioned the *Telegraph* yet.'

'Thank God, indeed. Where's Jeremy?'

'He's across the street, getting us some coffee— Oh, hey, my pager is going off, I got to go!'

Admittedly, I was insanely jealous. I looked out the back door where the sun glared. Instead of being on the road beside my partner, chasing a lead, I was stuck inside my own house, which now felt more like a prison. I had half a mind to call O'Brien back and ask if I could tag along, but he'd only say no. It would never be 'official' again. I returned to the couch and looked around the room. It was quiet. A little too quiet. And then, just to really stick it to me, police sirens wailed in the far distance. My spine straightened over my siren song calling me.

How I missed being official. There was nothing else to compare. Nothing in the world was more exhilarating than being on the force, believing I was making a difference.

Gritting my teeth, I closed my eyes as the siren faded. I then glanced out the door and spotted Bogart lying on his back, belly facing the sun, getting his tan on. I stared at him as a wall clock ticked with mechanical precision. Eventually, after I don't know how long, I headed towards the study to feed my addiction.

CHAPTER TWENTY-SIX

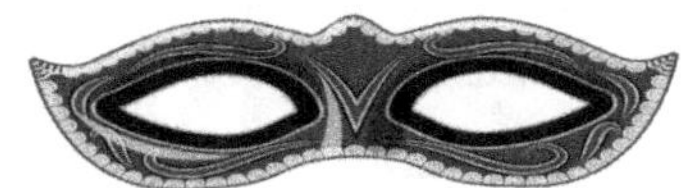

YAWNING LOUDLY, I closed the book. By the time I emerged from my study, it was dark. The house was eerily silent. I couldn't even hear any traffic outside, nor bicycle bells, nor dogs barking.

I made my way to the downstairs bathroom to relieve myself, and then grabbed a beer from the fridge. My beer supply was running dangerously low; I would have to rectify this soon.

At the back door, I saw Bogart trotting over to his water bowl.

'Here, boy,' I called, opening the door.

He looked up and bounded over.

'Want some din-din?'

His tail wagged like windscreen wipers on MAX. I couldn't help but laugh. 'C'mon, then.'

Bogart followed me inside, almost tripping me over in doing so. I sorted out his meal – chicken and liver from a can – in no time flat.

He guzzled it down as though starved. 'You'll be eating better than me tonight, boy.'

Thankfully, the leftover roast and accompaniments were still wrapped up in the fridge on plates. It was only a matter of spooning pork, mash and beans onto a plate and heating it up. There was no crackle left. Nor pepper gravy.

'Thanks a lot, Roberta,' I mumbled, slamming the microwave door shut and pressing the 2–MINUTE button.

I tipped the bottle back until my mouth was full, swallowing as the phone rang.

Ava! I snatched it up, smacking myself in the side of the head with the receiver.

'Hello, this is the Matthews' residence.' Squinting, I waited for the person to speak. 'Hello?'

Then it came to me, softly. Someone breathing at the other end.

My fingers tightened around the phone. 'Who is this?'

A faint chuckle floated down from the other line. My stomach muscles tightened.

I held the phone hard against my ear. 'It's you, isn't it?'

'Mm-hmm …' said a deep voice. Almost seductive, but in a morbid way.

Swallowing hard, I almost dropped my beer before I caught it by the damp rim. Beads of sweat dotted my brow and upper lip, tickling my flesh.

My lips curled back and a sickly chill ran up my spine, like someone doing itsy bitsy spider with skeletal fingers. 'Listen here, you sick *fuck*. You ever come here again and you'll be signing your own death warrant – got that?'

A deep, sinister chuckle caused my teeth to grind, but I realised it was muffled. Something was placed over his mouth. Something like a mask.

'Fucking coward. You ever go near my dog again and you're a dead man. Understand?!'

He tutted like the second hand on *60 Minutes*. *Tut-tut-tut-tut-tut-tut* he went on, reprimanding me.

'Can't speak, can you? *Fucking* yellow-belly. That's what I am dealing with, isn't it?'

'You will see.'

The dull, continuous disconnected tone rolled into my ear as I stood, frozen. That voice was not normal. It was not a man speaking to another man. It sounded evil, belonging to a black soul.

I hung up and turned to the back door, cursing myself for not locking it. I hurried over and locked it, gazing outside as leaves swayed in the dry wind. Tall trees created dark silhouettes against the blue-black panorama. Shit, where was my head at? I'd spent thousands of dollars on new state-of-the-art, burglar-safe gizmos, and I couldn't even lock the back door.

The phone rang again. I sprinted to it, beer spilling on the carpet as I made my way over. With my heart drumming and mouth dry, I reefed the receiver off the cradle, grappling with it in my sweaty hand before placing it to my ear. 'What do you want?!'

'Eddy?' A timorous voice said a beat later.

Realisation set in that this was a woman's voice. Shit! 'Oh, um, hello?'

'Ahh, it's O-Olivia Hitchcock ... from the library?'

I closed my eyes, grazing the wall in front with the fist holding my bottle. 'Jeez, I am really sorry about that, darlin'. God, I feel awful now.'

'Having a bad night?' Faint amusement laced her tone instead of panic.

When the microwave blasted a shrill *ding*! beside me, I almost crapped myself.

Placing a fist over my thumping heart, I said, 'You could say that. Look, I apologise; I don't usually answer the phone like that.'

'I don't know about you cops,' she said, laughing.

I laughed, too, wiping my damp brow with a forearm. 'Sorry. Anyway, do you have anything useful for me?'

'I do.' My heart kicked up a notch, but my hands still shook. 'I actually found some interesting patterns. I started with a simple search of the man I'd served. While he has only checked out one book pertaining to the occult, I decided to check his history.'

This was it. She had something for me, the undertone of teasing was unmistakable.

'Before this, he took out a book on Adolf Hitler.'

I frowned. 'Right ...?'

'Then a book on Stalin. Then one on Lenin.'

'Hmm. Okay, well, not too much—'

'I'm not finished.'

'Yes, of course, I'm sorry.' Raising the bottle to my lips, the cold liquid slid down my throat, warming my insides.

She chuckled. 'The time before that, however, he took out three books in one go. A book on the human anatomy, a book on the SS in Germany, and one on Friedrich Nietzsche.'

I rubbed my pinched forehead. 'I don't get it.'

'There's a link here, Eddy. Aryan themes. One race. Purification of societies.'

'Purification?'

'The cleansing of society. Eugenics. The *Übermensch*. Creating the superior race. Exactly what Hitler did with the Jews, eradicating society of the degradation and filth they brought upon the world – his words, not mine. I'm just telling you.'

'Yeah, no, I understand. I'm familiar with Hitler and Auschwitz. But this purification thing interests me.'

Cleansing society of sin. All three victims were not notable characters. But how would 'Jerry' know this about them? What was his selection process? What was the link I was missing?

'Anyway, are you ready for his name?'

'Am I ever!'

She laughed again, almost in a giddy way. For a librarian, this was probably the most exciting thing she'd ever done on the job. Of course, I was assuming here.

'His name is Joseph Fisher.'

CHAPTER TWENTY-SEVEN

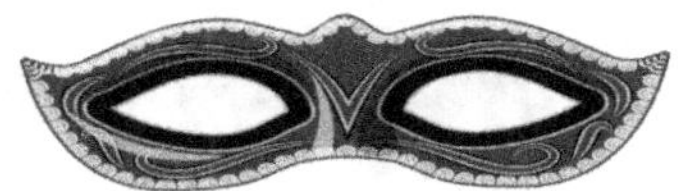

LATER THAT NIGHT, I double-checked every window and door, but I left the deadbolt unlocked in case Ava came home – she didn't have the new key to open the door. I'd eaten in the study while researching more about Satanism and the occult, as Bogart lay at my feet. The pork had dried out since refrigeration – but it was an automatic thing: food in mouth, swallow, belly + brain = happy. I tried to call O'Brien several times, but to no avail, so at about 11 pm I called it a night.

Reaching the bottom of the stairs, I peered out of the glass panel beside the front door, dismissing a profound sense of sadness that Ava had not returned. I'd thought about calling Hayley, but then convinced myself otherwise. Ava needed to cool off; I wasn't going to bug her to come home if she were still huffy and puffy. Plus, I'd had uninterrupted study time. Not that I was any the wiser; I found nothing that correlated feathers and crowns with the occult.

Inside the bedroom, I grabbed the gun from my dresser – it was hidden under my winter pyjama pants. Unlatching the safety, I placed it on my bedside table. I undressed and climbed into my pyjamas, and stared at Ava's side of the bed. I switched off the light and peered through the venetian blinds. This high vantage point gave me a view of the tops of a few trees in our front yard and across to the other side of the road. A woman dressed in gym clothes passed under a streetlamp.

I looked down onto the driveway; only my car sat there. As I'd spent all day doing research, I still hadn't cleared out the garage. I'd have to do that tomorrow afternoon. First thing I would call O'Brien and tell him about the phone call, and pass on the name of Joseph Fisher – then I would sort out the five grand for Heath.

Dropping onto the bed, I yawned. God, these past few days had taken it out of me.

I'd no sooner fallen asleep than the cover was pulled away from me. I awoke with a start, about to reach for my gun.

'Shh ... it's only me,' Ava whispered, climbing on top of my body. When she kissed me, I held onto her waist.

I could tell she'd been drinking by the faint smell on her breath. Not much. But a little.

'What's got into you?' I whispered. Was I still dreaming?

'Nothing.' She rolled onto her back, so I turned to face her.

'Did you lock the front door?' I whispered.

'Is this your idea of foreplay?'

Giving her arm a quick shake, I repeated, 'Did you?'

'Yes, sir.'

'Good. Where have you been?'

'I'm still mad at you!' She poked my arm in a childlike manner.

'Seems like it.'

'Oh, Eddy!' She gasped, her fist punching the mattress. 'I *hate* fighting with you!'

'Me too. Where were you?' Before she could reply, I added: 'I love you.'

She shook her head, slapping my upper arm. 'Oh, you big buffoon!'

'That's not very nice.'

She smiled lopsidedly. 'Handcuffs ... you and me.'

Chuckling, I said, 'Just like the old days, huh?'

She sucked in air and then hissed through her teeth. 'Gosh, I miss it.'

'We did it not too long ago.'

She shook her head and her face contorted. She was crying. A little too heavily. God, how much had she had to drink?

Then she passed out and I held her, cradling her head, kissing her hair, telling her how sorry I was for being a downright arsehole, and it's only looking back now that I realise, she never did end up telling me where she'd been.

CHAPTER TWENTY-EIGHT

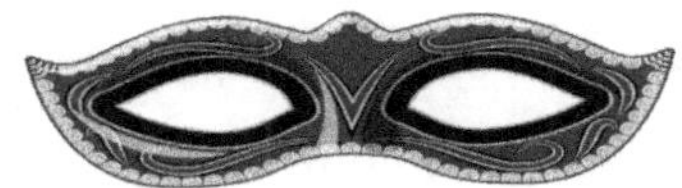

As I MADE MY way down the carpeted staircase, the scent of pancake batter and chocolate chips tantalised my nostrils. I felt like the sagging middle section of a bookshelf trying to hold everything up. Playing on my mind was the call from Olivia Hitchcock about Joseph Fisher, the fact I needed to withdraw five big ones for Heath and, of course, that creepy phone call.

I walked into the kitchen to see Ava dressed in her robe, flipping fluffy pancakes.

'Mornin', little lady.'

She looked at me but didn't smile. 'Morning.'

I smiled, staring at her bloodshot eyes.

'Hungry?'

'Famished.'

She motioned to a bubbling pot on the stove, and the aroma of bitter chocolate hit my nostrils. 'Coffee's ready.'

'Thank you.'

She handed me an empty mug with a downturned mouth.

'Feeling better after drowning your sorrows?' The urge to probe her about her actions yesterday rose to the forefront of my mind, but something lingered in the air between us like a permanent miasma. Tension. Anger on her behalf; shame on mine.

She gave me a deadpan expression. 'We still need to talk.'

'I agree. I'm all ears.'

She flipped the first batch onto a plate. 'Here. Sit. Eat.'

Taking the plate, I said, 'Yes, ma'am.'

'The paper is on the table, along with the maple syrup.'

'Thank you.' I poured myself a mug of coffee, added milk and sugar – which she'd also placed on the table – and sat down. 'Did you end up finding that copy of the *Telegraph*?'

'No.'

God, that irked me; where the bloody heck had it gone? There was no way in hell I'd miss a picture of myself next to the article headline. Had someone ripped out the page?

'I gave Guzzle Guts some kibble,' she said from the stove.

'Ah, excellent. That'll keep him going for the next twenty minutes.'

'He was inside the house again.'

A thin line of steam ribboned in front of me from my coffee mug as I picked up today's paper. I stopped on page three at an article about our first victim: *MURDERED MAN LINKED TO EXTORTION.*

'Eddy?'

'Mmm?' My eyes sucked up everything over the article relating to Norman Colbert.

'Bogart was inside when I got home last night.'

I forced my attention away from the article, but it was like a suction cup on a glass door. 'Must have slipped my mind.'

She sat beside me and wrapped her hands around a mug. 'Are you going to tell me what's really going on, or are you going to make me play guessing games?'

Putting the paper beside me on the table, I said, 'Love, I have the money. It's not like I'm taking out a second mortgage for this extra security. Things around here are changing; the streets aren't the same as they used to be – like when we were growing up.'

'They've always been bad; that's why you were able to keep your job for so long.'

'True, but there's no harm in ramping up security, is there?'

She studied my face, using her X-ray goggles to delve inside my psyche. She knew I wasn't being totally forthcoming; I was as see-through as a woman's underwear on her wedding night. 'Is this to do with the case you've been working on? You know, the one behind my back …?'

I picked up my knife and fork. 'I guess I still feel like I need to do more.'

She placed a hand over my wrist. 'You've done your time protecting the innocent. Let the others do the work now. I still don't understand why Mitch called you in the first place.' She removed her hand.

Shovelling a mouthful of pancake into my gob, I said, 'It's really not a big deal, is it? So what, we have a few extra cameras – oh, by the way, I have your new key to the deadbolt over there.' I pointed to the table near our front door and then reached for my steaming coffee.

She looked at the silver key and rose to her feet. 'Excuse me. The pancakes are burning.'

Ava left the house soon after breakfast. This time, she told me she was visiting her mother in the nursing home. She didn't ask me to tag along, and I was grateful. It allowed me to start on my errands. First thing was to try O'Brien again, then to withdraw five thousand dollars from the bank.

'O'Brien here ...'

'It's Eddy.'

'Hey! How are you?' He slurped on something; coffee, I guessed.

I sucked in air through my teeth. 'I've been trying to reach you. Last night, I received a call from Jerry.'

'Wait, what do you mean?'

'I mean, he's got my private number and he called me.'

'What did he say?' His tone was urgent, panicked.

'Hardly anything; some heavy breathing and chuckling, trying to freak me out. And I believe he wore a mask to disguise his voice.'

'We'll get a phone tap ASAP. Did anyone else call you?'

'Olivia Hitchcock from the library. She narrowed it down to a guy who has interesting ideas for bedtime stories.'

'Like what?'

'Like eugenics.'

'Huh?'

A plane soared overhead, and I shifted my weight to the other foot. 'Ever learn about what Hitler tried to do, creating a super race? Wiping out Jews, homosexuals, Gypsies. His Aryan Brotherhood. The SS. Auschwitz-Birkenau?'

He hesitated. 'Yeah, but what's that got to friggin' do with our psycho killer? Hitler didn't wear a mask – although he fucking should have with a moustache like that.'

'This bookworm is reading about ridding the world of evil. Hitler was all about creating a superpower, but he only believed he could do so by ridding the world of the filth. And our victims have less than outstanding morals. Whether it be extortion, drugs, cheating. It makes sense.'

He groaned. 'Eddy, I just don't see it, I'm sorry.'

'Red feather? Red is associated with communism, and this guy borrowed books on Lenin and Stalin. The upside-down bodies indicate evil. What if our guy sees these people as evil and – it's like he thinks he's doing this world a favour by cleaning up the streets?'

'By killing people?'

'It's ironic, I know. But you can't plead with psychos. In his own twisted mind, he probably sees himself as some type of leader or saviour – the next Jim Jones.'

'Man, this is getting way out of control. Furthermore, from memory, Hitler wasn't a commie.'

'Point taken.' I raked a hand through my hair. 'All right, let's swap names. What about Mustafa from Bondi?'

'Zilch, my friend. It *was* his van across the road, yes, but he said he was visiting an old friend of his whose girlfriend just had a baby. They used to go to school together way back in the day. Showed me a picture of them together and everything. I called in on the friend to verify it, and it all checks out. Cute baby, too.'

'I didn't think it'd be a lead, but we have to cross everything off.'

'Agreed. You?'

'My guy's name is Joseph Fisher – eighteen Norfolk Road, Cambridge Park.'

'Hmm ... not too far.' I heard his pen scratch this down on paper and waited for him to finish.

'Local indeed. You know serial killers work better on their own turf. They don't like to venture out; it causes too much suspicion. Plus, there's taking time off work, and hey, maybe this guy *is* married.'

'Wouldn't be the first husband to kill behind his wife's back – look at the Yorkshire Ripper.'

Girls outside cackled with delight – they could have been on my driveway by the closeness of it. Boys often tooted pretty girls along this road. 'Is there any way you'd let me tag along?'

'You mean, come inside for the interview?' His pager beeped in the background.

'Yes.'

He groaned in the back of his throat. 'I'm sorry, Eddy, you know the rules. Davies would make matzo soup outta our testicles if he knew. I *still* haven't shown him the letter – I'm technically withholding evidence here, God help me.'

Nathan Davies would make matzo soup out of anyone's balls given the chance – he thrived on seeing fear in people's eyes. Wasn't it Machiavelli who said 'It is better to be feared than loved'? Yep, that was Nathan 'Dickhead' Davies, all right.

'Worth a shot,' I said.

'Hey … are you okay?'

'As well as I can be, considering a serial killer knows everything about me. By the way, I left my book at your place.'

'Shit, yes, I was meaning to return it. Oh crap – almost forgot. I have info on that licence you gave me. You ready?'

'Hit me.' He rattled off a name and an address. 'Great, you beauty. Maybe I can swing by later to collect my book and have a chat?'

'No problem – oh, wait, we have people coming over for dinner. Sorry, pal.'

I rubbed my forehead. 'No problem.'

'I'll get the book to you soon.' His doorbell chimed in the background. 'Got to go, Jeremy is here. Ciao!'

After I hung up the phone, I turned around and leaned against the humming refrigerator.

Bogart peered inside the house again, so I walked over to let him in. 'Now, be a good boy while I'm gone, or Mum will chuck a stink, okay?'

He jumped up at me.

'That's not what we spoke about.' I kissed his wet black nose and pushed him gently off me.

Another five minutes of rushing about and I was out the door, keys tinkling in one hand, wallet in the other. I'd hoped Ava wouldn't arrive home before me and discover Bogart in the house. She knew I wasn't being truthful, but I'd rather tell a white lie than risk my dog's life.

I turned the ignition and '(Don't Fear) The Reaper' by Blue Öyster Cult came over Air FM. As the engine idled, I reversed down the driveway, stopping to let three young girls pass by on roller skates. Checking all was clear, I backed out and headed down River Road, a voyeur to the familiar scenes on a continual loop along the footpaths: a girl walking her dog, a boy holding his girl's hand, a steroid-munching jock in short shorts flexing his muscles at other pretty girls, a middle-aged man power-walking down the street. Brilliant rays glittered on the rippling water of the Nepean River, like a blanket of reflective diamonds. Speedboats cruised along past the designated five-knots-per-hour signs posted everywhere. A group of young boys took turns using a swing tyre on a rope attached to a tree, and a group of eager kayakers passed under Victoria Bridge, their arms and oars in perfect tandem.

My life wasn't perfect, but it was manageable. I believed everything would improve. How foolish I was. How naive to think everything would magically work itself out. Hope is like a safety net. You're never fully sure if you can trust or believe in it, and then when you do, it is ripped out from under you so all you can see is darkness upon descent. Hope – it's a destructive thing for a man to believe in. A fool's notion, really.

An hour after I'd set off from home, I knocked on the door to Heath's apartment and this time, a fully clothed Lorraine answered.

'Oh, hello again!' she said, her blue eyes wide. Today, she wore a black two-piece business suit, looking every inch the bank teller.

'Morning. Is Heath here?'

She shook her head. 'No, and I'm just about to head to work.'

Her sweet perfume reminded me of Rowntree's fruit gums. 'Ah. Where's Heath, then?'

'At his mate's place.'

Cool your jets; it could be nothing. 'I see. Any idea where that is?'

Her cool eyes regarded me with overt suspicion. 'What do you want, Eddy?'

'May I come in?'

She shifted on her feet, her eyes screaming impatience. 'I have to go to work.'

'It'll only take a minute.'

She sighed theatrically, as if her disposition wasn't obvious enough, but she opened the door just the same.

'Aaron at your mother's?' I asked, eyeing the apartment. It was tidy, I would give her that. The pungent aroma of garlic had knocked me about the senses when I'd entered the building, but inside the apartment the smells of burnt toast and stewed coffee overrode all else.

My back was to her as I eyed a framed photo on the wall of Lorraine, Heath and Aaron, taken with Santa, Christmas '81. Aaron was captured mid-bawl, his face redder than Santa's suit, tears streaming down his chubby face as he stared wide-eyed at the frightening, white-bearded stranger.

'I don't mean to be rude, but I really don't have the time.'

I turned to face her as she grabbed her brown leather handbag from the couch. 'Sit a minute.'

She folded her arms across her chest, her foot pointed outward in defiance. 'I'll take a seat then, if I may?'

She inhaled, swinging one arm out in an arc as if to say *'Be my guest'*.

Sitting back, one ankle across the knee of my other leg, I said, 'Right. I'm going to come out with it, seeing as you're in a hurry, and seeing as how we probably won't be having too much to do with each other in the future.'

She frowned, lips parting. 'Why do you say that?'

'I know what you've been up to.'

She stared at me, her mind in overdrive as she tried to act dumb, trying to work out how I knew her secret. 'What do you mean?'

'I know about Heath's little problem.' I let that settle to the bottom like sugar in an espresso as her chest rose and fell. 'Which means it's *your* little problem, and I know what you've been doing to supplement your income.' She arched an eyebrow. 'You've been selling yourself.'

Her cheeks spooled purply red, arms dropping to her sides. 'Excuse me?'

'Let's stop the theatrics. You're in a hurry, and I have a son I need to get to before he ODs.'

Her face resembled Aaron's in the Santa photo, except without the tears. 'How dare you!'

I ran the pad of my middle finger across my damp brow, eyeing her body's reactions: red-faced, short of breath, fidgeting. 'There's no way you can afford the rent on this place, to feed Aaron – plus yourselves – and the car, and electricity bills, et cetera. Does the name Jay Mason mean anything to you?'

She glared at me, her mind ticking over behind those stormy blue eyes of hers.

'The only question I have is, does Heath know?'

Her eyes shone with blatant anger. 'I am not a whore.'

'Oh, so, you're cheating on my son with another man, is that it?'

'No!' Her teeth overlapped as she spat this out.

'Then what? Come on, you'll be late for work.'

She hugged herself, as if to put a protective barrier between us.

'Lorraine, trust me, it is not you I am concerned about here. I only invite you and Aaron in because of Heath.' I held up a hand. 'Don't get me wrong,

I do like you. But I am not your father. I am not going to lecture you about this, but let's cut the shit.'

Tears cascaded down her cheeks, taking her mascara with it. 'He doesn't know.'

'Are you sure?'

Her eyes expanded. 'Are you kidding? He would *kill* me. It would break his heart.'

'Gee, I wonder why ...'

She blubbered, shaking her head.

'Thank you for being honest with me. Now, one more question: where is he, Lorraine?'

Her arms went to her sides, her fists clenched. 'I can't tell you! He'd know it was me!'

'I am an ex-detective, remember? I have ways of finding out. Like with Jay Mason.'

'Then do it!'

It took all my inner strength not to jump up and slap her across the chops. Hard. My anger wasn't half as fierce as my feeling of being shit-scared. 'And if he ODs in the meantime?'

She grabbed a tissue from the bookshelf, cluttered with everything from baby books and baby wipes to fantasy novels and Marvel comics. 'I can't.' She dabbed her eyes, the white tissue turning black and tan from her mascara and foundation.

'Do you love him?'

'Yes!' She turned to me, snivelling. 'Heath is my everything. He is terrific with Aaron, and such a wonderful partner. But when he's on drugs ... there's no stopping him.' She grabbed another tissue to blow her dripping nose with.

'I'll stop him.'

'I *can't tell you*!'

They hadn't called me 'Steady Eddy' for nothing. God, I deserved a Logie for this shit. 'How do you think he'll react to finding out about your services while he's shooting up?'

Her eyes widened. 'No! Please don't tell him! It's not like I *want* to do it, but what choice do I have? I've already borrowed three thousand from my parents to help Heath with his debt. They won't give me any more! We were about to get evicted from this place because the rent wasn't paid on time. We had nothing in the fridge! I have a son, Eddy! I didn't know what else tuh-tuh-to do.'

She collapsed onto the couch beside me. Christ, three thousand from her parents? I'd have to pay them back; that was not right. Had I ever been more ashamed of my son? I held her tight as she wept like a child, her whole body heaving into mine. It reminded me of Hayley when Heath had ripped the head off her Barbie doll. Or the times when she was convinced there was an evil monster under her bed that kept touching her feet as she tried to sleep. Turned out the monster was Heath. And boy, didn't he cop an earful from me when I busted him one night.

'Shh, it's going to be okay.' I rocked Lorraine back and forth as her arms squeezed the breath out of my lungs.

'It won't; he's too far gone.' She inhaled shakily. 'He cannot live without it.'

'Tell me where he is. I *promise* I will not mention you. No-one needs to know why I am here.'

She leaned back, sniffling. 'Are you going to kick us out of the family?'

The pain in her voice was enough to make any grown man cry.

'No. Besides, it would crush Ava.'

'And you?'

'It would devastate me to never see my boy again. I could never turn my back on him.'

She gasped for air, then sniffed hard once more. 'All right. If you promise not to tell him ...'

'Scout's honour.'

'The guy's name is Timothy Sharpe. He lives at forty-two Evensong Crescent, Bidwill.'

Using the pads of my thumbs, I swiped the wet mascara from her flushed cheeks, then wiped it onto my pants. 'Thank you. You might have just saved his life.'

Lorraine stared with doleful eyes, her nose red and wet. 'Do you think you'll be able to cure him of this thing inside of him?'

'I'll never give up, Loz. Never.'

CHAPTER TWENTY-NINE

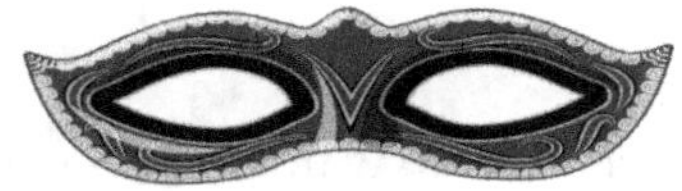

MY HANDS THROTTLED the steering wheel as I drove to Evensong Crescent, a UBD Gregory's Street Directory splayed out on the seat beside me. I tried with all my might to focus on 'Mandy' by Barry Manilow as I drove, but I was angry. The type of anger a father can only experience that is borne from the depths of being shit fucking scared. I'd never feared for my son's life more than I did at that moment. Ropable didn't cover it; I feared I would kill this 'Timothy Sharpe' with my bare hands.

My anger only augmented when I saw my son's car parked in the driveway, the broken back windows taped over with Scotch tape mocked me. The cops could book him for that shit.

I pulled up behind Heath's car, killed the engine, and hopped out without a game plan. Trembling, I walked down the driveway towards a putrid house with an overgrown front lawn, and banged on the door. The sound of scrambling ensued inside, like people stashing stuff, hiding evidence.

I knocked again. Waited. 'Open up, I can hear you.'

'Who is it?' a man with a deep, accented voice said.

'Saint Nicholas, now open up.'

The door opened. Through the gap emerged an ebony face from which brown eyes with yellowish sclera peered out. 'Wot cho want?'

'Timothy Sharpe?' My eyes roamed over his smooth face and plump lips.

'Nah, cuz, he out back.'

'Get him.'

'Sayz who?'

'Says me, dickhead, *obviously*! Who else do you see here, or are you that cooked up on drugs you're seeing two of me?'

Eyes widening, he opened the door in a flourish. He had those fucking corn-rows – worse hairdo than the mullet. 'Cho wanna be startin' sumthin', homie?'

Inhaling, I took off my Ray-Bans like a man who had nothing but time and nestled them in the V of my polo shirt. 'Listen up, dipshit, the longer I stand here, the angrier I get. Okay? It's quite simple. In plain English, I am asking you to get me Timothy. Comprende, shit-for-brains?'

'Hey, Jerome, who is—' Heath halted, eyes wide. Jerome turned from me, to Heath, bewildered.

My jaw clenched over Heath's bloodshot eyes and pallid complexion. 'Do you want an arse-kicking inside or out?'

Shit-for-brains jerked a thumb over his shoulder at me. 'Bro, is this yo dad?'

Heath pushed past Jerome. 'Dad, I can explain! I came to tell Tim I'd have his money.'

My fists clenched hard enough to pulverise a stress ball. 'You're a goddamn liar. Look at you! Imagine if Mum saw you like this. A pitiful disgrace.'

'Yo, you better re-lax, homie.'

I squinted at Jerome. 'What drugs are you on, cock breath? Shut the fuck up and let me speak to my son before I give you a permanent gummy smile.'

Heath pushed Jerome further inside the house. 'Go! It's okay, go. I'll be in soon, bro.'

Jerome glared at me, tight-lipped, as he disappeared inside the darkened house.

Heath turned to me, his face as white as marble. 'Dad—'

'You can kiss this goodbye.' I held up the envelope stuffed with the five thousand dollars.

His bloodshot eyes widened. 'No, wait!'

I turned away, heading up the driveway. His footsteps followed.

'Did Lorraine tell you where I was?'

I turned back, frowning. 'Lorraine? I haven't seen her.'

'Then how did you—'

'Is that really what you want to ask me? I agreed to save your arse, and this is how you repay me? By spitting in my face after everything I have done for you?' I shook my head as I looked his tatty clothes up and down. 'I don't even know who you are anymore.'

'I'm still *me*!' His eyes shone with unshed tears.

'No.' I shook my head. 'I see nothing of my former son in you. No trace of that boy who sat on my knee, showing off his new G.I. Joe that Santa gave him.'

'Stop!' His hands flew to the sides of his head, gasping for breath.

'Or the boy who would run into my room on Father's Day after making me breakfast in bed.'

He spun around, heaving in oxygen.

'What happened to that considerate young man who used to take his grandmother by the hand and help her with grocery shopping?'

'Don't talk about her!'

'Do you think she'll be looking down on you with pride – or disgust?'

'Shut up!' Spittle flew from little white pools collecting at the corners of his mouth.

'She loved you the most out of the grandkids; you know that, don't you?'

'Fuck off!'

'When she knew it was the end, I sat by her bed and she specifically told me to take care of you. Not Hayley, *you.*'

He charged at me. My own flesh and blood lunged, but I side-stepped. He howled from somewhere deep inside, somewhere a man cannot access without digging as far as he can go. The first place to get covered over, forgotten by the ravages of time.

He came at me again, but I blocked his arm, pushed his shoulder so his back was to me, then I shoved him on the ground where he emitted an *Oofff*, air tearing from his lungs – what was left of them, they were probably as black as the tar my wheels sat on.

I bent down so my clenched teeth were near his ear. 'Don't make a god-damn fool of yourself!'

He wailed, but I had his arms pinned out in front of him. 'Get the fuck off me, old man!'

I dug my knee into his back as I sat up. 'I am your father! Whether or not you like it, I am!'

'Not anymore!'

'Fine, you want to do it all on your own, huh? Then remember our deal. Don't ever walk back inside my house again. You can kiss family dinners, Christmases and birthdays goodbye!'

'I don't need you!'

'Then I guess I'll just take this money with me now, and you can sort yourself out.'

'No!' He stopped struggling but panted. By now, people were coming over to inspect the hullabaloo. Jerome stood at the door, clearly deciding whether risking a pummelling was worth it.

'Hey,' a guy yelled. 'Get off him!'

I turned as some junkie lad swaggered over, parachute pants trying to catch up with his legs.

'It's okay, we're learning self-defence. Wanna join in? I'll pin you to the ground and teach you how to get out of it.'

His face bunched up, showcasing yellow teeth. 'You're insane, man.'

'Nah, I'm just hepped-up on blow. Man it feels good. *Woo*!' I swivelled my head to address the gathering onlookers. I held up a palm and said, 'Don't worry, folks, show's over.' I got off Heath's back, panting, too. 'Bow for everyone.' I held Heath's arm, and he bowed along with me, as people dispersed back to their caves and crack dens, mumbling, shaking their pathetic heads at me.

Heath turned to me, lips pursed. 'That wasn't funny.' He wiped the tears and debris from his face using a forearm.

'Neither is this.' I brandished the envelope in front of him again. 'Take the money and pay off your debt. Or use this to get high, but know that you've turned your back on the family. And don't think I'll recant later. I am deadly serious. It's drugs, or your family. One is killing you slowly, the other is trying to give you all the love in the world. You decide. But if five thousand is worth more to you than family, then maybe I never really had a son to begin with.'

CHAPTER THIRTY

A FEW DAYS later, after reading Thursday's edition of *The Daily Telegraph* and another of Liz Fulton's damning articles, all I longed to do was collapse on the couch and hibernate until the shitstorm blew over. The sun may have been shining, but somehow it did not reach me; I felt no warmth, no joy from the glowing orb. I felt stuck in some H. P. Lovecraftian gothic horror where monsters and demons roamed free.

Just as I opened the fridge door, looking for a beer, the phone rang.

'Dad?'

I smiled upon hearing Hayley's voice. 'Afternoon, love, how are you?'

'Just wondering if we were still fine to come to dinner tomorrow?'

My memory hit REWIND. 'Ah, I don't know; didn't Mum come and see you today?'

'Today? No …?'

My mind scrambled to recall our conversation over breakfast in which I was damn sure Ava had told me she was going to see Hayley. 'Oh. Yesterday?'

'No, I haven't seen her all week, which is why I'm asking you for confirmation.'

I held the phone against my ear. Debilitating thoughts fuelled my over-excited imagination.

'Dad?'

I blinked twice, breathing in as inaudibly as I could.

'Dinner tomorrow?'

Leaning back against the wall, I said, 'Sure.'

She waited for what seemed like an hour before saying, 'You okay?'

'Mm-hmm.'

She hesitated. 'Okaaaay. Um, I guess we'll see you tomorrow, then?'

'You will. Bye.'

'Wait—'

I placed the phone in its cradle and stared at the kitchen bench, connecting things in my mind's eye to help draw my own conclusions. Either Ava had forgotten about Hayley, or she was lying to me. But Ava had been forgetting a lot lately, which raised alarm bells because she always jotted everything down in a small diary, which she called her Alzheimer's Antidote. If she was developing a habit of forgetting important things (Hayley's place for one, and let's not forget the Book Club fiasco), then something weighed on her mind. If this wasn't a simple case of my wife forgetting things, then she was lying to me. The question was, why?

***

Ava's keys jingled in the lock as I patted Bogart lying beside me on the couch. The door opened and closed, and she gave a huff as though it'd been an effort with the new lock.

'Hello,' she said tonelessly.

Heat pooled in my cheeks, causing me to sweat; my innards swarming with butterflies. My hand patting Bogart had a momentary attack of Parkinson's.

'Eddy?'

I swivelled my neck to look at her. How small she appeared standing so far away by the door.

'I said hello.'

'Hello.'

She blinked several times. 'You all right?'

My lips tightened as I smiled. 'Right as rain.'

She stared at me, frowning. 'What's the matter?'

I shook my head, my bottom lip protruding. 'Why would anything be the matter?'

Ava shrugged. 'You seem ... off.'

'I'm just thinking.'

'Fine. I'll start dinner then, shall I?'

I faced forward, continuing to stroke Bogart's soft fur as she made her way up the stairs. She came back down about two minutes after I heard the toilet flush. She headed straight for the kitchen and opened the refrigerator.

Rising, I walked to the archway, propping myself against the wall and stared. 'Had a nice day?'

'Yes, I did, thank you.' Her back was to me.

'What did you get up to?'

'I saw Mum again, remember?'

Pig's arse! 'How is she?'

'About as well as one can expect for her age. She keeps asking for Dad – poor thing.'

I glared at her as she opened butcher paper to reveal sirloin steaks. My grinding teeth sent volts up the sides of my face. 'See anyone else?'

She turned to me. 'No. Why?'

'You didn't see Hayley?'

She frowned, shaking her head. 'No? Was I supposed to?'

I bent forward. 'I thought you said you were going to see her?'

'No, I didn't. Why, what's up? Why are you acting funny?'

I stood upright, folding my arms over my chest. 'Didn't you tell me you were going to see her?'

She sighed. 'No, Eddy – jeez, what's gotten into you?'

Had I made a mistake, then? Had I misheard her? My heartbeat slowed. Now *I* was the one feeling like an arse. 'Sorry – guess I'm hearing things.'

'You are getting on, honey,' she said, smirking.

I laughed, more out of relief as my stomach muscles unfurled. 'So you didn't see Hayley, huh?'

She chortled. 'No, nor did I say I was. Why? Is something wrong?'

'Not at all, but Hayley called before.'

She sprinkled our steaks with salt and pepper before massaging them with garlic-infused oil. 'What did she say?'

'Asking if tomorrow night was still on.'

She stopped rubbing. 'Oh yes, of course!' She fixed me with a stare. 'Is that why you were asking if I'd seen Hayley? Do you think I've been lying to you?'

I'd never felt more like a dickhead.

'You think I've got a side-hunk? Hmm?'

'It's not funny, Ava. You have been acting just as weird as I have.'

She walked over to me, slick oil on her raised hands. 'Kiss me.'

I did as I was told.

She gazed back at me, still smiling. I'm glad she could; I'd made myself sick to the point of chucking up. I've always had a bad habit of assuming things (hey, it comes with the territory), but until I have solid answers, that's all a man can do in some situations, especially throughout his career.

'Dinner will be ready in thirty. Take a bath and cool down; you know I'd never lie to you.'

As I was halfway up the stairs, the telephone rang.

'I'll get it,' I yelled down the stairs. I entered the bedroom and answered it on the fourth ring.

'Eddy!' O'Brien said. 'We need you down here.'

My pulse quickened. 'Where? What's happened?'

'Another one. Or shall I say another *two*.'

My legs gave way under me; thank God the mattress was there to protect my arse. 'Double homicide?'

'Yep. No doubt about it. It's our guy.'

I breathed in through my nostrils, my breath quickening. 'Where?'

'Nineteen Wintergreen Row, Werrington Downs.'

God, I'd promised Ava I wouldn't. But ... my mistress was calling, my heart already palpitating from thinking about it. 'I'm on my way.'

I hung up and sat there, waiting for the shakes to subside. It was probably the first time in my career as a detective that I felt like a case was above me; we were in way over our heads. But that's what'd make the catch taste all the sweeter. After a few minutes, I headed downstairs, ready for battle.

I appeared around the archway and caught Ava smiling to herself, unwrapping corn from its cosy husk. She looked up. How much of a big, fat, hairy, unwashed arsehole did I feel at that point?

'What? Who was it?'

'I need to, ah, duck out for a while.' I waited as the seconds drew out. She didn't scream, or cuss, or even bang a fist on the bench. I chanced a look at her.

'Okay, Eddy,' she said upon an exhale.

I hesitated, waiting for an onslaught of verbal abuse. 'Are you sure?'

She bobbed her head once. 'Fine. Sure. Do whatever you want.'

Taking a step towards her, I said, 'I'll make it up to you.'

She went back to husking the corn cob.

My mouth had the texture of teddy bear stuffing. 'How about I cook for Hayley and David tomorrow? How about I do us a nice barbecue?'

'It's fine. Go. Run.'

Her lack of aggression somehow made me feel even worse. I'd rather she yell, or get angry – not that that was why I was doing it. It would have felt more right to have been torn a new one. But no, she took it on the chin. She didn't even ask where I was going.

Closing the distance between us, I kissed her temple. 'I'm sorry. I promise I will not leave the house tomorrow, and that I will take care of all the cooking and cleaning.'

She remained focused on the husk, ripping the last of it off with robotic tugs.

I waited a minute longer. 'I have to go now. Make sure to lock all the doors and windows, and keep an eye on Bogart. Please?'

'Sure.'

I couldn't fucking stand it. But I left, anyway. 'Jerry' was right; I would run to him every time he beckoned. I was too involved now. And what's more, Ava knew that, too.

CHAPTER THIRTY-ONE

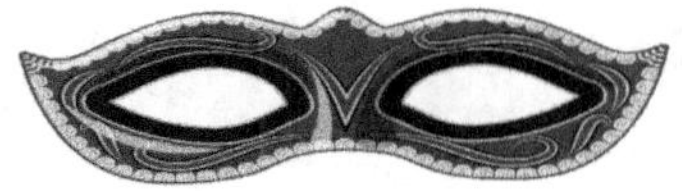

INSIDE THE BEDROOM lay a couple who had now joined the list alongside Norman, Ian and Mark.

According to O'Brien, Raúl and Juanita Martínez owned this modest, one-storey fibro dwelling. Jeremy informed me their two daughters were staying at Juanita's parents' place over in Merrylands.

I'd walked through the house, passing the CSU members already at work, and was led to the bedroom, third door on the left.

I attempted to stay out of people's way while the forensic photographer, Harold Lucado, snapped multiple angles of Raúl and Juanita Martínez. Their eyes wide in fright, their throats each with a gaping hole like a second mouth. Their bodies once again lying with their heads facing the door, but this time there was only one prop: a dead green tree snake, which lay coiled between them.

Jeremy walked up behind me as I crouched beside the bed. Hair and Fibre had finished with this room ten minutes ago.

'Michael Wong is on his way over from his in-laws' house to do the prelim.'

Nodding, I stared at our victims.

'He's deviated from his usual M.O.,' Jeremy whispered as I looked around the room. Black fingerprint powder smudged the windowsill and doorframe and light fixtures.

I gazed into Juanita's lifeless eyes. 'Just like the letter foretold.'

'A married couple. Non-Caucasian. Children. And they had a pinscher – at the vet's now.'

'Who called it in?'

'A neighbour. She's with O'Brien now, giving a statement. I don't know much else.'

I closed my eyes as my head swam with uncertainties, unanswered questions. The letter. Warning me this would happen. I believed he may have targeted a gay couple – seeing as in the eyes of religious folk, being gay is a sin. Never would I have expected a married couple with children. He'd upped his ante.

'What's with the snake, do you think?' Jeremy asked as I opened my weary eyes.

'Snake. Garden of Eden. Temptation. He even mentioned the Garden of Eden in his letter to me. He's taunting me.'

'Or ... or these props are nothing more than plain old rubbish. A red feather. A crown. A snake. A dog. I think it's designed to throw us off course.'

'No. It's not. This is all premeditated.'

O'Brien appeared at the doorway. 'Eddy. Jeremy.'

We walked over to him. His white shirt was missing the top button, his black necktie askew. 'We have a neighbour in the living room – Lauren Edgeworth. All shook-up – says she saw him.'

My ears pricked up. 'Our guy?'

He jerked his head to the side. 'C'mon.'

Jeremy and I followed O'Brien (and the scent of his underarm sweat patches) out to the living room where a frail, elderly lady sat hunched on the couch, crumpled tissues in her shaky hand. Hordes of police officers and CSU members were dispersed in different parts of the house, and some were in here, dusting for fingerprints by the windowsill.

O'Brien stood in front of her and then crouched to gaze into her watery eyes. 'Mrs Edgeworth, thank you for waiting. I've brought my partners here.' He motioned to us. She looked vulnerable, as if she didn't know who to trust. 'If you'd so kindly repeat what you saw, this would be appreciated.'

Jeremy took out his notepad and a pen from his top pocket – always at the ready.

Lauren lowered her fistful of balled-up tissues. 'I-I heard a scream at around four o'clock.'

'Male or female?' I asked in what I hoped was a soothing tone.

'Juanita's scream.'

Jeremy wrote this down as I gave her a tender smile, prompting her to continue.

'I didn't think much of it. They sometimes have big blues – you can hear them up the street.'

'They argue a lot?' I asked.

'But she gives it to him as much as he gives it to her. One time she threw a lamp at his head.'

'While the kids were home?' Jeremy asked.

At the mention of the word 'kids', she sobbed again. She bobbed her head as tears rolled down her time-weathered face.

'So they had physical and verbal fights ...' I continued for her.

'Y-Yes, that's why I thought nothing of it. But then, a short while later, as I was in the front garden, a man walked out of their house!'

'Did he see you?' I asked.

Lauren cowered into the couch. 'Y-Yes. He walked right up to me.' She emitted a choked squeal as her body shuddered.

Every hair on my body stood at attention. 'Go on, ma'am.'

She cleared her throat. 'I was crouched low behind my hedges. My hedges circle the front yard.' She used her weathered hands to demonstrate.

'What were you doing crouching behind the hedges, ma'am?' Jeremy asked.

'Putting out containers of water for the birds and leaving sugar spoons for the bees.'

'Sugar spoons?' Jeremy said, eyebrow raised.

'Mm-hmm, I leave all sorts of things in my front yard for animals. I have a birdbath in the backyard, too. I lost my husband, Keith, a few years back, and, well, I only have the animals now.'

Jeremy scribbled in his notepad, then looked up. 'Okay, so you were in the garden, tending to the insects and bugs, when *what?*'

'When I saw some movement near their front porch. And so, I looked up as a man dressed in black closed the door behind him. But wouldn't you know, he turned to me. He walked down the steps and crossed the front yard. He stood opposite me as I was on my knees. I tried to scream but n-nothing came out. I couldn't turn away from his eyes. But I did notice something peculiar.'

I breathed out steadily. 'What did you see?'

'He had a nervous tic in his eye.'

'Nervous that you busted him coming out of the house, perhaps?'

'I am sure he was nervous, but it was as though he knew I was there the whole time. He didn't turn his head around to check the coast was clear; he looked directly at me as I stared. When he stood before me, his eye did this flicker-thing, like a twitch – maybe he could have been on drugs? Then he strolled off, as casual as anything after slaying these two poor people. Oh, the rotten monster!' She sobbed again, hand to her mouth.

'What else can you tell us about him, ma'am?' I asked as gently as I could.

'Was he white? Black? Asian? Hispanic?'

She sniffled, steading her breathing. 'That's just it, he was black ... and white.'

Jeremy frowned. 'Like a panda?'

She wiped the base of her dripping nose with ruffled tissues. 'No, his mask. He wore a mask.'

'Like a stocking mask?' I said. 'A ghoulish mask? A balaclava?'

Lauren squinted, sniffling. She shook her head. 'It was like one of those gag masks.'

My head tilted, mind reeling. 'A gag mask?'

'Like something a person would wear to scare somebody. It scared *me*! Lord, was I scared, especially when he towered above me, breathing heavily. I thought my time was done, so I said a silent prayer to the good Lord above.'

'Anything definitive about this mask?' Jeremy asked.

'The eyeholes were black stars, and it had a long, pointed nose – you know – those clown types?' Her hands fell to her lap in frustration. 'No – not a clown – what they use for entertaining kings and queens.' She placed a hand to her forehead as though this was exhausting. *Welcome to my world, lady.*

Jeremy squinted. 'A jester?'

Her eyes lit up. 'Yes! That's exactly what it was! Thank you, yes, he wore a black-and-white jester mask, and it had a pointed nose, like the Wicked Witch from *The Wizard of Oz*.'

O'Brien turned to me. 'Another sighting of a mask.' He turned back to Lauren. 'And tell me again what time was this?'

'I'd say about an hour after I heard the scream.'

'It was still daylight though,' I said, glancing through the windows that faced the front lawn. 'At the time, anyway, it would have been light.' I locked eyes with O'Brien. 'He's becoming more brazen now.'

A couple of Forensic team members walked past the doorway, one being a bald man with a silk tie and a clipboard.

O'Brien inhaled through his nostrils before focusing on Lauren. 'What happened next?'

'I got this eerie feeling things weren't right, so I looked to see where he was going.'

I wiped my sweaty palms over my pants. 'And what did you see?'

'He walked that way.' Lauren pointed to the left as she faced the windows.

'He took a left up the road?' Jeremy asked.

She nodded while chatter in the hallway floated by in nonsensical snippets.

'And then what, Mrs Edgeworth?' Jeremy said. 'Did he leave via car? Or motorbike?'

'He hopped into a car.'

My heart raced; adrenaline pumped through my veins. I wanted to shake her so hard that all the information would spill out like coins from an arcade game. But if there was one thing I could boast about, it was my patience: *Steady Eddy*.

'Did you see the colour of it?' Jeremy asked, pen at the ready to jot this down.

'Dark. It also had black windows.'

'Tinted windows?' he asked, raising the pad higher.

'Yes. Tinted. And he took off without a care in the world.'

As Jeremy scribbled, I took the reins. 'He took off up the road, or did he swing back?'

'He kept going up the road. I couldn't see the numberplate or what kind of car it was, but it was on the darker side – blue, or black, maybe even dark green. With tinted windows – well, at least the back window was.'

'And then what?' Jeremy said.

'After I saw he'd left, I ran to this house. I rang the doorbell, and when I didn't get a response, I immediately called the police using my house phone.'

O'Brien patted her knee once more. 'And we're thankful you did.' He stood up to face us and whispered, 'Let's proceed with door-to-door now.' His eyes pinned mine. 'I can't ask you to—'

'Oh, I'm coming. I am quick. Useful. And we can cover more houses – fuck what Davies says.'

'Yeah, he's only the supervisor – fuck him!' O'Brien shook his head, grinning.

A few suited members of the unit stopped at the doorway, appraised the situation, then moved on. Harold's camera clicked as he continued working his way around the house. Anyone could guess the kids had decorated the Christmas tree over by the front window, and pain choked me seeing the wrapped presents. Mummy and Daddy would not be appearing for Christmas this year. Seeing the various presents of all shapes and sizes filled me with carbonated determination. This had been going on too long; even the papers were making a mockery of us, claiming that chimpanzees could work out this puzzle before we did.

I walked over to stand beside Lauren. 'Was there anything else about him that could help us?'

She tilted her head to one side, eyes narrowing. 'Just that he was tall; I'd say about six feet or more – Keith was that height, so I know.'

'And his build?'

'Medium. Not fat, but not skinny, either.'

'How did he move? I mean, was he agile, heavy on his feet, a lightweight?'

'He didn't exactly have a youthful bounce; he may well have had a bit of a hunched back – I'm not too sure, though.'

'Hair colour? Did you see his skin tone?'

'His hair was covered by one of those hood things.'

'Like on a jumper?'

'Yes. Black. So were his pants and shoes.'

'Skin tone?'

She shrugged apologetically. 'Black gloves ... I have no idea.'

'So, he *was* using gloves?'

'Yes.'

'Did you see a weapon?'

She shook her head. 'No. But he had a briefcase.'

My left eyebrow fish-hooked. 'A briefcase?'

'A black one, swinging in his hand.'

'Could explain the hunched back if he carried something heavy in that briefcase,' Jeremy said.

'But I am certain his eyes were light brown. Lord knows, I stared into them long enough.'

I placed a hand on her bony shoulder. 'You've been most helpful.'

She peered up at me with red-rimmed eyes. 'What kind of person would do this?'

My face turned hard. 'An evil one.'

O'Brien leaned forward to speak to Jeremy and me in a hushed whisper. 'Let's proceed with interviews. Jeremy and I will take the left side; Eddy – God, I hope this doesn't bite me in the arse – you take the right. We meet at the end of the street when we're done.'

'Agreed,' I said as that old familiar sense of importance crept up my spine. It was like the rush leading up to an epic orgasm. There was nothing like it.

I halted and turned to face them both. 'Why did he let her live?'

They were silent as a stern-looking redhead rushed past the doorway, pager in her hand.

'If what Lauren says is true, why did he let her live after he saw her? That's another witness right there, and he walks away?'

'Broad daylight, perhaps?' O'Brien said. 'Doesn't want to draw too much attention to himself. The more crimes he commits, the more evidence he leaves behind. Maybe old grannies don't do it for him? We haven't had any old folks yet. There's no sport in bumping off the half-dead.'

Shaking my head, I said, 'It's not that; he has no moral scruples, anyway. It's exactly what that homeless guy Fuzzy said about being spotted at Ian's. Our guy probably spent days scouting the area; I find it difficult to believe he didn't notice a drunk lying in the street mere metres from the exit of Ian's complex. No, the reason he lets his witnesses live is because they aren't part of his master plan.'

Stephanie May

CHAPTER THIRTY-TWO

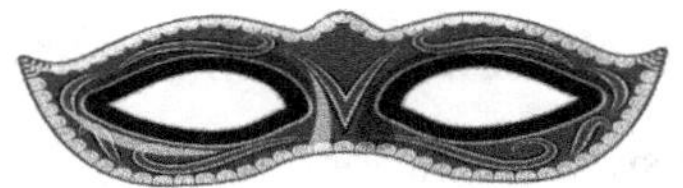

IT WAS MIDNIGHT by the time I arrived home. Panic seized my stomach over the absence of Ava's Honda in the driveway. I had yet to clear out the garage for our cars; I'd get on to that first thing tomorrow morning. Exhaustion consumed me, but how could I sleep without Ava beside me?

As I approached the front door, the automatic light sprang to life, momentarily blocking my vision. I eyed my keychain and found the shiny silver key for the deadbolt, as well as the key for the normal lock – the same key I'd been using since we'd bought this place.

A dark, empty house welcomed me. I called out to my wife anyway, though I knew I would be met with silence. I flicked on the light before making my way over to the kitchen. There was no note pinned to the fridge, yet the dinner she'd been preparing appeared to have been eaten; a stack of dishes and pans drip-dried in the wash-up tray. Had she invited someone around to take my place? I turned around as Bogart whimpered at the back door. I bolted across the dining room to let him inside, tail wagging as he jumped up and pawed my chest.

'Down, boy!' After closing the back door, I patted his rear. I turned around, yawning, and then the tiny hairs on the nape of my neck ruffled as I eyed another envelope addressed to me on the coffee table. But this time, a small mahogany box sat beneath it.

READ ME FIRST was written in that same neat-style handwriting across the envelope beneath my name.

I ignored Bogart's yips to play with him and ran to my study in the darkness. I flicked the light switch, grabbed the letter opener like a madman, and ripped open the top. Beads of sweat perforated my temples and forehead, dripping from my chin. My breaths came out harsh and ragged as I held the paper before my eyes.

Dearest Eddy,

My old friend, have you been keeping well?

No, I suppose not. I imagine you're positively fraught with emotion. How are you advancing so far? Not any closer to catching me, are you, old boy?

How was it seeing those two tonight? Yes, I was watching from afar. Have you put on a little weight, my dear old chap? But then, if my wife's cooking were as good as yours, I think I'd have packed on a few by now, too.

By the way, speaking of your wife, you ought to tell her to make sure all the windows are locked. You didn't spend money to have the house under heavy surveillance, only to have her leave a window unlocked, did you? Silly woman. And in case you were wondering, she left a short while ago. Pretty little thing, isn't she? Even if she's a bit long in the tooth.

Now, I do not want you to worry. I am a gentleman, and if I give you my word that I shall not do harm to you or your wife, then you need not worry. I solemnly declare that I will not be responsible for either of your deaths. I believe that some things in life are worse than death. Do you agree? How do you think Abigail's parents are coping? I read in the papers they were getting a divorce. Now, to me that would be worse than death, don't you agree? To know someone out there raped and murdered your daughter — never to be caught. Have you called her parents recently, Eddy? Have you been monitoring their mental wellbeing? No, I'm sure you have more pressing things to percolate over.

I suspect you were hoping the last letter would be a fake. Am I correct in this assumption? You were hoping it was a crackpot. Well, no, Eddy, I am the real deal. And to help you believe, I shall leave you with two things: The box contains one of my most prized possessions; the other is a clue to your next victim. I cannot tell you where, I cannot tell you when. But I have my sights set on someone older than yourself of the same sex.

Oh, this is just starting to get really interesting — don't you agree?

You sounded a trifle stressed when I called you. Do take care of yourself, won't you?

That's enough from me, I imagine you must be exhausted. Get some rest. We have a lot more work to do — you and I.

Ta-ta, old boy!

Yours sincerely,

Jerry.

Stephanie May

CHAPTER THIRTY-THREE

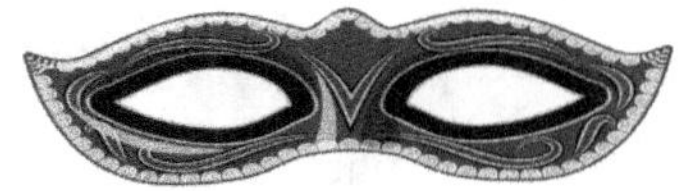

THE SQUARE BOX fitted inside my quivering palm; I felt like I were holding a strain of smallpox. If I unleashed it, all hell would break loose. I popped the lid, gagged, and placed a fist to my mouth as I dropped into my chair. Two shapes cut out of human flesh taunted me. One was a circle, the other a triangle.

All the remaining breath I held in my diaphragm was reefed out of me by an invisible force. My head spun and my spine extended taut. It was not the worst thing I had seen during my time on the force, but this solidified what I had been keeping to myself: that *I* was the one he had been competing with from the start. This flesh had to belong to the first victim, Norman Colbert (technically the first victim *found*; Ian had been killed days before). And even though Basil Humphries could be a prick most of the time, there was one thing he'd told O'Brien that rang true to me. He was competing against us. He was the director, producer and performer in his own dark and twisted theatre of cruelty. But was I the one audience member who mattered most? This wasn't my show – why wasn't O'Brien receiving this vile shit? Because it was to do with *me*. I believed it now more than ever. God, how long had he been planning this? The Jester would be his name from now on – courtesy of Lauren's account. Jerry the Jester.

Running to the wall phone near the fridge, I spun O'Brien's house number.

Janice answered in a groggy voice. 'Hello?'

'Janice, it's Eddy.' I rushed the words out as my heart pummelled my chest, stumbling over my words like a runner with his own two feet. 'Sorry to call so late.'

'Eddy? What's wrong?'

'I need to speak with Mitch, please.'

'He's not back yet. What's the matter?'

'Can you have him call me when he gets in?'

'Sure.' She yawned.

'I'm sorry; go back to sleep now.'

She sniffled, then swallowed. 'Get some rest, Eddy. The last time I saw you, you looked peaky.'

'Yeah, will do. Thank you. Goodnight.'

'Night!'

After I hung up, I dashed up the staircase, taking two at a time. I grabbed my gun and just as I turned, something caught my eye from the window. On the other side of the street, directly below a halo of a streetlamp, stood my adversary.

He gazed up at me, and even though he wore the mask Lauren Edgeworth had described – white with black stars around the cut-out eyes – I sensed he was smiling. He raised a hand and waved it like the Queen would wave to a crowd. Slowly. Methodically.

Without forming decent cognitive resolutions, I shot off, almost ripping my bedroom door off its hinges as I bounded down the stairs, tumbling once before I grabbed hold of the banister, until I landed at the door. I fumbled with both locks – the deadbolt, and the normal lock – emerging from my house, gun in hand. I sprinted across the street without looking, Bogart's paws padding the asphalt behind me like we were playing a game. I ran to the exact spot where the Jester stood – his energy lingering in the air, pulling in everything around it like a black hole. I spun around; houses, cars and trees flew into one conglomeration of blurred shapes and objects. How my heart hammered, but I took off running, Bogart at my heels, scouring everywhere until a horn tooted twice from behind. I spun so fast I thought I'd drill a hole in the tar, and Bogart crashed into me. A dark car up ahead, its red taillights a stark contrast to the darkness of night, stood out. A hand popped out of the driver's window and he waved again, that mocking, slow, cordial wave before he sped off. I sprinted back to my house, ran through the door, and grabbed my keys.

I leaped inside my Statesman faster than I could say 'You're under arrest', Bogart acting as my partner as he jumped in and sat on the passenger seat. I reversed without looking for pedestrians. The gun lay on my quivering lap as I took off, smoke wafting in the air in the aftermath of my screeching tyres. I hit eighty kilometres faster than a sneeze. River Road hosted numerous bends either way, designed to slow drivers down in places children and cyclists often frequented. My rear tyre clipped a concrete island as I swerved left, then right – arm propped against Bogart's chest to keep him from sliding around until I had to change gears. My foot was plastered to the floor until I reached a set of traffic lights. I had no idea which way he would have gone, but my guess was left because there were less traffic lights, and there was Old Bathurst Road, which would take him up the meandering mountains. After running the red light, I put my foot down. I hadn't been able to see the numberplate, but it was indeed dark blue (as Mrs Edgeworth had said) and now I knew what model we were looking for: a dark-blue '83 Plymouth Turismo. A car designed for speed. A car not so conspicuous as to draw attention. And the beauty was, there weren't too many out this way, I was sure of it!

My hand quivered against the gearstick. 'You just made a *big* mistake, cocksucker.'

Bogart looked at me, as if to show his disapproval of my language.

'Don't forget what he did to you!'

Bogart gazed back out the window as cars that were travelling along looked to be stationary as I shot past them.

I drove and searched every side street and cul-de-sac, until eventually Bogart fell asleep, and my eyes struggled to stay open after the adrenaline had waned. As my petrol light flashed red, I resigned to the fact that he'd escaped me.

Sighing and punching the steering wheel, I headed back, dejected, pulling into an Ampol petrol station along the way to refill.

As I held the bowser, listening to the guzzling, regurgitation sounds, my head kept drooping. My eyes were stinging. My legs were aching in pain from running, so were my damn knees and back.

I ducked inside and paid for the twenty dollars' worth of fuel to a spaced-out teenage girl, who probably didn't even know what day it was.

Bogart's head shot up as I slammed my car door shut.

'Sorry,' I whispered, taking in a lungful of air. Jerry had escaped, and he'd been mere metres from me. God that burned me.

Bogart's head tilted, his pointed ears sticking up.

'Sorry, boy,' I repeated before starting the ignition. Only then, as I drove towards home, did I realise I still didn't know the whereabouts of Ava. Despite the disappointment in my failure to catch 'Jerry', I was also pissed off. She'd left no note, but had left a window unlocked. How else would he have been able to get inside the house? And that's what pissed me off the most: that fucking prick had been inside my home. He could have done anything. Anything! He could have sniffed Ava's underwear for all I knew, he could have poisoned the food in our fridge, he could have set up a bomb – how would I get shut-eye now? Where the hell was she?

CHAPTER THIRTY-FOUR

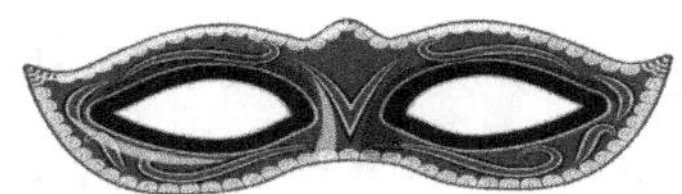

AFTER REFUELLING AT the service station, I drove home. The fact I could have missed a call back from O'Brien played on my mind; no doubt he'd be home by now, but 3:17 am was an unacceptable time to try him again. Besides, I needed to check out the house. I needed to inspect everything from top to bottom. A shudder assaulted my body as I pictured him in this house. All alone. Looking at our family photos. Sitting on the couch in smug glee that he'd entered so effortlessly. The money I'd spent on security may as well have been pissed away. And hadn't I warned Ava specifically before leaving, to make sure all the doors and windows were shut? Yes, I goddamn had!

I loved Ava more than anything, but Christ ...

I inspected all the windows, trying to work out which one she'd left open. But all of them were locked as far as I could see. I also grabbed a torch and headed to the side gates with Bogart at my heels. The thick padlocks were secure, which only made me scratch my head.

Once inside the house, I headed upstairs, dragging my throbbing feet. I checked every window, but they all seemed to be locked from the inside. What the bloody hell was going on here? How would I have a go at Ava about security if I couldn't even tell which one she'd left open?

In my delirium, I had half a mind to unlock one and say she'd left it open, just so I could drive home the point about conscientious safety, but I wasn't that big of an arsehole.

Then I opened the fridge. I didn't trust this madman about not harming either of us. He was a bona fide psycho, so I did the only thing any sane man would: I grabbed the bin, and with big sweeping arcs, chucked everything into it. Bottles clinked together as a packet of ham fell to the floor and liquids spilled, gushing about. I filled up the garbage bag in no time flat, then with a new bag, I went back for more. And more, this time to our pantry cupboard. Soon four chock-a-block bags of rubbish were lying on the kitchen floor like cadavers waiting for an autopsy. I ran to both the upstairs and downstairs bathrooms and shoved our toothpastes, mouthwash and toothbrushes inside as well. Then all the chemicals; they could have been laced with explosives. Bleach, toilet cleaner, even the goddamn washing detergent. Everything went like a clearance sale. His residue tainted this house.

Then I started checking the phones, the vases, the hanging pictures adorning our walls, the Christmas tree, anything at all that could conceal a wire or a small bomb. I would not take this lightly. He was luring me into a false sense of security by telling me we were not to be harmed. Fuck that! He was full of shit. He was pure evil. And then, to watch me from across the road. And wave – that fucking cocksucker had *waved* at me. In a flash, I grabbed the nearest framed photo I could get my hands on and smashed it against the floor.

Panting, I fell against the wall. I shut my eyes while breathing through it all, in through the nose, out through the mouth. Lethargic was an understatement, but I could not sleep. My brain would not shut off, as this was taking its toll. It weighed me down like an anchor, and as I picked up the frame on the floor, surrounded by broken glass, I turned it over to see our family portrait staring back.

CHAPTER THIRTY-FIVE

AVA'S LOUD GASP awoke me, followed by the sound of the front door closing. In my mind, it was like a gunshot firing in the dead of night.

'Eddy!'

I blinked rapidly, taking in my surroundings of the living room. My back and legs throbbed from excess use last night, my mouth as dry as the Simpson Desert.

'Why are there plastic bags all over the front lawn, for goodness' sake?'

Sunlight streamed in vibrantly behind me. Bogart raised his head, but did not move.

'Answer me!'

Moaning an old man's chorus, I sat up, blinking away the grogginess. 'What time is it?'

She tsked. 'Nine o'clock.'

I inhaled and took my time standing on shaky legs, easing out the kinks, rolling my neck around. I don't think I had ever truly felt my age until that moment.

'Answer me! Why is all our stuff on the lawn?'

'Where were you?' A yawn crept upon me. Christ, I'd have been surprised if I had slept at all.

She glared at me. 'I told you: I went to stay with Gracie-Ann from the Book Club.'

Shaking my head, I shuffled over to her. 'No you didn't.'

Her lips pursed as she regarded me. 'Yes, I did. I left you a note on the fridge.'

'You left a note?' I said patronisingly.

'Yes! Right there!' She went and pointed to the bare fridge, halting. 'Oh ...'

'I didn't see any bloody note!' Then it dawned: *He* took it down, that's why. He came into my house and took down the note. Probably scrunched it up while laughing his arse off, that fucking—

She opened the fridge door. 'Have you been drinking?' She turned to me, squinting as she closed the door.

'No.'

'You look like death warmed over. What's gotten into you? Why'd you throw out our things?'

'Don't worry about it; I'll go shopping today.'

'What?' She walked into the living room again.

'I thought we had a gas leak; I was worried. I didn't want to risk anything.'

'So, you threw everything out?'

Shuffling by, I said, 'Yes, but I will fix it. Calm down.'

'Calm down?' She inhaled, then exhaled, hands out beside her body, steadying her emotions. 'Have you forgotten your promise?'

'Which one? Be more specific.' I stood in the kitchen archway, inspecting my handiwork.

'About the barbeque tonight.'

'Oh *that*, no, of course not.' *Crap, was that tonight?*

Through thin lips, she said, 'I am going to head out again now.'

Standing taller, I turned to her. 'No, you're not.'

Her hand flew to her throat. 'Excuse me?'

'I don't want you going anywhere.'

'And who are you now; my father?'

Storming over, I grabbed her shoulders. 'I am your goddamn husband! And it's high time you start remembering that!' Her eyes portrayed fear as she stared at me like I was the *Creature from the Black Lagoon*. 'Where do you keep disappearing to? What's with all the secrecy?'

She breathed in through her nose as her chest puffed out. 'You are not in a position to keep badgering me with questions.'

My brows shot skyward. 'So, you're going to keep going out and not tell me where or with whom, and you think that's perfectly acceptable? Does it look like I have a penis on my forehead?'

'Why would I want to stay at home with someone who doesn't even acknowledge my existence?' Her face turned redder with every word. 'You do nothing! *We* do nothing together, so excuse me for wanting some fun and excitement in my day!' I released her and stood back. My drowsiness had disappeared – her words like a slap across the chops. Now, she became the aggressor. 'If it were up to you, you'd stay in your pyjamas reading books all day! I want to eat at fancy restaurants, go shopping, watch new movies, smell the ocean breeze, but it feels like I may as well be a widower!'

She fell against the kitchen archway and held her head in both hands, weeping. And not lightly, either; this had been building for a damn long time. All I could do was stand there and watch her wail until I pulled her in close. She didn't wrap her arms around me, but my hug must have offered some comfort, some soothing effect.

'I'm so sorry,' I whispered, my throat closing up on me.

'That's the thing,' she choked out. 'You keep saying that.' She sniffled, wiping her cheeks before peering up at me with doleful eyes. 'You keep apologising to me.'

'I don't know how to make this right. I keep stuffing up.'

Another tear fell, her lips quivering. 'Yes, you do. And then you tell *me* not to go out.'

'It's more than that, love. I'm not trying to tell you what to do for the sake of it; I am concerned about your safety.'

She pushed my hands away. 'Is this to do with what I keep seeing on the news? That masked man who's murdering all these people?'

This I could be truthful about. 'Yes, he's on the loose. Of course I care for your wellbeing. You're my wife, goddammit, of course I care! You need to be more vigilant when you go out. You need to lock all the doors and windows.'

'I did. And then I wrote you a note.'

I held her gaze. 'Did you really stay at Gracie-Ann's last night?'

'Yes.' She turned away from me, so I kissed her temple.

I stepped back, brushing my knuckles over her splotchy cheek. 'Shh, don't cry. I will fix everything, okay? I will go to the supermarket right now. Everything will be fine for tonight's dinner.'

'Fine.' She sniffled, clearing her throat. 'Is Heath coming?'

Hearing his name gave me unwelcome visuals of his bloodshot eyes at Timothy's place and I stiffened. I was still waiting to hear from him, to see what path he'd decided to take. 'You can call and ask him.'

She stepped away from me, drying her eyes with the palms of her hands. 'I am going to head out for a few hours, and when I get back, I expect everything to be sorted. Deal?'

'Promise.'

'And dinner will be ready by six-thirty, yes?'

'Yep, you bet your sweet arse.'

She held my gaze. 'Don't let me down.'

Raising crossed fingers, I shook my head and said, 'I won't. Go and enjoy your day, but be careful. I'll see you tonight. Just please, *please* be careful.'

'Just answer me one thing ...'

'Yes?'

'Is there anything you're keeping from me? And don't lie. Eddy, are we in danger?'

Steady Eddy made an appearance as I smiled, close-lipped. 'No. Not at all. I promise.'

Stephanie May

CHAPTER THIRTY-SIX

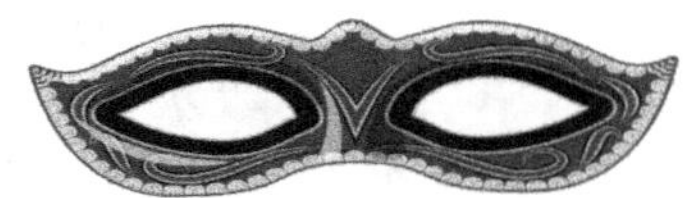

ONCE AVA HAD DRIVEN off, I ran inside the house to the telephone. I caught O'Brien at his office, just as he was on his way out.

I divulged everything about last night, from the letter, to the flesh souvenirs, to the car chase. He was speechless, judging by the silence at the other end; all I could hear were telephones ringing in the background and the clicking of computer keys.

'Okay,' he said after an age. 'Okay-okay-okay. I will start a search of all registered Plymouth Turismos around the Penrith district. Then, I'm afraid, you'll need surveillance.'

'At my house?'

'Yes! He's been inside your house; he's addressing you personally. We'll also need to send the CSU to your house as soon as I can arrange it.'

'How will I explain that to Ava?'

'Don't you want to feel safe in your own home, without looking over your shoulder?'

'Of course. But I don't want Ava to panic. I've got things under control.' I fingered the gun burning a hole in my hand.

'Don't be naive! You're not a fool, Eddy!'

My stomach gurgled its displeasure at being deprived of food and coffee. 'I went through the whole place myself. If he happened to leave prints, then I am sure I've bungled it up by now. I trashed the place myself; removed anything he could have tainted.'

'Better to be safe than sorry, but I think you're going to have to come clean with Ava. Tell her what's been going on, tell her about the letters. She's your wife; she deserves to know.'

I shook my head as I eyed Bogart squatting on the lawn, a big grin on his face as the brown log shot out of the chute. I'd left the back door open, and the cool summer breeze brought with it a mirage of pleasing, perfumed garden smells that aired out the stuffy house.

'What's your plan of action for today?' I asked as Bogart used his hind legs to flick back grass.

'We're going to track down this Joseph Fisher – the one borrowing all that weird shit from the library. I'll get the guys looking up vehicles registered in the district. Then I'll send some boys to exotic pet shops to see about that green tree snake. Also, Eddy, I've been thinking … if he's not out to harm you, then why is he stalking you? What's his fixation?'

'If he wanted me dead, he could have done it. He's fucking with me.'

'Hey, I agree; if he wanted you gone, he could have done it, but you know how cats like to play with their prey before they kill it.'

'Yeah … yeah, I guess so.'

'Can you get down here today so we can send off the samples of flesh to the lab? We won't have any time to come to yours.'

'Yeah, can do.'

'Be vigilant while you're here, yeah? Give me two hours. Jeremy and I are on our way to Joseph Fisher's house.'

'And nothing else from any neighbour – apart from Mrs Edgeworth?'

'Nope. But hey, feel free to do a door-to-door in your street to see if anyone saw anything from last night. Even if it's a partial numberplate.'

'Will do.'

'See you soon.'

I hung up and slid my gun into its holster. Was I allowed to have this? No. Was I a paranoid guy who wanted to protect his family? Yes. So, I also donned a jacket to conceal my weapon. The weather was too hot for a jacket, but I didn't want to risk it being seen by anyone – especially a cop. I was no longer authorised to carry a firearm; it was something I was going to have to get used to.

Seeing as the Penrith Police Station was only about a ten- to fifteen-minute drive away from mine, I did what O'Brien suggested. I started off with the houses near where Jerry the Jester had sat in his car when he waved to me. If he'd parked his car there while he taunted me from under my own window, then chances were someone who lived there may have seen something.

Fortunately, I did not know the names of many of my neighbours – except the old battle-axe, Mrs Murphy. I'd been too busy chasing bad guys to ever properly introduce myself, so I felt reasonably confident that my inquiries wouldn't be reported back to my wife – or Nathan Davies.

I walked by the aesthetically impressive houses along River Road. Red brick with white shutters. Immaculate lawns. Vibrant trees. My adjacent neighbour gave me a wave as I walked on by, and I returned it. I think his name was Ron, or Don – one of the two.

As I passed the fourth house on my left, I deduced this was roughly where Jerry had parked last night.

Following the narrow gravel drive, I passed a black Pontiac and walked up to the front door. I rang the doorbell and an elderly man answered soon after.

'Yes?' His frown indicated I'd probably interrupted him on the throne.

'G'day, my name's Eddy. I live a few houses down the road' – I turned and pointed – 'and I was wondering if last night, you may have seen anything unusual?'

'Be more specific!' His Coke-bottle glasses amplified his myopic grey eyes, and his coffee-and-cigarette breath packed a punch.

'A strange car that didn't belong here.'

'We get cars all the time; it's the Nepean River, for God's sake.'

'Sorry to have disturbed you. Have a nice day, sir.'

When he slammed the door in my face, I let out a frustrated sigh. I cut across his manicured lawn towards the adjacent house – a two-storey brick home with a Jeep and a Fairmont using the driveway as a tanning bed.

'Come on Eileen' played over the radio in the background as I waited.

Soon enough, a young, attractive woman answered. She was a redhead with unblemished skin and green eyes, dressed in tight gym clothes.

'Hello?' she said cautiously. A chihuahua yipped from the white tiled hallway a few feet away.

'Morning, ma'am, my name is Eddy and I live down the road.'

She turned to where I pointed. 'Right ...?'

'Yes, and I had a bit of a scuffle with some man taking drugs out the front of my place last night, and I wondered if you happened to see or hear anything?'

She turned her head to the yipping dog. 'Hercules, calm down!' She turned back to me once the dog quit yapping. 'Depends what time?'

'Well, what did you see?'

She twisted her lips. 'Hmm, it was around ten-thirty. I was waiting for my boyfriend, who was due home from work, and I was peering out the window when a car with no headlights did a U-turn in front of my house, and parked there before the driver hopped out.'

Sweat trickled behind my earlobe as I stared at her. 'Did you see what he looked like?'

'Well, from my second floor, I thought his face was really pale, and that he had black around the eyes, like a panda or something, but they weren't circles.'

My weight shifted from foot to foot. 'Did you get a good look at the car?'

'It was dark-coloured. I can't swear on what shade. Could have been dark green, or black.'

'When he hopped out, was he carrying anything?'

Her eyes flew skyward, winding back the clock. 'Yes, a briefcase.'

I discreetly wiped my sweaty hands on my pants. 'Was anyone else with him?' By this time, Hercules had approached us, peering at me with suspicious eyes and a twitching nose.

She shook her head. 'Just him and the briefcase.'

'And that was all you saw? Did you see him again?'

'My boyfriend, Ted, came home soon after, and he had a trunk full of food – he's a chef, and the restaurant where he works is closing for two weeks because of renovations, so his boss let him take home food – otherwise they would have thrown it all out, see? So, Ted comes in and tells me he has a trunk full of goods – boxes of tomatoes and mushrooms – stuff like that. And while I was down the driveway about to collect boxes with Ted, I *did* check if the car was still there.'

'And it was.' It wasn't a question. She nodded. 'Did you see the licence plate?'

She grinned. 'I did.'

'And do you remember it?'

A plane flew overhead, so she waited, but my gaze was fastened to her flawless face.

'I do, because it was unusual. It said J3ST3R. And at first, I didn't get it because I was kinda wiped out, but then I realised it was supposed to spell JESTER.'

CHAPTER THIRTY-SEVEN

ITHANKED THE LADY for her time and returned home to collect the letter and box of human goodies from my study. It sickened me knowing I carried around human flesh, but I was glad to pass it on to Forensics. I knew I was carrying remnants of Norman Colbert, but what else would this sample tell us? I still had to go shopping for tonight's dinner. I hoped Heath and Lorraine would make an appearance, but I still hadn't heard anything from him, which pissed me off.

I locked Bogart inside the house, triple-checked all the locks and windows, and then took off down the road, reliving the events of last night as 'Africa' by Toto played in the background.

A raging fire ignited in my belly. I now had that son of a bitch's number-plate, and that was as good as gold. Three confirmed sightings of a tall man wearing a jester mask.

How funny would this dickhead find it being behind bars for the rest of his life? I, too, would send him taunting letters from the outside and ask him how it feels.

It was an odd feeling parking out the front of the headquarters, alas, not in my usual designated parking spot. I hopped out among the frantic Christmas shoppers, carrying more than their body weight in plastic bags, and made my way across High Street and into the building; a building that still felt like home. It's like living with your parents, and then moving out to start your own life. It's always strange going back, and having to knock on the front door instead of letting yourself in.

I said hello to Maura Bacia, the receptionist. A flashing Christmas tree was perched like a silent soldier beside the desk. Bing Crosby sung 'Silent Night' over the speakers, and tinsel was sticky-taped like a crawling worm stretched to either end of the reception desk.

'What brings you back?' Maura asked with a cheeky grin. 'Can't keep away from us, is that it?'

Smirking, I said, 'Something like that.'

'You're missing your partner, huh?' Her flashing Rudolph earrings swung on her every move.

'Is he in?'

'Yep, came back with Retmeyer about twenty-minutes ago with lunch. I'll buzz you in. Wait, are you carrying?'

'Old habit.'

She grinned, shaking her head. 'Always the troublemaker, Matthews. But I'll let it slide.'

'You're a peach. Is Davies in?'

She rolled her eyes. 'He's *always* in; I don't think he ever goes home.'

'Well, he never did marry, did he?'

She laughed just as the phone rang. Thank God, too. She had no idea the box I held contained human flesh.

'Oh, by the way' – she reached for the phone – 'I saw your photo in the

Telegraph about, you know, the case you're "not" investigating.'

Shrugging, I nodded. 'What can you do? Old habits and all that.'

The door clicked open as Maura buzzed me inside. I travelled the same corridor that the soles of my shoes had scuffed over the past few decades. It was a strange kind of familiar. People looked at me over the tops of their cubicles as phones, printers and fax machines whirred in the background. Some folks smiled and waved, some pretended not to see me, some looked shocked to see me back here. The endless chatter and trilling phones had not changed; it always used to remind me of a newsroom. There were a few fresh faces, but thank God, I had not bumped into Davies. Considering I was carrying an unlicensed gun and cookie-cutter pieces of human flesh, he was the last person I—

'Matthews?'

Fuck! And here we go.

I turned as my ex-superior, Nathan 'Dickhead' Davies trotted over, belly leading the way.

He stood only a few feet away, his pudgy hands settling on his wide hips. 'My office, now.'

A sea of heads swivelled as I followed behind. I remembered his office well. He slid open the glass door where his name was painted in gold block letters: CHIEF SUPERINTENDENT NATHAN DAVIES, and let me enter first. I gave him a cheery smile as I walked by and took a black leather chair. Among other things, Davies was one of those pompous pricks who had a head full of black hair, but a totally white beard. I'd thought about telling him to let it go many times, but he was touchy about his appearance, always one of those guys who told you he was six feet, when really, he was five-eight – with shoes on, yet he had no problem looking like a walking advertisement for a gym's 'before' photos.

I sat in front of his cherrywood desk. No pictures of a wife or children adorning it, and the walls displayed his merits like badges of honour, and so he should. I did when I was here, too.

He sat opposite me, giving an exaggerated moan as he sank into his black swivel chair, the horizontal desk cutting into his gut. His insignia of his rank of chief superintendent stood out on his navy-blue jacket. He sweated like a bastard in that thing. He placed his pudgy hands on the desk on either side of an open planner. A Macintosh computer cluttered one side of his desk, and a tin of pens, pencils and highlighters was on the opposite, next to two trays labelled IN and OUT. A stack of files two phone books high sat neat and tidy in front of the tray. Nothing out of place. Nothing askew.

His blue eyes resembled a raging storm out at sea. 'What are you doing here, Matthews?'

'I came to say hello.'

'Bullshit!' Spittle flew from his mouth and landed on the desk, inches away from me. 'Everyone here has seen the paper with your photo in it.'

Shrugging slowly, I said, 'I happened to be walking by when the photographer got me.'

'Cut the fucking crap; I've already spoken to O'Brien and Retmeyer.' A fat sausage finger rose, directed at me. 'I know Mitch called you on the case because of your expertise and long-standing friendship. But let me tell you something, Matthews: the walls have not collapsed since you walked out. We're doing just fine without you – you shouldn't feel any qualms about going back to your normal, quiet life.'

My hands rubbed the chair's arms back and forth. 'No problem.'

'What do you have with you there?' He pointed to the box and envelope on my lap.

My heart pounded harder, mind scrambling to put something believable together. 'A little thank-you card and gift from Ava, to pass on to Janice O'Brien. I was in the neighbourhood doing some Christmas shopping and decided to pop in to see Mitch. Is that okay?'

A fat fist collided with the table. 'Do you understand how much shit we could be in if we organise a sting and you're involved? Do you understand this could be thrown out of court if the defence ever got wind? Do you understand my arse could be wiped over the floor because of you?'

'I do.'

'Then don't you fuckin' lie to me. And don't you dare think about working on any more cases. I will let you see Mitch and Jeremy this one time, but don't think about coming in again. No more popping in for a chat – got it? You want to catch up with everyone, then do it on your own goddamn time. We have work to do. Go home and fuckin' bake cookies while watching *A Country Practice*.'

I glared at him with a facile smile, imagining what it'd feel like to drive my fist into his mouth. We'd never gotten along since the get-go; he was nothing like the superior I'd had before. 'No prob.'

He shook his head. 'Get out of my sight, and don't be too long!'

'Yes, sir.' I stood, leaving his office as silently as I had walked into it.

I hurried along back to the cubicles and headed straight for O'Brien's office. I knocked on the door and heard an abrupt: 'Come in!'

When I entered, I almost double-checked to make sure I had the right room. O'Brien appeared to have tacked an extra ten years on to his life, and Jeremy's baggy eyes conveyed he'd been working round the clock. Greasy Hungry Jack's wrappers adorned a mountain of paperwork and what looked like today's paper.

'Hey, Eddy,' Jeremy said, holding a paper takeaway cup of dark liquid – my guess: Coke. I shook his other hand, and then O'Brien's.

Jeremy used the corner of his free hand to wipe the side of his shiny mouth. 'Mitch told me about what happened to you last night.' He offered me a seat by pushing it out, and I took it.

'Thanks. Yes, I brought the letter and the box.' We both sat facing O'Brien's cluttered desk.

O'Brien took the box from me. He placed it on the desk, sat back down and burped into a fist. He rolled his shoulders before opening the box, as Jeremy stood to lean over the desk.

Jeremy's hand went to his stomach as he turned away. 'Shouldn't have had those burgers …'

O'Brien shook his head as he stared at the contents. 'Christ almighty.' He turned to me, hand outstretched. 'Now … the letter.'

I handed over the envelope, and Jeremy walked behind O'Brien's chair to read the letter over his shoulder. When they were done, Jeremy looked as pale as a Nord. He ran a hand through his dark hair, tongue pressed against the inside of his cheek.

'And I have something, too.' I waited for them to look at me. 'A numberplate.'

'Fucking-A!' O'Brien slapped his desk. 'We are, right at this moment, expecting a fax from the RTA.'

'How'd you go with Joseph Fisher? Anything?'

O'Brien shook his head. 'Not a damn thing. He was a weird character, all right, but I think he's just trying out to be a Neo-Nazi. Besides, he drives his mother's car – an old fender-bender Pontiac, plus … he's about five-six. Way too short for our guy – according to the witnesses.'

Jeremy pointed to me. 'We did get him on having illegal reptiles, though.'

'We searched his bedroom and car; he has a swastika flag hanging in his room, but too piss-weak for this type of case.'

'It was a long shot, but had to be done,' I said.

'Agreed. It's all about elimination – but we have something else.' O'Brien's eyes glittered. 'We did background research into Raúl and Juanita Martínez, and turns out they were not exactly law-abiding citizens, either.'

Sitting forward, I asked, 'What do you mean?'

'Drugs. Money laundering. Her eldest is not Raúl's, either; she was from a previous relationship.'

'Where's the biological father?'

'Prison! For murdering his drug dealer.' He reached for his drink. 'He'll be out in five.'

I steepled my fingers under my prickly chin. 'Once again, we are dealing with shady victims, which still leads me to believe these murders are some sort of punishment. He sees them as evil.'

'How is he finding them, though?' Jeremy said. 'Is he selecting them at random?'

O'Brien offered the remainder of his box of salty chips to me.

I shook my head, raising a hand before turning to Jeremy. 'No, he watches them. Same as he watches me.'

'By the by,' O'Brien said, 'all local exotic pet shops turned up nothing useful. No-one has sold any green tree snakes recently. Perhaps our guy acquired it illegally?'

The fax machine whirred, so O'Brien swivelled to the right. He jumped up and waited for it to finish. He grabbed the piece of paper with both hands, staring at it.

'What?' Jeremy said.

He flicked the paper and looked up. 'The names registered to Turismos in the Penrith district.'

Using the chair for help, I rose to my feet. 'What do you have?'

'Only five names.' He handed me the paper, and I scanned the names and licence plates. There was no J3ST3R.

'Doesn't make sense,' I whispered.

'*Or* it isn't registered in Penrith,' O'Brien said.

Shaking my head, I said, 'He's a local boy, I can feel it. It's his hunting ground.'

O'Brien cleared his throat. 'Let's start by paying these five blokes a visit, shall we?'

My head jerked up. 'I want to come.'

O'Brien looked at me as he shrugged on his jacket. 'Look, mate ...'

'Don't start!'

O'Brien placed his hands on his hips, head tilted as we lost eye contact. He turned to Jeremy. 'Son, send these off to the lab.'

'Right.' Jeremy held the box far out in front with both hands.

After he left, I turned to O'Brien.

'Don't put me in this position, please,' he whispered.

I held up my hands. 'I won't say a word.'

'Then why bother? Let us handle it.'

'No.'

His arms fell to his sides, turning away.

'This fucker has been inside my house.' My fingertips pressed into my temples. 'He has been inside my *mind*.'

He leaned against his desk, staring at me. 'We still have to organise surveillance and have your house combed over.'

'It won't do shit, and you know it.'

'I've already been in the shit, thanks to that newspaper article!' He shook his head. 'I can't let you, mate.'

'You can. Please. Just this once. I'll know him as soon as I see him. Trust me, I will know.'

He hung his head, exhaling. 'Why do I have the feeling this is going to bite me in the arse?'

'No-one will know.'

'Oh yeah?' His tired eyes found mine. 'They're already onto it being connected; they've even given him a nickname.'

'What is it? I didn't have a chance to read today's paper.'

His lips twisted in a bitter smile as he held up a copy of the *Penrith Press*, issued Friday, December 14th:

POLICE STILL HAVE NO CLUES TO THE WHEREABOUTS OF THE PROP MASTER.

I pinched the bridge of my nose. 'Christ, that moniker is friggin' awful.'

'Tell me about it.' He paused, deliberating. 'Do us a favour and take your own car, okay? Wait for my car to pass you on High Street and then follow me until we get to the first house. We will have to organise the CSU to go to your place—'

'No-one is home. C'mon, let's do this; I still have to go grocery shopping.'

He looked at me for a moment, contemplating, then shook his head. 'Who's the first guy?'

I glanced at the fax sheet. It was black and white, so I couldn't see the grainy pictures well, but I could see the ages from their birth dates. They ranged from 20 to 74.

Glancing towards O'Brien, I said, 'Thomas Allgood of Kingswood. Almost due for rego, too.'

CHAPTER THIRTY-EIGHT

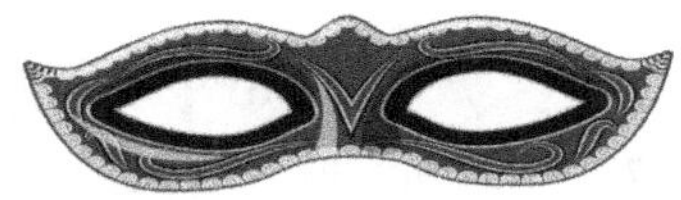

'AVALON' BY ROXY MUSIC played over Air FM as I waited in my Statesman for O'Brien and Jeremy. Behind my Ray-Bans, I kept scanning the throng of people travelling up and down High Street. *How many of these are sinful people? Why does this Jester fuck take it upon himself to judge others for their sins? Hypocrite award for 1984 goes to …*

I popped a piece of Juicy Fruit into my dry mouth. I typically did this while interviewing suspects, as a matter of having something to do. Some people smoked. Some people chewed pens. I remained calm on the outside while chewing ferociously on the inside.

Not long after I'd rolled down my window, O'Brien's Ford Fairlane appeared in my dusty side mirror. He even flashed his lights to make sure. I indicated after he drove past, then pulled out and cruised not far behind him. The sense of thrill dominated all other emotions; I imagined it was how a lion felt, getting a whiff of a fresh carcass on the savannah winds. Nothing could deter me from that point on, I *had* to follow the scent, no matter what danger lurked ahead in the shadows.

We reached Kingswood not long after; about eight minutes thanks to the traffic lights in between. We pulled up alongside a damaged white picket fence. It wasn't anything to write home about, this house. Small. Fibro. Neglected. Noxious weeds monopolised the lawn; dog shit that'd turned to alabaster-white coated the concrete path, and the front window had a broken, gaping hole stuffed with an oily rag.

They hopped out first as I gathered myself together, breathing in and out, trying to keep myself under wraps. If Allgood was our Jester, I'd know it upon first sight. And he'd know me, too, and that's exactly what I wanted – for this guy to look me in the eye without his mask to hide behind.

'Here goes nothing,' O'Brien said, pulling up his pants by the belt. 'Remember, don't fuck this up, Eddy. If it's our guy, let us handle this. Deal?'

'Deal.'

He nodded, and that was as good as shaking hands. We made our way up the crooked path, dodging canine crap. Jeremy *tap-tap-tapped* on the dirty fly screen as we peered inside. The smell of faeces made Jeremy turn away, there were nappies full of hardened shit lying about in the hallway. In the lounge room to the left, we could make out a pile of rumpled clothes; the dusty floor looked like it hadn't been swept since the time of the house's erection, and mould spooled in the corners of the ceiling, indicating water damage. The pungent smell of cannabis wafted throughout the house. I don't understand how people can smoke and eat in the same space. To me, it was like shitting where you cooked, and from the smell of shit, I'd say this assertion was right.

Jeremy cupped the corners of his wide gob. 'Hello?'

'Hang on, fuck ya!' a man yelled.

O'Brien turned to me, raising his brows as if to say 'Here we go …'

A man emerged from a room along the hallway, shirtless, pulling on his jeans as he walked towards us, zipping up his fly. A tuft of pubic hair stuck out above the hem of his jeans. Classy.

'Yeah?' he said, squinting, mouth open to reveal yellow and chipped teeth. Bits of meat stuck between his crooked teeth. Yuck, who'd want to stick their tongue in that bacteria-riddled mouth?

'Thomas Allgood?'

He folded his arms across his scrawny chest and straightened, revealing a tattoo on his upper right bicep – a bulldog with boxing gloves on, posed to fight. 'Who wants to know?'

'We're detectives with the Penrith Police Department – mind if we ask you a few questions?'

He dipped backwards, slapping his hands by his sides. 'Aww man, if it's about our fuckin' neighbour again – tell him we fuckin' stopped playin' the stereo so loud, bro!'

'Sir?'

He scratched his bare chest with dirty fingernails, squinting hard. 'He fuckin' complains all the time, bro! He needs to chill – Mötley Crüe is the goddamn balls, ya know what I mean?'

I glanced past Thomas Allgood, a man who was clearly not over-burdened by intelligence of any kind, as a woman with platinum-blonde hair with black roots emerged from the same room that Thomas had a moment prior. She adjusted an orange summer dress and stormed down the hallway. She lit a cigarette as her bare feet slapped across the filthy linoleum. I wagered the soles of her feet would resemble black soot by the time she reached us.

'Who are these gronks?' Her perfume was a scent of sweat and semen. God, these two were a blight on society. To top it off, she was braless.

'Ahh, fuckin' Mr Have-A-Whinge has dobbed on us again!'

The woman pushed Thomas out of the way and stuck a finger towards us, her nose wrinkled and one knee pointed outward, other hand raised in the air like she was some female activist telling the crowd to keep on fighting the good fight! 'You tell that mongrel to shove it up his clacker!'

'Ma'am, keep your voice down,' Jeremy said. 'We're not here about any music disturbance; we're here to ask about your car.'

She took a drag, eyeing us before blowing plume through the fly screen.

Thomas frowned, wheezing a laugh shortly thereafter. 'What fuckin' car, mate?' He hooked a thumb over his bony shoulder. 'It's been out the back since the missus smashed it.'

She turned to him, pushing his chest. 'I told ya I was sorry, Tommy! I fuckin' said I was ...'

When a baby somewhere inside bawled, O'Brien turned to me. 'Clearly not who we are looking for.'

'Let's have a quick look, anyway.' I pointed towards a back fence that lay slumped backwards like a limbo dancer, as Thomas and his girlfriend argued. The three of us walked along sunken pavers at the side of the house and arrived at the back gate. Under an oak tree sat the Plymouth Turismo in a sad state. Windscreen smashed, bonnet caved in. Judging by the concentrated impact, I'd say she'd slammed into a tree trunk or telegraph pole.

'Next ...' O'Brien said, checking his list under the glaring sun as we made our way back past the front door where yelling and baby wailing continued.

'Who's next?' Jeremy asked, looking left down the quiet street.

'Brian May, over in Cambridge Park. We have two in Cambridge Park, and then one in Werrington Downs – the last is in Orchard Hills.'

One down, four to go.

CHAPTER THIRTY-NINE

Ten minutes later, we arrived at the residence of Mr Brian May (not the guitarist of Queen, I assure you) in College Street, Cambridge Park.

The Turismo sat in the driveway, yet I noticed with disappointment that the windows were not tinted. Still, none of the cars were registered with the numberplate J3ST3R either, so I wouldn't let this deter me.

We headed down the charcoal-coloured brick driveway and O'Brien knocked on the door.

A man wearing a Vietnam veteran's hat appeared. His grey bushy moustache resembled a giant caterpillar, and wiry grey hair sprouted over the neck of his white singlet.

'G'day, fellas,' he said, glancing at each of us. 'What have I done this time?'

'G'day, sir,' O'Brien said. 'Would you happen to be Brian May?'

'Depends what you want him for. If Madonna is asking, then sure, you've got him!'

O'Brien forced a chuckle. In the space of five seconds, we didn't need to be told this was not our guy. For one, he was too short. Second, I was sure he was too old – but I didn't rule that out – Lauren Edgeworth said he could have been older. But, third, my gut instinct told me this guy was genuine, and there was no look of shock when he saw me. And finally, his right arm was bionic; there was hell's chance he could have overpowered men twice his size and half his age with one arm. I deduced he'd lost it in the war.

'Battle of Long Tan,' Brian went on to explain later as he showed us the car. 'Goddamn bastards tore off my arm like someone pullin' on a wishbone – one bullet, that's all it took!'

We left after five minutes.

O'Brien and Jeremy leaned against my warm bonnet, as did I.

'Hot day,' Jeremy said, wiping the sweat from his brow with a hanky.

O'Brien gave a watery snort. 'You can say that again. I feel like Earth's getting hotter and hotter as the years roll by. Sure could go for a Cola Sunnyboy right about now.'

Birds twittered in a nearby tree, sprinkler systems in front yards quenched thirsty plants, and I rubbed the base of my sweaty, itchy neck. 'Who's next? I still have to shop for tonight's dinner.'

'Are we invited?' O'Brien wiggled his brows.

'Don't even think about it – who's next?'

O'Brien consulted the page. 'Kenny Longbottom.'

'Right.' I clapped once – the thunderclap sending birds flying. 'Let's do it!'

I waited for Jeremy to search on the map where O'Brien was to head, as I sat there drumming my fingers on the hot leather steering wheel. Of course, I thought about dinner with my family, but the lads and I were playing a game of Hot and Cold, and baby, we were definitely getting warmer. We had the car. We had the numberplate (*a* numberplate, anyway). We had reported sightings about his mask – soon his capture would be over the news quicker than Liz

Taylor remarrying.

Nathan Davies was due to give a press conference this afternoon outside the Penrith Police Station, and he was in for some serious questioning. Already the public were quick to lash out at the cops, saying this has been going on for too long, without any leads. That we (yes, 'we') were lying down on the job, where in reality, look at what was happening to our families. They had no fucking clue, the public; didn't have a goddamn iota what it took to keep the streets safe, and how much time with our families we sacrificed. In many ways this job was rewarding, but if you fucked up just *one* time, they'd hang you against a pole and start lighting torches. Trust me, I wear the mental scars from what happened with—

O'Brien pulled away from the kerb and I wiped my forearm on my long sleeve. It was only a two-minute drive to Kenny Longbottom's house, but I couldn't wait; he was person of interest number three on the list of five. God, I hoped it would be this guy. How I prayed to God it would be as we pulled alongside a peach-coloured fibro house on the corner of Barry Street. It faced a line of shops on the intersection of Oxford Street. A football oval stood before us, and the smell of Chinese food wafted through the air from the takeout shop.

The Turismo sat on the front lawn. Peering inside the car, I shook my head. 'Nope.'

'Why not?' Jeremy said, coming in for a look-see.

'First, no tinted windows. Second, look at the muffler. It's illegal. Trust me, I would have picked up on that. Third, look in the back seat.'

'Oh ...' Jeremy said, heavy-lidded as he eyed the baby seat and diaper bags.

O'Brien loosened his collar, his chest heaving. 'Don't you even want to go in and see him?'

'Nope, because look ...' I pointed to the console, and there, sticking out, was the identification card of a Timezone employee with his photo next to it. It showed a pimply-faced geek with oily blonde hair. This was our twenty-year-old. Nevertheless, we'd needed to see for ourselves.

'The Jester is not some kid who works for an arcade game company.'

'You're right.' O'Brien rubbed his eyelids back and forth before putting on his sunnies again. 'Fuck *me*, it's bloody hot.'

Jeremy placed his hands at the back of his head and leaned backwards, stretching.

Three down, two to go. The sooner this ended, the sooner we could all reclaim our sanity.

CHAPTER FORTY

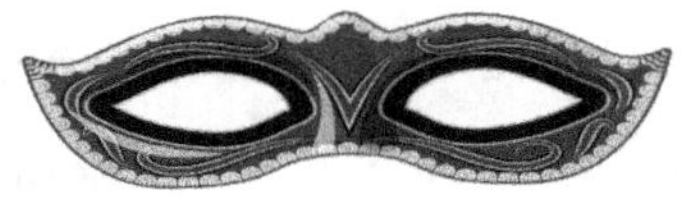

FIVE MINUTES LATER, I switched off my engine with a sense of dread. This was going nowhere. We were wasting our goddamn time, but if not this, then what else? Publish an article in the papers, sure, but then what? Sit by the phone and wait?

As they hopped out of O'Brien's car, I approached. We stared at number ninety-two, which was situated down a crooked driveway. Due to all the over-hanging trees, the archaic house had a sense of abandonment, pushed aside and forgotten.

'Hey, look at this,' Jeremy said, pointing to the letterbox: chock-a-block full. It was clear posties had tried to shove letters as hard as they could into the mess, rather than head down the driveway and leave it at his door.

'Gone away, has he?' O'Brien said. 'Or hiding out, perhaps?'

We headed down the wide concrete pathway that led to the house. This place was closed off from the world; it became darker and cooler, as slivers of sunlight infiltrated the small cracks between the trees in their tangled embrace.

'Place looks deserted,' I said. No cars sat in the driveway, and the garage roller door was down. There were no signs of movement, and the deeper and darker it became, the more something sinister tickled the top of my spine, making me shiver violently.

'Whoa,' Jeremy said, eyeing my body. 'Who stepped on your grave?'

'I just had this feeling.' It metastasised as we got closer and closer to the door. As we crept on, a black cat screeched as it darted in front of us, jumping over a fence.

'Little fucker,' O'Brien said, placing a hand over his heart.

Upon stepping on the tattered WELCOME doormat, the smell of putrefaction punched me in the nose.

Jeremy stepped back, wide-eyed. 'Holy shit!'

O'Brien reached for his gun. 'Stay behind us, Eddy. Jeremy, get your arse here.'

Jeremy used his hand to create a dome-shaped mask over his mouth and nostrils as I stood aside to let them enter.

O'Brien opened his mouth, raising his head. 'Hello? Mr Pratt?'

The door opened with no resistance. Flies buzzed like one continuous droning hum. The smell was bad enough to make my eyes water. There isn't any other foul smell like that in the world – the smell of a rotting corpse.

Jeremy doubled over and dry-retched. God, it was enough to make our skin peel away, so I held my forearm over my nose and mouth.

'Hello?' O'Brien yelled again. 'Elliot Pratt?' His face was scrunched up that tight, I thought if he released the muscles he'd shoot off into the stratosphere.

I followed O'Brien and his drawn gun. Without being able to use mine, I felt as superfluous as a used condom. I hated this feeling of letting other people get their hands muddied as I stood back and watched. Of course, I'd brought my gun, but pulling it out in front of the lads would be moronic.

We travelled a narrow hallway, peering into the rooms on our right, and then the left. We kept on until the smell intensified. It became sicklier, like wading through acid.

'Here!' O'Brien yelled behind a crooked arm, standing in an open doorway to the right; the lullaby of the blowflies serenading our victim more pronounced now.

I stepped in behind O'Brien to view the most recent artwork of our perpetrator.

As we stepped closer, eyeing the remnants of an elderly man who lay on a single bed in front of us, we had to bat flies out of the way. His hollowed face a waxy yellow, his chest undulating from maggots. The top of his white head faced us, and he had a prop with him: a lantern. A walking stick lay beside him on the bed, too. Was that also a prop? Elliot Pratt appeared feeble; old enough to need the aid of a walking stick. The lantern I had no clue about. I began to turn away when something lying on the blood-splattered sheet called out to me. Holding my breath, I bent over Mr Pratt, careful to avoid transferring any hair or fibres, and stared at an object. It was small and cut out of what looked like plain old white cardboard.

'What is it?' Jeremy said, entering the room, pale as a beluga whale. 'What do you see?' He came by me, wiping his watery eyes with the back of a hand.

'Is that a star?' O'Brien said, squinting from this height.

Jeremy stepped closer. 'A star with six points … I don't get it.'

I stood, spine extending as flies buzzed a harmonious tune. 'The Star of David.'

Jeremy squinted. 'Of *who*?'

'The symbol of the Jews. The Star of David has six points.'

O'Brien glanced at the star. I closed my eyes for a moment to get a hold of myself. And then, with eyes refocused, staring back at me from a dresser was a ceramic doll of a jester, dressed in a black-and-white costume with a frozen, sinister smile looking directly at me.

I turned to Jeremy, who was doubled over, coughing into a fist. 'I think we know where our guy got the Turismo from.' I pointed to the dead man. 'He stole it, then used his own fake plates just to screw with us.'

CHAPTER FORTY-ONE

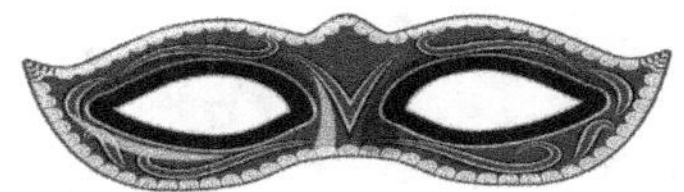

OUTSIDE ELLIOT PRATT'S house we would have sworn Mel Gibson was here. What a fucking media circus. Dozens of reporters. Dozens of cameramen. Police lining the street, and many of Pratt's neighbours rubbernecking. The street was now cordoned off, while CSU vans lined the kerb – the Mercedes-Benz belonging to medical examiner, Dr Michael Wong.

Sitting on a stool at the kitchen bench, I surveyed the room, noting the magnets and reminders on the victim's fridge, and his collection of souvenir mugs on a wall-mounted shelf. Then, Nathan Davies stormed inside. He glared at me, tight-lipped, before disappearing down the hallway. I sat still, as if in a vacuum while everything crumbled around me. I was pissed off because the Jester had warned me it would be an elderly man, and I couldn't stop it. I couldn't save him from death.

The pressure surrounding this case kept sucking me back to Abigail. How useless I'd felt. How utterly despicable I could not bring a child's murderer to justice. Those were some of the darker times I'd had during my career. And he knew that. He *knew*.

As though a door opened and then slammed into my face, Ava and the family dinner brought me back from my reverie. Shit. I'd blown it again. There was nothing I could do now. The wall clock said 4:20. Not enough time to head to the shops and buy a whole fridge-worth of provisions, and then go home, and then prepare everything, *and* have it ready by 6:30. There was no way. Not when I was still needed here. We had nabbed ourselves a neighbour who had been a witness. Or so he claimed. He was only a young boy from across the street. He was about to be called upon to give us his account of what he saw – his mother reckoned he could help us. I needed to be there for the interview at all costs.

I waited inside Pratt's kitchen, feeling like a spare cock at a wedding. I tried to use Elliot's landline to inform Ava I would not be home, but the telephone cord was cut. The prick had cut the landline, as he had done in all the other victims' places. As soon as we were done with the kid, I would drive to the nearest public payphone and call her. It would not be pretty. But as 'Jerry' said in his letter, we were like illicit lovers, and I would go to him every time he beckoned me. I loved my wife and children more than life itself, but this *thing* inside me, God, it had a voracious appetite. It kept eating and gnawing away at my insides. It was an appetite for destruction. But what I thought about most, as I listened to endless chatter, was *him*. The one who eluded me; the one always two moves ahead.

'Eddy?' Jeremy's voice floated down the hallway above the white noise before his head poked through the kitchen entrance.

He stared at me, blinking several times. 'The kid and his mother are ready to talk now.'

My head jerked towards Pratt's bedroom. 'What about Davies?'

'He's with Michael Wong. He already knows you're here. Let's go; Mitch is coming.'

I rose from the stool and tried to roll out the kinks in my neck. I heard a snap that sounded like a wooden ruler and it took me back to my schooldays when I'd been a naughty boy. O'Brien appeared at the doorway, brushing past Harold Lucado and his camera, and headed straight for the front door.

'Ready?' O'Brien said, throwing his shoulders back. 'It's a goddamn madhouse outside.'

We exited the house and followed the driveway. Dozens of people were gathered out the front, standing behind tape that cordoned off the top of the driveway.

Already, people were shouting and shoving microphones in our faces. Bulbs flashed, cameras followed our every move like magnets, and people hollered. I made eye contact with that bitch blonde, Liz Fulton, as others shouted to us.

'O'Brien, can you tell Channel 7 viewers what the nature of the murder is?'

'Macintosh Matthews, have you come out of retirement?'

'Is this the Australian version of Son of Sam?'

We ducked under the crime scene tape and followed O'Brien to the house across the street. The front yard had signs on pickets welcoming Santa and his reindeer; unlit fairy lights covered the roof.

A brown-haired woman waited behind a fly screen as the vultures stood behind us, shouting and taking pictures.

'Quickly,' she said, ushering us inside. The lady appeared to be in her mid-thirties, wholesome and well groomed. 'My son's in the living room.' She closed and locked the door. As soon as I stepped inside the kitchen, the smell of freshly baked cookies made my stomach gurgle.

O'Brien turned to me. 'This is Margot Average, and her son has some information.'

I shook her small hand. 'Eddy Matthews. What's your son's name, ma'am?'

'Noah.' Margot Average led us into a moderately furnished living room, where a young boy – no older than seven, I guessed – sat on a one-seater. His knees were scraped and his feet swung back and forth, shoulders bunched, a protruding bottom lip dominating his facial features. The room could have been mistaken for Santa's workshop, with reds and greens covering every horizontal inch. Fake snow settled in the corners of the windows, mistletoe swung from a ceiling fan, and the tree, which was surrounded by a train track with sleighs, had more presents than you could poke a stick at.

'Honey, you need to tell the lovely policemen what you saw, okay?' Margot bent forward, hands on knees. 'Tell them what you told me and Daddy. You're not in trouble, just say the truth. Then we can get pizza for dinner – how does that sound? Pizza and ice cream!'

He peered up, those big chocolate-brown eyes wide and innocent, untarnished by the harsh realities and mishaps of adulthood. Milo and milk smudged his blue-and-white-striped shirt.

'Hey there, squirt!' O'Brien said, sitting on the three-seater couch positioned beside Noah. 'Your mummy tells me you have a story to tell us. Well, we like stories, don't we, fellas?' O'Brien turned to us, so we nodded enthusiastically.

'Love 'em!' Jeremy said.

'You should hear some of mine, buddy!' I added. 'Woo-hoo, you'll think it's a right laugh!'

Noah's eyes relaxed, and a cheeky grin crept onto his face. Margot Average stood near the archway, a dainty hand to her slender throat as she watched on with encouraging eyes.

'Go on, honey,' Margot whispered, smiling.

'I can't – I can't remember when, buh-buh-but I sawed a man in front of Mr Pratt's place.'

O'Brien nodded. 'Right, and what kind of man was he?'

Noah shrugged. 'Don't know. He was in his car.'

'Do you know if he was tall? I mean, was he down low in the chair, or higher up so his head was near the roof?'

'Head near roof.'

'You'd say tall?'

He sucked his lips in, bobbing his head.

'And do you remember what Mr Tall was wearing?'

He crinkled his brow. 'Mmm, dark stuff.'

'Right. Okay, good. And did Mr Tall see you, or say anything to you?'

Noah nodded, serious now. 'He seed me, 'cause he-he did this.' Then he put his index finger to his lips as if to silence those around him.

'He told you to be quiet? Or to not speak to anyone?'

'Yeah!'

'Which one, buddy?'

'Be quiet.'

'Right, and how did you notice he was there? What were you doing?'

He sat straighter in his chair, wiggling his bum. 'I was riding my bicycle up and down the street with my older brudder.'

O'Brien let Jeremy scribble this info into his little notepad before continuing. 'What's your brother's name?'

'Owen. He's at Beau's place right now. I wasn't 'loud to go.'

'Did Owen see Mr Tall, too?'

He shook his head adamantly. 'No, 'cause – 'cause he rid off without me!'

'Oh, he sped off, did he?'

'Yeah! And Mummy told us not to do that! So I turned around to come back home, and that's when I sawed him.'

'Mr Tall?'

Noah nodded, scratching his earlobe.

'Sitting in his car?'

'Yeah! Across the road!' He pointed past his mother's frame.

O'Brien paused. 'He sat in his car across the street when you came by on your bike?'

Noah nodded, chin tilted.

O'Brien continued as Jeremy scribbled. 'What did he look like, Noah?'

He twisted his hands, eyes wide like he was sorry he couldn't help us. He was unsure.

'Do you remember his hair colour?'

He smiled then, and the hands stopped twisting. 'Same as Mummy's.'

We glanced at Margot Average as she looked back at each of us.

'So, on the lighter side of brown?' Noah nodded. 'Did you see his eyes?'

He shook his head. 'Glasses. Black ones.'

'Right, so he wore sunglasses. Do you remember what his car looked like?'

He sat up and smiled gleefully. 'Yup! I got it; I can show you!'

We watched as Noah ran off, shoulder bumping the doorframe.

O'Brien stood. 'Ma'am, do you remember when this was?'

Her mouth twisted, shaking her head. 'I can't be too sure – nothing really happened, so I didn't mark it down. Noah just told Clint and me that some man across the road told him to be quiet. We thought it was odd because Noah wasn't causing a ruckus, so we looked outside but the car was gone. That was it.' She shrugged. 'Thought nothing of it until now. And that's when I realised: I think that man was casing Elliot's place. Maybe a burglary gone wrong? I don't know, but I thought if this information helps you, then why not?'

'Any information right now could be vital to us,' O'Brien said. 'We have solved some big cases with the smallest amount of evidence.'

She fiddled with the puffed sleeves of her yellow dress, adjusting them as though the elastic was pinching her. 'Clint and I have been watching the news – about the one they call Prop Master.'

'Ma'am,' O'Brien said, 'do you have any objection if we got a sketch artist in to meet Noah?'

She showcased her lovely smile. 'I don't have a problem, but I wonder what you'll get out of it. He sat in a car with glasses on. And it was a few days ago now – I'd say at least five – possibly longer.'

'It would help us tremendously if we could arrange it, nonetheless,' O'Brien said.

'Then sure, no problem. Anything to help you catch him. No-one has the right to take a life away. Gosh, I feel terrible for old Elliot. He had no family. Nothing. He sat on his porch drinking and smoking his life away. To be honest, probably hoping that he'd kick the bucket. But not by murder.' She closed her eyes. 'Gosh, he was too good for that; he even went to church on Friday nights.'

My ears perked up. 'He went to church on Friday nights?'

She opened her eyes, a fine layer of tears forming. 'A spiritual-type of thing.'

My heart reacted to this. 'Spiritualism?'

'I attended myself a few times to heal when my brother died in a motorbike accident.'

'I'm truly sorry to hear that.'

She smiled softly, looking downward. 'It was a while ago now, but it helped me. The service went for two hours in total. They dedicated an hour and a half to things like singing spiritual songs, meditation. Then we would heal – an act where people stand up and can heal others with their hands while a song plays. But the last half an hour was the interesting part.' She stood taller. 'Each week we had a different medium come in and they spoke to us through others.'

'Like psychic stuff?' Jeremy said.

Her lips twisted as her head tilted skyward. 'Um, it's not so much like predicting who will win the State of Origin, but the person on the platform communicates to us for the dead. They channel the voices from the other side.'

'Really?' Jeremy said with a deadpan expression. I shot him a warning glance.

She chuckled. 'I know what people say about it, but there was one night where I had an excellent medium. Ruby actually won Psychic of the Year. And I am telling you, Ruby told me things about my life that she would *never* have known just by looking at me.'

'Like what?' Jeremy asked.

'Like my great-grandmother's name, for instance – Flo, as in short for Florence. How would she have known that? And then ...' She took in a huge gulp of air. 'Then there was Leslie. My brother. He came through, too.' She swallowed deeply before tilting her chin and inhaling deeply.

'No shit!' Jeremy said.

I glanced at him again; O'Brien nudged him in the ribs.

She licked her lips. 'I kid you not. I'd never met this woman before in my life, and then here she is, passing on messages from my late brother and all. It was crazy.'

Glancing about, I asked, 'Where is this church?' Behind her on the wall hung a framed picture of a good-looking bloke. It was a candid picture of a young guy with a moustache and sideburns, taken mid-laugh. Was that her deceased brother? How many of us walk with the fallen beside us?

'Over in Werrington. Why?'

Shaking my head, I said, 'Just curious about it, that's all.'

'Who's the head ... um, leader? Medium?' O'Brien asked.

'Facilitator – Len. He isn't a medium, but his wife was, so he created a meeting place for like-minded people.'

I turned my attention back to Mrs Average, who was by no means average in the slightest. She reminded me of Ava's younger self. 'If Elliot Pratt attended, then can I assume he wasn't a Jew?'

'Jewish? Pratt? Goodness, no. He may have been with his money, but of the Jewish faith?' She shook her head. 'Not that I'm aware. But we have had Muslims attend before, so I suppose anyone is welcome. Anyone who believes in the other side. It gives us hope after death.'

O'Brien turned to me.

Margot cleared her throat. 'Why do you ask if he was Jewish?'

I turned from O'Brien to her. I trusted she'd keep the props to herself – I didn't see Margot blabbing to Liz Fulton. 'Strictly between us; we found the Star of David inside his house.'

She shook her head. 'I would have been surprised. And his last name – Pratt. That's not very Jewish, is it? I thought Jewish surnames typically ended with Stein, or Man, or Son. Not Pratt. I believe that's more Anglo-Saxon.'

'Where exactly is the service held, if you don't mind my asking?'

She gave a closed-lip smile. 'Not at all, it's the Werrington County Spiritualist Church near Victoria Road. Every Friday night, starting at six o'clock. There are other churches around; a lot up at Springwood, too. I don't go anymore; it was just to help me get through those dark times when I couldn't see the light.'

Jeremy's brows shot north. 'It's Friday today!'

'Oh, so it is!' Margot said, chuckling. 'I have no idea of time, as you've probably gathered.'

At that moment, the sound of small feet running echoed from the hallway. Noah came bounding in through the archway, almost tripping over the train track around the Christmas tree.

'Found it!' he said proudly, holding up a little Diecast model of a yellow Holden HG Monaro GTS 308 Coupe. Two black stripes ran the length of the body, ending at the back window.

'This is the one you saw Mr Tall sitting inside?' O'Brien said, pointing.

'Yup!'

'He loves his cars,' Margot said, beaming. 'Asks Santa for those types of cars every Christmas – don't you, sweetie?'

'When I'm good, I get presents!'

O'Brien chuckled as I stared at the miniature car. Thanks to my books and general passion, I too knew a lot about cars, and I knew damn well that the HG was the third facelift of the HK/HT series, introduced in the mid-seventies to coincide with the new tri-matic automatic transmission, replacing the old two-speed powerglide, designed for high performance. It was installed with air conditioning and came in numerous colour options – including the stripes. But despite all the bells and whistles, the HG was replaced by the HQ in 1972. Which meant *this* type of car would be easier to locate than the prick would have thought possible. Boy, I was excited. Boy, I was full of exhilaration! *Fuck yes, we're coming for you!*

'I am sorry to ask this of you, Mrs Average, but will I be able to use your phone? I must call my wife, because if I don't …'

Margot chuckled. 'Say no more, it's right over there.' She pointed to the kitchen.

'I am happy to pay for—'

'Don't insult me, please.' She laughed. 'By the way, would anyone like any coffee or tea?'

I made my way to the kitchen, feeling a paradoxical mix of excitement and dread. Reluctantly, I picked up the phone.

As I pressed the receiver against my ear and spun the dial, I pleaded for Ava not to pick up.

Her sweet voice answered after the third ring. 'Hello?'

I pinched the bridge of my nose. 'Hiya, little lady, it's me.'

She inhaled sharply. 'Where are you?'

Closing my eyes, I said, 'Ask me no questions and I'll tell you no lies.'

She tsked. 'You're not going to be here for dinner, are you?'

Despite the invisibility between us, I shook my head. 'I'm sorry.'

'No, that's fine, Eddy, really.' It wasn't. I didn't need Captain Obvious to tell me that. Her short-clipped words running into each other like a fender-bender said it all.

'I feel like the biggest letdown,' I whispered.

'Ha! You leave me with *nothing* in the fridge, with two hours to go before family dinner ... why on earth would you feel like that?'

I stole whatever oxygen my constricted throat would allow through. 'I could tell you a million times over how sorry I feel for doing this to you, but it won't make a difference. It's not as simple as just walking away from this case.'

She paused, deliberating. 'Is this to do with Abigail?'

My pulse quickened and my heartbeat thundered. 'No,' I whispered as a steel talon tightened around my throat.

'Are you doing this because of your demons?'

Scrunching my eyes, I tried to dodge haunting visuals. 'Can we please not talk about her?'

'No, we will! Because I went through this with you before. All those sleepless nights alone in bed wondering where you were. Asking myself if this job was worth the time you spent away from your family! We are flesh and blood, Eddy. *They're* dead. I'm sorry to say it, but they are. They cannot love you like we do, yet you put *everything* into them and I have to ask myself, why? Why are we not good enough for you? Do I need to be six feet under before you pay attention to me? Are you not capable of loving the living?'

My head spun; it felt like a blood clot had burst. God, I needed aspirin, fast.

'At least,' she said, lowering her register, 'I think I could accept it more if it were another woman. Then, at least it could have reasoning behind it. But this, *this*, I just don't understand. Especially not now that you're retired.'

'There will *never* be another woman.'

'But in some ways, it would be easier for me to cope with, knowing that some young thing took your attention – from a logical point of view, it would be more comprehensible.'

'I am *so* close here, Ava,' I whispered, my free palm on my forehead.

'That's what you said during the Abigail case.'

My spine stiffened and my fingers tightened around the phone. It was like she'd touched an exposed nerve in my tooth with an ice cube. *Please don't talk about her.*

'Even when you were here with us, your mind was elsewhere. You almost drank yourself to death. But who was there for you through it all? *Us!* Your family.'

'She was only six years old.' I fished for air, hooking oxygen through my nostrils and dragging it in. Floating body. Mocking newspaper articles by Liz Fulton. Grieving parents never afforded solace or justice.

'I remember it, Eddy,' she said, her voice quivering. 'Because I was right alongside you. I was there the day you found out Abbie was missing, to the day they found her floating in the lake. I was there the day they buried her, to the days where you got so drunk I had to hide the kids away from you.' She sucked in air with great force. 'I remember it all.'

Tears threatened to spill; I had to go. I had to cut this off now before I unleashed it all in Mrs Average's spotless kitchen. 'I love you very much, but I have to go now.'

'Fine. I won't wait up. You go ahead and enjoy your night. I know *we* will.'

CHAPTER FORTY-TWO

WHILE SITTING IN my car on Victoria Road at ten to six, I popped another Juicy Fruit into my mouth as vehicles drifted into the car park. It was not yet dark, but the sun was close to clocking off. I'd parked adjacent to the Werrington County Community Hall. It wasn't a church as such; peering through the binoculars, I couldn't see any steeples or Christian crosses, or symbols of Jesus on the crucifix.

I'd lied to Jeremy and O'Brien, as they knew me well enough to predict I was going to investigate this angle. I gave my word I would *not* enter the hall. But that didn't mean I couldn't park across the road and spy on everyone. That didn't mean I couldn't bring my gun along, either, just in case.

My gut instinct had led me down the path of religion all along. And something about this meeting place made me feel hot – like the game of Hot and Cold. I still had no idea what the red feather or dead dog represented. But what did I actually know about spiritualism? That it was based on the belief that we, the living, could communicate with the dead? I personally thought it was all bogus, but Margot Average seemed taken in with her experiences. Did they use a Ouija board? Did they perform a séance? Did they sit around in a circle holding hands while some gypsy person with a purple hood spoke to everyone? And what did a jester have to do with spiritualism? What did the Star of David have to do with it?

The people walking into the hall seemed fairly normal. All dressed nicely, no-one outrageous-looking so far. But I was not here to judge anyone on their lifestyle or clothing choice – I'd done that already during the seventies. I had not missed out on a family barbecue to listen to people sing 'Kumbaya, My Lord' and talk about the dead.

The dead. Abigail. I closed my eyes and told myself to breathe, just breathe, and let the pain pass. Emotional pain often came in waves. I couldn't stop it. It was like being strapped into a rollercoaster as someone else manned the controls. You had to just sit back and wait till the rising and falling stopped. It was also her 'anniversary' soon – a word I used to associate with good connotations, like buying cards, roses and gifts. I gritted my teeth as grief tried to swallow me whole. I'd often thought of Hayley during that time, seeing my own girl whenever I saw Abbie's photo. That's what they called her affectionately: Abbie. I wondered how I would have felt, being a father, knowing that some man had snatched your only daughter, unzipped his pants, and then had his way with her. A six-year-old child. As a father, I felt that was something I could never get over. I think I would have honestly drunk myself to death – heck, I almost did, and she wasn't even mine. And what got me more fired up than anything was whenever a judge granted a murderer or rapist a release after serving a few piddly years. There was no justice in that. After all the hard work and sleepless nights that went into taking someone down for taking away a life, only for them to be back on the streets a few years later, free to carry on with his life while everyone else suffered. No, Ava, you are wrong. I *am* doing this for my family. You just don't see that.

Heart rate decreasing as I pushed Abbie's visual aside, I opened my eyes and, through blurred vision, ahead a set of headlights approached. The car slowed down as it passed, and as it rolled alongside me, I habitually noted the colour and model, then my eyes connected with *him*. When he looked straight at me, recognition flashed across his dark eyes.

It all happened too quickly. Once I saw the black stripe, on a knee-jerk reaction, I started the car, flipped on the headlights, and did a sharp U-turn, but cut off another car that'd been travelling in my lane. They blasted their horn as I flashed an apologetic hand, shifting into second as I sped after the yellow flash of lightning. He was going for it, pedal to the metal. My Statesman caught up to the Holden HG Monaro, flashing my high beams for him to pull over. He drove faster.

Victoria Road was a long stretch of road, one-lane going either side. So, when he kept on flying, I drove alongside him – no-one else was travelling in the other lane.

I manoeuvred my car so we were parallel on this two-way stretch of road.

'Pull over!' I yelled through my open window.

He flashed me an *Up Yours* grin, then turned his eyes back to the road. His hands looked like they were vibrating on the steering wheel. Christ, we were now up to one-twenty in a fifty zone.

He swerved at me. My car moved when he did, manoeuvring right, then drifting left again. My heart was jabbed with a full shot of adrenaline as I kept looking at the road, then back to him.

'Pull over now!'

He gave me the bird, and then laughed – not that I heard over the pounding of blood in my ears and the wind whistling through the windows. He pointed up ahead where a car was now travelling in my lane, high beams blinding me.

I didn't have much time. Wetting my dry lips with my tongue, I pressed the brakes and moved back in the left-hand lane and slammed on the brakes when he did the same – only inches away from his rear. My body flew forward but settled back as the hunt recommenced, sweat dripping from my hairline. My mouth was as dry as a cotton jumper, heart leaping, toes tingling. We soon flew by the car in the right-hand lane, barely registering the driver blasting his horn.

Throttling the steering wheel, I gritted my teeth. 'Come on, prick! Where's your mask now?'

As I manoeuvred around his right side again, the left side of my bonnet clipped the back of his car. His tyres squealed in fright as he lost control and veered straight into a telegraph pole with an almighty *BANG*! My heart fell through my sphincter. My mouth flung open as I slammed on the brakes, changing back gears before I chucked a U-turn. I parked on a grassy knoll, reefed up the handbrake, and jumped out, handcuffs and gun at my side. The smell of burnt rubber fouled the air. The bonnet of his car was smashed in, and white smoke billowed out like a gassy sigh. Thankfully it hadn't burst into flames with the force of the impact. I raised my gun as I walked around to the driver's door.

'Hands up; you're under citizen's arrest!'

A coal train rumbled by on the tracks beside us. The squealing of metal on metal was loud enough to drown out everything else, including the harshness of my breathing.

Gripping my gun, I crept towards the door. The man lay crumpled against the steering wheel, no signs of movement.

'Hands up!' Sweat dripped into my eyes, so I used a forearm to wipe my face, waiting for any signs of life as my chest expanded and deflated. Expanded and deflated.

Yanking open the door, I pressed the nozzle of my gun to his limp head. Blood rushed over the steering wheel, his face was tilted to the left, so I had no way of knowing if his eyes were open or closed. I grabbed his shoulder and used it to push him backwards.

His limp head fell against the headrest. A fine horizontal gash marred his forehead where blood flowed like some morbid water feature. A blood mask.

Swallowing, I tried to gain control over my breathing as pinpricks of light flashed before my eyes. He produced watery gargling sounds in the back of this throat as he, too, struggled to breathe.

Panting, I lowered my gun and reached for the handcuffs when my eyes travelled to a bone on his left wrist sticking out of the skin, completely snapped.

I crouched to my knees and glared at him as a gust of wind from the rumbling coal train blew over me like an elongated sigh. Could this punk be Jerry the Jester? Jumping up, I scanned the interior, as the thrill of the chase faded and panic took its place. As far as I could see, there were no masks or props, or briefcases.

That didn't mean they weren't stashed in the boot, though, so I took another look at this guy. The length of his lifeless arm draped by his side suggested he was tall. Not all of his brown hair was covered in blood, and he wore black clothing. His gold earring gleamed with fresh blood, and I guessed him to be about twenty-five to thirty. But did this scrawny fucker look like he could take down those grown men? But then, what brought on this chase in the first place? The flicker of recognition. He'd tried to outrun me. Innocent men did not speed off if they had nothing to hide.

Sirens floated from the west like some transient melody. The darkening sky in the fading horizon lit up with red and blue flashing lights.

Two police cars and a paddy wagon screeched like circling eagles around me. An officer opened his door and used the window frame as a shield and a place for him to prop his gun as he yelled: 'Drop your weapon!'

Bending down, I placed the gun and set of handcuffs on the grass before stepping back. By now, they'd aimed more guns at me.

'Hands up!' someone else yelled.

I did, and I also spread my legs apart as I turned around. Someone came up behind me and shoved me over the dented bonnet.

'You're under arrest! Don't move!'

Swivelling my neck, I said, 'Guys, I'm Eddy Matthews. I've caught him!'

'Do not speak!'

He manhandled me, but I wasn't too worried. They'd take one look at me and realise who I was, and more importantly, who I'd caught – the one the papers had dubbed Prop Master.

The male officer swung me around.

'My name is Eddy Matthews,' I repeated as he led me to the paddy wagon, ambulance sirens wailing in the distance. 'I've placed this man under citizen's arrest.'

'Save it, pal!'

A female officer opened the doors before the man shoved me inside.

'That man is the Prop Master! I'm an ex-detective—'

The doors slammed. I fidgeted on an uncomfortable bench and peered out the back window as onlookers gathered around. Thirty seconds after being locked inside, the ambulance, in all its blazing glory, pulled up alongside the Monaro. 'Jerry' hadn't moved, not even while they placed him on a stretcher and loaded him in the back.

It seemed like hours before we finally took off, heading for the Penrith Police Station on High Street. Closing my eyes, I calmed my nerves. Sure, I was locked up now, but soon they would pat me on the back for this. And so what if I wasn't a cop anymore? This was a fair-and-square citizen's arrest. Sure, Davies and the team might be pissed off that I was the one and not them, but this was still a valid arrest. I had not busted into this guy's house. I had not stalked him, per se; I was just a guy, about to go into the hall and start praising

Jesus when he happened on by. Speeding, he was, that's why I took him off the road, in case he hurt anyone. And then, lo and behold, look who it turned out to be? The fucking Prop Master, that's who!

Elation soared through me, as things could return to normal. I'd surprise Ava with tickets to Aruba. I'd even ask the kids to come along, too, if they wanted. Sure, Ava was pissed at me now, but thank goodness this would look like a mote of sand in the Gibson Desert once tomorrow came. It'd be so far behind us she wouldn't even remember why she'd been mad at me in the first place.

Exhaling through a smile, I thought, *Thank you, God, or whoever the hell You are up there.*

I always had a helping hand in many arrests, but I'd never been on the other end of it. I had to go through the whole rigmarole: mugshots, fingerprints, locked inside a cell. Tell you what, if only you could have seen the faces of my ex-colleagues; I mean ... cut them off and put it on a board, and they'd look like a line-up of stunned mullets.

I told them all not to worry. I told them I'd done my job as an upstanding citizen; that we could all rest easy tonight because I'd finally found the one terrorising our neighbourhood.

As I sat inside my cell, I wondered what stories were being swapped around my dinner table. I wondered what excuse Ava would have said on my behalf, and I wondered if perhaps they were missing me as much as I missed them. I had seriously fucked up, but hey, look! *It's over and done with now, Ava! I caught the bad guy! We will be okay from now on, my love; everything will be fine.* I leaned back against the wall with my eyes closed. *Everything will be peachy.*

Stephanie May

CHAPTER FORTY-THREE

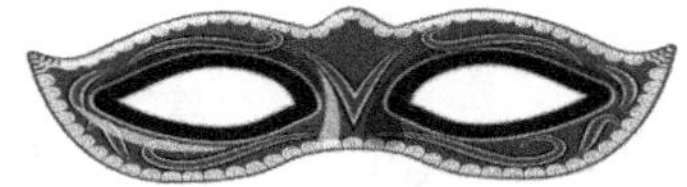

NATHAN DAVIES STOOD at my open cell door. His presence alone had woken me up. He regarded me with disapproving eyes.

'Come with me,' he said.

I hadn't a clue how long I'd nodded off for, but the events of the car chase seemed like a distant memory. I waited for the good news, but Davies' red face and set jaw made me wonder if I'd killed the Prop Master. But even if I *had* killed this prick … who cared? One less murderer on the streets to be worrying about.

He ducked into a conference-type room and I followed. O'Brien and Retmeyer sat waiting, their gaze downcast at the oval table. A Styrofoam cup waited for me in front of a chair at the table.

'Sit,' Davies said. A glass of water sat before him.

I pulled out the blue upholstered chair and sat opposite the lads, as Davies plonked his wide rear on a chair at the head of the table. Behind him stood an overhead projector and a whiteboard.

He didn't waste any time. 'What the fuck happened?!' Spittle ejected like the human cannonball.

I looked him square in the eye. 'It wasn't pre-planned.'

'Bullshit!' He banged his fist like a judge's gavel, the water in his glass quivering. 'Does it look like I have the word *moron* tattooed on my forehead?!'

Oh, how I wanted to answer that. 'It's the truth. Scout's honour.'

He glared at me. 'You happen to have a gun and handcuffs on you at all times, do you?'

'Yes, lately, I do.'

'I know, Eddy. About everything.' He pointed to a manilla folder sitting on the table beside his water. I assumed the letters would be inside, and who knew what else.

'We told him,' Jeremy said, chancing a look at me. 'About the letters, and the box you received from "Jerry".'

Davies was tight-lipped; he looked like he'd been sucking a sour gumdrop. 'We'll get to that in a minute, but Jesus fuckin' Christ, who do you think you are? Do you understand the gravity of what has happened? Of how it'll look in the papers that an ex-detective of ours is now playing *Magnum P.I.* and running people off the roads?'

If I'd side-swiped his own precious car, I don't think I could have seen him angrier. I had serious concerns for his heart and blood pressure; I half-expected his head to smack down on the table from an aneurysm.

'He's a killer, Davies. He's off the streets now; you should be thanking me!'

'That's just it, you piss-weak geezer, he's a fucking nobody! He is *not* the Prop Master, you imbecile! The station's janitor has more form than this bloke.'

I looked at O'Brien.

He shrugged slowly, upturned palms lifting. 'It's true.'

It took a while before I could speak, trying to process the facts. 'He was there at Elliot Pratt's house. He sped off once he saw me; I didn't chase him until he gave me a reason to!'

'He's nothing but a lowlife druggie. That's all we can pin on him! All he had in his glove compartment was some blow and some weed. Not even enough to fill out paperwork over!'

'He was out the front of Pratt's place casing the joint. He stole the man's car, then put fake plates on it. Did you ask him about that?'

Through clenched teeth, he said, 'He was waiting for his girlfriend. She lives on the same road as Elliot Pratt, you moron.'

Shaking my head, I said, 'But he told Noah Average to shush. He was outside of Pratt's house, wearing sunnies, making sure that little boy didn't say anything about seeing him there.'

'It's been confirmed,' O'Brien whispered. 'His girlfriend lives three doors up from Elliot's place. She'd just moved in and was coming home from her afternoon shift. We've already spoken to her and checked out her address; it's on her driver's licence. That's why he was there, Eddy, to surprise his girlfriend.'

I shook my head adamantly. 'But he shushed Noah.'

'So fucking what; are you gonna take the word of a seven-year-old boy? How do we even know he silenced him? Even if he did put his finger to his lips, so goddamn what? Does that make him a murderer?'

Everything crumbled down around me; the pressure on my chest was immense. Disbelieving, I shook my head again. 'But he sped away from me.'

'Because he had drugs on him! And he's as skinny as a rake from all the meth. Hardly the type of guy to mastermind an elaborate plan such as what we're dealing with!' Davies then waved a dismissive hand towards me.

'I can't accept it,' I whispered, my eyes roaming the table.

'You almost killed a man and you're saying you can't accept it? Jesus, give me strength!' As Davies sat back in his chair, it gave a squeal of protest. He leaned forward on a better thought and grabbed a silver foil packet from his breast pocket, pressed the blister seal, and out popped a white tablet. As soon as it hit the water it sunk to the bottom, leaving a fizzing stream. 'How the fuck do we explain this, once it gets out? I'm *glad* the pipsqueak had drugs on him, because maybe, just *maybe*, we can strike some sort of hush-hush deal. Imagine if it had been your average law-abiding citizen going for a drive to pick up a roast chicken for dinner!'

I leaned forward, the side of my hand connecting with the table. 'He sped off. He saw who I was and sped off. He was speeding in a fifty zone, flipping me the bird and all sorts.'

Now it was Davies' turn to shake his head. 'You're losing it, Matthews. So, it will not come as a shock when I tell you I've already told these two' – he pointed – 'that if they so much as page you about this, then they'll be suspended without pay. No questions asked. I *never* want to see your face inside these walls again. Have some respect for the law! And stop trying to stroke your ego. You're retired now; let us handle it. Got it?'

I opened my mouth, but his eyebrows rose, daring me to challenge him.

'I already told you that you could fuck this up for us. Things could be thrown out of court with your interference, understand? If you want the bad guy caught, then keep out of it.'

'Sir, that's understood, and we gave you our promise we will not discuss this case with Eddy anymore,' O'Brien said. 'But these threats are real.' His forefinger stabbed the manilla folder. 'Those flesh trophies belong to Norman Colbert. This is a serious matter; Matthews *is* being targeted.'

Davies' hand shot up to stop him. 'I said I was getting to that.' He turned to me, bringing his hand down. 'I appreciate your fragile state of mind right now, although I am *pissed off* this wasn't brought to my attention sooner.' He paused for breath, throwing back more cloudy water. 'We will organise surveillance for your house. From what I understand, you've added additional security measures to your property, yes?'

I nodded, assuming O'Brien or Jeremy had told him.

'Where else are you up to on this? Sorry, I was too busy chatting with Dean in the hospital!'

O'Brien coughed, cleared his throat and sniffed hard. 'Sir, we have experts working on the letters, trying to identify his writing style and patterns. We have yet to pull any discernible prints from either of the two letters – or the envelopes, but we are working on it.'

Davies turned his attention back to me. 'And you received a call from him; is that right?'

Staring at the table, I nodded again – more like jerked my chin.

Nathan Davies leaned back in his chair. 'Oohhhh, this is a shitstorm.' He sighed and shook his head. 'Do yourself a favour and leave the rest up to us, okay, Eddy?'

Focusing on my thumbs, I bobbed my head once.

'Do I have your word?'

My teeth ground together as I turned to him. 'Yes.'

'And if I catch wind that you three are up to no good, I'll come down on each of you like a mountain of bricks – got it?'

'Yes, sir,' we chorused.

'Good.' He locked eyes with mine. 'Your car is to stay here with us. And your gun is confiscated – I don't even want to know where you got it! You can either catch a cab, or I'll get two officers to drive you home. I personally do not give a dribblin' shit; I just want you out of sight.'

'I'll walk.'

'Eddy, no!' O'Brien said. 'It's four in the morning! Your house is miles from here.'

'I do not care.'

'Neither do I,' Davies said, scratching the top of his head. 'It's settled then. I'll be in contact so we can bug your phone, and I'll get surveillance happening.' He waved a hand in the air. 'You're dismissed.'

I grabbed my cup, took a long, drawn-out sip of bitter coffee that by now tasted like something dredged from the bottom of the Nepean River, and stood up. As I exited the room, I felt three sets of eyes on my back.

CHAPTER FORTY-FOUR

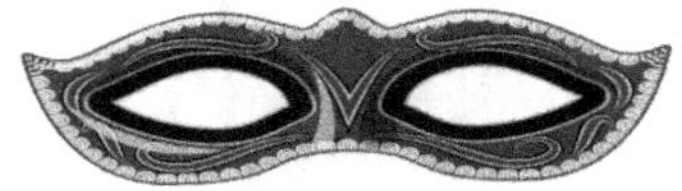

I COULDN'T SPEAK TO the receptionist as she buzzed me out, or even wave goodbye as I left Penrith Police Station. I made a right and travelled along High Street with my head down, gazing at chewing gum stuck to the pavement as a car cruised by. I kicked a crumpled Pepsi can, and it travelled alongside me – my only companion on my lonesome journey home during the dark, early morning hours.

As I made my way across a footbridge sometime later – I don't want to guess how much later – I eyed the ink on my fingertips as I walked under streetlamps. My knees throbbed, my back ached, and I hovered on autopilot. My breath thinned out; my heart struggled with exhaustion by the burden of stress I had placed on it. Sliding into bed with Ava and holding her was all I focused on. Soon the sun would rip open the sky; it already seemed to tear a slit over the eastern horizon with a faint orange glow, but Ava's warmth was what I craved. Her comforting embrace and loving touch were all I needed to keep going.

And I admit, I was hungry. I couldn't remember the last time I'd eaten, and that coffee back at the station only served to move my bowels. God, I was in pain in more ways than one. My aching feet scraped along the road, facing a string of cars with their headlights shining on me – people probably on their way to work in a factory. No-one of importance would be up this early, except tradies and shit-kickers. And I was definitely a shit-kicker. How had I fucked up so badly? Going off the word of a seven-year-old boy.

Dean had been the guy's name. I came close to killing Dean last night, and he would not have known why. But I accepted he was not the man I was looking for. Not the man I needed. And here I was, still speaking as though I was going to keep looking. How much strife had I placed O'Brien and Jeremy under? They could barely look me in the eye. O'Brien – my loyal now ex-partner for more than a decade – almost suspended. Because of what? Some guy who didn't even have enough grass to bother a lawnmower with … I'd have to make it up to my buddy. But first, there was Ava. My little lady. My everything.

Just when the pinpricks of bright spots in my eyes intensified, I reached the beginning of River Road – thank fuck for that! A group of keen female joggers in Spandex with voluminous hair ran up the road wearing legwarmers, yet I was sweating worse than them. My eyes drifted skyward as a bird's caw captured my attention. Drawing oxygen into my screaming lungs, I closed my stinging eyes and trudged on, breathing through the stitch that held my sides hostage. My house was more than halfway down the winding road and God, it seemed distant, but the thought of Ava in bed waiting for me gave me my second wind. I threw my head back, breathed in some of that early morning freshness, and pushed on the rest of the way until I spotted Ava's car in our driveway. Home! I was finally *home*.

When I unlocked the door with a quivering hand, Pizza Hut boxes stacked on the coffee table caught my eye. Was that a guilt trip? She hated ordering takeaway instead of cooking.

I made my way up the stairs, breathing through the stitch in my side, feet dragging as I blinked away the drowsiness. Before climbing into bed, I'd have to shower; I smelled worse than the armpits of my mechanic.

I needed to see Ava first, though, to check on her.

The handle squeaked as I turned it. Ava sat on the side of our bed, gazing out the bedroom window as a bird twittered.

I flipped the light on. The bed was still made, and two suitcases sat by her feet. She twirled her wedding ring around and around on her finger as her eyes focused on the window to my right.

I licked my dry lips before holding onto the doorframe for support. 'You don't have to do this.'

She turned to me. Her nose was red and tears had left track marks down her cheeks. 'I would ask where you have been. But I don't care anymore, Edward.'

'Please don't go.' I took a step closer as my chest expanded, my knees only moments away from failing me.

'You and I both know this has been on the cards for a while.'

'I didn't want to believe it could be true,' I whispered.

Her smile was mirthless. 'This life isn't a practice shot for our next, and I have spent the better years of my life on you. Now I think I will start to focus on *me*.'

'I don't want you to go.' My oesophagus felt like the size of a straw as I tried to swallow. Panic arrested the muscles in my hollow stomach. 'Please, I promise it's over with. I won't ever take another case again.'

She shook her head. 'The damage has been done. My mind is made up.'

Images flashed across my mind's eye in rapid-fire shots: Divorce papers. Family divided. Selling the house, moving to an apartment. Images so vivid I swore I'd seen them in a recent movie. 'I wouldn't know how to live without you. I don't know how to do that, or where to even begin.'

'It's not like I didn't try to warn you. You can't tell me this is a complete shock.'

'But I love you.'

'It's one thing to say it, Edward; it's another kettle of fish to show it. I was stupidly hoping that after our chat on the phone yesterday afternoon, you would walk through that door and prove me wrong. But it's now' – she glanced at the neon clock on our bedside table – 'almost six o'clock. I have not slept, despite me telling you I would not wait up.'

My head snapped up. 'You can't just walk out on me; I'm your husband.' I swallowed in an act of trying to stall my erratic breathing, while I blinked away the mote of speckled light in my eyes. 'We've been through ups and downs before.'

'It's too late. I will not keep listening to you saying the word "sorry".'

I took two steps, dropped to my knees, and held her legs. 'Give me another chance.'

She looked down and removed her wedding ring. The exact one I slipped on her finger decades ago, when we'd vowed to love each other forever.

She held it between thumb and forefinger, inspecting it. 'This isn't exactly a joyous feeling for me, either. I put a lot of hard work into this marriage while trying to maintain a happy family. I feel like I failed.'

'Don't say that. It's me, it's all me. You were wonderful; the most amazing, kind-hearted person I have ever met!'

She sighed, closing her eyes. 'I was worried you'd say that, because then that means there's no appreciation if you can so easily toss me aside like yesterday's paper.'

I squeezed her legs tighter. 'Don't do this, please. What can I do? Tell me what to do!'

She inhaled through her nostrils. 'You need to let go of me and try to move on.'

'How the hell can you ask me to do that? You are part of me; you're the air that I breathe. I am sorry for hurting you, but it's who I am. It's all I know how to be.'

'And what about what I need? What about who I am?'

'You're my wife. You can't just *leave*.'

Ava placed her wedding ring in the top drawer and closed it. 'I need to go before the sun comes up and everyone sees. It'll be gossip for weeks around these parts.'

'No fucking way, you're not going.' I dragged air into my lungs. 'As your husband, I forbid this!' Despite an aching back that screamed for rest, I got up and moved to the bedroom door. 'I'm putting my foot down!'

She rose, grabbed the suitcase handles, and walked towards me, avoiding eye contact. 'Move.'

'No.' It was more like a sound being dragged out of my throat, being torn by some unknown spirit, than a word.

'Don't be a fool, Edward.'

'Stop *calling* me that! Stop speaking like I never existed.'

She gritted her teeth. 'Move aside.'

'No. It'll be the end of me. Please. Think about the kids; what will they say if we divorce?'

'I already spoke to them about it last night.'

My gut tightened as I felt the impact; it almost knocked me on my arse. 'Them? Heath came here, too?'

'With Lorraine and Aaron. He looked so well. If you only could have seen – oh yes, you were supposed to be here, but you were too busy. Again.'

'You told them you were leaving me?'

Her chin jutted. 'I did.'

My nostrils flared. 'You'd already planned it. Meaning it didn't matter if I came home or not—'

Her eyes met mine. 'Don't try to wriggle out of this. I said it had been on my mind for some time now. Last night was the final straw.'

My tongue clicked, mind in overdrive. 'I see. What did they say?'

'Hayley said she could see the cracks in the foundations; Heath said we all need to do what's best.'

I swallowed past the knot in my throat. They'd all stabbed me in the back. An irrational feeling perhaps, but that didn't make it hurt any less. 'So that's it, then? There's nothing I can do to change your mind?'

The resolute look in her eyes rather than her words convinced me. She'd checked out of this relationship, and in hindsight, how could I have blamed her?

Defeated, I stepped aside. I didn't give up easily, but the last thing I wanted was for the Penrith Police to receive a call that I was holding my wife hostage. And what could I do – apart from chain her to the bed to make her stay?

'Thank you,' she whispered. Normally I'd have carried her suitcases, but this was no trip she was taking. She was leaving me. I did not want to aid her in that, not when my heart was breaking.

There were so many things I should have done and said when I look back now. But I can still remember the determination in her hazel eyes.

I stood at the top of the landing and gazed down as she descended the stairs one by one, struggling with the heavy load. She placed them on the ground and unlocked the front door.

She moved her suitcases to the doormat outside and turned around, hand on the doorknob. Her eyes swept up towards mine.

'Goodbye,' she whispered before closing the door.

I fell back on the top stair and stared at the same patch of wallpaper until sunlight shone through every window of the house. I did not cry. I did not make a sound. The rumbling, almost purring sound of her car engine idled before she'd backed out of the driveway, and that was the last thing my brain distinguished for hours after. I half-expected her to walk back inside and ask where my car was. But she either didn't notice, or didn't care.

It was only when my bladder and bowels began knocking that I stood up and blinked before I stumbled to the bathroom.

Every breath from this point was an effort, like I had to keep telling myself to breathe. After I flushed the toilet and washed my hands, I walked outside to stumble down the staircase to let Bogart inside. His paws padded my feet and ankles, but I pushed him away and ambled to the fridge.

What I had done the day before came back to me – God, that now seemed like last week! Inside the fridge lay one pizza box. In the bin lay two empty bottles of Sunkist, which must have been ordered with the pizza, and the foil Pizza Hut wrap the garlic bread came in, lay crumpled on top.

I grabbed the cardboard box. It felt empty, but when I lifted the lid, there was one slice waiting for me. A Hawaiian, and they goddamn knew I hated pineapple on pizza – that shit was for kids. It was deliberate, just to stick it to me. An isolated piece, alone in an empty box – a fucking metaphor, damn them! I slammed the door shut and picked off the slices of pineapple one by one. By the time I was done with that, I was too damn tired and miserable to do much else, so I sank my teeth into the soggy pizza slice as my stomach gurgled. I chucked the box on the kitchen bench, but it fell off. After kicking it aside, I headed towards my study, slamming the door shut as soon as Bogart was inside.

My expensive bottle of whisky called out to me, so I popped the top before downing whatever I could, scalding my throat worse than apple cider, until I couldn't breathe anymore. My head fell forward as I coughed, feeling as though a flammable liquid had gathered in my stomach, followed by a lit matchstick.

I collapsed into my chair as my hands flopped to the sides and I sat there, breathing. Blinking. I made the mistake of glancing up and met Abigail's eyes staring back from the corkboard on the opposite wall. I laughed and took another swig, spluttering as cold liquid ran down my chin, and then I laughed again until I cried. Cried is maybe too tame a word. I bawled. Poor Bogart had no idea what was going on. But I sat there, drinking, staring into nothingness, swallowed into a deep abyss. Grief had hold of me; Christ, did it have a chokehold.

'Wasn't even him,' I said to Abigail, who looked back at me. I chuckled again, tears drenching my shirt. 'Wasn't even the Jester, Bogart!' I laughed louder – it sounded mad even to my ears. I took another swig, moaning as it went down. 'It. Wasn't. Even. Him! How do you like those apples, Bogie, huh?' I hiccupped, stomach roasting over hot coals, pain dwindling. Cheapest therapy out there. 'How's that for irony?' I finished the bottle and chucked it in the bin with a dull *clunk*, but it tipped the bin over before rolling on the floor.

'C'mon, boy! Let's have a bath!'

I fumbled with the door handle until it eventually opened. With a spinning head, it seemed to take me an age to locate my bathtub, and when I staggered across the tiled floor, I flopped over the sides of the porcelain tub. Panting, I laid there in a world of pure darkness as I fumbled to turn on the taps. Cold water shot up my body while my mind swam, alcohol seeping into my blood, tainting it. When I reached down to pop the plug in, I realised I still had my clothes on. I laughed hysterically as water filled around me.

'What a dickhead!' I laughed and cried at the same time. I somehow reclined my head without throwing up, as the cold water turned hot. When it reached my armpits, I leaned over with what felt like way too much effort and turned off the faucets.

With that task out of the way, I once again reclined and closed my eyes, mouth hanging ajar as water swished around me. Ava's face was the last image I grasped before drifting into a world free from pain.

CHAPTER FORTY-FIVE

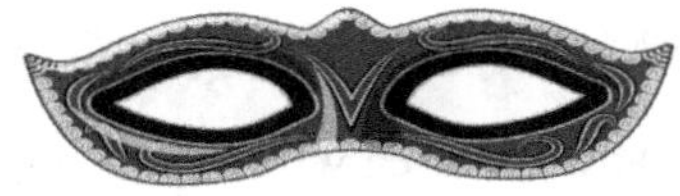

THE TRILL OF my house phone stirred me from slumber sometime later. I opened my bleary eyes, confused as hell, with no idea where I was, or even *who* I was. The shrill ringing continued, but I made no attempt to answer it. I looked around, soaked to the bone, in my bathtub, fully clothed. With each ring, my head pounded even more. I raised my hands to my throbbing head, my tongue superglued to the roof of my dry mouth.

The last time I'd drowned my body in Instant Amnesia was when, after years had dragged on, Abbie became a cold case – told I had to move on; that we had tried everything. We'd interviewed hundreds of suspects, to no avail. We'd checked every registered car in New South Wales with those that matched the tyre prints we'd picked up in the dirt leading to the lake where her body was dumped. A six-year-old girl raped in the worst way possible (not that there is a good way), and then thrown into the lake and left to drown. We'd known this from her autopsy. Fluid in her lungs. How long had she been alive for? Was she thrashing about in the murky water as her killer stood there, watching?

These thoughts sickened me to my core. I'd renounced God – rejecting all faith from then on. I still grasped the belief that one day, somehow, we would catch him; that there'd be a new breakthrough in forensic science that could help us. And then, earlier this year we were told about this new DNA analysis breakthrough over in America. Like any new thing at the time of its inception, there were flaws. But despite its infancy, it still gave me hope. Personally, I had not closed the file on Abigail Jerkewitz, and I would not with 'Jerry'. Dean may not have been the Prop Master, but I was getting closer with every new lead.

The telephone stopped. No idea who it was, nor did I care.

I gripped the sides of the tub and lifted myself up as my teeth chattered. Water poured off every inch of my wrinkled clothing.

I began the daunting task of undressing. I peeled off my shirt. Then I sat on the edge of the tub facing outwards, unlaced and removed my shoes, took off soaking-wet socks to reveal purply white feet. Last were my pants and jocks. I chucked the heavy clothing in a discarded heap on the tiled floor with a *splat*, grabbed a towel and dried myself as best as I could. My mouth tasted foul, and I needed to piss. Even the tinkling of my urine hitting the water in the bowl disagreed with my ears. I was well and truly hungover. Completely fucked. I was of no use to anyone, including myself, in this state of torpor.

After switching off the light (it'd remained on since Ava left) with an anguished groan, I ambled to my bed and collapsed on top of it as Bogart looked at me from the doorway.

With no more strength than a newborn, I tapped Ava's side of the bed. The covers were still cold. And now they always would be. She'd made up her mind about us before I even had a chance to change it.

'C'mon!' I said to Bogart, once more tapping the bed. He was never allowed in here, let alone on the bed, so he jumped up and looked at me with wide eyes, waiting for Ava's automatic 'Get off!'

'Sleep now,' I whispered through a dry mouth. Then I opened my eyes, elevated my head, and took the phone off the hook. No disturbances. Not now. Not ever.

'I'll feed us both later,' I mumbled, my eyelids fluttering as I tried to hold on in vain. Once again, it was lights out for both of us.

Hours later, I pried my heavy lids apart, floating into the land of the living. My head no longer ached, and I did not feel like my mind was weighed down, but drowsiness subdued me. I wanted to sleep it off and wake up to a world where the sun was shining, Ava was downstairs cooking us breakfast, and to a world without crime. No murderers, no drug addicts, no child molesters, no rapists, no terrorists. It brought me back to Lennon's song 'Imagine'. Yes, John, *let's*!

Rolling over, I glanced out the window. The sun had shifted, the sky a hazy purply red. Spectacular. A stark contrast to inside this house, which felt like a black hole where everything was being consumed by darkness. My eyelids felt like soggy puff pastry, but I forced myself to wake the fuck up. My forgotten stomach gurgled, and I knew Bogart must be hungry, too. He was no longer on the bed beside me. Another one to leave me.

Once upright, I groaned into my hands, and Christ, didn't my back and neck feel as aged as a bottle of vintage wine. How the hell had that happened? When had my grey hairs sprouted? When had my eyesight started failing? When had my skin started to sag? I'd been too busy to even notice.

Bracing myself on the bed, I rose and shut the blinds, flinging off my towel. I was now stark naked – as naked as I felt in this world after Ava's abandonment. Walking to the sliding closet doors, I grabbed a dressing gown – a green one that Hayley had given me as a present on the day of my retirement. Embroidered on the back was COPS ARE TOPS. The warm cotton caressed my wrinkled, cold flesh, with its sunspots and scars – badges of honour from decades on the force.

Descending the stairs barefoot, I caught sight of Bogart at the back door.

Poor bugger must have been dying for a whizz.

I headed over to him as fast as my aged body would allow. 'Sorry, boy,' I whispered, unlocking the door. He sprinted out and squatted, so that's when I closed the door.

Already the house seemed so empty it felt like a death had occurred. And hadn't it? Hadn't a death happened here in the early morning hours? For me, it had. I didn't know about Ava; she seemed all too keen to abandon ship and give up on our marriage, which I felt I'd worked hard for.

I left Bogart to do his business in peace and staggered to the kitchen fridge. Oh yes, that's right. I'd emptied the fucker the day before. Was it? Surely not the day before; it seemed like aeons ago. But I was correct. I'd emptied this only yesterday.

Irritated, I slammed it shut and walked to the top cupboards, blessed to find a box of overlooked Jatz crackers. I shook my head and grabbed the box all the same. Clenching my eyes shut, I blew dust off it. Still within the expiration date. Barely.

Plonking on the couch, I ripped open the box and the foil packet and shoved my hand inside. One by one, I robotically brought each cracker to my lips. It could have been cardboard for all I cared. As I chewed, I glanced about the room, picturing what had transpired here the night before. Ava, being too flustered to run to the shops and buy all the ingredients, had ordered pizza. The boxes were still stacked here with hardened crusts inside. Hayley, I thought. She always hated the crusts, but loved Hawaiian ... go figure. I pictured my family sitting on these couches. And Heath! That's right, Ava said Heath had been here with Lorraine and Aaron, too.

I pictured my children's faces as Ava told them she was leaving me. She'd proved me wrong; I'd never known her to speak ill about me, or speak of our marriage woes to the kids, but there you go. Everyone had known before I did.

Didn't I feel like a jackass, expecting to come home and snuggle with my wife after being locked up for the first time in my entire goddamn life.

I picked up another cracker and popped it in. My jaws masticated without thought, and I inhaled deeply, vaguely aware of the sound of cars passing by out front.

Surveillance! Maybe that's who'd called me: Nathan Davies, to tell me about it. Fuck it. I didn't care. I did not give a shit at that moment. Let the Jester find me and finish me.

Hell, I'll open up the doors right now. Come and get me, motherfucker, here I am! The fool in all his glory. Abandoned by his family. Shunned by his ex-colleagues – I won't even move. How's that? I will sit here with the front door wide open, and you can waltz on in, put the nozzle to my head, and blow my fucking brains out. Would that be better? Then come on! *Finish me!*

I threw the packet of Jatz beside me, the remaining crackers spilling to the carpet. I sat forward and held my buzzing head in shaky hands. I wanted to weep, but I was running on empty as I gulped for oxygen. There was nothing left for me to give. Bogart was at the back door, scratching the glass to let me know he wanted in. But I couldn't move. I lay back on the couch and closed my eyes again. I was already as full as a goog (as my late grandmother used to say) from those few pitiful crackers. My stomach churned, but I was done. Over it. Over this life. Once again, I drifted into a painless chasm, an existential void of nothingness.

CHAPTER FORTY-SIX

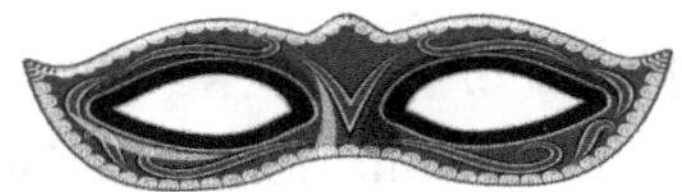

IT WASN'T UNTIL days later that I started to feel better, but if I said I'd bounced off the couch, full of beans, I'd be full of shit. Once again, I'd passed out during the late-night movie. The awareness of what today meant – 21st December – weighed on my mind like wet cement.

Stumbling in my half-asleep state, I made my way to the laundry where we kept Bogart's bag of dry feed, scooping up extra before taking it out the back laundry door to the yard.

Bogart ran in a circle when he saw and smelled what I carried. I walked over the dewy grass and peered at the sky – it resembled a turquoise ocean on a calm day. Not a cloud, nor bird disturbing it.

My knees popped as I deposited his breakfast into his silver bowl. His water dish also needed a good clean-out and refill, so I hopped to that afterwards. I re-entered through the laundry door and made my way back to the kitchen. On my toes, I spied a tin of Campbell's country chicken and vegetable soup in the back corner of a cupboard.

Good enough for now, but today I would have to go shopping again. I also needed aspirin. These past few days, I'd survived on frozen dinners. Just because I felt better, didn't mean I was about to break out into 'What a Wonderful World'. My future looked bleaker than a winter's night. I guess when you're married for decades, it lulls you into a false sense of security. You don't think that when you reach your sixties, you'll ever have to worry about things like divorce. Heck, I never thought I'd get arrested either, but yet ...

I walked by the front door and peered through the glass panel beside it. My heart thumped on seeing my car sitting in the driveway, the new scratches visible even from here. Unlocking the front door, I walked outside towards my car, fear constricting my throat as I noticed a white note pinned beneath the wipers. Glancing around, I approached the windshield. Unfolding the white piece of paper, I let out a gush of air upon reading Davies' handwriting:

This is the last favour I _ever_ do for you. Stay the hell away from the case! And next time, answer the damn door!

Davies

Scrunching up the note in one hand, I surveyed my surroundings again. Nothing took my interest, only a few joggers and a muscular man walking his rottweiler. No cars across the road appeared to be part of any surveillance. Turning around, the sunlight bouncing off my silver keys inside a terracotta pot plant beside the door grabbed my focus. Had that been Davies trying to call me about putting a wiretap on my phone days ago? Even if it was, I had been too pissed to speak. The logical part of my brain understood it; if I'd been in his big loafers then, from a legal point of view, yes, I could have jeopardised the whole outfit. But it didn't mean I had to be happy about it. Call it petulance, call it what you will. I was being personally targeted; 'Jerry' had gone to O'Brien's house to fuck with me by releasing Bogart from the side gate. He'd sent human flesh to my house like it was no more than sending grandma's panettone. He had been watching Ava; even knew how good her cooking smelled.

Could anyone with half a brain out there listening to my story have blamed me for wanting to be as involved as I had been? Could anyone understand my consuming need to be at the forefront of the investigation? If anyone said no, then they should turn away now. I wish *I* could have.

After I consumed the soup and took a much-needed shower, I resigned to visit Flemings and purchase the essentials. As I pushed my squeaky trolley with a possessed mind of its own out through the gravel car park, I eyed an elderly couple beside an old-school V-Dub. The husband packed the things his wife handed to him into the boot, moving at a glacial pace. That got me. Oh boy, did that get me. How could I not picture Ava? How could I not have hoped that would have been us in, say, fifteen years' time? But then it occurred to me: When was the last time we *had* done the shopping together? Fuck me dead, I couldn't remember. A plastic bag drifted around the cars, and that's how I felt: floating through life with no clear direction. I shook that thought from my noggin and loaded my car, by myself, as a thought kept popping into my mind like a flashing neon light. Initially, I wasn't going to, but then I asked myself what else was I going to do today? Before that, though, I needed to unload this lot before the ice cream melted.

Bogart bounced up and down like a pogo stick as soon as I opened the front door. Once again, his nose was pressed to the back door, his row of short front teeth showcasing a smile as his rump jiggled up and down.

I had no energy to even laugh. After dumping the four plastic bags on the kitchen bench, I went back outside to grab today's paper from the lawn, and then locked the front door. I made my way over to Bogart and unlocked the latch before allowing him inside. He jumped up, but I couldn't play with him.

I just … couldn't.

After dumping a bunch of Scotts heat-n-eat TV dinners into the freezer, I ripped open a bag of doggy treats and held one out to Bogart. He almost bit off the tips of my fingers.

'I'll be back,' I said. 'Be a good boy.' His head bobbed on each chew, paying me no mind. 'Ah, fuck it, you can come with me.'

Five minutes later, I pulled out of the driveway and headed to Dan Murphy's. After loading the beer into my car, 'I'm Not in Love' by 10cc played on the radio as I headed south. However, after I hit Mulgoa Road, all thoughts of my surroundings vanished, and all I could focus on was Ava and the kids. What the hell was I going to do about that? What would I say if Ava came around?

I wound down my window to let the breeze in, propping my elbow on the frame as I drove, consumed by sadness, guilt and anger. It was like watching myself in a movie; I could do nothing about what would happen to me.

Luckily, the drive to Campbelltown was pretty much one long stretch of road, with a few bends and roundabouts in between. On either side of the road, for most of it, were meadows and the occasional farmhouse, with cattle roaming and sheep grazing.

I loved this area many years ago. I remember taking Ava on random car trips before I made detective, and this route was always one of our favourites; hardly any traffic, no matter what time of day. It used to fill me with a sense of calmness, and sometimes on our way back late at night, we'd find ourselves pulled over to the side of the road to take a little adventure in the back seat. And I still loved it even after the passion dwindled; a chance to clear the mind and listen to music as the tyres hit the bitumen – until a few years ago, when this route became no longer what I intended it to be.

Now it led to something far more sinister – a one-way road to my living nightmare. I hadn't been down here in a *very* long time.

Around forty-five minutes later, I pulled up alongside the cemetery gates. Because I was not letting Bogart come with me, I left my window down.

'I'll be back in a minute,' I told him as I hopped out into the sun's warmth. Retrieving the case of beer from the back seat, I breathed deeply. After closing the door, I made my way over to Abigail's grave. A few other people were here, visiting loved ones who were now departed.

I remembered how to get there like it'd been yesterday. I closed my eyes as I made my way down the aisle of those who had now turned to dust. Luckily, no-one was around, except for a woman, one lonely red rose in hand, a black veil covering her head. Who was she here for? A husband? A father? A child? This place ... it invited the living to commemorate the dead. How many souls were laid here to rest? How many reservoirs could be filled with the tears that'd been spilled by mourners here during the years? It was not a nice place to be, but it reminded me of one thing: we all have scars. We all have wounds that probably wouldn't ever heal. We were all headed this way eventually. It was only a matter of time. I believe we all have an invisible countdown timer above our heads from the moment we are born. So, when someone takes it upon themselves to speed up someone else's fate, it makes me a little mad. More than a little mad, actually.

Before I knew it, I stood before Abigail's headstone, spotting fresh daisies. That familiar tug on my heartstrings played havoc, so I didn't waste any time. I plonked my arse on the warm grass and cracked open a beer, and it hissed a gassy sigh of relief while I gazed at her plot. I re-read the words; words so familiar to me they may as well have been my own. But they'd been pulled from the mind of a grieving father.

'Every day, every place, every thought is connected to you, beautiful girl. Like sand dancing in the sunlight, you drifted through our lives, captivating us, giving us joy, and to everyone you touched. Goodnight, Abbie. Love Mummy and Daddy.'

My tightening fingers crinkled the aluminium can as I blew out a pent-up rush of emotions. Angry tears clouded my vision as pain scraped its claw over my heart and stomach. I lifted my beer and downed half its lukewarm content in one gulp, hissing after I swallowed.

'Oh God,' I whispered, heaving for oxygen. 'I am sorry I let you down.' With a trembling hand, I wiped my nose and mouth.

I stared at her name chiselled into the stone. I stared at the two most important dates any person will ever have etched against their name: Date of birth. Date of death. It wasn't fair, the shortage of her years.

'I tried, you know that? I tried hard to bring you justice. I gave it everything I had.' Tears dripped over my hand. 'There's not a day that goes by when I don't think of you. Not a day goes by when I don't hear your name in the back of my mind.' I took another sip, baring my teeth on a hiss. 'I did not give up. They told me to move on, that we'd exhausted every avenue.' My face contorted of its own accord as I drowned in the sorrow that clutched my throat. 'I didn't give up. How could I? To see their faces – your mummy and daddy – oh God! *God,* you have no idea ... I tried. Help me, Abbie. Help me find him. Where is he? *Who* is he?'

I glanced about the cemetery, and noticed a family of four – Mum, Dad, son and daughter (or so I presumed) – over by a gravesite a few metres away from the entrance.

'Tell me what to do here,' I said, turning back to Abbie's headstone. 'I'm failing on another case, too. I've now failed at my marriage. Where is the light at the end of the tunnel?' I waited for a response as wind whispered a chorus around my ears, carrying with it a bouquet of sweet, perfumed scents from nearby roses. 'Will you come and find me in death? Will you tell me you for-give me for failing?' My head dropped forward as I whimpered. I wept until

I'd polished off three cans of beer.

The sun shifted in the sky, on its trajectory to the west.

My head mimicked a fuzzy, static TV again, my eyes sore and puffy. I am grateful her parents buried her far out south. There was too much media presence back in Penrith; they wanted to grieve in peace without photographers in their faces. Their choice gave me peace here, too.

'I will find you up there in Heaven when my time is done. I will hold you and tell you how sorry I am. You believe me, don't you, sweetheart? I have never been sorrier over anything in my life.'

A gentle breeze blew over me, soothing me like the touch of an angel. People came and went. I was now alone with my dangerous thoughts. Wondering if her parents would visit, to allow themselves to fall apart before going back to their shattered lives – *separate* lives now. Could I have done more there, too?

After using the backs of my hands to clean my face, I turned to the headstone again. 'I better go now, Abbie. Sorry it's been a while. But you know, don't you? The pain it causes me. It eats away at me every single day. But one day, I'll make it up to you. I couldn't catch your guy, but I will catch mine. Give me some guiding light there, too, please. I want to catch him, and I want my family back.'

***

When I arrived home sometime later, I let Bogart out the back and placed my remaining beer in the fridge, then made my way upstairs – even *that* was a gargantuan effort. I needed to lie down. I was in no mood to do anything apart from crawl under the covers and sleep everything off.

I sat on the edge of my bed and looked at my phone still off the hook. Fuck it. No-one needed me anymore – that part was as obvious as dogs' balls. I removed a spare unlicensed back-up gun no-one knew about from my jacket and placed it beside the phone.

After kicking off my shoes, I crept under the covers, pulling them under my prickly chin. I lay with my head on the pillow, missing Ava sleeping beside me. I gazed out the bedroom window, to the sky producing sepia tones – like a picture from the 1900s. I blinked once, and drowsiness sucked me under. The light outside was fading, and so was mine. Fading into obscurity, powerless to stop the eclipse.

I blinked once more, but this time my heavy lids overpowered me. I drifted into a never-ending void of impermeable darkness, and I kept descending. Falling with my arms and legs outstretched as wind whistled past me. My eyes were open, but I saw nothing. Not even my hand in front of my face. I heard nothing except my own heartbeat, and the wind shooting past me as I fell from a great height. Here, in this black pit of despair, I grew numb. No pain, no remorse, no guilt or even anger. I was just there. Existing in this other realm, but I was not dead. Oh no, I was very much alive, but the meaning of me being in the other realm was not understood. My existence seemed superfluous; an accidental design in this creation of the abstract. I tried to reach out all around me, but I was alone, being swallowed by something, down the oesophagus and destined to land in its belly. The giant monster laughed at what he'd captured: Me. Hook, line and sinker as a strength far superior to mine washed me down. I collided with a thud as I fell on something bulbous and wet beneath my hands. It undulated, as though I'd fallen on a heart – the heart of a monster. Dazed, I stood on sea legs. Cackling laughter exploded around me, and I realised it was not a heart, but a stage. A stage where I looked up and peered out through the opening of the monster's mouth, and the light that shone through was my spotlight.

My arms lifted as though supported by strings, and my body danced. Not by its own accord; forced into a sickly, macabre dance as I was connected to strings from every which way, even my head as I bobbed and nodded along to an accordion. Who played that music? More importantly, who controlled me? Who was my puppeteer?

I managed to gaze up as my head bobbed to and fro. High above me, peering down, was the most sinister smile from Jerry the Jester. His teeth as long and sharp as a lion's incisors. The grotesque smile made me shiver with pure fear. His face was deathly white, there were black stars for eyes, and his nose was long and pointed like the bowsprit of a sailing vessel. His eyes were obsidian black, but something moved in the pupils. That eerie music from the accordion played some awful, sinister circus song, like the devil's minions were behind an orchestra for the damned. Jerry the Jester moved his head sharply from side to side, like a bird keeping an eye out for predators, as his lips remained pulled back in a nasty sneer. His head lowered, his breath foul – from carrion meat that'd been decaying between his razor-sharp teeth since he'd devoured their souls ... and then I saw it: the angel among the fiery depths of hell. His pupils were not pupils at all, but the miniature faces of Abigail. She shone through his black eyes, but as beautiful as ever. Her fine blonde hair in pigtails, and she stared at me with a look of pure innocence, her hands outstretched. The image was the same in both eyes as his face came closer and closer to mine.

'Help me!' she squealed before the Jester opened his mouth wider and swallowed me whole.

Stephanie May

CHAPTER FORTY-SEVEN

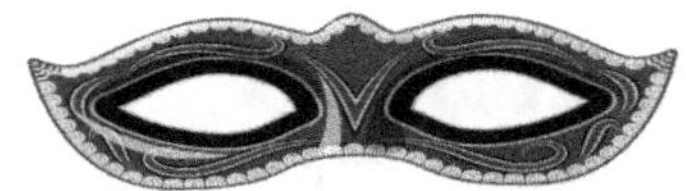

I SAT BOLT UPRIGHT upon hearing the front door close. Heart pumping, I jumped out of bed and grabbed my gun, then yanked the bedroom door open to see Ava standing at the bottom of the stairs.

She looked up and her eyes narrowed in on my gun before whispering, 'Planning to kill me?'

I glanced down at the gun. 'I'd rather use it on myself.' I looked back at her, hope soaring through my veins for the first time in days. 'What are you doing here?'

She fidgeted with her soft-pink summer dress. 'I came to collect more of my things.'

I turned away and headed to the bathroom. After shutting the door and placing the gun on the sink, I gazed into the mirror. Staring back was a sight I could not have picked out from a line-up of my former self. Thick bags hung under my bloodshot eyes and I hadn't shaved in days; I was pretty sure I'd earned myself a few extra lines from that whacked-out dream I had, and I smelled bad, too. A pitiful sight, even *I* turned away in disgust. As I grabbed my new toothbrush and toothpaste, I heard Ava rummaging in the bedroom.

I spat out the bubbly paste and stuck my toothbrush under the running faucet before brushing some more. A knock at the door made me freeze. I didn't want to see her. I didn't want to notice things like the colour of her lipstick. She didn't wear it willy-nilly, so had she put it on for me? Had she come back to collect more things, or in the hopes I would grab her and never let go?

I dunked my face in a handful of cold water, then patted my face dry and walked to the door.

I opened it and stared at her. I was hurt, yes. And I was angry at her for running away from what we had spent decades together making.

Her hazel eyes roamed over my face and dishevelled hair.

'Have you come to see what you've done to me?'

She closed her eyes. 'I don't want to argue.'

'Who's arguing? I'm not. Excuse me ...' I brushed past her. God, I wish I'd have known she was coming so I could have shaved, or at the very least, showered.

'Can we talk, please?'

'Sure.' I descended the stairs with a pep in my step. 'What would you like to discuss?'

'Mind if we sit on the couch?'

'Fine.'

I sat first, in my usual one-seater, and sighed – feigning carefree and relaxed.

She walked past me and sat on the other couch in the furthest end away from me.

Clasping her hands together in her lap, she said, 'Have you been keeping well?'

Glaring, my jaw clenched, I replied, 'What do you think?'

She shrugged, tears surfacing. 'I thought maybe you could work better if I wasn't around. That you would have a clearer mind – in case you were feeling any guilt.'

'Don't blame me for *you* wanting to give up on us.'

'How dare you?' she whispered. 'How dare you say I am the one who gave up?'

'You'd already decided for the both of us, and like an idiot, I was the last one to find out!'

'Agreed; I probably shouldn't have told the kids first. But I was so angry.'

'Then get angry at me; it doesn't mean you go straight to divorce.'

'I have been unhappy for a very long time.'

I turned away from her mounting tears and swallowed. 'I can't apologise for who I am, Ava. In my mind, I tried to be the best person I could hope to be.' I glanced back. 'I wanted you to have a husband who you were proud of.'

'I am!' Her tears overflowed. 'I *am* proud of you; you put your life on the line many times. But why did you ever get married?'

Cocking an eyebrow, I said, 'Why? Because I *love* you! Is that not a good enough reason?'

Her hand went to her breast. 'But you didn't *need* me.'

Anger flared inside me, travelling up my throat, spreading to my ears; she'd come in with a matchstick and thrown it onto the bale of hay. 'What are you talking about?'

'You needed someone to fit the mould of what you were trying to project into the world: a great job, a pleasant wife, a beautiful house, well-behaved kids.'

'That's bullshit! Now you're deliberately trying to provoke me.'

'It's what I've been feeling ever since you made detective.'

'Well, you're wrong. I never once cheated on you, Ava, and let me tell you I could have!' She looked away. 'In some of my darkest hours, all I thought of was your face, do you know that? Like the time I got stabbed and thought it was all over, you were the last thing I saw!' Despite rubbery knees, I stood up. 'So don't you dare come back in this house and try to tell me what I feel. I *loved* you! I didn't want my life to be shared with anyone else. Even now, how can I think about anyone else? You and the kids are my *life*. I need you. And it's not for cooking, or sex, or housework, but because you're the light amid the dark. You help me breathe when it all becomes suffocating. So do not come back now and try to make yourself feel less guilty for quitting this marriage.'

She dropped her head, shielding her face with a hand.

I stared at her, my bottom lip trembling. My whole body shook with anger and guilt.

'Please don't cry,' I said in a choked-up voice.

Bogart whimpered at the back door as I headed to the coffee table and grabbed a box of tissues, handing it to her. 'I'm sorry.' I leaned down and clutched her shoulder. 'You know I love you,' I whispered against her hair. She shook her head, sniffling. 'We can still make it work, little lady.'

She erupted on that and crouched forward further.

'Shh, don't cry. I am sorry, Ava. You're right, it's all my fault – everything.' I held her tight, squeezing my eyes shut. 'C'mon, don't worry, everything will be fine.'

'It's too late.'

I released her from my hug and, with my hands on her shoulders, shook my head. 'It's not.'

She took a tissue and blew her nose. Then she also shook her head and peered at me like a timid mouse. 'There's someone else.'

My head reeled back and my first response was to laugh out loud. But I went rigid, my mouth fell slack. I stumbled backwards as though I'd been shot right through the heart. The backs of my wobbly knees connected with my one-seater and I went crashing down.

'I am sorry.' She blew her nose and continued to weep.

I sat there, expressionless and unblinking, my face frozen in a mask of confusion.

'I *tried* to fight it! I didn't want this to happen. But these past few months you've been so cold, and ... and when you retired and were home every day, that was when I began seeing how different we are; how many things we don't have in common. I never realised, because we have never spent this much time alone together since you became a detective.'

Rigidity took control as she went on. Marquis de Sade himself couldn't have tortured me into speaking. At a complete loss for words.

'I feel so ...' She sobbed, sucking back air. 'I feel like I've betrayed you, but I've spoken to some of the girls, and-and they believe life is too short to be unhappy.' She sniffled. 'And that life is meant to be lived, not just to *exist* in it, but to be explored. And while you were off making your dreams come true, I put my life on hold for three decades. *Three!* Well, I am sorry, but now I think I'll take a little time for myself ... to do the things I've always wanted.'

I choked out a wry laugh. 'You've been sleeping around behind my back? You? Ava? Of all people. You slept with another man?'

She shook her head. 'No! I haven't!'

'You bring him to the house while I've been gone? Fucked him in our bed?'

She licked her lips before biting down on them, tears flowing. 'We ... we haven't been intimate.'

Shaking through my lividity and breathing heavily, I spat out, 'Bullshit!'

'It's true! I swear it on the kids' lives!'

'But you've brought him back here to the house while I was out?'

Her nose and mouth scrunched up. 'But it wasn't sexual; it's emotional.'

I lowered my tingling head and laughed. 'I don't believe it ...'

'We have not!'

'No – I don't believe that you've got a boyfriend.' *Boyfriend*. There's a word to make a husband vomit.

'I … I don't know what he is to me. All I know is what he does *for* me.'

My head snapped back so fast I swear I time travelled. 'I don't want to hear it.'

'He is attentive, kind, doting, intelligent—'

'I don't want to *fuck*ing hear it!' She glanced up, stiffening. 'Did you come back to finish me? Then *here*—' I hopped up and stormed into the kitchen, vision blurring before returning with a knife. 'Here! Do it!' I placed the tip of the knife to my heart.

She broke down again, sobbing. 'Stop! *Stop* it!'

'No! No, you want to fucking kill me? Then do it fast! Finish me so I don't have to suffer anymore. That's what you want, isn't it? To see me suffer?'

'No!' She stood up and slapped me hard across the chops – the hollow sound echoing around us. Bogart yipped, his nails scratching against the glass door. 'I loved you, Eddy!' She pummelled my chest. 'I tried to be the best wife and mother, and it still wasn't good enough!'

I threw the knife to the carpet and grabbed her hands. I shoved her into the couch, on her back, and sat on top of her, pinning her hands above her head.

'I hate you! I gave you everything, but you didn't care!'

While pinning her wriggling arms, she squirmed beneath me, my harsh breathing rippling the hair beside her red face. 'You don't hate me.'

She wept, her neck stretched back taut, making feeble sounds. 'I gave you *everything*,' she whispered again, no longer struggling against me.

I hopped off her, pulling her up to a sitting position as I kneeled before her. What the fuck was going on here? Whose life was I living?

'Give me another chance,' I whispered, my heart pick-axing my chest as I pushed unwanted images aside. 'Please. Don't go.' I moved my hands to cover her kneecaps. 'I can do better.'

'It's too late,' she whispered, shaking her head.

'Let's go to Aruba.'

She laughed mirthlessly. 'Too little, too late.'

'Stop saying that! It's only too late if you want it to be.'

She shook her head. 'He makes me happy. He dotes on me; God, he actually pays me attention, and he makes me feel beautiful. Something I haven't felt in years. I am only human.'

I rubbed my hot face, my heart only one beat away from collapsing. 'How long has it been?'

She exhaled and snivelled. 'I met him about, maybe, seven months ago.'

I sat back on my haunches as my trembling hands curled into tight fists.

'We met while I was at my favourite coffee shop. He approached me while I was minding my business, eating a croissant with my head in a book.'

'He didn't notice your wedding ring then, I take it?' My jaw tightened at the mere thought of another man ogling my wife, closing in on my turf.

She closed her eyes. 'He asked about the book I was reading and we got to talking about Dean Koontz.' She opened her eyes again. 'It was innocuous, I swear. I did not plan this; I even told him about you, but things developed naturally.'

'And you've been meeting up in secret?'

She bobbed her head, swallowing once more.

I stared at her like she was one of the criminals I'd dealt with: with disgust. 'You know what, Ava? Just go. Go be with him. If this guy who you've only known for a handful of months is worth more than the decades we have shared, then piss off back to lover boy.'

She turned to me, open-mouthed. I had never directed profanity towards her. Not once.

'No, honestly.' My spine straightened. 'I will not stop you. Take what you need and go. It's clear this has been in the making for a long time – you've been making a fool outta me.'

She stared, wide-eyed. 'I was hoping you'd make good on your promise to Aruba.' Her eyes leaked again. 'That you'd plan to do nice things for me. I was hoping you'd change.'

A bubble burst somewhere deep inside me. 'I can't change if I don't know what to fix!'

She flinched. 'I shouldn't have to tell you how to appreciate your wife. And you can blame Bill all you want, but if our union was strong, this would never have happened.'

'Bill? *Pffttt.*' I shook my head.

She turned away. 'I am staying with Lyndell from the Book Club. I can give you the address if you like—'

'No need.' I waved a hand in the air. 'Just go and live out a happy life.'

She stared at me, chewing her bottom lip. I hopped off the carpet and sagged into the couch, my sanity hanging on by a mere thread. 'I tried to call you a few times.'

In my periphery, I saw her staring at me.

'Go,' I whispered.

'I still—'

'Yep. Sure.'

She whimpered, gasping back air. 'That's all you have to say?'

'Guess so. But don't come crawling back; that's the only thing I'll add.' I turned to her with thin lips. 'Do *not* come crawling back when it doesn't work between you two.'

Her chin tilted. 'And why do you think it won't?'

'Because he will never be able to love you the way I do.'

She turned away and stood, but more tears fell, despite her bravado. 'I guess I need to be shown, rather than told.'

Gritting my teeth, I said, 'Don't you need to run along to Bill? Don't wanna leave his bedsheets too cold now, do you?'

'It's *not* sexual.'

'Oh, fuck off, it isn't! You didn't leave just so you could hold some guy's hand.'

'It's true! But you won't believe me, so there's nothing left for me to say. I'll just grab my ...'

I remained on the couch as my soon-to-be ex-wife trundled up the stairs and shut the bedroom door. My eyes closed as I breathed through the agony. Bogart's whimpers floated through from the back door as my chest expanded and fell on every deep breath. Ava soon made her way down the stairs, but I kept my peepers fixed on Bogart's wide eyes.

'I put the phone back on the hook,' she whispered.

I could not speak to her; couldn't even look at her. Who was she now? Who was I?

'I am going now.' She waited, silent. 'Please take care of yourself.'

My knees bobbed as I clenched my throbbing jaw to refrain from screaming. She waited for a response, but I was done. Nothing left to say.

Eventually she shut the door and once again I closed my eyes, the pain unlike anything I'd ever felt before.

Stephanie May

CHAPTER FORTY-EIGHT

SOMEWHERE IN THE distance, the trill of a telephone pulled me out of a black hole. Wait – it was *my* telephone! I opened my weary eyes and turned to gaze at the wall phone near the kitchen, letting it ring out. I'd hoped that when I awoke, I'd be saved and this had all been some horrible nightmare. But the raw agony was as sharp as ever. My broken heart like shards of jagged glass, and no amount of sleeping it off, or pills, or booze, could blunt the edges. Pain ached inside of me like a throbbing pulse. The thought – oh, the thoughts they were plentiful. I wasn't oblivious to Ava's pain, and perhaps she *did* feel guilty, but how was that supposed to help me? Where was the comfort when we could not suffer our failed marriage together? She'd taken off, and then tried to convince me she hadn't lain with him. The thought of my wife's lips wrapping around another man's—

'Arrghhhh!' I sat up, grunting in agony, hands to my stomach as my insides stretched in a game of tug-o-war. Pacing the room, I ran a shaky hand through my tousled hair. The thought of this fucker putting his hands on her. Of robbing me of the right to sleep next to my wife. This homewrecker taking her out for meals. So … they'd met in secret, had they? Well, how about I secretly rock up to his place and rearrange his teeth? How about I shoot his dick off, so he'd know to leave other men's wives alone? Where was his own wife? And … Christmas! It was days away. What was I going to do? Did this Bill fucker have kids of his own, or would he steal mine also?

Everything in life I'd worked so hard for, gone. A king abandoned by his loyal subjects, left to fight the battle solo. I thought retirement would be a semi-good thing; turned out it was the worst thing I'd ever done. I hadn't a clue where Bill lived, but if I ever drove past them on the street, I'd happily go to jail for murder. Infidelity was cruel. It was filth; disgusting, amoral, a fucking sin. It *should* be a straight-up capital offence to fuck another man's wife.

'*Cocksucker*!' I huffed as murderous thoughts infiltrated every part of my damaged mind, my body boiling rapidly while I paced, kicking out at a table. Sweat clung to my temples; any hotter and I'd self-combust. I had to calm the hell down; I was on the verge of committing premeditated murder.

Shaking with fury, I made my way to the fridge and yanked it open to grab a can of beer before slamming the door shut, muttering expletives as the fridge wobbled. I wandered down the hallway to the left and entered my study.

Plonking on the chair, I cracked the beer open, chugging it until I finished it. I burped, welcoming the carbonated comfort with bunched-up lips. I crumpled the empty can in my fist and slammed it in the bin; this time it didn't miss, unlike my bottle of whisky, which still lay on the floor.

My knees bounced with agitation as I pulled the chair closer to my desk. What the fuck was I going to do? I rubbed my flushed face, scrubbing at invisible dirt.

How would I find the strength to carry on? What was the goddamn point anymore, anyway? The light was gone. There was no sunshine anymore. Everything in my life had gone tits-up; I'd been bent over and cornholed by

Satan himself.

After about an hour of enduring the explicit images hijacking my mind's theatre, someone knocked loudly at the front door. Fuck it. Even if it was the undercover surveillance team, I didn't care anymore. Let Jerry the Jester finish me, please!

But the banging persisted, followed by muffled shouting; a feminine voice calling out to me. Moaning, I rose and made my way to the front door. It was only when I stood a few feet away that I recognised Hayley's voice.

'Dad, open up!'

I reached the door in no time, yanking it open – still unlocked since Ava left.

Hayley breathed a sigh of relief, a hand flying to her breast. 'Dad!'

I smiled for her sake as best as I could. 'Hiya, sweetie.'

'Oh, my God.' She teared up as her hands cupped her mouth.

'Don't worry, everything is going to be okay.'

'You look awful!' She wept, hands now clutching her cheeks. 'I'm so sorry.'

'Hey, look, it's for the best.'

She shook her head, causing tears to fan out everywhere. Then she halted and pushed my shoulder. 'I've been trying to call you!'

'Sorry. I needed a little time.'

'I was so—' She sniffled, head tilted skyward. 'I was worried you'd done something stupid!'

Maybe later tonight. 'No. Just needed time.'

She palmed away the tears. 'You look like shit.'

'Well, I've felt better. Come inside, don't stand there crying on my doorstep.'

She threw her arms around me. My little girl throwing me a ray of sunshine; it peered through like a light at the end of the tunnel. 'I love you, Dad!'

I patted her back, the tears once again brimming at the surface. 'Love you, too. Come inside.'

Her forehead rumpled. 'I can't stay for long; I've got to get dinner on and bathe Lucy.'

'How is she?'

'As long as *Mr. Squiggle* is on, she's fine. But it's *you* I want to talk about.'

'What do you want me to say? That I'm doing well?'

She closed the door and we walked inside. 'Even if you did, I know you're not.'

'Apparently, you told her you could see the writing on the wall.'

She wiped her wet eyes. 'I did. I won't lie, Dad, I could have seen it coming. I didn't say anything because sometimes people just go their separate ways.'

'That's nice.'

'Don't be sarcastic. It's not a place for a daughter to interfere with her parents' marriage, and I am sorry to say this, Dad, because I love you, but if I saw it, how could you have not?'

Shrugging, I said, 'Guess I'm not husband material.'

'I didn't say that.'

Throwing my head over my shoulder, I said, 'Would you like a drink?'

'What do you have – I can't stay for long.'

Cracking a grin, I said, 'Beer?'

She smiled, nodding. 'Sure, why not?'

I cocked an eyebrow. 'Really?'

Her glare translated to: *Don't fuck with me; I am not in the mood for wisecracks.*

'Two beers coming right up – shall we sit in my study?'

Hayley glanced around, arm swinging in an arc. 'Why not here?'

'Here currently reminds me of things I'd rather forget.'

'Fair call.' She adjusted her brown shoulder bag and took off down the hall.

I grabbed us two beers and cracked them open before joining her in my study.

'Ta,' she said, taking the beer I held out. 'What do you want to happen from here?'

Exhaling, I dropped into my chair. I settled back and forced a gentle smile. 'It's not a case of ask and you shall receive. Do you know the whole truth?'

'Yes. You, too, I take it?'

'About as much as I can stomach. I know there's a new man – boy that's going to take some getting used to.' My stomach churned, my pulse quickened, and I gave an involuntary shudder.

'I know. Mum came clean today. Oh, Dad, she looked awful!'

'Can't understand why; she started telling me all these things before about what he does for her, and how well he treats her.'

Hayley took a sip of beer, her eyes on mine. 'Don't you understand women at all?'

'Apparently not.'

'When Heath and I came around to dinner and she told us she was thinking of leaving you, I swear, she was staring at the front door, waiting for you to come home.'

'Probably worried I'd overhear her plans.'

'No, you fool! She was hopeful. I think in her mind she was giving you one last chance. She was waiting for you to come home and be with us – as a family.'

'Guess I screwed that up then, didn't I?'

'If she'd made up her mind, then why was she waiting for you to change it?'

'I can't answer that.'

'You were a good father. But perhaps a better father than a husband.'

My eyes trailed away to safer ground. 'I don't know what to say to that.'

'I will not badger you with the list of things that you missed in my youth that were important to me – things a father *should* have been there for. Because

I get it. And I know you love us, but sometimes *knowing* and *feeling* are two completely different things. And Mum needed to feel it. You can't just tell someone you love them a hundred times a day and that makes it true.'

'But I do love her! I love you all; you're my—' My throat closed like a fist, blocking off air. 'Dammit, you're my family.' I swept my hand out before me. 'I created this – *we* created this.'

'I didn't come here to upset you; I came to say I still think there's hope. There's light for you guys. Have you given up the case?'

'I was kicked out of the circle we had going on. So yes, like my marriage, it is over with.'

She took another sip of beer, and I followed suit.

After swallowing, she said, 'It doesn't need to be.'

'Do you think I want to touch her after she's been with another man? It's tainted now.'

She tsked. 'Get real; this isn't some hot love affair … God, she's early sixties! It's more of a comfort thing, I'd say. Two lonely people coming together. She swore it was platonic—'

'I don't want to know …'

'What I am saying is, I think this is purely emotional, and from what I hear, they share many things in common – he also reads lots of books.'

I raised my hand and pointed to my large bookcase.

She glared at me. 'I don't mean about murderers. Classic literature; things *she* loves.'

'Then maybe we're not compatible. Your make-up is running, by the way.'

'Thanks.' She leaned down to her handbag and rummaged around, pulling out diaries and baby wipes, lipstick and perfume, until she found a packet of tissues. Removing one, she dabbed her eyes with the corner to remove her running mascara.

'I don't have the will to fight anymore. I love your mother, but I feel like I have been fighting my whole life.'

She removed a glob of black mascara from the corner of one eye. 'Dave and I are hosting Christmas this year. How is it going to feel with the family divided? How would you be, alone on Christmas? Think about it. Something needs to change.'

'This is her choice.'

She lowered her hand. 'Do not blame it all on Mum. Same as she shouldn't blame it all on you. We're all adults here; let's start acting like it, okay?'

'Jeez, when did you grow a pair?'

She chuckled. 'I learned from you. You're the strongest man I know.'

'Yet a woman can bring me to my knees.'

After consulting her wristwatch, her bottom lip protruded. 'I am so sorry, but I have to cut this short. I wish you'd answered the damn phone!'

I shook my head. 'I don't; I'm glad you came.'

She smiled, holding the eye contact. 'Please call me if you need me, yes?'

'Sure.' We both knew I wouldn't.

I kissed her cheek as we stood at the threshold, a gentle summer breeze billowing around us.

'Love you, Dad. Please take care. And think strongly about what I said.'

'Will do. Love you, too.'

After closing the door, I locked it and leaned against it, facing the back door where Bogart stood, demanding to be let in. So I acquiesced, and then retrieved a can of dog food – beef and kangaroo – before dumping it on a plate.

'You can eat inside tonight, mate.' I grabbed another beer from the fridge.

I made my way back to the study while Bogart inhaled his meal. In my chair, I closed my eyes as my mind tried to absorb what Hayley had said and yes, there may have been a ring of truth to it, but God, I was exhausted. Mentally.

Physically. Emotionally. These past few days had siphoned everything out of me. And then, the image of Ava and this faceless man, Bill, in his bed – it was more than I could take. I downed the beer in three gulps, chucking the can against the bookshelf as I stared at the spines. Then I got up and went to my liquor shelf. I was running low on supplies; I'd have to remedy that later on. But first … I picked up a bottle of Jack and ripped off the cap. I drank like a sailor, pushing every graphic image out of my mind, but those images – how could I stop them? After decades of marriage, she leaves me for some bloke she's known for seven months. What a goddamn insult!

I collapsed in the chair, my thoughts whipping about inside my cranium. 'Likes books, does he? What about his cock, do you like that? *Huh*?' I took another swig as the room spun like a vortex. Inevitable hot tears streamed down my face as a pain so intense crushed me, I felt like I needed an oxygen mask to breathe. No adult male should be caught blubbering like this, but I was in *hell*. Next thing I knew – I swear I didn't even know how it got into my trembling hands in the first place – my gun was pointing at me.

I blinked several times, trying to see through the tears.

'Hope he was worth it, darlin', ' I slurred. 'The kids. The fucking kids. Our marriage!' Bulbous tears obscured the gun barrel wavering in front of my face as I heaved, gasping for air. 'How *could* you?' My face contorted before expelling a primal scream. And then the nozzle lay inside my mouth. Breathing through my nostrils was difficult due to the tears and mucus. My finger began to squeeze the trigger as I looked up to make my peace with God – or whoever the hell was lying down on the job – but as I did, the picture of Abigail stared at me from the corkboard. *'Don't do it'* she seemed to say.

I blinked in confusion, mouth wide open to the gun that was about to blow my damn brains out through the back of my head. Would I end up looking like JFK, bits of flesh hanging everywhere?

Abigail smiled at me. Fresh tears poured down my face as I thought of her, and like darkened clouds parting to reveal the moon, it came to me: if her parents could both find the will to live after someone had raped and murdered their child, then where the fuck was my courage? How utterly selfish! I removed the gun from my quivering lips and stared at her picture, my jaw aching. *'My parents somehow found the will to live. So why don't you?'*

I placed the gun on my desk with a metallic *clank* and stared at it in horror. Oh, my good God. My hands covered my face as I let out a startled cry. What the hell was I thinking? It'd all happened too fast; I didn't even remember getting the gun. My hands quaked in disbelief, and when I lowered them, something on the corner of the chair opposite stole my focus, where Hayley sat not long before. A folded paper. I sat there for a moment, blinking as I expelled the bad thoughts from my damaged mind, warm snot running down my lips.

Shaking my head, I said, 'I'm sorry, Abbie. I didn't mean—'

After I don't know how long, I wiped my face and rose unsteadily to see what the piece of paper was; I didn't want Hayley missing a business invoice.

I staggered over and bent to pick it up, sniffling hard. Unfolding it, I blinked several times – too blind drunk to read; I could not make out B from P, so I threw it on my desk, near my loaded gun, and somehow made my way up to bed with the help of invisible hands.

CHAPTER FORTY-NINE

MY LIFE DIDN'T magically turn into an Andrew Lloyd Webber musical the morning after. It was no Disney movie either, but I felt a tad better than I had the night before. Even one per cent was marginally better, right? As I turned over in bed, images bombarded me as sharp as the sun infiltrating the gaps in the curtains, the main one being – I'd almost killed myself. I'd almost splattered my own brains across the wall. God, it's incredible how the mighty can fall. One minute you're standing, the next you're on your knees. It all happened quicker than a fart; I'd been seconds from death. I would not have opened my eyes this morning – damn, that was a scary thought. And would I have regretted it? Hell yes. Despite the internal pain that felt like it'd never let up. Despite feeling alone. Despite knowing I was a failure in many aspects.

Today was a new day.

I unlocked and opened the front door and peered outside, but I couldn't locate any surveillance cars on the street; however, today was the epitome of summer: sunshine, birds, a cool breeze from the river. Jerry the Jester would not be paying me a visit in broad daylight, we both knew that. We all knew that, which was probably why Davies hadn't given a toss about organising anybody to watch the house.

The *Telegraph* lay rolled up at my feet on the mat. Jeez, it'd been a while since I'd read the paper (the one from yesterday had not been touched). I grabbed it, went inside and relocked the door. Once I'd let Bogart outside to run and play, I put the kettle on. A strong cup of coffee and eggs on toast would go down well.

A knob of butter slid into the hot pan with a sizzle, followed by three beaten eggs with a splash of milk and salt and pepper. I popped two slices of fresh white bread into our toaster and grabbed a mug (the one that said: *I've still got it … Now where did I put it?*) and dumped in two teaspoons of sugar. My body knew nothing other than numbness, like a tooth dulled by a local anaesthetic before it's yanked out. Could anyone blame me for wanting to curl up in a foetal position and hibernate until it passed? Until I could manipulate my brain to feel something other than dread?

Holding my plate in one hand, coffee in the other, and the rolled-up paper under my arm, I headed for the study. Although the memory of my darkest hour was now imprinted in this study (and probably always would be), it was still a more ideal place to sit than in the lounge room – a constant reminder of what my life should be. Or the dining room, with the sun's warmth flowing in through the back door, picturing my wife by my side as we ate breakfast and talked about our plans for the day. The dining room was a place where we'd created many memories. Where we all used to sit as a family, and talk about good times and bad while eating Ava's incomparable cooking.

No, the study was my sanctuary now. In this study, I had always been alone. Breakfast, lunch and dinner would now be eaten here, and even Abigail could join me. I wouldn't be *totally* alone. She'd never abandoned me. She stayed with me. Every. Single. Day.

Placing my plate and mug on the desk, I dropped into my chair with a prolonged sigh. What to do today? What to do indeed. Slicing into the buttery toast, I spied a piece of paper on my desk, next to my gun. Then it came back to me: Hayley left this here last night. I'd been too soused to read it. While chewing my toast, I picked it up and flipped the rumpled paper over to smooth it out. My eyes narrowed in on the words:

NSW SPIRITUAL GROUP INVITES YOU TO OUR

CHRISTMAS IN JULY DINNER

WHERE: Springwood Hall, Macquarie Road

WHEN: Friday, July 13th

TIME: 6 pm

THEME: Masquerade Ball

Included in this year's event:

* *Mediums* * *Psychics* * *Tarot Cards* **Fortune Tellers* * *Palm Reading*
* *Healing* **Tasseography* * *Meditation* * *Prayers*

Have your loved one drawn by our psychic artist – Evelyn DuPont
(Recipient of the Psychic of the Year Award 1979)

$10 entry p.p. (Wheelchair access available.)

To book your own marquee, please contact Rosie.

WE HOPE TO SEE YOU THERE!

Frowning, I stared at it. Hayley hadn't attended this, or had she? It was odd she still had this on her, but then again, it was all scrunched up; probably shoved at the bottom of her bag among the baby wipes and make-up.

That date ... Had Ava gone out then, too? Something rattled in the back of my mind like a faint knocking – somewhere in the far distance. Where was it coming from, and where would it lead?

My mind was still hazy from last night, so remembering something that happened months ago was impossible. Besides, Ava had been going out a lot more frequently these past few months – now I knew why. I stiffened at the thought of the lies and backstabbing, so I put the piece of paper out of sight and grabbed the newspaper – today's date: Saturday, December 22nd.

I held it in front of me with one hand, picking up my mug in the other as my tongue dislodged a bit of toast stuck between my teeth. 'Let's see who killed who today.'

The scalding, rich coffee slid down my raw throat about as smoothly as razor blades, but it hit the spot. Putting the mug back down, I turned the front page and something slipped out.

Recognising that elongated handwriting on the envelope, my eyes widened.

I turned it over, front and back. No return address, no stamp.

My letter opener was in my hand before I knew it, and I sliced the top off the envelope as quickly as 'Jerry' slashed his victims' throats. There was another smaller envelope inside, but I picked up his letter first, held it up to my face and wasted no time in reading it.

Dear Eddy,

I would ask how things are, but by the looks of it, they're hideous. Am I mistaken? The wife's gone, hasn't she? It was only a matter of time, old boy. Found another man, hasn't she? I saw them, you know. Once. They do look like a cute couple, I must admit. But this is the price you pay when you take on a mistress; you can't divide your time between us adequately.

I am more thrilling though, aren't I? Ah, don't worry about her, Eddy; you're with me now. But I must say, I am a trifle surprised. I thought I'd at least have someone knocking on my door by now. I even gave you a clue last time, too. This is getting to be wearisome, old chap. But look, just for you, how about I do one more? Furthermore, I will give you some insight, because it seems to me that you're struggling worse than I thought. But we cannot compare a bull to a calf, can we?

It is not the kill that makes my appendage stiffen. But you know that, don't you? It is not the feel of their warm blood spraying on my flesh as I snuff out their life like a candle's flame. It's not even the look in their eyes upon the realisation they're about to die. It's what I do afterwards. The power of it. Knowing that I can get away with murder; knowing that this is eating you up inside. I love the thrill of almost being caught by the great Macintosh Matthews.

How about I give you another clue? Being this far ahead of you is not fun for me. So here goes: I knew all of them. Everyone. I met them, then stalked my prey. I watched their sinful lives and decided to do them a favour. But what's more, they invited me into their own house. There's no bigger agony than to wear a mask to hide who you really are. I've seen the composite sketch in the paper. I knew witnesses were watching me and yes, even I will admit the sketch circulating in the media is mostly accurate. Not perfect, but close enough. Black and white. Light and dark. Good and evil. Heaven and hell. Everything is a juxtaposition in life, wouldn't you agree?

Well, I best get going now. My time could run out, and sooner or later I could be caught. I can't have that just yet. You could have ended it, though. Yes, you laid eyes on me not too long ago. I was watching you. And you turned to me. I was the 'woman' in black at the cemetery with the single red rose.

How did I know you would visit Abigail? You, too, are predictable. I knew you'd be there on the anniversary. I saw you weep. You drank at least three cans of beer as you spoke to her. I captured the image forever. It is like watching Goliath fall. I've enclosed the picture for you and I, too, have a copy.

I laugh when I think about how close we were to each other. However, I shall leave you be, while I plan my next murder. Hurry up, old boy, for this will be my last.

Yours faithfully,

Jerry.

fall. I've enclosed the picture for you and I, too, have a copy.

I laugh when I think about how close we were to each other. However, I shall leave you be, while I plan my next murder. Hurry up, old boy, for this will be my last.

CHAPTER FIFTY

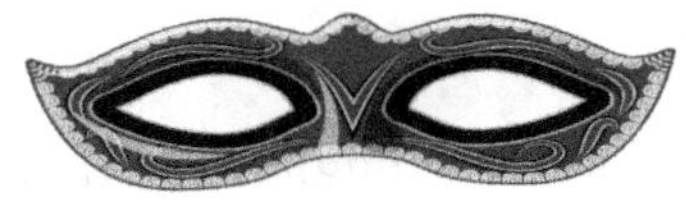

SCRUNCHING UP THE note, I clenched my eyelids. He'd spied on me at Abigail's resting place?

I fumbled to open the other envelope and sure enough, there was a black-and-white Polaroid taken from afar of me sitting on the ground in front of Abigail's grave.

'Mother*fucker*!' I thought back to the 'woman' I'd seen with the rose. Yes, I remembered, but only vaguely. Tall. Dressed in black. He'd had his head down, a single red rose held up to his chin as he said a silent prayer. Like fuck he did. Where did he stash his camera? No-one was there by the time I got up and left, so he must have been watching, and waiting. In the distance, in the car, who bloody knows? But Bogart had been in my car, too. 'Jerry' could have easily taken him. Maybe he was worried Bogart would bark again? All it would have taken was for me to look over, see someone stealing my dog, and then reach in and pull out my gun. No, he was playing his cards right. But this ... Abigail ... it was the most personal intrusion. In a way, I felt more violated than when he had been in my house. Abigail was personal to me. It was the biggest invasion of privacy. Not the graveyard. Not there.

This letter, meant to provoke and taunt, gave me my second wind, breathing life back into my soul. A renewed vigour into my outlook on life had been hand-delivered. The sneaky fucker had put it inside the morning paper. He knew everything about me, from where I would be, to what I did in the mornings.

I no longer had an appetite for cold eggs and soggy toast. I did, however, down the rest of my lukewarm coffee and said aloud, 'Right ... you wanna play? Then let's dance!'

After removing my plate and mug, I cleared everything off my desk with one big sweep of my arm, including pictures of Ava and the kids. Everything was strewn on the floor like the aftermath of a tornado. Glass cracked and splintered, but picture frames could be replaced.

Reaching into my filing cabinet, I pulled out every file pertaining to the case that the fellas had copied for me, plus my own notes. I opened the blinds and made sure I had enough light to read over every single goddamn thing. Every clue. Every prop. I would die here trying to find it, so help me God.

Having poured an hour into the Norman Colbert case, nothing new jumped out. Nothing in the crime scene photos, nothing in the coroner's report.

'C'mon, c'mon!' I grabbed Ian McLaughlin's file, starting with the initial report followed by the crime scene photos, and re-read his girlfriend's official statement. Everything the fellas could have done was ticked off.

I grabbed the file on the third victim, Mark Andrews, and applied the same methods, asking myself different questions. Anything I could think of. But it appeared everything was accounted for. I raked a hand through my hair, my lips thinning. *This is not going my way*, I thought, as I grabbed the stack of duplicated crime scene photos. I went from one corner of the photograph to the next, trying to pick up something with fresh eyes. And then, I eyed something that made my body ripple with goosebumps. I squinted hard, but I couldn't be certain. Maybe it was my overexcited imagination.

Opening my desk drawer, I pulled out a magnifying glass. As I hurried over to the window, Bogart pranced around outside from left to right, then right to left, trying to capture my attention. I held out the photo of Mark's office and raised the magnifying glass. There! I closed my eyes and my heart started doing backflips. I told myself to calm down. This could all be a coincidence. I breathed in and out through my nose, enthusiasm racing through me. I opened my eyes once more and checked again through the glass to make sure. And there it was: sticking out at the edge of a corkboard, underneath other papers pinned there. Remember that game – Hot and Cold? Well, I was now boiling – any hotter, I'd blister. But this wouldn't stick. The cops would probably laugh at me if I ever told them the connection I'd made.

I needed more proof. More! I grabbed the other files, not bothering to read what the report said, or what the autopsies revealed, but the photos. That's what I needed.

Next came Juanita and Raúl Martínez. I searched every pixel in all the photos, but it wasn't there; however, that didn't mean it didn't *exist*. Same with Norman and Ian.

Then there was Elliot Pratt. Because I'd been shafted from the group, O'Brien hadn't provided copies of that crime scene. However, just as I tried to conjure memories of being inside the house, the image came to me: Elliot's fridge. I'd seen it while sitting on a kitchen stool, gazing about the place while the others were working, and Nathan Davies stormed inside. And it was there, I was one hundred per cent certain. On the fridge, attached by a magnet. If I closed my eyes, I could visualise it clear as day. It was in none of the other victims' photos, but I would have bet my life if we were to go back and check out the places, we would find one – if it hadn't been thrown out already. But

I'd bet there were still ways to prove it – an event diary, a wall calendar.

Getting to my knees, I flicked through the pile I'd created on the floor until I found the invitation Hayley left behind. I held it up in my left hand and glanced at Mark's photo in my right.

'I know how you met them.'

CHAPTER FIFTY-ONE

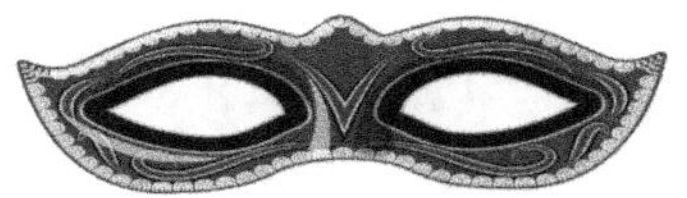

THE PHONE QUIVERED against my ear as I eyed the piece of paper with all the important numbers I'd ever need stuck to the wall. Ava had an excellent memory, but I, for one, couldn't guess Hayley's number if I had a gun to my head; the only one I knew off by heart was O'Brien's house. Hayley was the third one down, after Heath, then 'Mum Nursing Home'. With the phone in the crook between my ear and shoulder, I spun the numbers.

It rang four times before David Warner answered.

'Dave! It's Eddy, mate; how are you?'

He paused, no doubt baffled – testament to how often I called. 'Oh, *Eddy*! Fine, fine, thanks, and you?' The put-on voice was not welcome to my ears. 'Sorry to hear about you and Ava ...'

'Yeah, me too. Listen, is Hayley there, please?'

'Sure. Hang on – oh, and take care of yourself. We missed you at dinner the other night.'

Why don't you punch me in the gut with knuckle dusters next time? 'Appreciate it, and I missed you guys, too.'

'One second.' He put the phone down with a dull thud.

Hurry up, hurry up!

After a beat, Hayley picked up the phone. 'Dad?' Her voice a falsetto. 'You okay?'

I smiled so it shone through my voice. 'Fine, pumpkin. You?'

'Um, yeah, not too bad, I guess. Have you spoken to Mum yet?'

'No. Look, you dropped a piece of paper here when we were speaking in my study.'

'I did?'

'The invitation to the Christmas in July dinner.'

'Oh! Must have left it in my diary – that was ages ago, obviously ...'

'Did you attend?'

'We all did.' Her tone said she was as confused as a lab rat in a maze.

I licked my lips, trying to live up to 'Steady Eddy'. 'Who's "we"?'

'Everyone. Mum, Dave, Lucy, Lorraine, Heath – I think Lorraine dragged him along.'

'You all went?'

'Yes – Mum would have told you.'

'My mind is like a sieve in my old age. You know this.'

She sighed pitifully, lowering her register to one of sympathy. 'No, Dad, Bill didn't come, if that's what you're wondering.'

At the mention of *his* name, anger surged in my chest like reflux, but I pushed past it. 'I'm not, actually. Tell me about it.'

She sucked in air abruptly. 'Huh?'

'Tell me about it. How was it?'

'Why? What's going on?' She now sounded a bit agitated.

My nostrils flared in a vain attempt to pull back the reins on my anxiety and impatience. 'Honey, please.'

She tutted. 'Um, well, Mum came and picked up Dave, Lucy and me. Heath, Lorraine and Aaron went in Lorraine's car. Um, what else … we had to pre-pay because they organised dinner—'

'But what actually *happened*? What went on?'

'We all entered the huge hall, and the place was decked out with stalls, marquees outside, even – once you'd ticked off your name at the front door, of course.'

I licked my parched lips. 'So, there was an RSVP list?'

'Yes. We had to pre-pay, and when we arrived, we lined up at the doors as a young girl marked us off on her clipboard before giving each of us a wristband. Then we basically wandered around until dinnertime.'

'Was there a host?'

'Rosie Weatherstone.'

'Any males?'

She chuckled. 'Um, there were a few male speakers, but I can't remember their names. They were spiritual leaders of other chapters, for lack of a better term.'

'Tell me about the stalls.' I wished I'd had a notepad with me; I was loaded like a gun with questions, ready to fire 'em off.

'You didn't have to go to one, but they had *everything* there. All set out around the walls of the hall, and you could line up at anyone you wanted to and have, like, your fortune read, palm reading; they even had an elderly lady reading tea leaves from a cup.'

'Did you have to pay money each time?'

'Yes, a small fee, depending on what you wanted. The initial cost was just to cover dinner.'

'Which ones did you guys go to?'

'Gee, um … personally, I went to a psychic named Cora. She told me good fortune was coming my way, but then, get this: she sensed that a death was foreseeable. Bizarre, huh?'

I squinted as my heart rate kicked up a notch. 'A death? *Yours?*'

'She didn't say; she couldn't see it properly. But she said she saw tears and sadness, and a grave in the near future. Morbid, huh?'

My whole body tightened and my stomach cramped. 'I'll say.' I gripped the phone tighter. 'Did Cora say anything else?' I heard Lucy gurgle in the background, followed by David's soothing coos.

'She honestly looked shaken, but I don't know whether it was an act. She left it on a high, though; said she could see a baby boy surrounding the family. But I don't know if that's me, or Heath, or … or anyone, really.'

I used my free thumb to scratch my jawline. 'Hmm … fancy that. Did you attend any other stalls?' I stared at the invitation on the kitchen bench. Had Hayley kept this from me because she knew I thought they were nothing but charlatans, taking advantage of the vulnerable?

'No, Lucy was restless that night. Mum went to a few, though. Said she tried old runes. She said the woman was eerily accurate.'

'Remember what she told your mother?'

'Umm … yes, actually. Something about her marriage being on the rocks – I know, irony right; she was looking at rocks?' My stomach contorted tighter than a bowline knot. 'Mum said the woman told her a new change was on the horizon.'

Did Ava leave because she thought it was prophesised? I tried to keep the anger from my voice. 'That's not an exaggeration. Anyway, what about the others?'

'We all went to stalls, but by the time I had taken Lucy off Dave, she was really restless, so I can't remember what they'd all done, or where they'd been to.' She hesitated. 'Dad, you're awfully keen on this. Does this have to do with the case?'

'I won't lie, sweetie, I think so. I need to speak to the event organiser.'

'That can be arranged! I know the lady who ran it. I have her address if you want it?'

My ears pulled back. 'Yes! Honey, thank you, yes.'

'Let me get my address book. One moment.' I held on with bated breath, listening to the *Inspector Gadget* theme song in the background. Not everything was wrapped in a red bow, but damn I was close. She returned after what felt like minutes, whereas in reality, it was probably seconds. Women always knew where their address and phone book were.

'Okaaaaay, here we go: Rosie Weatherstone of eighty-nine Cox Avenue, Cambridge Park.'

'Cambridge Park?'

'Yes, she runs classes here.'

'But it was up the mountains, wasn't it? Springwood?'

'That's just where this festival was held. It's been an annual thing for God knows how long. The leaders or facilitators of every group take turns running it, but Christmas dinner has always been based in Springwood, though – the bigger hall, see?'

'Do you have her number?'

'Sure, here it is.'

In my frenzy to call Hayley, I hadn't thought to bring a pen, so I told her to hang tight while I searched for one. As my daughter rattled off the seven-digit number, I scribbled on a notepad.

'Got that?'

'Yes, thanks. One more thing ... I need Lyndell's number. I need to speak to your mother.'

'No problem!' She was smiling her arse off; I could hear it in her elated voice. She gave it to me ten seconds later, as it was also in her book.

'Pumpkin, I couldn't love you any more if I tried. Thank you!'

'I'm glad I could help you with whatever it was you needed help with. Take care. Love you.'

'And you. Bye-bye.'

After I got off the phone to Hayley, I called Rosie Weatherstone, thanking my lucky stars that she answered quicker than David had; I was that excited I needed to piss.

'Hello, Rosie speaking ...'

It was on the tip of my tongue to say 'You should already know who this is', but I refrained. This needed to go smoother than the lane of a bowling alley. I had no badge to flash her. No warrants to go snooping about her place. I had to be sweeter than apple-cinnamon pie. My life depended on it.

If there's one thing I know about people, it is that they hate feeling inferior. Cops have a certain way of speaking – always being the alpha. Yes, I wanted to come across as professional, but the preferred way to yield results was to speak to people like they were just a normal, average Joe Blow. But of course, I kind of was now, wasn't I?

'Hello, my name is Eddy Matthews. We've never met, but I saw your flyer about the Christmas in July dinner, and wondered if I may ask you a few questions?'

She took a moment to answer. 'Questions like what?'

'I am interested in the other side, see? And, well, um – look, I'm going to level with you ... I am a detective for the Penrith Branch.'

'A detective?' She chortled. 'What on earth does this have to do with the dinner, Eddy?'

'It's probably nothing – there wasn't an incident or anything – but from what I understand, there was an RSVP list to the dinner, wasn't there?'

'Correct.'

'And since I see your name on the flyer, I can only assume that *you* would have kept a record of said list?'

'Why, yes. Yes, I have the list.' She sounded mighty chuffed.

My heart jumped. If I had the list and I saw the names of even one or two of the victims, I could be moments away from making an arrest. Well – not me, but O'Brien and Jeremy. Fuck the credit; it was the principle of bringing down the bastard.

Licking my parched lips, I asked, 'And would I be able to see the list?'

'You still haven't told me why. And how do I know you're really a detective?' She didn't sound rude or curt; more or less covering her bases, I thought. She didn't know me from Adam, and let's be real, how often would a detective ask about a simple dinner?

'I've been on the force for over three decades. Unfortunately, for confidentiality purposes, I am not at liberty to divulge reasons why – just shitty protocol, I'm afraid. I promise I don't need a copy, just a quick squiz at the list of names. One brief glance, and then I'll be out of your hair.'

'Wait – Matthews ... Not *the* Eddy Matthews – father of Hayley?'

'One and the same, ma'am.'

'Please – Rosie.' She chuckled. 'Why didn't you say so? Of course you can have a look! I'll make you a copy. I also have photos.'

This was too good to be true. 'Photos?'

'My son was the photographer for the night. We love scrapbooking, and you're in luck because we haven't even put them in the book yet.'

This euphoric feeling was better than an orgasm. 'Rosie, you may be a lifesaver.'

'Eddy, please tell me what this is about.'

'As much as I would like to, seeing as how willing you are to help me, it could actually incriminate you.'

'Oh. I see.'

'Perhaps we can arrange for a time to meet up? Full disclosure: Hayley gave me your address.'

She chuckled. 'That's fine. How does tomorrow sound – say noon?'

'That sounds perfect to me. Thank you, Rosie.'

'I look forward to finally meeting you, Eddy. Ta-ta!'

After we disconnected, I took a moment to calm my erratic nerves. I was fucking onto something. My fingers tingled, but there was still something I needed to do first.

I picked up the receiver again and exhaled before I spun the dial.

On six rings, just as I was about to chicken out, Lyndell answered.

'Hi, Lyndell, it's Eddy Matthews – Ava's ... um ...'

'Oh. Hi.' Tone as flat as a discus. 'Suppose you want to speak with her?'

No, I called to ask you about chicken cacciatore. 'That would be lovely.'

She chucked the receiver down so it would cause discomfort to my ear. Jeez, what yarns had Ava been spinning? I was nervous as hell, like I was my nineteen-year-old-self about to take Ava's virginity. I'd been with girls before, but she was the only one who mattered. I recall wanting to rush, because I felt like I was going to explode in my high-waisted pleated trousers. And I remember my heart. It was all hers, every damn bit of it belonged to her. It was the hardest thing ever to go slow, and a few times I had to grit my teeth against the agonising thought of just fucking going for it, but I refrained. I can still remember she came close to weeping in my arms afterwards—

'Hello?' Hope soared through that one word. Or was that what I wanted to hear in her voice?

'Hi.' My throat clicked; I had to swallow. 'How are you?'

'I'm well. Dare I ask about you?'

I stole a shallow breath. 'Look, we need to talk. I need to come clean about something.'

'What's happened?'

'Nothing to be alarmed about.' Ha, what a joke that was. 'But we need to talk.' Glancing out the back door, I said, 'Meet me tomorrow.'

She hesitated. 'I can't. It's too late.'

'This isn't about *us*.'

'It's not?'

Was that disappointment? 'No. I know you've made up your mind.'

'What is this about, then? Are you planning to kill me?' She chuckled softly.

The corner of my mouth twitched. 'I thought about it.'

'Oh, Eddy ...' She sniffled, exhaling through the phone.

'Meet me tomorrow. You ran out, and I didn't have time to tell you things. Important things.'

'Do you have someone?'

'Tsk! It's like you don't know me at all.'

'Perhaps I don't, no,' she whispered.

Gritting my teeth, I inhaled through flared nostrils. 'Don't get me angry. I don't want to argue. Meet me tomorrow so we can talk.'

'Fine. Say lunchtime?'

'Ye— oh, actually no, that's no good for me. Dinner?'

'What are you doing at lunch?'

'Don't ask me questions if you won't answer mine.'

'Like what?'

'Like how's Bill?' Even saying the prick's name made my jaw clench.

She tutted. 'Oh, for heaven's sake ...'

'Let's not argue. Please. Have dinner with me.'

She hesitated. 'Where and when?'

Gripping the receiver in one hand, I gave Bogart the thumbs-up with the other as he stared from the back door. 'Seven o'clock – Sizzler.'

'Okay.'

My heart palpitated. 'You'll be there?' God, it felt weird to be asking my own wife out for dinner; I had to keep a close check on my tone. Over-anxiousness doesn't suit anybody. Not even a man begging to be with his wife again.

'Yes. Yes, I will have dinner with you.'

Dry swallowing, I closed my eyes in utter relief. 'Great. I'm glad.'

'I guess I will see you tomorrow, then.'

'Until then, please, *please* be careful and keep your wits about you at all times.'

'You're scaring me – tell me what's happened.'

'Promise me!'

She deliberated, testing my patience. 'Promise.'

'Good. Until tomorrow, little lady.' When I hung up, I banged my head against the wall with a great gush of pent-up relief. I closed my eyes and focused on steadying my breathing. Dinner. Tomorrow. With Ava. With my *wife*. But before that, Rosie. *Please, Rosie, may you save me from this hellhole nightmare.*

CHAPTER FIFTY-TWO

EATING BREAKFAST IN MY study the next morning, I felt like a man at a crossroads. I didn't know what that Sunday would bring. Nervousness in the form of bile coated the back of my throat – the type of nervousness that turns your stool to liquid. I was fearful, too. Of what I was capable of, if Rosie had the answers I sought. How would I explain it to O'Brien I'd still been working on the case after having received strict orders to stay away altogether? At the end of the day, it would be case solved – drinks all around for catching the bastard who had been terrorising our community.

After downing my plate of eggs and bacon on toast with a cup of bitter coffee, I had a bath so I could also shave. My suit and tie gave the appearance I was still an active homicide detective. I even dabbed a spot of cologne behind the ears; it was like going on a first date – hoping that everything went well and I got lucky afterwards. I returned to the study and prepared a dossier to present to Ava tonight at dinner. There was no telling how that was going to go down, either. It was clear from yesterday's phone call tensions were still high. There was now a toxicity between us, and as much as I was still hurting over her leaving,

I did not want to engage in a public spat over steak and wine. I wanted it to be as amicable as possible, but I was worried that seeing her again and then, thinking of her lover, there'd have been less tension during the Cuban Missile Crisis. I'd chosen a public place to help entice her to the idea of meeting up with me. Perhaps she was now a little scared of me after I had pulled out the knife.

I put the latest letter from 'Jerry' into the file I was going to hand to Ava tonight. It still left a rancid taste in my mouth when I thought about him being there at the cemetery, watching me.

Time moved slower than a sloth. I could barely concentrate on anything except the clock, but time gave me an opportunity to clean up the mess I'd created in here yesterday. Broken glass and stationery littered the floor.

Despite tidying up, I still had a good hour to go before I was due to set off for Rosie's place. So, what else was there to do in my suit at 10:30 am? Vacuuming, of course. At least it got my mind off things; the humming and concentration of picking up every dog hair and mote of dirt was sort of therapeutic. There's something I never thought I'd admit to.

Once the clock ticked over to 11:30 am, it was time to leave. Sure, I'd arrive early, but why wait any longer? What else was I going to do; squeegee the windows? Clean the bathtub?

At ten to twelve, I pulled up out the front of Rosie's house and hopped out of the car. The house looked welcoming, one that would beckon anyone inside for milk and bikkies. That's the vibe I got from one glance at the one-storey fibro house on brick stilts on this warm summer's day. The front yard, encased by a yellow-brick fence, was immaculate. A lot of tender, loving care had gone into this place. Not just the house, but the front yard and gardens, too. The lawn was a luscious green – the type that looked too good to be real. Adorning it were gnomes and ornaments, including a concrete boot with a mouse sticking out of the hole in the big toe.

I plodded up a path of white Cowra pebbles surrounding large circular stepping stones, which led the way to the awning porch. The front door had an angel-shaped knocker. Something about this place exuded good vibes. A tonic for the soul.

Opening the fly screen, I rapped on the front door, bypassing the knocker.

A moment later, a woman wearing a floor-length burgundy dress answered with a smile as welcoming as the house.

'Eddy?'

'Yes, I know I am early; I hope that's not a problem?'

Her hazel eyes twinkled. 'Ten minutes? Not at all, don't be silly. Please, do come in!'

She stepped aside so I could cross the threshold. My nostrils were assaulted with the scent of candles and burning incense. I couldn't tell shit from sandalwood, but sometimes Ava used to burn this stuff when people were due to come over for a Tupperware party or for her Book Club buddies.

'Find the place okay?' She overtook me so we could walk down a short hallway and into a country-style kitchen. My eyes focused on her waist-length ginger hair until she turned to face me.

'Yes, no problems. Hayley lives near here.'

'That's true. I don't see her much now that she has Lucy, but it was so good to see her and the family at the dinner.' She brushed aside her fringe. 'Did you not want to attend?'

'Ah, well, I didn't get an invitation, to tell you the truth.'

'Is that right?' She motioned for me to take a seat at the teakwood table. I did so and inventoried the kitchen as she turned her back to me. It had a homely feel, like this was the way grandma's place should be – mind you, Rosie couldn't have been more than fifty. Still, it reminded me of a grandma's place. Lots of doilies and crocheted lace against a backdrop of oakwood. A purple butterfly wind chime took up much of her window space, and there were inspirational quotes sewn into cloth that hung about the walls. My favourite: *Life is 10% what happens to you and 90% how you react to it.*

'Tea or coffee?' Rosie asked over her shoulder.

'Coffee, please.'

She went to work fixing us two cups of coffee. It was the instant kind, but I was not here to critique her barista skills. I wanted to delve into things right away, but felt it would have been rude. Besides, I'd specified my urgency to her the day before.

'So, you didn't get invited, huh?' she said with her back to me, grabbing a jar of sugar to the left of her. 'Is that because you're a non-believer, perhaps?'

'Depends what you mean.'

She turned to me, leaning against the bench while holding the sugar. 'Do you believe in God?'

What should I say? After seeing what I have during this lifetime, I can tell you one thing: I may not believe in God, but I sure as hell believe in the Devil.

'I am psychic, so don't lie because I will know.'

Stifling a smirk, I said, 'Is that so?'

She nodded, eyeing me. 'Mm-hmm ... since I was a little girl.' Without taking her eyes off me, she placed the jar on the bench beside her. 'Tell me, what *do* you believe in?'

'Maybe it's because of all my years on the force, but I believe in the tangible. In things I can touch, see and hear, not take the word of a book that was written thousands of years ago.'

'So, you don't believe in Jesus Christ?'

I held her gaze as I tried to remain relaxed. 'Where is Noah's Ark? Or the Holy Grail? Or the Ark of the Covenant?' I shrugged slowly, to show I meant no offence. 'We don't even know where Moses' body is. We have no actual *proof* apart from a book written by man, and what do men do best? Lie.'

She cocked an eyebrow. 'That is fair enough – I am not trying to make you a believer.'

I sat forward. 'But you believe?'

She smiled serenely as the kettle whistled. 'Oh yes, I know He is real.' She swivelled her neck to the left, grabbing a mug with an angel printed on it.

'And what about spiritualism? How does that tie into it?'

She circled the lip of her mug with an index finger. 'People like me are different from others because we're seen as sinful. As something akin to Black Magic. We believe in God, but we also know that once we pass on to the other side, then life is eternal. Our body is just a vessel for us in this lifetime, but the soul can never perish. And that's what I do for a living. I communicate with the other side. I see things I could have no possible way of knowing.' She poured steaming water into our mugs; the high-pitched sound soothing.

'There's a lot of controversy around it, from what I've been reading.' I tried to say this as diplomatically as possible, because whenever someone says 'No offence', it's right before they say something that is, in fact, offensive. But whether she was psychic or not, she was human first and foremost – she could see through my bullshit.

She smirked as she poured the milk. 'It is said they are not the spirits of our loved ones, but ghosts. Evil spirits trying to take over the living. I know that is hocus pocus.' She walked to the table and handed me my coffee.

'Thank you.' I took the mug and placed it before me on a daffodil coaster, peering into the swirling mass of brown and white clouds.

'My pleasure.' She sat opposite me and shuffled the chair forward. 'It gives people hope. And it also takes away the fear of death – and why is that? Because people will always be afraid of the unknown. Of what death really is.'

'Our spirit passing on to the other side?'

'It is true. I can see people around you now.'

I raised a brow. 'How does it all work, then? Tell me.'

'It's different for everyone. But I really *am* a psychic medium. I daresay I could not keep up with the mortgage if I were a charlatan. And yes, there are many fakes out there. For every one legitimate psychic, there may be twenty who are phoneys. But people need to believe in something. People need to hang on to their loved ones in order to go on. But it is real, Eddy. We're surrounded by the dead all the time. Psychic abilities have been tested and proven.'

'Hmm …' I blew on the steam before taking a sip.

'I can see you don't believe.'

I eyed my mug as I placed it back on the coaster. 'I wouldn't say that, necessarily. We have used psychics to assist us with an investigation or two.'

'And how did that pan out?'

'Hit and miss. You ever hear about Gerard Croiset?'

She shook her head, bottom lip protruding. 'I don't believe I've met him.'

'You wouldn't have. He was some Dutch clairvoyant flown over to help solve the disappearance of the Beaumont children – remember that Adelaide case from '66?'

Her whole body shuddered as a hand went to her throat. 'Who could ever forget it?'

'Right, well, he stated the kids hid inside some barn thing and they fell down a shaft, which has now been turned into a factory, and guess what? There's no way to get to them, as it's all concrete. There's public pressure to do whatever the hell Croiset said and excavate the concrete floor to search, but I can tell you right now how that debacle will turn out. Convenient, if you ask me. Picks an inaccessible place and then pisses off back to his country – now he's passed on. Shame on him, and shame on others like him – forgive my scepticism here.'

She threw her head back and laughed. 'Never let it be said I don't appreciate honesty. But they should have called me. I am quite good. But you have to understand it is not an exact method. I cannot tell you every single thing you need to know. I cannot tell you the winning lotto numbers – which is a fairly common one asked.'

'How can you see some things, but not others?'

Her eyes flew to the ceiling. 'The brain can handle sense data the other five senses cannot. Spirits find this sixth sense the easiest to use as a channel of communication; however, what is not commonly understood is that thought transference is a physical phenomenon. Thought has substance, and the substance of thought is vibrations. Our body is like one great big antenna with specialised receivers to collect these specialised vibrations. Like radio waves, these vibrations can't be seen, although they are around us. Everything in this world has its own unique vibration, its own special frequency, and because each frequency is different, the brain is able to physically sort one thing from the other. When a ghost communicates via telepathy, it is no more or less than the transfer of vibrations from one mind to the other – hence the result of communication.' Her hazel eyes pinned mine. 'Shall I prove it?'

This was not what I goddamn wanted. I didn't want to waste another second on this subject, but the coffee had been made and I wanted to seem as cooperative as could be.

'Let me ask you, what harm is there? If I am no good, then call it a hoax. But if I touch on subjects I would have no way of knowing, then you may walk out of here a happier man.'

But I didn't know that, see? She knew my daughter. I'd never once heard Hayley speak of Rosie, but that didn't mean they weren't close. How much do we really know about the friends our children keep company with?

Offering a close-lipped smile, I said, 'Sure. Why not?'

She licked her lips, lowering her mug. 'Come with me.'

I followed her, convinced this was all a big set-up – that she'd be asking me for money before this visit was done. Ah well; I owed her something for the list, which she had yet to give me. Hadn't even mentioned it, in fact.

She led me into a room to the left of the kitchen, a room with a round table and a purple velvet tablecloth. A red candle sat burning in the middle of the table, a black cloth concealed the window, even a curtain of red beads covered the doorframe. A chill set in; it was nothing like the friendly and warm atmosphere the rest of the house exuded. There were only two seats on either side of the table.

'Sit here, please.' Rosie pointed to the chair closest to the door, so my back would be to it.

I sat, mentally rolling my eyes. *How much cash do I have in my wallet, anyway?* My thoughts were disrupted when Rosie wrung out her hands like she was flinging off flaming oven mitts, and then she rolled her head down and around. With closed eyes, she emitted a low moaning sound, like she was on the verge of climaxing. To refrain from smirking, I clamped my jaw.

Her eyes popped open. 'Ready?'

Yes, and let's make it snappy! 'Only if you are.'

She pulled out the chair and sat, inhaling deeply through her nostrils. She sat back and regarded me. She regarded me for so long I thought she'd had a stroke. I shifted uncomfortably because she wasn't even blinking, and then I wondered if she was trying to recall everything Hayley ever made a comment about in passing. But then, as I was about to tell her to just forget it, she opened her mouth.

'There's a young girl around you.' She said it so low that it sent the tiny hairs on the nape of my neck standing on edge.

My breath caught in my throat, lodged there by the fear of the unknown. Was I supposed to say something back? Was it a question or a statement? I'd never done this before.

Before I could respond, she looked at me with worried eyes, her mouth downturned. 'Brutal. I see violence. She was young. Blonde.'

I sat forward, mind reeling with questions. I don't even recall that I blinked. Had Hayley told her about Abigail? Although, why would she? Why *would* she?!

Rosie's eyes roamed the carpet as if searching for something lost on the dark floor. 'I am getting an A.' Her hand went up in the air as though air-writing this to me. She squinted, eyes still narrowed and focused. 'Someone is drawing me a picture of an A. I'm certain it's an A.' All the while her hand made the motion of the letter. Then she looked at me. 'Does this make any sense to you?'

My heartbeat was louder than my breathing. 'Yes.' Wide eyes glued to hers. 'Go on.'

She closed her eyes, then frowned. 'I am cold. I am freezing; submerged in water.' She wrapped her arms around herself. 'Creek? *Lake*! I am in a lake. My whole body aches. Raped.' She opened her watery eyes. She swallowed, hand to her throat. 'She was raped.'

I, too, was on the verge of tears; one blink and they'd be let loose. 'Go on …'

Her eyes went to the right-hand side of me, as though looking at someone. 'He is … friendly-looking.' Her voice had still not elevated above a certain register.

'Who is he?' I whispered, my eyes bulging as my fingernails dug into the tablecloth. 'Tell me.'

She shook her head, trance-like. 'I don't know. But …' Her hands began working again. 'I am getting the feeling of familiarity. There was a cover-up, I think.' She spoke as though she was on drugs. Very slow. Very soft. 'It was hush-hushed. I think – I *can't* be too sure.'

My spine straightened; my clenched toes were throbbing. 'What does he look like?'

She pursed her lips, eyes still avoiding mine as her mind's eye showed her pictures I could not access. 'I can only see parts. Average height. White male. I can't … see much else.' Then she looked at me, shaking her head apologetically.

'Wait! Look harder, please!' God, I needed this more than 'Jerry'.

'Parents divorced. She blames herself.'

'No! No! Tell her—'

'Oh, she can see you.'

My back collided with the chair as the candle's flame flickered between us. An icy wind caressed my skin, like a lover's silk nightie, sending goosebumps from top to bottom. 'Pardon?'

'She can see you. She's right behind you.'

I turned. It was fucking stupid looking back now, but God help me, I did. There was nothing, of course, nothing except the red beads overhanging the doorframe. My breaths were coming in shallow and quick; my body gave an involuntary shudder as I grappled with these revelations.

'You have a picture of her,' she continued. 'I can see it through her eyes. I see pigtails.'

I turned back, cracking my neck. 'Yes! Jesus Christ, tell me! Tell me who it is, *Abbie*, I can put him away! I can make him pay, *please* tell me!'

She scrunched her face in concentration. 'I believe I'm hearing the word … uncle.'

My lips tried to speak the words my brain hadn't caught up to yet. '*What?*'

'Uncle,' she whispered again. She peered up, teary-eyed. 'It was her uncle.'

'*What?* Are you sure?' A million fucking titbits of information were sucked up into a cyclical wind tunnel inside my mind. *Her uncle? Raped her? He was married with his own kids – why? Why would he have done this?*

'I think so,' she whispered.

'You *think* so?' My palm collided with the table and she jumped. 'I need to know!'

'I-I don't … know for certain.' Her head tilted; eyes focused on the flicker-ing orange wick. 'I think she is showing me her uncle, but that doesn't mean it was *him* who attacked her. I see the letter B – but again, it doesn't mean he is responsible—'

B? I uttered a groan. 'Robert,' I said, panting; sweat trickling down my spine. 'She has an uncle called Robert – as in B for Bob.' I sprang to my feet; my chair fell backwards. 'I need to go.'

She glanced up at me with puppy dog eyes. 'What about your list? And the photos?'

My light-headedness unbalanced me as I stooped to pick up the fallen chair. Nothing else mattered to me, nothing!

Uncle Bob? No, it *couldn't* have been … he'd helped search for her! But then, I knew of cases where that had happened. It was sickening, but not uncommon. Hiding in plain sight. Looking for the one they themselves had murdered and dumped, joining in with all the other volunteers, sniffer dogs and specialists.

Rosie stood up too, and in the dull lighting, her pale face in the candle's flicker gave her the appearance of an apparition. 'I have them in a plastic bag, ready to go. And, I also printed a spare copy of the RSVP list.'

I raked a quivering hand through my hair, my other hand flat against the table for support as briny sweat trickled into my eyes. 'I cannot thank you enough.'

'You're very shaken. Are you going to be all right?'

Taking her hands in mine, I said, 'You may have saved my sanity. I am speechless.'

We walked out of that room and I took in a deep lungful of clean air to prevent myself from passing out. My knees shook like telephone wires during a windstorm.

'You must know I cannot always be one hundred per cent correct; even I'll admit this. Sometimes names and places sound the same to me. I can't always get a clear picture. But if I have helped you in *any* way—'

'You really ought to look at employment with the homicide department.'

Her smile didn't reach her eyes; we were both shaken to the core.

We headed into her living room, where she collected a plastic bag from a cherrywood table. 'I hope I can trust these will be returned – the pictures, I mean. I didn't make copies of those. And I suspect I could get in trouble for handing these over; I have no written consent from the guests to take their pictures for distribution, you see.'

'Understood. I give you my word.'

'In that case' – she handed me the plastic bag – 'may you find what you are looking for.'

CHAPTER FIFTY-THREE

IT WAS JUST after 2 pm when I arrived home. I didn't want to look at anything until I reached the safe confines of my house. I could have been watched, and even though I could have been holding proof of how 'Jerry' found his victims right here in my hand, Abbie took precedence over anything. She was the thorn in my side; I needed to solve it once and for all.

Once inside my study, I went straight to my filing cabinet. There, I took out all my copies of the police records pertaining to Abigail's case. Every bit of information I'd stored over the years was once again in my trembling hands. At my desk, I flipped through the mountain of paperwork. I tried not to look at the crime scene photos; instead, I searched for the witness reports and family member statements. I knew Robert had been interviewed because *I* had been the one to speak with him.

My hand quivered when I held his statement in front of me.

I skipped the questions and read his answers, absorbing each word as though reading for the first time.

Interviewee: Robert Anthony Jerkewitz

08:45 am. Friday, 7th January 1977, led by Detective Chief Inspector Edward Matthews, and Detective Snr. Sergeant John Barrie – Penrith Police Station.

'Where was I on the twenty-first of December? I was in Canberra for a conference.'

'My vocation? Travelling salesman.'

'My brother called me and told me about her disappearance. I raced back as soon as I could. When they discovered her in the lake, we were shattered. We were devastated that someone out there could have picked her up and done these unspeakable acts to her. She was such an innocent and sweet child.'

'I participated in the search because I felt that, as her uncle, it was my duty. I had a loyalty to my brother like no other. Abbie was my only niece, and my kids adored her, of course.'

'The last time I saw her? Yes, it was only a few weeks before she ... Abbie told me what she wanted from Santa – a Ballerina Barbie because she liked the tutu and red ribbon.'

I sat back, staring at the words he spoke to me years ago, in Room 4, as we recorded the interview on a tape-recorder. I did not have the tape in my possession, but I didn't need to; this transcript was sufficient.

Could it really be him? He said he was in Canberra at the time. Trust me, we'd followed that up – I'm sure of it. There was a note in the file that his wife, Bertha, corroborated his story. He wasn't even in town when the murder happened. But when exactly had he left? The estimated time of death was only an approximation due to her condition. But her date of disappearance was due to the fact we collectively agreed she'd been killed shortly after being kidnapped – he wouldn't have kept her around. It was a snatch, rape and drown. As simple as that. That's all it took for her to leave her earthly abode – a place where she was supposed to die of old age, not after six years.

We found her a week after she'd been dumped – 28th December. How could it be possible that Robert was in Canberra at the time? Either he and his wife were lying, or Rosie had fucked up. But Rosie had gotten everything else right, right down to Abbie's pigtails!

No, I'd left Rosie's house a believer, after entering as a sceptic. Didn't she say she lived her life off the money her customers gave her?

But then ... what if Hayley had mentioned it?

What if Rosie had re-read a few newspapers with my face and name attached to it? What if she'd done her research on me beforehand? It was a national outrage at the time; the public wanted vengeance. Of course, Rosie would have read about it and seen my photo in some articles – thanks to Liz Fulton, who vilified me for not finding Australia's most hated killer.

No! Rosie said 'B' as in Bob. How could she know that? And even if my daughter *had* spoken to Rosie about the case, I hadn't divulged much information to begin with. Not even Ava knew the half of it. I tried to keep the two worlds separated ... ironically, now I was separated from *them*.

It was all doing my friggin' aching head in, so I closed the file and grabbed the plastic bag that Rosie gave me. Inside, there was a box of photos and one piece of paper. As I took out the RSVP list, I inhaled and exhaled steadily before unfolding the paper, and searched the long list of names, a blob of sweat hitting the page:

Quentin Harris
Madeline Barker
Faith Habberfield
Mary-Jane Kelly

John Kelly
Valerie Burnett
Mark Andrews

Breath catching in my throat, I stopped. I'd almost missed it; my mind was turning to mush. I swallowed and grabbed my highlighter, gliding the yellow tip over his name as my flesh tingled. Mark Andrews. The third victim. As my knees bounced, I continued. No longer surprised, but expectant:

Jimmy Bleeker
Susan Bleeker
Harold Longstreet
Elliot Pratt
Megan Blatchford

I went back. There! Elliot Pratt.

'I've got you now.' I ran the highlighter over Elliot's name, lips shrivelled. 'I have got you!'

Then I swallowed deeply on seeing my family's names. I stiffened at the sight of Ava's. And no Bill had been associated with the booking, so Hayley was honest about that.

I read past them, determined to find the rest – my panting blowing against the paper.

Maxine Prance
Stephen Prance
Norman Colbert

BINGO! I highlighted his name, and then continued while picturing

O'Brien's face when I told him the news. A sneer spread across my lips. 'This cat is coming for you, fucker!'

Candice O'Rourke
Ian McLaughlin
Raúl Martínez
Juanita Martínez

I sat back with the list of over ninety names, but only six highlighted. This was Christmas, Easter and my birthday all in one. It was too overwhelming; finally we were narrowing in – Merry fucking Christmas to me. It was indisputable proof they had all attended this dinner. And now, I had to zero in on who would have been there to commit such acts after meeting these people. It also meant someone on the list would become a future victim. One of these people had a date with destiny. But who?

I took out the thin cardboard box from the plastic bag and sat back as I held the collection of 4 x 6-inch photos.

The first image was of the hall's interior. Nothing out of the ordinary, just a large communal hall with ceiling fans, overhead fluorescents, polished floorboards with a few scuff marks, plus banners and streamers placed around the room. A small Christmas tree covered in baubles stood in the corner, underneath hanging mistletoe. Very nice, Rosie. Nice touch.

The second photo showed Rosie speaking to guests, her waist-length ginger hair shining – these people wore stickers with their names in black ink.

The third image was another of Rosie and a few other masked attendees, the next was an elderly couple smiling for the camera – his nametag said Hubert – hers said Anna.

The next was a photo of people lining up at a marquee – by the looks of it, it was for palm reading. Masks concealed the guests' faces – glittery ones, feathered ones, some scary-looking, like something you'd only wear on Halloween night for trick-or-treating.

I flipped through the next few and stiffened at a photo of the Martínez couple. It was morbid to think only a while ago they were out and about, sipping on champagne, living life to the full. The reports stated they'd quarrelled, but I did not get that vibe here. Raúl had his arm draped over his attractive wife's shoulder. They had their masks in hand as they spoke to one man, caught amid something that appeared humorous. Their smiles were wide, their eyes half-closed.

Pushing on, I vowed to seek justice for those who had fallen prey to this madman. The next five photos were nothing too exciting, but the sixth was a spearhead to the heart: my family. Everyone except me. Why hadn't I been invited? They looked to be having a genuine blast – Ava *did* resemble Ava Gardner with her hair all done-up, her green silk dress flowing. God, she was a stunner. How had I fucked this up? And Hayley, the apple of my eye, her brown hair shimmering like her ever-ready smile. An unmasked and unsmiling Heath stood between Ava and Lorraine, who wore a distractingly low-cut top, and I noticed David was furthest away from her – no doubt a deliberate act by Hayley to keep her husband's wandering eye out of Lorraine's cleavage.

A grin fought its way onto my face over that. But I also had to push on; there must have been at least a hundred photos in my hands. I flipped over the next few images, studying every face. I'd forgotten to ask Rosie about her son; he'd slipped my mind. He'd been the photographer, but I had yet to see him – not that I should have known who he was, or what he even looked like. But if Rosie was around fifty, then presumably her son would be around, what – thirty? Give or take.

I dropped the image of a young mother holding her son up to a masked man, when my body went rigid, and my back arched like a frightened feline.

I grabbed the photo and stared at a familiar white and black mask – the same one that had peered up at me with that God-awful, sinister smile across the street from my house.

It was a mainly front-on view, but slightly turned so only one side of his face was visible. The picture was not a George Hurrell by any standard, but enough to see that he was dressed all in black, and the camera's flash highlighted his visible eye. So, they *were* light brown, but they looked older – not young and sparkling – on par for the formalised writing in his letters. He was not some fucking kid, let's put it that way. His nametag said 'Jerry'. Had I seen those eyes before? How could you tell one set of brown eyes from the next? Wasn't brown the most common eye colour? Everyone in my family had them; even O'Brien and Jeremy had brown eyes.

I grabbed the RSVP list off my desk and eyeballed all ninety-odd names. There wasn't a single man by the name of Jeremy, Gerry, or Jerry. How far in advance had he pre-planned this?

And more importantly, how did he select his victims? Had they spoken to him? What was his selection process? How could he pick them out of a crowd and decide 'You're next'?

There were many lingering questions, but I was closer than ever before. And to think I'd wanted to blow my brains out not too long ago; now, here I was bouncing back like a cat dropped from a ninth-floor window, landing on my feet with crucial evidence in my hand.

I flipped through the rest of the photos, but saw no more of 'Jerry'. He was somewhere on this list. Now it was all about the process of elimination. Start at the top and work down. One by one, the males on this list would be tracked down and questioned.

I raced to the kitchen phone and spun the rotary dial. Thank God they had not bugged my phone; I was more grateful for that than anything.

After six rings, it went to the answering machine.

'Hi, you've reached Janice and Mitchell O'Brien. Unfortunately—'

Gritting my teeth, I hung up, opened the fridge, and was pissed off to see no beer.

'Gimme a break, for fuck's sake!'

Pacing the living room back and forth, I tried to place the items of information I'd obtained into separate mental files. It was too much overwhelming shit. Uncle Bob/Robert. Jerry the Jester.

I needed booze like a diabetic needs insulin. The wall clock said I still had a few hours to go before dinner with Ava. I would not miss that for anything.

I looked up Sizzler in the Yellow Pages and then made the reservation. With not much left to do, I settled on taking Bogart for a walk. I needed to clear some space in my head. With two recent revelations, I was in danger of power overload. Short circuit – no thank you!

I ran upstairs to change my shirt and tie. No-one wants to look like Clark Kent when they're taking their dog for a walk, because there's one word for people like those: wankers.

Within five minutes, Bogart and I were strutting our stuff along the Nepean River, blending in with the crowd, no way of knowing who the person huffing and sweating next to us was. To distract my overloaded brain, I slipped into musing: Does that middle-aged guy watch kiddie porn? Does that young man dress in his wife's nylon stockings while she's at work? Does that mother pushing the pram sneak out behind her husband's back to visit his brother? As O'Brien said to me on the phone: 'You just never know; it's always the ones you least expect.'

CHAPTER FIFTY-FOUR

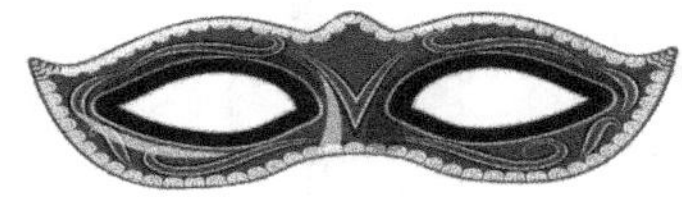

WAITING FOR AVA was as nerve-wracking as waiting to get test results back for an unusual lump detected by your doctor. The files were on me, and my beer was half-empty. That sickly butterfly effect was in full swing in my stomach, prancing around like dancers on a stage. I kept checking my wristwatch as my fingers drummed the table. Sizzler was already at full occupancy. The air was redolent of fried onions and char-grilled sirloins, the chatter like incessant cicadas on a warm summer night. Glancing at the people seated around me, I asked myself, How many of them are sinners? How many men are here wining and dining their wife while keeping a whore on the side named 'business trips'? How many people have stolen? How many have lied? While glancing about the animated faces as they guzzled wine and swallowed food, I deduced: we are *all* sinners. Every. Single. One of us.

It was eight minutes past the hour when Ava walked through the doors. She gave her name to the man at reception, and he pointed to me. She smiled at him and gave her thanks before making her way through the tables. At that,

I downed the rest of my beer.

Ava's knee-length yellow dress with white flowers swayed as she walked, and a touch of pink tainted her lips. Her hair had been blow-dried, and I waited for the characteristic lopsided smile she usually reserved for me.

When I stood, I had no idea how to proceed. Should it be with a kiss? A hug? A handshake? She gave a lukewarm smile and hugged me briefly. Too briefly for my liking, but enough to get a whiff of her sweet perfume. A new brand, one I'd never smelled before. A gift from her lover?

I squashed the notion; we had important things to discuss.

'How are you?' I asked, sitting while staring at her.

She eyed my now-empty beer glass with foam around the sides. 'Fine, thank you. And you?'

'I've been better.' She licked her tight lips. 'Thank you for coming.'

She shrugged nonchalantly. 'I'm curious to hear what you have to say.'

'You want to get right into it? Can we not have an enjoyable meal over some drinks, too?'

She regarded me, then nodded. 'I suppose I am a bit peckish.' I handed her a menu. 'Thanks.'

I'd already studied the menu during the minutes I'd been sitting here, waiting to see her again.

'Where's Bill?' I knew as soon as it tumbled out of my mouth like explosive diarrhoea, it'd been a bad idea. It was yanked out of me by its own accord. But as much as I thought I'd blown it, she answered me civilly.

She peered up from the menu. 'Tonight he is volunteering at a soup kitchen. Satisfied?'

'How nice,' I said through clenched teeth.

She eyed me for a moment before gazing back at the menu. God, why couldn't my glass of beer be the magical refillable kind? I was so parched I thought about sucking the condensation from the table where my beer glass had been.

After a minute, she put the menu down, then folded her hands together on the table. 'I know what I want.'

'So do I.' I wasn't talking about food, but I don't think she cottoned on.

She pushed the menu aside. 'What do you need to speak to me about; is it about Heath?'

I inhaled, clenching my toes. 'Thought you might like some answers.' I placed my hand on the file beside me on the seat. 'I haven't been entirely honest with you.'

Her shoulders pulled back. 'About what?'

'About the reason I have been acting so weird as of late. The reason for the amped-up security on the house, for one.'

'It's regarding the case you're working on.' It wasn't a question.

'Yes.' Clearing my throat, I held up my other palm. 'Before you get mad, think about what was going through my mind. About how much I love and care for my family, and would do anything to protect them. I know you think I don't care, but I do. And I was worried sick, but in doing so, I wasn't behaving rationally.' I picked up the folder beside me. 'Here ... read this. But first, would you like a drink? I think you'll need it.'

She took the file off me. 'Yes, please.'

'Your usual?'

She nodded, swallowing – already looking paper-pale.

'Okay, you start on that and I'll be back.' I slid out of the booth and headed towards the darkly lit bar where a middle-aged man stood, wiping the inside of a beer glass with a white cloth. 'Another one for me, good sir, and I'll have a chardy for ... the lady.' *For my wife!*

The barman smiled, revealing his gapped front teeth. 'Coming right up.'

While he went to work, I glanced about the restaurant. Its clientele would not be the likes of high school kids, out for a night on the town. The demographic was probably around thirty and upwards. People had dressed in their finest attire, which was fine by me, because I could fit in. I'd changed back into a suit after the river walk, looking every inch the homicide detective I used to be.

'On your tab, sir?'

'Thanks.' I grabbed the drinks in each hand and took off. Ava's eyes darted across the page, absorbing every word. She was still on the first letter from what I could gather.

'Here,' I whispered, placing her wineglass on a coaster. I started on my second beer, looking at her as she read. When she was done, the waiter made his way over. She glanced up at the young lad with braces.

'Howdy, folks, are we ready to order?'

Ava's pallor mimicked the white of a nun's habit, but she nodded just the same.

'You go first,' I said to her.

Her rumpled forehead told me she was trying to act social in an unusual situation. 'Um ... I'll have the, ah, lobster mornay, please.'

I knew she'd go for it, and that's what I'd selected, too.

'Excellent.' He turned to me. 'And for you, sir?'

'Make it two, please.' And then my eye caught his name badge: *Jerry*. I gazed into his eyes as my stomach clenched. I blinked once. Twice. And it was only when I shook my head that I saw it actually said 'Terry'. His name was *Terry*, and thank fuck for that. God, this was getting to me ... I needed another – wait, I already had a second beer. I reached for it and took a deep gulp.

He bowed and held out his hand for the menus. I placed them in his hand as I drank from my glass with the other. Terry walked off, jotting down the order in his notepad.

She glanced at me with a hard look and thin lips, yet her eyes conveyed a nervousness. 'The killer wrote to you?'

While using a knuckle to remove foam from the corner of my lips, I bobbed my head.

'And you didn't think this was important enough to tell your wife?' She breathed through her nostrils and turned back to the file, shaking her head. She picked up the next letter, and kept quiet as she read the fresh revelations, but her set jaw said she was on the verge of abusing the crap out of me.

Ava finished that one and closed her eyes before shaking her head again. As she picked up the third letter, I sat in anguished silence as she read on, the sound of cutlery on chinaware tinkling around us, laughter floating like pollen. Even as I drank more beer, my gaze never left hers. In this lighting, she appeared fragile. It didn't show the fighting spirit she possessed, but she looked like a suspect being questioned – a guilty one at that. There was a spotlight on her face from a hanging downlight, and her complexion resembled a seasick sailor.

After finishing the third letter, she put it back in the file. She reached for her chardonnay and downed the lot in one go. She placed the glass back on the table with a *clink*.

She closed her eyes and tilted her head as she began. 'So, he's been inside our house. He knows our phone number; he knows what we do – that you take Bogart for walks along the river.' She opened her eyes. 'And for the record, I never left any darn window or door open!'

'Look, that's not important now.'

She let out a short, sarcastic laugh. 'I love what you consider "important"! You'd think some crazed psycho entering our home would be important enough to tell your wife, but there you go ...'

'Can you at least try to understand why I didn't tell you?'

'Because you're pig-headed and always think you can do things your way?

That you'd rather do things alone than tell your own wife?'

'No. I was frightened for you. I thought I could protect you without having to worry you.'

She banged her small fist on the table, causing my beer to quake. 'You should have told me!'

'Perhaps I should have, but that can't be changed now.'

She glanced about the room, licking her lips. I'd guess, to her, any one of these fine people could have been Jerry the Jester. 'So, what now?'

'Ava, I think I've found him.'

She turned back to me. 'Really?'

'Yes. And you may know him, too.'

Her eyes widened. 'Me?'

'I don't know his real name. He only goes by Jerry.'

'You used to work with a Jeremy – sorry, "work" present tense.' I smiled bleakly. 'Other than his nickname, I don't know any other actual "Jerrys".'

'Not him, of course, but someone who has assumed the alias Jerry – from *Tom and Jerry*.'

Her fingers pressed against her left temple. 'The cat-and-mouse cartoon?'

'Exactly. I'm the cat, he's the mouse. Do you remember when you all went to the Christmas in July dinner at Springwood?'

She frowned momentarily, but then nodded. 'Yes, of course.'

'By the way ... why didn't I get invited?'

She blinked, her hand lowering. 'I did invite you! I invited you to everything.'

'I don't recall this conversation.'

She smacked the table lightly. 'Because you had your head stuck in a book at the time! You laughed it off, then went back to reading your stupid crime book. I even remember that it was called *Crimes of the Twentieth Century*!'

I thought back, and yes. Yes, I *had* read that book months ago. Had she really asked me? For the life of me, I could not remember. Now the haze surrounding the image of our marriage dissipated. It was hard to accept it, but stuff like this really shone a light on how I'd behaved as both husband and father.

Guilt swirling within me, I reached for my beer. 'Okay, I believe you.'

'I did invite you. I always invited you to those things, but you were never interested.'

I swallowed, returning my beer to its coaster. 'Look, it's not important now, but what is, is I have proof he was there with you that night.'

Her eyes enlarged. 'Jerry?'

Leaning forward, I said, 'Yes. I spoke to Rosie today.'

Her back stiffened, her head tilted. 'Rosie Weatherstone – the host?'

'Yes.'

Her brows shot north as her lips parted. 'I didn't know you'd been speaking to her.'

Shrugging, I said, 'Is that a problem?'

'Did you go to her house?'

'Yes.'

She sat straighter. 'Was anyone else there?'

'Jealous?'

She scoffed, then leaned forward and looked around before turning to me. 'Don't be ridiculous, but you wouldn't be the first married man she's slept with.'

My back slammed into the wooden board behind me. 'Really? She didn't seem the type.'

'Why did you go to her house?'

'To gather evidence. And guess what I discovered? The RSVP list of all the attendees, and you know what? All the victims' names were on there. Everyone. They all attended *that* dinner.'

Her lips parted. 'You don't say!'

'Look' – I pointed to the file – 'I included the list in there, too.'

She grabbed the pieces of paper and flicked through until she picked up the sheet and gazed over the names.

'Did you know any of them?'

She shook her head, looking at the list. 'No, but there were many people there that night, and I mainly stuck to our little group.'

'What did you do? Who did you see?'

'You mean, what activities did I do?' I nodded. 'Um, I saw a fortune-teller and had a reading using runes. Both females.'

'I still don't know for sure *how* he selects his victims. I tried calling O'Brien to speak to him about the list, but until we know for sure how he does it, we have to warn every single person who attended that dinner. Any one of these people could be at risk.'

She gasped. 'Including *us*?'

'Yes. Everyone. I need to know the names of all the stallholders who were present. But in the meantime, I have a photo of him. See if you can remember him.'

She picked up the file again, and inside an envelope lay the picture of Jerry the Jester – the only one captured during this set of prints.

She lifted the flap and pulled out the picture, wincing. 'The mask certainly is ghastly.'

'Do you remember seeing him? Did you talk to him, perhaps?'

She studied it with intensity. 'I can't remember if I saw him that night, or whether I think I did because I've seen this sketch on the nightly news. This image is everywhere now. I can't be too certain one way or the other.'

'But you didn't see him at any stalls?'

She shook her head. 'No, not me – look, his nametag says "Jerry".'

'Yes, but look at the list.' I pointed to it. 'No-one there is named Jerry.'

She inhaled through her nose. 'So, what do we do? Have you told Rosie?'

The usage of the word *we* was not lost to me. It gave me hope. More fool me. 'No, I am waiting to speak to O'Brien. But I need to warn these people – the sooner, the better.'

Her lips twisted. 'What now?'

I waited until a waitress carrying a drink tray walked by. 'Move back in with me.'

Her lips parted as colour rushed to her cheeks. 'I … I can't.' Her eyes diverted from mine. 'It's too late for us.'

'No, it's not. You are my wife, and to me, you always will be.'

'I'm …' She inhaled as her eyes flew to the ceiling. 'I'm with Bill now.'

'Fuck him. I want you back. I want you under the same roof as me so I can protect you in case anything happens. I'd never forgive myself if—'

Her tears descended. I handed her my napkin from the table. 'I'm not happy with the way things are.' She dabbed her red-rimmed eyes, tears absorbing into the napkin, turning it almost see-through.

I leaned across the table and grabbed her other hand. 'I will do whatever it takes. And if you say yes, then tomorrow I am booking us tickets to Aruba. Hell, invite the kids along, I don't mind. I *will* make this work between us.'

She continued to dab her leaky eyes and let me hold her other hand. 'You don't want me … you just don't want anyone else to have me.'

'That is *not* true. That is so far from the truth, it's insulting to me you say that.'

The waiter walked over with our two plates. '*Annnnd* here we are.' Terry placed our meals in front of us – Ava first, then me. 'Two lobsters. Enjoy!'

'Thank you,' I said to him, staring at the bright red-shelled lobster.

'Looks delicious,' Ava said, shielding her face.

'You're welcome – would you like another drink, ma'am?'

I cleared my throat. 'Yes, one chardy for the lady, and another beer for me.

Thanks, mate.'

Terry retrieved his notepad and pen from his apron's front pouch. 'You got it!' He sauntered off to the table adjacent to us.

I turned back to Ava as steam rose in front of my face. 'I miss you.'

She lowered her head, clenching her hands into tight fists. 'I feel like there's a part of me that has died from being married to you.'

I sat back in the booth as my jaw lowered. What a slap in the chops.

'I'm sorry, but that's the truth.' Her eyes fluttered to the ceiling. 'Oh God, I kept every letter you ever wrote. There were times when I stared out the window of my parents' place waiting to see your headlights coming up the road.' She closed her eyes. 'I couldn't believe someone as handsome as you could ever be interested in me.'

'Are you kidding? *I* was the lucky one!'

She continued like I hadn't even spoken. 'But then one day it slowly started to die, like a flower deprived of water.'

It wasn't easy bearing the brunt of her words, but she needed to get it off her chest, so I listened to every hurtful thing she had to say, despite the discomfort it caused me. Truth was always a bitter pill to swallow.

She opened her eyes and stared at her lobster, not seeing it, just staring. 'The feelings I had grew dull. There were many instances where I was waiting at home, and you never turned up.'

'I was on patrol,' I said, choking on my words. 'Not sleeping around with other women.'

'And when we had Heath, I thought that maybe you'd want to be at home more often.' She shrugged, face contorting. 'But I was wrong. You were promoted and soon I felt like a single mother.'

I leaned forward, the smell of lobster plugging my nostrils. 'I never meant for it to go down like it did. And when I was on the job, of course I thought about you.'

'And then you started forgetting important dates and anniversaries. I felt so alone.'

I stared at her while servers walked past, patrons rose to pay their bills, or made their way to use the john.

'Our marriage was not how I pictured it. But I still stuck by you. I still made your dinner every night; I still did all the housework, *and* I took care of both of our children while you were out. I put my life on hold for you. Now I feel like I have a second lease.'

I lowered my weary head. No longer did I have an appetite for this lobster with green beans and potatoes au gratin.

'We did go on family vacations,' I said, speaking to my thighs. 'Remember when we did that road trip to Ayers Rock with the kids and we camped out under the stars? Or when we crossed the ocean on the *Spirit of Tasmania* – you and the kids were seasick, remember?'

Her hands flew up. 'You can't say a one-week trip compares to fifty-one weeks of neglect!'

I reached for my beer, swallowed, then slammed the empty glass on the table. 'No, it doesn't. You're right. I was a shitty husband. But do not mistake the fact that I sincerely love you and the kids. No Bills or Bobs could ever change that fact. We shared our lives together.'

'But the happiness ...'

'I can still remember when I first met you in Gardenia Café in Toongabbie, you know that?' Because I could see she was not eating, either, I picked up my cutlery. I didn't want for us to quarrel; I had planned for it to be an apologetic gesture in the hopes she would see I needed her in my life.

'You were so damn cute and innocent, and I thanked my lucky stars I got to you before anyone else did. I knew upon first sight that you were "the one", do you know that? As clear as day, I could picture us growing old together, surrounded by grandkids.' I shrugged. 'But, if you're not happy …'

I cut into the tender white lobster meat, smothered in melted cheese and parsley.

She raised her napkin once again to her eye.

I shovelled a forkful of green beans and lobster into my mouth and peered up to catch her sniffle. She placed the napkin on the table and grabbed her cutlery. Thank Christ for that.

'Here we go, folks,' Terry said, and Ava reached for her wine before he'd lifted it off the tray.

'Thanks,' she said, bringing it to her pursed lips.

He placed my beer on the table, giving me a quizzical look.

'Thanks, mate,' I said, reaching for my third beer of the night.

Ava placed her glass on the table, picked up her knife and fork, and sliced. 'It's not like I wanted to give up. I did try.'

'Then don't give up.'

'I'm with Bill now.'

'*Fuck* Bill! You're not his wife, you're mine!' I stared at her, feeling the pulse in my neck throbbing. 'Have you slept with him?'

She held her fork mid-air, her greasy lips shimmering. 'It's not a passionate relationship.'

I closed my eyes and inhaled. 'Don't say that, it's too weird – you in another relationship.'

'But I am. It may be platonic, but I am seeing someone else.'

I opened my eyes. 'Not anymore. I need you, Ava. I will book us the tickets to Aruba tomorrow, I swear to *God* I will.'

She reached for her glass of wine, and in the process of me shovelling lobster meat into my gob, I glanced throughout the seating area as my second nature to survey my surroundings kicked in.

'I just ...' she trailed off.

Something up ahead arrested my attention and I stopped chewing. By the register, a man stood with his arm around his wife's waist. Ava's voice was now distant; I couldn't hear a single thing she said. My eyes were glued to Robert Jerkewitz – Abigail's uncle.

My eyes couldn't be trusted; I'd even seen 'Terry' as 'Jerry'. Yet, Robert was paying the bill, about to leave, and I was mere metres away from it happening.

'Eddy?' Ava said. At least I think she did, far off in the distance carried away by the wind, it seemed.

But I was rigid with haunting memories of Abbie's bloated body. My mouth hung open, my eyes pried wide in disbelief, and heat boiled below the surface of my skin. I had purposefully chosen not to talk about that case here tonight; I wanted Ava to know only what she needed to. I was prepared to take care of Robert myself. And now, leaving the restaurant was the man I had been chasing for eight years – a man who now had a face, a man who'd haunted my dreams. Something grotesque akin to the monster Cthulhu possessed me as my fingers clamped around my knife.

And before I knew it, a blast of warm air hit my face as I bounded through the front doors, chasing after him as I spat out my half-chewed lobster. I spotted him and his wife walking across the parking lot hand-in-hand, her heels scraping against the tar. Pulling Abbie's body out of the murky water was the last image my mind's eye conjured before I power-walked up behind him and stabbed him in the ribs before the couple even had time to respond to the approaching footfalls.

'This is for Abbie,' I whispered through clenched teeth as his warm blood cascaded over my hand that had plunged the steak knife into his ribcage. I kept it there as he fell to his knees with a grunt.

I think his wife screamed, or it could have been another female witness. My knife scraped against his bone as I kept it in him while I stood, then raised my heel and slammed the sole into the protruding knife handle. A red mist washed over me, like fog flowing down the mountains on a winter morning.

The guttural sound he made was something I could not dare try to describe, but I had never heard another sound close to that being emitted by another man. And I hope I never do again.

'Stop!' a female screamed. But I was too far gone; I knew that as I raised my heel again and slammed it into the side of his head.

Blinding, fiery rage dominated every part of my former self. I dropped to my knees as people screamed around me, but it sounded far off, like echoes from the past.

'Your own niece? How does it feel to die?' I saw nothing but red. 'Rapist!' I repeatedly punched him in the windpipe as more piercing screams erupted. His thick blood soaked into the knees of my pants while I kneeled beside him.

I clutched his throat and choked him until someone grabbed me around the neck from behind with the crook of an arm and hurled me backwards.

The stars winked at me sporadically until a man sat on top of me, bounding my hands above my head with his own. 'Calm down!' I grappled with this man sitting on my chest. 'Stop struggling!'

'Fuck off! He's a murderer! A child rapist, you *prick*!' Spittle flew from my mouth. I continued struggling, and something flickered in the man's eyes over my words, it said: Oh shit, what have I done? He turned back to Robert, and I, too, looked at his wife crouched beside him, screaming at the blood on her raised hands.

'Call an ambulance!' a bystander screamed.

'He's dead!' a female yelled.

And because of that one second where this hero on top of me dropped his guard, I threw him off; call it adrenaline. The guy fell onto his back and I jumped to my feet. I then planted the boot into his ribs as I turned back to Robert, intending to finish the job. For Abigail. For me.

When I stormed back to where he lay, his wife screamed: '*Martin!* Can you hear me?'

I halted abruptly, as though I'd hit an invisible wall while her falsetto wails filled the night sky – hazy mind trying to decipher what had passed through it.

'Martin! Oh, God! Oh, my *God*, please help – someone help me!' She collapsed onto his motionless form. I blinked once and stood there, panting like an enraged beast, as adrenaline continued pumping through my body, riding the waves of my blood. I shook my head. *No.*

She turned back to me, panting. His blood streaked her face. 'Why? What do you want from us?' She wailed open-mouthed before throwing herself over her husband, shielding him from any more harm. She wept uncontrollably, a piercing scream that shot straight into my head and heart. I turned around as the red neon lights from the restaurant flashed on and off with an electric buzzing. I could now pay attention to the fact at least a dozen people milled about, murmuring incoherently – cupped hands over mouths; a mother shielding the horrified eyes of her children. I looked inside the restaurant where people gazed in disbelief from their booths, like I was a chimpanzee on this side of the glass at a zoo. The man at the reception desk had the phone to his ear, hand flailing about like a conductor as his lips moved.

'Don't leave, Martin! Stay with me, puh-lease!' She gasped for breath. 'Help is coming, honey. Martin ... Martin, oh, *God*, why?'

A lady pushed through the crowd in front of the restaurant and stared at me. Ava, with a hand to the base of her neck, glanced at the dying man on the ground, then back to me. Tears fell from her wide eyes as she collapsed into the man standing next to her – he grabbed her and held her upright, her face a mask of bewilderment – her eyes peeled open, lips parted.

Staggering off, I squinted away sweat from my eyes, feet shuffling along the tar, kicking up pebbles and fallen leaves.

'He's getting away!' some bright spark from the group yelled.

'Are the coppers coming or not?' a man screamed.

The car park grew darker and darker as I travelled away from the restaurant and towering streetlamps, but there was another exit around this corner. After swallowing bile, I made my way, like someone on a rocking boat on an angry ocean, through the rows of parked cars, as in the distance from behind, wailing sirens approached.

Despite the sweet taste of payback, I knew that at that precise moment, my life would never be the same. And it had all happened in a flash. I had been so fucking certain it had been Robert. Sure of it. Bet my life on it. Felt it, didn't I? Maybe he'd changed his name in the past few years?

The sirens hit a crescendo, and that's when I hot-footed it. I needed to clear my head before I spoke to anyone, because this was it. This was some real, big, deep shit, and I was only making it worse, but I needed more time. I was onto it! This could bring them all down, if only—

I needed to change course, as the patrons would tell the police which way I headed. Instead of going straight ahead, I backtracked and took a left, down through the dusty alleyway that led out to one of the main streets. I kept running and staggering, looking behind me periodically as sweat slid into my eyes, causing them to sting. At any moment, I expected to see flashing red and blue lights chasing after me, but I realised it had been an ambulance siren, not the police. Not yet. That would buy me some time, at least. I kept on, at least giving myself the chance to mentally break down what had happened. In one instant, I was dining with my wife, the next I was in the car park stabbing an innocent man.

'No!' I yelled, huffing while sprinting. No, it wasn't Martin; it was *Robert,* the child murderer! Maybe the wife was covering for him? Maybe she knew who I was because she remembered me! Yes, that was it, now I knew – she remembered me from the investigation. That's what I'd tell the police when they caught me.

'That *bitch*!' I roared, running as far away from the scene as I could while wheezing. 'You knew! Didn't Rosie say there'd been a cover-up? Ha-ha, I've got you now! You lied! You changed your name from Robert to Martin, you *fuck*!' I waited for a red Ford Falcon to pass me before darting across the road. Home was to the right-hand side of me. No, not yet. I needed to call O'Brien – he needed to know what I'd discovered. Those people on the RSVP list were in danger. This would be my only hope – but *fuck!* I'd left the files and photos back in the restaurant with Ava. No matter! I had it all in here. I tapped my temple while running, blending in with the sinister shadows like some night stalker. Now came the police siren. I would not head home now. Not tonight, even. Tonight, I had to find a payphone and call O'Brien, and tell him the good news about Robert. Not Martin – the lying *bitch* – but Robert Jerkewitz – the one who killed Abigail.

CHAPTER FIFTY-FIVE

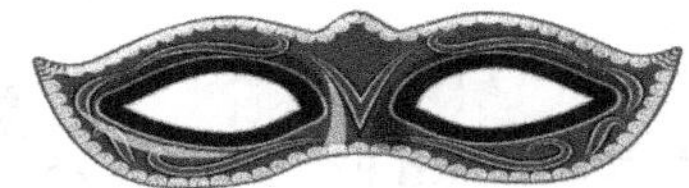

ACCORDING TO MY wristwatch, it'd ticked over past midnight, which meant it was Christmas Eve. I'd stayed hidden behind a foul-smelling dumpster for hours, and during that time I'd found a discarded bottle of rum. Only a few inches of amber liquid remained, but I'd picked it up and swallowed what was left. I'd stayed out of sight, having time to think. I'd turn myself in tomorrow, but only after I called O'Brien and relayed everything about what I had learned. It was important to notify those who had been at the dinner; one of them had a date with the Grim Reaper. I'd blown it with Ava, but if only she would heed my advice and keep her wits about her. And Christ ... what was going to happen to Bogart?

The sirens had long since died down. I'd polished off the rum and was feeling drowsy from those beers and lack of sleep, but I had to keep alert. This was a waiting game.

Just as I'd decided to press on and find a payphone, a ginger cat sauntered down the alleyway. I'd peered out moments earlier to check the all-clear when I had seen it, looking for food scraps.

'Got nothing on me, pal,' I said. The cat peered up from a squashed Hungry Jack's paper cup, hissed, then ran the other way, but as it did, a pair of headlights rounded the entrance. I sat back as my heart raced. I moved my whole body to shield it from view behind the dumpster. The tyres rolled along the ground, making its way up the alley. Back against the cold steel, knees to my chest, closing my eyes and praying to God. The tyres crunched various bits of debris – broken glass, sticks, paper cups, as it approached.

'Not yet,' I whispered. No, I wasn't ready to turn myself in. Not now. I was so close. I waited with bated breath in a state of anxiety as a white Mitsubishi Delica drove past my hiding place. My body tensed, my breath quickened, but thankfully it drove on, and I let out an elongated, gusty sigh when I eyed the name stamped over the van's back doors: WYNDLAM FLOWER DELIVERIES.

Only after it made a right at the furthest end did I allow myself to breathe. I peered out the side of the dumpster – now I had the all-clear.

Hopping up, I staggered along the dark alleyway, an alleyway that smelled like urine and faeces, the walls covered in bright neon graffiti with Prince's iconic purple symbol. Thankfully there was a tap, which I used to wash my bloodstained hands. The water was freezing, but it was a relief to rid myself of the dried blood. I wiped my wet hands on my pants and turned off the faucet.

I hurried towards the direction where the van had turned. Peering out from behind the corner of a brick building, I saw no-one else about; not even a damn helicopter patrolling the skies with a searchlight.

I slid along the side of the jagged brick wall, peering back and forth as I made my way towards Henry Street. This was called hiding in plain sight, with the station on High Street parallel to me, but I was certain they'd be at my house, waiting, searching. No way would they assume I'd be anywhere near such a hot spot; it was my stroke of genius.

I sauntered along Henry Street with my head down and collar up, avoiding showing my face at all costs. Most of the shops adorned with Christmas decorations were closed, except for seedy pornography stores and a jazz bar, but even that had a small occupancy. I walked in virtual darkness when I stumbled upon a shop with a red neon sign on the door reading OPEN.

I suppose it was like seeing the Christian cross when you desperately need to ask for penance. I stopped and took a proper look inside the store called ESTHER'S PLACE.

In the two shopfront windows on either side of the door, books were displayed and a poster hung in the left-side window of the zodiac signs displayed around a circle. The books on display pertained to witchcraft. I took a step back and walked to the other window; as far as I could see, no-one was in the dimly lit store. This window contained more books: *A Guide to Fortune Telling*; *How to Read Your Destiny*; *Tarot Cards Explained* and many more. A poster stuck to the window showed images of tarot cards placed in a circle with the name of the book and artist inside that circle.

Taking a step closer, my heart rate tripped as I focused on one image. A cold seizure hit my body. In front of me was a picture with a caption at the bottom: THE HERMIT. It was an elderly man all alone, holding a staff and a lantern in front of him. As I peered at it, the man's face morphed into Elliot Pratt's.

My skin developed goosebumps as my body gave an involuntary shudder.

'*What the …*' I whispered as it all came into startling clarity. The next picture below it had a caption: THE TOWER. A large grey tower stood ablaze, having been struck by lightning. A man and a woman were falling from the tower, but what got me was there was also a crown that fell from the tower. But that didn't make sense. The crown was not at the murder scene of Juanita and Raúl Martínez; it had been on the body of Mark Andrews. Still … it was a crown.

I scanned the other images and saw TEMPERANCE – the image on the card showed an angel with cups of flowing water. *Water?* I thought – *The water flowing from Norman Colbert's en suite!*

I looked more thoroughly at the image and two things made my pulse quicken: on the angel's chest was a triangle, and on its forehead was a circle.

'Holy fuck!' I whispered as a young couple in Santa hats strolled by, arm-in-arm. I was too exposed here; I needed to hide inside on the double.

A bell attached at the top tinkled as I pushed the door open. I was going out of my mind with jubilance and disbelief; I had done it. I *finally* solved the missing piece.

Jerry the Jester *had* been following instructions, like I'd assumed. He'd used tarot cards, placing the props from his chosen affiliation.

As I closed the door behind me, I was inundated with the scent of incense sticks burning and the sound of meditative music. Two bookshelves facing each other stood on either side of me. To the left was a table covered in crystals and rocks; to the right was a glass cabinet containing good luck charms, tarot cards in different packs, and a row of candles of all different shapes, sizes and scents.

'Hello.'

I turned as a woman approached. Her flowing white dress reached her ankles, exposing her bare feet; her light-brown hair was long and frizzy like a mad professor.

Clearing my throat, I said, 'Oh, hi.'

'Welcome,' she whispered – her voice like a tranquiliser dart. 'I'm Esther. How can I be of service?'

'Eddy.'

She bowed. 'Eddy, welcome.' God, she looked and sounded like she was as high as a cloud.

'Yeah, ah, look …' I swallowed, buying time, still not completely comprehending. 'I am interested in tarot cards.'

'Oh yes, that is a preferred favourite for many of my customers.' She walked between the bookshelves towards me.

'Well, see, I don't know much about them. How do I play?'

She stood before me, and even in this dull lighting, it showed the airy-fairy look in her eyes.

'You don't play them; you read them. I can teach you.'

'Well, I was wondering, do you have a book I could squiz through?'

'Yes, of course, we have many. Come with me.' She turned around and walked back through the aisle between the bookshelves, over towards her counter. Behind the counter hung a curtain of black beads, just like in Rosie's place. A large red candle perched on a gargoyle's head, which I thought would seem more fitting in Dracula's castle, burned beside the cash register. Behind the counter stood a display cabinet of jewellery, with pendants, earrings and rings. A few posters adorned the walls, and under the glass display cabinet, where we faced each other, were rows of incense sticks and other assorted spices, all bagged up, ready to chuck into any bubbling cauldron.

'I have one I show the curious who enquire about such things. It is not for sale, but I am happy to let you look over it as a guideline, then you can ask me anything you like.'

'Thanks,' I said as she walked backwards through the beads. Blinking once, I shook my head; this Esther lady was a bit too freaky for my liking. But not long after her disappearing act, she came out carrying a battered book that looked like it had been written at the turn of the century.

No wonder it wasn't for sale.

'Here,' she said, flipping the book over and then placing it on top of the glass cabinet so I could bend and read. 'You will find everything you need to know. And then, of course, I have many books that you can purchase if you took home a tarot pack.'

'Thanks.' Trembling with adrenaline, I reached for the book. There was a table of contents in the front, and a foreword by the author. Then there was a section on INTRODUCING THE TAROT, which rambled on for a few pages, explaining all about the astrology and kabbala. It dissected the difference between a major arcana versus a minor arcana.

Step Two was HOW TO BEGIN; Step Three was CARD LAYOUTS, then there was the chakra spread. I blew hot air out of my mouth, hopping from foot to foot, wiping away the sweat tickling my cheek. I just wanted the friggin' answers all at once.

Step Four was CARD INTERPRETATION: THE MAJOR ARCANA, which started off with The Fool on page thirty.

My body jolted at the first card. There, in plain sight, was a red feather. And a dog.

'Holy shit.' A hand flew to my rumbling stomach.

'Are you okay?'

'Huh?' I looked up. 'Oh, sure. Um, do you mind if I grab a pen and a piece of paper, please?'

And a bottle of whisky, I wanted to ask, but didn't want to push my luck.

She leaned underneath the register to a hidden shelf and pulled out the stationery.

'Thanks,' I muttered, placing the yellow pad beside the book in front of me, where I jotted down:

Ian McLaughlin - The Fool.

'Are you looking for something in particular?'

'Actually, yes, Esther. What is the significance of this being upside down?'

As I looked up, she grinned. 'The reversed meaning.'

'Pardon?'

'It's reversed to what you see now. It explains it on the next page' – she turned the page – 'each card is different.'

REVERSED MEANING – *The Fool reversed brings out his irresponsible side, as his mouth works ahead of his brain. The reversed Fool leaps without awareness, and so becomes the literal idiot, sabotaging his chances due to desperation and irrationality.*

Standing taller, I ruminated. Ian had accused his girlfriend Candy of cheating on him with some bloke, and it turned out the bloke was a homosexual. Was that it?

'You look a little shaken, Eddy.'

Waving a hand, I shook my head. 'How many cards in a deck, Esther?'

'Seventy-eight – twenty-two for the major arcana, the minor has fifty-six.'

'Wow.' My lids flickered. 'Okay.' I went back to the book, flipping over pages, studying each one until I stumbled across The Emperor. The tarot card depicted a man on a throne with a crown, a red cloak, and the ankh in his right hand.

I flipped the page.

When in reverse, The Emperor is excessive in his demands, and represents the negative traits associated with traditional masculinity, such as being domineering, greedy, controlling and even cruel. The reversed Emperor does not know where to draw the line …

Mark Andrews was cheating on his wife. He had a beautiful family, but it wasn't enough.

Grabbing the pen, I jotted down:

Mark Andrews - The Emperor.

Esther played with her hair, picking up strands, finger-brushing the tips while I flipped through the book as ethereal music filled in the silent gaps.

'You're not interested in these books for your personal use, are you?'

I flipped over from The Hierophant to The Lovers, and halted. 'No, I am not, but I will buy a book off you after this. In the meantime, I just need to find what I am looking for.'

'So, you'll buy a book?'

I peered up, smiling. How could she have known that a pleasant man like me took away someone's life? 'Yes, I'll buy a book. Why don't you find one like this where it explains everything?'

'Excellent. Business has been slow lately – despite it being Christmas.' She took off down the aisle of books behind me as sirens wailed in the distance.

'Make it the most expensive one, in that case,' I yelled as I studied The Lovers: Adam and Eve and the Archangel Raphael looking down over them. There was the snake. Garden of Eden. Lovers ... I flipped the page.

When The Lovers card reverses, relationships go out of balance, and the shadow side of your personalities enters the equation. A relationship in crisis – there may be betrayal, inequality, and dishonesty.

Man, I was cooking with gas now. This was indisputable. God, this was liberating. My heart and head had been shackled, but now I was free. Finally. Fucking. Free.

Juanita and Raúl Martínez - The Lovers.

Page 66 featured The Hermit.
When reversed, you may be feeling alone and unsupported ...

Elliot Pratt - The Hermit.

Esther returned with a giant book. 'Twenty dollars. But it's the best one out there.'

'That's fine; I have the money, but listen ...' She walked behind the counter and leaned in close. 'Do you think it'll be possible for me to use your telephone?'

She surveyed me. 'Why? There are payphones ...'

I shook my head. 'I will give you ten dollars if—'

'Done. It's out the back.'

Grinning, I shook my head. 'You beauty. Thank you; I am almost done here.'

Her eyes dropped to the pad. 'Looks like you've got a long list happening there. I'm glad you're finding it useful.'

'Sweetheart, you have no idea.' I went back to the book.

Page 86 showed Temperance – the card displayed on the poster in the window. The water. The circle and triangle. I had practically pulled my remaining hair out trying to decipher what it all friggin' meant. Remember when I first spoke about fate? If I hadn't killed that guy, it would never have led me here.

'Esther, how long have you been open?'

'Since ten o'clock.'

'Sorry, I mean, in general. This store.'

'For three years.'

'Wow.' And I hadn't known it existed. And why would I? I never surveyed the shops as I drove past; I surveyed people. And even if I had seen this shop of voodoo and magic, I would have dismissed it. Yes, I'll admit I would have laughed at the thought. And now ... after everything Rosie told me, my eyes had been opened wider than ever before. I saw our existence in a whole new light.

Temperance reversed shows imbalance and unfairness in relationships, and problems with money ...

Norman Colbert - Temperance.

There, I was done. I closed the book and looked at my list. No denying this. Not for a second.

'All done now?'

'You have no idea how much you have saved my life, in more ways than one. This' – I brandished the notepad – 'will save my reputation, and my marriage.'

She frowned. 'Really?'

'I could kiss you right now, that's how happy I am! But I need to make that important phone call – actually, two quick calls.'

'Um, would you mind ...'

'Oh! Of course.' I grabbed my wallet. I skimmed through the notes, and it occurred to me I'd skipped out on paying for the meal. Funny thing to think about, huh? But it's true, I had. I'd withdrawn money from the bank in preparation for Sizzler. I always paid for Ava whenever we went out. God, what was Ava thinking right now? Was she on the blower to the kids, telling them she watched me stab and beat a man to a bloody pulp outside the restaurant? Was Bill holding her, kissing her, telling her everything was going to be all right?

'Eddy?'

I peered up. 'Sorry. Um – screw it, here's a fifty.' I handed Esther the fifty-dollar bill.

Her eyes widened. 'Wow. This is too much, just for a book and phone call? Wait – where is it to; not overseas, I hope?'

'Parramatta. The other will be to the taxi company.'

Her shoulders relaxed and her eyes softened. 'Oh, in that case, go ahead. And thank you for the generosity, friend! Merry Christmas.'

I walked around the counter, through the waterfall of black beads.

'Just through here,' she said as I found myself in a small cupboard-type space before Esther opened a door on the other side, which led to a small kitchen area.

'You keep the phone out here?'

'There's usually more than one person on duty in the shop, so yes, it is kept in the staffroom.'

'Suits me fine.'

'Take a seat,' she whispered in her hypnotic voice. 'Would you like a tea or coffee?'

The phone sat on a square table with only three seats, as it was pushed against the wall. I picked up the receiver, shaking my head. 'No, thanks.' I spun Mitchell O'Brien's number on the rotary dial and closed my eyes as it rang.

'Hello?' Shit. Did Janice know about me being kicked off the case?

'Janice, hi, it's Eddy.'

'Eddy? You okay?' Her tone was one of sympathy; no hint of sleepiness considering the hour.

'I'm not too bad, thank you. Is he there?'

'Yes, he got back not too long ago. He misses you. He tried to call you a few times, but he said it didn't even ring out, so he assumed you'd taken it off the hook.'

Bunching up my face, I said, 'I did, yes.'

'I'll get him.'

I glanced towards Esther. She gave me the thumbs-up with questioning eyes.

Smiling, I nodded: yes, all good. She squealed over my good luck, then turned around to the cupboard and reached for a herbal tea bag. On the kitchen bench near a small sink stood a silver urn – red light illuminated, ready to go.

I placed my hand over the mouthpiece and whispered to her. 'Esther?'

She turned on a smile. 'Yes?'

'Changed my mind; mind if I grab a coffee?'

'Of course! How do you like it?'

'Milk and sugar, please.'

She squinted hard. Then she made her way over to me, index finger rising.

I leaned back, my pulse quickening. 'What?'

She leaned in close, her eyes mere slits. 'There's blood on your neck and ear.'

Shit! 'Oh, I was helping a mate who busted his nose earlier on at the pub.' I rubbed my skin.

She leaned back and waggled her finger. 'Fighting, I guess?'

I rolled my eyes and sighed theatrically. 'Yeeees. Drunk.'

She nodded, but pursed her lips disapprovingly. 'I thought so.' She walked off, shaking her head as the receiver picked up at the other end of the line.

'Eddy? How are you?' There was no mistaking his relief.

'Mate, I cannot even begin to answer that. I am up and I am down, but ... take a seat for this ... I know who he is.'

'Who? The Prop Master?'

'You bet your arse. I have all the evidence with me, except where he lives, or his real name.'

He laughed, then stopped as though cut-off midway. 'You're pulling my leg, right?'

'Nope. I need you to do the rest. You take all the credit – you and Retmeyer, I don't care. With a bit more research, you could nail him any day now. But I need to see you. Tonight.'

He moaned deep in his throat. 'Jeez, Eddy, you heard what Davies said—'

'Stuff him! Aren't you aching to find out what his motives are? How he met them? He knew them all, and I can prove it. I know where and when he met them.'

'Tell me ...' His voice deep and pinched.

'It's tarot cards.'

'What?' His tone in that one word conveyed the level of his confusion.

'He places the bodies on the bed upside down, staging them like tarot cards. I've got all the evidence I need.'

Esther glanced over her shoulder, her eyes wide with fright.

'Are you serious?' O'Brien said.

'It's all here. In my hand. I've done my research, now we need to talk. I promise it will be worth your time. Just gimme ten minutes to explain. No-one needs to know.'

He sighed, then groaned. 'Ten minutes, buddy. I can't afford suspension without pay—'

'I'll be there within half an hour.' I slammed the phone down. Liberation. Sheer liberation, but there was one thing that stood out ahead of the crowd.

The Jester said there was one person left. One more person to make an example of. Out of the ninety-odd people he met at that dinner, who the hell would it be, and why?

CHAPTER FIFTY-SIX

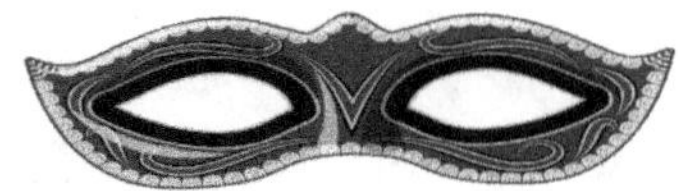

AFTER PAYING THE taxi fare and thanking the driver, I stepped out onto the kerb. All I had on me was the notepad and the book on tarot cards. I hoped Ava had taken the other files with her. But if not, Rosie had said she'd made a copy of the RSVP list, anyway. And although she didn't have a spare set of the photos, she'd still be able to retrieve the roll of film. Of that I was certain.

Standing on O'Brien's porch, I knocked on the door as the taxi driver took off. A split second later, O'Brien answered as though he'd been waiting behind it. He peered behind me with an outstretched neck before ushering me inside without another word, as though I was some hired prostitute he was worried the neighbours might see.

He closed the door, then locked it before turning to me. 'Eddy ...' He embraced me in a man hug. 'Oh Christ, I've been worried. I've felt guilty as hell for what happened that night. I've been trying to call you!'

I stepped away from him. Poor bugger was still in his suit and tie. 'Don't worry about it. Thank you for letting me come over.'

'Let's go into my office.'

'Where's Janice?' I asked as we made our way down the hallway.

'She's gone to bed; it's early morning. I didn't tell her you were coming over; I didn't want her to bombard you with questions.'

We stepped inside his office, where I took a seat.

'How are you?' he said sincerely, appraising me, the skin between his eyes pinched.

'I am better now I've found the proof we've been looking for.'

He fixed us a drink each, grabbing a bottle of his finest. 'How? What did you find?'

'It's a long story. But through a chance visit from Hayley, I found out everything.'

'Okay, hit me.' Ice cubes rattled against the glass before he poured in the dark liquid, but as he turned around, he froze. He raised an index finger from the glass he held and pointed to my shirt collar. 'Is that blood?'

My spine stiffened, but I held his gaze. 'That's another story.'

His mouth flew open. 'Christ, what is going on with you?'

'Listen!' He remained silent and wide-eyed. 'There was a Christmas in July dinner organised by a psychic medium: Rosie Weatherstone. They had this masquerade dinner at a hall in Springwood.'

He squinted. 'Spiritualism?'

'Yes, we were on the right track. I went to Rosie's house, and she gave me the RSVP list, plus photos from that night.'

'And?' He seemed to remember he was holding our glasses; he handed one to me and took a liberal sip of his own.

'And they were all on there.'

His forehead smoothed out. 'The victims?'

'Every one of them.' He blinked, taking it all in, eyes roaming the carpet. 'I even had a picture of the Jester in my hand. He was there that night, O'Brien; *that's* how he chose the victims.'

His pupils expanded. 'Where is the list?'

I licked my lips, tasting the sweet honey, shaking my head. 'There was an incident a few hours ago and unfortunately, I left those in the care of Ava. But I saw it with my own two eyes. He was there, scouting for victims. My assumption is he ran a stall reading tarot cards.'

'You really think so?'

'He was there in his mask, and that's how he chose his victims. I think they must have had their future read by him. They may have even joined up to some mailing list; something that would have given him their name and address. It also explains why there was never any sign of forced entry. They opened the door to their killer, exactly how he said in his letter.'

'But why kill them? What's the motive?'

'I think he was killing those who had dirty laundry. That was his justification. Every victim had shady dealings going on. I think he stalked them, then used tarot cards that closely responded to their reversed meaning.'

'Their *what?*'

I sat forward, now the sudden expert it seemed. 'With tarot cards, if you turn them upside down, it gives the message a whole other meaning. It's the exact opposite, like day turning into night. It's the amoral side, the one where people are deceptive, or cheaters, or liars and drunks.'

His mouth twisted. 'I don't know, Eddy ...'

'Here.' I presented him with the list. 'These aren't in victim order, but the order in which the tarot cards go. Like in a deck of cards – jack, queen, king, ace ... it's all there. The props. The upside-down bodies. The staging of it all.'

He took the pad off me and looked at what I'd scribbled down, taking another absent-minded sip as his eyes darted back and forth.

'Now, look at the book. Find the card, and you'll see the props that correspond with our victims' props. The red feather, even the goddamn water in Norman's bedroom.'

His head snapped back. 'If there's a list, then this guy must be on there, too.'

I shook my head. 'No "Jerry" is mentioned. He knew what he was doing. He knew that he'd walk in with a mask and a fake name, and then wait for people to come to him – Christ, do you realise that? People were lining up to set themselves up in his firing line. That's morbid as hell.'

O'Brien opened the book. He landed on Temperance and studied the notes. Then he moved on to The Lovers.

'I don't believe it …' he whispered, propping his arse against his desk.

'But it all makes sense now, doesn't it?'

'Except one thing: why were they all in their bedrooms? I get they let him in the house – he seemed innocuous enough – but how'd they end up in their own bedrooms?'

'That I do not know – maybe he gave false pretences of needing to view their sleeping conditions? Check the fuckin' *feng shui* – I don't know. Maybe he concealed a gun inside that briefcase of his. Once inside their house, he whipped it out instead of his tarot cards and forced them at gunpoint into the bedroom. It'd be easier for him to set the scene if they were already in there, as opposed to him having to drag their bodies.'

He shook his head, astonished, then looked at me. 'We need to warn the other attendees.'

I dipped my head. 'Agreed, but that is something I cannot do.'

'But how do we find this guy?'

'I need to speak to Rosie – she must know him. If he rented a stall at the dinner from her, he must have given his name. Maybe he even has business cards.'

He frowned. 'But his name wasn't on the RSVP list, you said.'

'No, but maybe this list was for dinner guests only? Maybe she has another list, one for the stallholders.'

'It's hard to picture some of these victims going to an event like that ... Mark Andrews; the slob, Norman Colbert. What interest would they have?'

'Maybe it was like with Heath: he didn't want to go, but Lorraine persuaded him. Mark Andrews didn't go with his wife; he went with his lover. Besides, everyone has a loved one we wished we could communicate with again, agreed? It isn't limited to one group of people.'

'You're right – spiritualism is for everyone; even Margot Average said she'd seen Muslims attend the church. Grief is ubiquitous; grief makes people do crazy things.' He clamped his jaw, his mind obviously working overtime as he looked at me again. 'I don't believe it.' He shook his head, giving a close-lipped smile. 'Thank you, Eddy. This is gold. This is *brilliant*. Macintosh Matthews has done it again, you bloody ripper!'

I settled back, wishing I shared his optimism. 'This cost me my family, this did. But I got there.'

He squinted. 'Your family?'

'Ava left. She found someone else.'

The paper fell from his hand, seesawing to the carpet as his mouth fell ajar. 'You're joking!'

My mouth twisted to one side. 'Wish I was.'

He continued to stare while I tipped the glass against my lips, craving that burning sensation.

'Who is he? When ... how?' He shook his head. *'What?'*

'Name's Bill-something. I don't think she's living with him just yet. But yeah, it's been going on for a while now.'

He opened then closed his mouth before opening it again. 'I-I don't know what to say ... Ava?' His eyes roamed the carpet. 'Really?'

'That's what I get for a lifetime of neglect. Anyway, that's another story.' I would tell him about Robert and what I had done to him, but not yet. Not at this moment.

'I'm sorry to hear that, mate.' He bent to retrieve the paper, then cleared his throat. 'So, this really is all to do with tarot cards?'

'At first I believed it was religious – and technically, I was right. It is to do with the realm of spiritualism. And it was so easy for him to find the sinners.'

'The sinners?'

'The ones who steal and cheat and lie, while they claim to be children of God. He's punishing them for their sins. Every one of our victims was involved in something they shouldn't have been.'

'He stalked them just to punish them?'

'That's what I believe. To make an example of them.'

'To punish them for their sins, yet he's a murderer?'

'You cannot reason with a psycho, as I said before. He's completely lost it. He has no touch with reality.'

'Tell me about it. I'm pretty sure slicing and dicing is a sin, too.'

'The thing is, how do we know who he is going to target next? He wrote me another letter telling me there would be one more.'

'He wrote you another?'

'After the car incident with Dean. But again, I don't have any of that on me. Just this.' I pointed to the page. 'But as I said, I can visit Rosie tomorrow.' *Before I hand myself in,* I wanted to add.

He raised a finger. 'I just have one question: were you his intended audience or not? Was this really all about *you*?'

'I believe he saw me as competition. Perhaps he tried to make it in the force but couldn't? Maybe he wanted to test the theory of Macintosh Matthews, to prove who the better man was? Who bloody knows, mate? It's been a mental mind-fuck this whole time – just the way he wanted.'

'But why *you*?'

'As a figure to compete with? Someone who is jealous of my accolades? Maybe some people are that fucked up they'd rather be remembered as a murderer than never be remembered at all.'

His eyes drifted away, nodding. Then he turned to me. 'Eddy, thank you for this, but you know Davies will shit bricks if he finds out you've been working on the case. Jeremy and I should take over from here. Davies is still going on about you running that dickhead off the road.'

'What ended up happening with that druggie, anyway?'

'Luckily for you, we managed a deal with Dean's lawyer. No arrests for drug possession in exchange for his silence. Department had to pay for a brand-new car, and we paid for his medical bills. He's fine, though; he'll probably live to the ripe old age of ninety.'

'That's how you know he's crooked.'

He stared, head tilting.

'If you die young and broke, then it's proof you've lived a saint's life.'

He glanced back at the book, shaking his head. 'You've really done it.'

'I know. Go get him.'

'At a more respectable hour, we'll contact Rosie, and I'll get Retmeyer to call the list of people who RSVP'd and tell them to be extra vigilant. We can't monitor them all; there's not enough manpower to keep everyone under surveillance. Just as long as they know what they're up against, and who knows, maybe they can give us more info about this madman. Did you see today's paper?' I shook my head. 'Whole new article in there by Liz Fulton about how we're nothing but useless pigs who couldn't catch a caged animal—'

The phone rang. He snatched it up mid-ring, no doubt to keep the noise from waking up Janice.

'O'Brien here …' He listened, then frowned. 'Yeah?' He remained silent, eyes narrowing. 'You're joking.'

The hairs on the back of my neck responded to his deadly tone.

'Okay … right. No, it's fine; thank you for calling me. What's the address?' O'Brien scribbled on a piece of random paper. 'That's not our jurisdiction, though.' He listened. 'Right, I see, and will you call Jeremy?' He paused. 'I think he said he was going out with friends tonight; I can't be too sure. Call him – get him on the scene; I'll be there soon. Bye.' He hung up and turned to me.

'Who was that?'

He shook his head. 'There's been another one.'

'Jerry the Jester?'

He bent his head, then rubbed the back of his neck. When was the last time this bugger had had a solid eight-hours sleep? 'Same M.O., props and all.'

I smacked my thigh, hard. 'Where?'

O'Brien shook his head, his hand flopping to his side. 'Eddy, you can't come with me, mate.'

I rose and stood, my face only inches from his. 'Don't do this to me. I was there every step of the way. I helped you with anything I could. I have lost Ava over this. Please. Please don't discard me, too.' He hesitated. 'I *need* this. I need to help bring him down.'

He exhaled through his nostrils as his eyes closed. 'Fuck.'

I grinned, heat swirling through me, flesh tingling. 'You won't regret it.' My heartbeat already erratic. 'Where?'

'Look, if you're seen with me and Davies is there, then it's bye-bye vacation—'

'I'll catch a cab.'

He frowned. 'Where's your car?'

Probably being combed over by Forensics right about now. 'Indisposed. But I'll catch a cab.'

'Davies will know that we've been speaking—'

'*Fuck* Davies! I'll say I was scanning the police radio.'

He shook his head, grabbing his jacket from the coat rack in the corner of his office. 'You're gonna get me killed one of these days.'

'Living is overrated. Where are we going?' I walked around to his desk and stared at the paper where he'd jotted down the address.

42 Evensong Cres, Bidwill

Frowning, I stepped back from the paper.

'What?' he said from the corner.

'Hang on ... I know this address.' I shook my head, screwing my eyes shut. 'I'm certain I've been there before.'

'You know the person who lives there?'

I placed my hands on my hips and threw my head back. When had I gone to this address? It wasn't too far back now, was it? But I was sure. Damn sure. *Bidwill ... Drugs ... Jerome.*

My eyelids tore apart.

'What?' O'Brien stared at me. 'Who is it?'

Shaking my head, I frowned as my gut tightened like a fist.

'Eddy, talk to me!' He held up a palm. 'Look, mate, I don't think you should come if you're acting like this. If you know this person, then you're not coming along.'

I inhaled through enlarged nostrils. 'He's a drug dealer by the name of Timothy Sharpe.'

CHAPTER FIFTY-SEVEN

O'BRIEN AND I had quarrelled in his office over whether he would let me come. But in the end, the determination in my eyes convinced him, and if it had so happened that I needed to pull a gun on him, then so be it. Jerry had taken all that was precious to me – now it was time to get it back.

In the end, he made the right choice and I sat in the passenger seat of his Fairlane as he sped along the Great Western Highway.

'This is a bad idea,' he murmured, overtaking a Linfox truck. 'I'm going to get in shit for this.' He propped an arm against the doorframe, head leaning on his fist as we approached a set of lights.

His car clock read 02:47 am, which meant I'd been awake for a shitload of hours. The moon took centre stage in the blue-black sky, and for the first time ever I thought how sinister it looked. Few cars were about at this ungodly hour, but the journey still seemed to take too long. 'Hold Me Now' by Thompson Twins played softly on 2WS as images of a dead Timothy Sharpe played before my eyes (not that I'd ever seen his face before).

'Explain to me again how you know this guy.'

As the lights turned to green, I glanced out the window. 'He's a small-time drug dealer.'

'Jeez, what the hell is a drug dealer doing, going up to Springwood for a spiritual dinner?'

He ducked back into the left lane and overtook a Shell oil tanker. I turned to him as wind rushed through the open window. Hang on, that was a damn good question. I blinked several times before turning back to stare at the open road. *Timothy Sharpe.*

There had been no Timothy Sharpe on the RSVP list. So, if Timothy hadn't been killed ...

I fell forward, a groan escaping from my tight throat.

'Hey!' His hand went to my shoulder. 'Hey, you okay?'

Invisible hands reefed the air out of my lungs. 'No ... please no,' I whispered, hands going to my sides as immense pain held me prisoner. I squeezed my eyes shut and leaned back against the headrest. 'Please Lord, don't do this.'

'Eddy! What the *hell* is going on? Are you having a heart attack?'

'Drive,' I whispered as the pain took a stronghold on my body. 'Hurry.'

'What the fuck is – *shit!*' He swerved, narrowly avoiding a taxi before straightening up again. 'Talk to me!'

'Hurry. Quick.' My head throbbed, my heart was on the verge of exploding, tears blurred my vision. All I could do was close my eyes and breathe through the mounting pressure, feeling the car rock as he changed lanes.

He opted for a gentler approach. 'Tell me what is going on, please.' But I couldn't verbalise it. It couldn't be true. No, not this. Anything but this.

I rocked back and forth, winding down the window fully to accept all the fresh air available. My mind was a maelstrom, thoughts as macabre as any Edgar Allan Poe story came to light like visions of the future, but I clenched my eyes harder.

'Stop it!' I yelled, shaking my head.

'Stop what? Fuckin' talk to me!'

A loud moan escaped me – it reminded me of the time I'd had kidney stones and ended up writhing on the floor. This was far worse than anything like that. A pain so raw it was rare.

'Hang on, we're almost there!'

After what felt like an hour, I pointed to the street he had to turn down before O'Brien's car screeched to a halt behind an ambulance. Members from the Mount Druitt department dotted the lawn like a kid's game of toy soldiers.

He turned to me. 'Right, remember—'

I jumped out of the car, running over to the crime scene. Neighbours wearing robes and hair curlers milled about on the pavement, some smoking, some even holding a stubby as though this was *Bidwill: The Late-Night Feature*.

'Eddy!' O'Brien screamed as he slammed his car door shut.

This couldn't be. It wasn't *him*. Anyone else in the world but him. Swallowing, I ducked under the crime scene tape as red and blue lights flashed across my face.

Nathan Davies stood out the front, dressed in a black suit. He spoke with other officers, but I didn't give a shit. I respected O'Brien, but fuck it. I'd deal with the consequences later, as with the Sizzler incident.

My feet trampled across the patchy lawn, and then down the driveway, where a policeman looked up. So, too, did Davies. His eyes widened, and that was the first thing I noticed. He wasn't angry, or ready to bash my head in. This was something else. Nevertheless, I pushed it aside.

'Stop!' Davies yelled, grabbing me by the waist mid-stride, pulling me back. 'Don't go in there!'

We grappled, struggling against each other, both emitting low wrestling moans.

'Don't! For your own good, I'm telling you, *don't* do it!'

Panting, I elbowed his eye as hard as I could. He yelped, and other officers rushed over while reaching for their guns. O'Brien approached, and the betrayed look in his eyes … I'll never forget it.

For a moment, Davies and I stared at each other, his palm held up to his eye. We both panted, and I expected anger to flash across his good eye. But there was only pity, and that's when my tears sprung forth. What had started as disbelief had skipped to highly plausible.

He sniffled and looked down. 'I am begging you, Matthews. Don't.'

'No!' He could no longer look at me as I stood there, shaking. 'You're wrong!'

He continued holding his eye as his harsh breathing dwindled. Two male officers went to grab me, but Davies held up a hand.

'Leave him.' Davies lowered his palm. His half-clenched, bloodshot, watery eye focused on me. 'Go.' He turned to face O'Brien, who had no idea what the hell was going on, and must have wondered why Davies didn't have me arrested on the spot for elbowing him in the face.

I turned around, my knees feeling gelatinous, and took in a deep, shaky breath, quivering with shock as my stomach squeezed tight, pushing bile up to my hot throat.

I crossed the threshold, a hand to my stomach, and began slowly making my way down the hallway. My head spun and through blurred vision, I saw people inside taking photos or dusting for prints. The smell of marijuana clung to the walls and carpet. The bedroom doorway loomed before me. I staggered towards it as officers turned to face me, confusion setting in. This was not my jurisdiction; this area belonged to the Mount Druitt department. But this was our guy; this was *my* scene. My knees buckled and I slammed into the wall, sending a photo frame crashing to the floor. The doorframe loomed an inch away, and a brunette female dressed in a deep-purple suit emerged through it, heading for the kitchen, where more officers milled.

'No-one else was home,' the woman said. 'The owner is out of town.'

My throat stung with the stomach acid crawling its way up, but before I passed out, I needed to see. With bated breath and my mind screaming, I turned the corner to see a message scrawled in dripping blood on the opposite wall. A message for me:

YOU LOSE!

Stephanie May

CHAPTER FIFTY-EIGHT

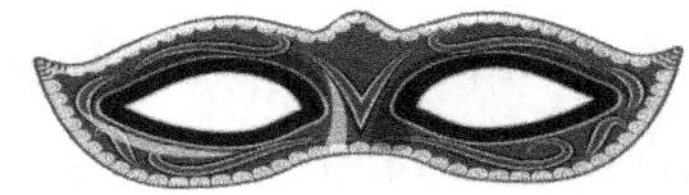

THE LIFELESS BODY of my son, Heath Matthews, lay sprawled on the bed. Every parents' worst nightmare had become my reality.

And that's when I turned and threw up on the shabby carpet.

I heaved up what little of the lobster I'd consumed (and the rum), all over the dirty carpet. I doubled over as the last bit of vomit erupted from my mouth, searing my oesophagus as pain tugged on every part of my body. The chatter in the kitchen ceased and confused whispers rang out. After spitting on the ground, I wiped spittle from my mouth with my shirtsleeve and turned as the brunette in the suit bounded down the hallway, frowning.

We locked eyes as I slammed the door in her face. Then, I turned around and surveyed the room through briny eyes. A mist seeped into my brain, blocking everything else out, a swirling cloud of red, blurring my vision, clouding my thoughts and clogging my senses. My sight. My smell. My hearing. Something transformed inside of me. Or died. One of the two. Then my head snapped back and my eyes flung open as I took in a huge gasp of oxygen and sighed it out.

That rancid acid taste in my mouth lodged there, making it hard to breathe. No longer was I Heath's father; I was now a homicide detective at a crime scene. Yes, that's what this was. This wasn't my son on the bed. I knew that. Same as I knew the man I had stabbed earlier was Robert. Not Martin – *Robert*, the child murderer – same as I knew it was a direct message to me: You lose.

'Ha! We'll see about that!' I chuckled. He thinks he got me. No, he hadn't. I was not licked yet.

And even as I walked around the bed, peering at the man with his throat slit and eyes wide open, I knew it was not Heath. Not my boy. God wouldn't do that to me. It was someone who *looked* like him. We all had a doppelgänger in life.

'C'mon and pull yourself together,' I whispered, breathing in through runny, clogged-up nostrils as I inspected the scene. The cut to the throat was so severe the head looked to be almost decapitated. And unlike in any of the other crime scenes, his face had been cut, too. A Glasgow Smile, the corners of his mouth cut with a knife to imprint a permanent grin. Just like Elizabeth Short A.K.A. the Black Dahlia's killer had disfigured her.

There was hardly any blood seeping from the sinister smile, which told me these cuts were made post-mortem. Next, I noted the props. In his pale hand lay a wand, and a red cloak draped his body. A mix of red roses and white lilies lay strewn around him.

Hmm … I wonder what card this could be. Thanks to Esther's book, I was going to find out.

I cleared my throat and began my inventory of the room as voices floated in from outside.

'No, give him time,' someone said. Davies, I think it was.

'But—' said a female – I presume the brunette.

'Just leave him be.' Definitely Davies.

Yes, piss off and let me do my job. Detective Edward Matthews is here. God, it felt good to be working a case again. And now it seemed Davies had finally learned my worth! He was even telling other cops to give me a wide berth so I could investigate. My, my, how things change.

Drug paraphernalia cluttered the dresser. A pipe, a needle and marijuana buds lay scattered next to a bottle of Calvin Klein cologne. I spied a can of Aqua Net hairspray, a ratty-looking tie, and a small doll dressed in a black-and-white jester costume. 'Jerry's' calling card.

'I'm not done with you yet,' I whispered.

Crumpled banknotes and loose coins adorned the other side of the dresser next to a male's brown leather wallet. I didn't have gloves, but it was clear the Jester hadn't taken the man's wallet out of his pants before killing him. No, the man on the bed took this out before he got loaded on drugs. I turned back and spied the arms of the dead man. Just as I suspected. Needle marks.

'Another junkie,' I muttered before grabbing the wallet and flipping it open.

My back stiffened as my lungs ceased working, brain bobbing like a buoy up and down on ocean waves. There, right in front of my face, was a picture in the plastic display pocket that I recognised as a Christmas photo given to me in 1982. A family picture of Heath, Lorraine and Aaron – a photo they'd placed inside our Christmas card.

I dropped the wallet and it hit the carpet with a soft thud as I turned back to the bed. The fog dissipated and rays of sun poked through the hazy picture.

'Heath?' I whispered, eyebrows raised.

He smiled back.

I cracked a grin as hot tears rained down my face. 'You're pulling my leg, aren't you?' I chuckled. Yes, yes, I could see the funny side of it. My son playing a prank on his old man.

Actually, that *was* quite funny, so I laughed hard enough that an endless stream of tears ran down my face.

Reaching the bed, I nudged his shoulder. 'Where'd you get your sense of humour from?'

The door burst open. Davies held the knob, his eye still red. He looked from me to my boy. 'Eddy?' he whispered, staring at me.

I wiped my eyes. 'It's okay, Davies.' I waved a dismissive hand before laughing again. 'My son ... You can call it off – my son likes to prank. Look!' I pointed to the wall with the blood-red writing. *You lose.* It was dry now, but it'd dripped down the peeling yellow wallpaper at the time it was written.

'There's your first clue! He played a prank; he's always wanted to run his own joke shop – Heath's Crack-Up!' I resumed laughing as more officers joined Davies at the doorframe, O'Brien being one of them, the corners of his lips as white as bone, his unblinking eyes on Heath.

'C'mon now, son, time to quit fooling your dad!' I playfully shoved Heath's shoulder, his big, goofy grin never wavering.

People wheeze-gasped as I gave Heath a little tap-a-roo.

Davies and O'Brien walked into the room as slowly as a lioness stalking a gazelle.

'Eddy,' O'Brien whispered, his arms outstretched. 'Eddy, it's me.'

I looked up and laughed, slapping my knee. 'O'Brien, you look like you're gonna cry! C'mon, fellas, don't go too harsh on him. It's just a prank.'

Davies walked around the left of me, and O'Brien on the right, both of them with arms outstretched, taking one step at a time, moving in a pincer attack.

'You're going to need to come out now, Eddy,' Davies whispered.

'Why? I'm just having a word with Heath.'

O'Brien looked at Davies, his nostrils flaring.

'Eddy, listen,' Davies whispered, enunciating every word. 'You need to leave this room *now*.'

I looked between the two of them; they always took things too seriously.

'Fine. I understand. But don't worry about the mess; Heath will clean it up – won't you?'

I glanced at the bed, and my boy grinned back.

Davies reached me before touching my shoulder. 'Come out now, mate.'

I was thankful I wasn't in too much trouble. God, I would have felt bad if O'Brien had lost his paid vacation time because of me. Janice would never forgive me, either.

'There's a good man ...' Davies whispered as I moved with him. O'Brien's face was as pale as cream – he could do with a good night's rest, poor bugger.

'Easy does it now,' Davies whispered as we began walking, stepping over the pile of spew. I turned to look over my shoulder at Heath, expecting him to stop this charade.

'Call me when you can, son!'

O'Brien snapped his head up to look at me.

'What?'

He shook his head, lowering it.

Leaning towards O'Brien's ear, I whispered, 'You look like you're about to cry.' I turned to Davies. 'You're not going to put him on suspension because of this, are ya?'

'No,' Davies whispered as he and O'Brien ushered me out of the bedroom. Other officers lined the hallway with startled expressions, staring at me like I was the fox in their chicken coop. Jeez, what a bunch of loonies in this department ...

'See? Told ya,' I said to O'Brien, who kept his head low as we headed towards the front door.

'We're, ah, going to take you to the hospital now,' O'Brien said.

'Why? I'm not hurt.'

His jaw clenched as he cleared his throat. 'We just, ah, need to make sure you're okay.'

'Oh, because of the physical between me and Davies – hey, sorry about your eye, Nathan.'

Another police car rocked up out the front. More residents had joined the rest to spy on the excitement. Lowlifes!

Two male police officers trampled across the yard, straight towards us.

'Edward Matthews?' one of them asked, hand on the butt of his gun. He was an odd-looking man; a weird face that didn't go away once you closed your eyes: severe black eyebrows, protruding Neanderthal brow ridge.

'Who wants to know?' Davies said, still supporting my lower back.

The other guy, a budget version of Mickey Rourke, took out a set of steel handcuffs. 'You're under arrest on suspicion of murder.'

O'Brien's eyes widened. '*What*?!'

'Turn around now,' Mickey Rourke said, as Davies and O'Brien let go of me.

'I demand to know what this is about!' Davies said.

Mickey Rourke shot him a stern look. 'We're bringing him in for the murder of Martin Kopek.'

'*Who?*' O'Brien said, deep frown lines embedded across his forehead.

Cold handcuffs slipped onto my wrists with a sickening metallic *click*.

'Let's go,' the officer said, turning me around, the knocked-for-six expression on O'Brien's frozen face was unmistakable.

'Is it true?' O'Brien whispered, walking alongside me. 'Is that why you have blood on your shirt? Did you kill a bloke called Martin?'

I leaned over as the two officers led me towards their cruiser, bubble lights brightening our faces with blues and reds. I shook my head and tsked. 'No, his name is not *really* Martin. It's Robert. Robert Jerkewitz.'

CHAPTER FIFTY-NINE

I HAD BEEN present when we first welcomed Heath into the world, and I was there when we sent him out of it.

There are parts of his funeral I have forgotten. Some moments are a blur – like a dream you only vaguely remember once you wake up. I didn't have any input into the funeral: Ava, Lorraine and Hayley organised it. I was grateful I could attend, but O'Brien and Davies had pulled the strings. Ha! Davies. Didn't he eventually warm to me. It only took the murder of my son for it to happen.

They flanked me on either side during the entire service; that was part of my day-release conditions. I could not be unescorted. They had allowed me out to attend the funeral, but not the wake. Apparently, Ava tried to object to me being there at all. I told myself it wasn't because she blamed me for his death. No, it was because good old Bill was right beside her. I saw him and her together for the first time as I rocked up to the Pinegrove Memorial Park in Minchinbury a few days after Christmas.

If it hadn't been the day of a funeral, one would say it was a glorious summer day. The kind of day where you wake up and feel inspired to make good on what Mother Nature has provided. Of course, I hadn't seen the sun until I walked out of the asylum. My home was now a padded cell. My clothing was no longer the suits I used to wear; it was standard issue white clothing.

O'Brien organised to bring a suit from my house. He held back on telling me what Ava was saying about me, and how she was handling it.

I believe I only accepted it myself a few days later. When I'd been taken in for another round of questioning with a psychiatrist. In my mind, I'd blocked it all out. I realise that now. I realise I'd blacked out in Timothy Sharpe's bedroom.

Everything was explained to me – that I'd snapped; I'd had a mental breakdown. But I am fine now. Truly. Everything is fine. I mean, sure, I still feel anger towards Ava. She brought her new lover to our son's funeral. I wanted to say something to them both, but O'Brien and Davies stood either side of me, holding my elbows as we made our way towards the North Chapel, where a congregation had gathered outside the doors.

There were many people I knew. Many people looking at me with pitiful eyes. I didn't want that; I didn't need it. I heard someone remark, 'Jeez, he's holding up well, considering …'

And I was. I had been. But then again, they didn't know I was pumped full of drugs. Full of Valium and other assorted goodie gumdrops to keep me from self-harming again. I'd tried. Once I understood the gravity of what had happened; once my psychiatrist smashed the walls down and I saw the crime scene photos of my son on the bed, I turned into the monster all men secretly fear lurks within us.

Something took over me as I wrapped a bedsheet around my neck, the same as something took over me in Timothy Sharpe's bedroom when I was no longer a father, but a homicide detective looking at another corpse.

I'd spotted Ava and Bill as I walked towards the chapel. No-one dared approach me. Some onlookers' jaws unhinged when they saw me; I suppose my hair wasn't looking too good, and the prescribed drugs disguised what *used* to be my face and eyes. How could I be the same man?

'Are you feeling okay?' O'Brien whispered as we both looked at Ava. She sobbed into Bill's chest. She only glanced my way when someone else – her goddaughter – approached her.

Ava lifted her head, and that's when her eyes narrowed in on mine. Oh, if looks could kill, I'd be free from this world three times over. She'd wiped her eyes with her handkerchief and then hugged her goddaughter in a tearful embrace.

A dirge played on the church piano inside the chapel as people wept. I'd spotted Hayley and David, who held Lucy. Gosh, my little girl looked pretty in that black dress.

They, too, spotted me, but turned away.

I stood there, peering around like *I* was the outsider. I had the sense that people did not want me there – at my own son's funeral. I wanted to lash out at this one woman who looked at me like I was a criminal. No, I wasn't. I hadn't done anything wrong. They'll see, once this all clears up, I said to myself, walking in behind everyone to take a seat in the back pew with Davies and O'Brien.

My son's coffin lay before the altar, and I shook my head as the priest approached the pulpit.

O'Brien turned to me, bending to my ear. 'What?'

'They'll see. They'll all see soon enough.'

After the procession finished, we gathered on a grassy hill, staring at a six-foot-deep hole in the ground. I told O'Brien and Davies I was going to stand beside the coffin, no matter what. They warned me to stay back, but then I warned *them*. In the end, the look in my eyes must have convinced them, as I demanded to pay my proper respects to my son.

So, there we were, directly opposite Ava and Bill, Hayley and David, and

Lorraine and her son, Aaron. Lorraine's father held her arms to keep her upright. She wailed, high-pitched, for most of it.

Ava glared at me across the pit. Bill avoided my eyes as much as humanly possible, but he still kept an arm around my wife's waist. Murderous impulses ran through my mind at what I would like to do to him.

Weak as piss he was, as soft as fucking butter – and my wife chose him over me? Ava stated they hadn't slept together, and by the look of him, I believed it to be true. He appeared as if you'd have to stuff a fucking rebar up his *schlong* just for him to get hard. Soft cock is what he was.

Just as I thought about what it would feel like to take Bill's life away with my bare hands, Heath's coffin was lowered and more sobs rang out. Ava fell into Bill's body and he held her upright. At that, O'Brien held me tighter, too, as if pre-empting I was about to jump across the divide and use the shovel to hack Bill's head off.

Red roses were thrown in as the shiny brown coffin lowered to the tune of 'Amazing Grace'.

I was allowed to throw one rose in, too, and I appreciated the fact Davies and O'Brien did as well. While this happened, people gave me a wide berth, like they were fearful I'd stab them with the priest's cross, which hung around his wrinkly neck.

As people ambled away, sobbing and sniffling, I stood there, staring at the open pit. Thinking of my son, unable to cry or feel anything but anger, really. And what a slap in the face it was for Ava to be so callous towards me. She was right to be fearful of me. If I were her, I'd be scared too. When a man has nothing left to lose, as well as nothing else to gain, he is capable of anything.

I didn't see Ava walk up to me from behind, as I was in my own little world as we strolled away, flanked by the men either side of me.

'Eddy,' O'Brien whispered, tugging my arm.

I turned to the left to see Ava standing there alone, trembling, tears streaking her face as she held a hanky to her blotchy nose. Her eyes so ablaze with physical pain, her expression alone made my anger dissipate.

'I will *never* forgive you,' she whispered, slapping me so hard I saw white pinpricks of light.

A few remaining guests gasped and some hurried away, but I clenched my jaw and watched her rush to the open arms of Bill.

And that was the last time I ever saw my family.

CHAPTER SIXTY

TODAY IS TUESDAY, 4th February 1986, and I have just received the newspaper. Staring back at me on the front page is one of the most beautiful women I have ever beheld. A nurse found murdered in a paddock out at Reen Road in Prospect. Lovely dark curls, a dazzling smile to crack even the Queen's Guards and make them blush.

Raped. Sodomised. Tortured to the point of near decapitation.

Anita Cobby.

Anger flares in the pit of my stomach as I read what she was subjected to. She was only twenty-six years old. Married. A woman spending her life taking care of others, and this was her fate.

Wrong place, wrong time. What a tragic waste of a beautiful soul. I close my eyes and think of Abigail. But of course, she watches over me.

After placing today's paper on my bed, I glance about the walls, trying to spot where I can make room for this new article. Since my time here at the institution, I have adorned the walls, mostly with newspaper clippings about various crimes, but also with pictures I draw in crayon of my sweet Abbie. She will always look down over me, and it makes this place seem almost bearable.

Ah, who am I kidding? It's not so bad here. I don't need a big fancy desk to work. No, this bed inside my room will do me fine. At least light filters through the window, and I no longer have to wear a straitjacket. Of course, sometimes I look at that window, expecting Bogart's nose to press against it. God, I miss my handsome boy; I hope Jeremy's parents are taking good care of him.

My doctor says he feels I am making improvement, and I feel that way, too. I have been saying so since the day they transferred me here after my son's funeral. Gosh, that was a while ago now. Every damn day, I think about Heath. I think about how he lied to me and reverted to drugs after taking my money. I think about him shooting up in Timothy Sharpe's place while Tim was away visiting his brother, about how Heath must have felt, opening the door and seeing 'Jerry' standing there. He wouldn't have known that his life was mere moments from ending. He should never have gone to the Christmas dinner; he should never have had his fortune read.

'Jerry' used an alias, I was told, when he booked a marquee at the hall. He had been hiding in plain sight, and no-one to this day knows his name. Incidentally, O'Brien told me Heath's tarot card had been The Magician, and if I've got my facts right, the upside down Magician represents a trickster. A manipulator. What you see is *not* what you get – it's all show. Magicians are also known for feeling torn between two paths. Sounds familiar, doesn't it? Ah yes, I think of Heath's follies often.

But I think of Ava, too. And Hayley and little Lucy. Do they ever think of me? It doesn't feel like it; I have no visitors anymore. My doctor forbade Jeremy and O'Brien after it was determined it wasn't helping my emotional state of mind. I'm damn lucky they let me have the newspaper at all!

I saw Davies sporadically, but only in the beginning, while they were still working on the case. There have been no arrests, but the killings have stopped.

'Jerry' told me he was going to commit the perfect crime. And it seems he wasn't wrong. Why did Jerry the Jester pick me? No idea. This was a challenge for him – and he won. I lost. And not just this fool's game, either.

Do you know what that feels like? To work damn hard, only to have no result? They are *idiots*, though! They *need* me to work the case. But they won't fill me in on anything else, except to say they haven't found him. At first I thought they were lying to me; after all, I gave them everything they needed to find the bastard, but the newspapers corroborate their story. Still no arrests in the case of Jerry the Jester – known to the public as the Prop Master.

God, that burns me. YOU LOSE, he wrote on the wall in my own son's blood. Those words above Heath's body gnaws away at my stomach.

But then I think about the other detectives before me, and personally, I think I am taking it remarkably well. Mental breakdown (so they say) and murder (of a child rapist) aside, I really do. I am not the only one who was outsmarted by 'Jerry', and there is comfort in that.

I think of Inspector Frederick Abberline, who worked on the Jack the Ripper case back in 1888. What would it have been like for poor old Fred to lie on his deathbed, never knowing Jack's identity? Did the stress contribute to his demise?

What about Eliot Ness and his mysterious man, the Cleveland Torso Murderer? Old Ness even had two torsos left outside his window, for Christ's sake. Talk about taunting. They never found the guy, of course. No, he probably lived to a ripe old age, knowing he'd outsmarted one of the finest men to step foot in Chicago. They say it hung over Ness's head for the rest of his life, too – his perp. The man who personally addressed him, antagonising him in every way possible. How could we not go a little crazy? So don't blame me. There are lunatics all over the place.

'Case in point,' I murmur, tapping the newspaper over Anita's picture.

I close my eyes and breathe deeply through my nostrils, the smell of chicken and vegetable stew wafts down the linoleum corridors, seeping under my locked door. The food isn't too bad here. Nothing like Ava's, but better than shit on toast. I am grateful I don't have to cook or clean, anyway. It gives me more time to do what I crave: to focus on my sole passion.

'Lunch is almost ready,' Abigail whispers. I smile and glance up to the wall.

'Yes, sweetheart, then we can work on this new case together.' I hold up the newspaper.

'She's pretty,' Abigail says.

'Yes. But food first, then we can brainstorm, all right?'

'Okay, Eddy. I love you!'

'And I love you, too, Abbie.' I begin tearing out the column dedicated to the nurse, glancing to my walls to see where I can stick it up. They won't let me have scissors or knives in here, see?

And you want to know something? Even if I do feel isolated and alone, it doesn't matter, anyway. Because I know one day the truth will come out, and I'll be as free as those birds who fly by my window. Oh sure, they can tell me all they like that I killed Martin Kopek. But I know it was Robert, and I avenged Abbie's death; they were too damn thick to see it for themselves! Oh, sure they tried to convince me they had the DNA to prove it was Martin, but that forensic crap is a new thing they developed over in America – trying to pass it off as 'science'. There are always flaws. I *know* it was him. Even as I looked at photos of him and his wife, and then photos of the crime scene during the trial, I knew. But it was one thing to *know* something, and something else altogether to *prove* what you know.

O'Brien came to pay me a visit one day and told me he'd rechecked Robert's alibi during the time Abigail went missing. Tried to tell me it had been airtight with witnesses at the conference or some bullshit.

They are plain dumb! Rosie Weatherstone wouldn't lie to me – Abigail told her to tell me. Spiritualism is real. I believe that now. But my lawyers told me to plead not guilty on the grounds of insanity. They had all sorts of quacks and fancy doctors come in and speak on my behalf – something about mental breakdown, completely snapped, blah-blah-fucking-blah. I knew it was just part of the protocol. It was all part of the master plan.

And that's why I am here, but you know what? I am glad I'm in an institution instead of an actual prison. Now I have all the time in the world to myself, and I don't have to shit in the same room as another bloke. How great is that?

I stop tearing the newspaper as an ungodly scream emanates from somewhere outside my room. Sometimes we have to put up with that nonsense – men screaming out or laughing hysterically throughout the night. But I shake my head and go back to tearing alongside Anita's photo.

I am no longer a burden to anyone. I do not have to be annoyed into anything – like going to Aruba, for fuck's sake. Christ, I can't believe Ava sometimes. *Aruba?* Why should I go anywhere when I have lots of work to do? So much work as long as people keep murdering. Because that's what I am, and always will be: a homicide detective. And now I can work on cases without any outsiders telling me what to do.

That's why I wait. I wait inside this room with Abbie for company, and we'll both wait, however long, for the truth to emerge. And it will. We will catch the one who outsmarted me. It will all come to light and then I'll be free again. The truth will set me free, and when it does, Tom will *finally* catch his Jerry—

A letter slips under my door, followed by a knock. 'Letter for ya, Eddy!' a male says before shuffling off.

Frowning, I drop the paper and retrieve the envelope. The wheels of the lunch trolley jangle as I stare at the same sinister handwriting written in a Sharpie. My pulse quickens, my lower jaw unhinges as I stumble backwards on the bed, which squeals as my weight crashes down. I flip over the envelope and rip the top open, yanking out the folded piece of paper and bring it towards my failing eyes.

Dearest Eddy,

How's life on the inside treating you? I'm sorry it's been a while, old chap, but I've relocated. Despite starting a new chapter of my life, I cannot help but think of you — wondering how far your mind has gone. Have you worked it out yet? Do you know why this happened? Considering I am a gentleman, let me give you peace of mind — it's the least I can do.

That the victims all had a shady past was irrelevant. But it sure made me tingle with glee over the fact. I met them under a disguise at an event, and subsequently stalked them for months before I made my move — no, let's call it a Blitzkrieg, shall we? We all have a past, isn't it so? None so as illuminating as yours. When I first heard about you, I had to test the theory of who the better man was; who was more deserving of a wonderful life filled with love — surrounded by children and a wife who cooks and cleans and caters to your every need. I never knew such love; the mention of my wife in a previous letter was a red herring, old chap. Once I delved deeper into the history of Eddy 'Macintosh' Matthews, the wheels were already in motion to test this theory of mine. You did not deserve the life you were given. You were selfish and too arrogant for your own good.

Still to this day no-one knows my true identity; I did not have a helping hand, nor have I confessed to anyone what I did during the summer of '84. But with the precautions I have taken, I dare say I shall live out my life as a happy fellow who proved who the better man — the more deserving man — truly was. Sincerely, I had fun with you while it lasted. I often wonder what you think about with the abundance of time on your hands. The thought of never contacting you again crossed my mind, but alas, I could not help myself. You may not believe me, but in some ways I am fond of you — you gifted me with the very things I'd always dreamed of. I wanted to help clear up those burning questions that no doubt linger in your damaged mind. How much medication do they have you on? Too much to ever be taken seriously again, I'd imagine. Incidentally, I am sorry about Heath — call it collateral damage, dear old chap. No matter. You still have <u>life</u>, and now I have finally begun to know the meaning of the word.

I shall close by saying, do take care of yourself. Ta-ta, old boy, this shall be my last letter, so keep it safe and read it on those lonely nights.

Fondest regards,

Jerry.

P.S. We simply <u>adore</u> Aruba.

ACKNOWLEDGEMENTS

It was always my intention to write a story in which the detective 'failed'. Call me a pessimist, but it is my obsession with Jack the Ripper that led me down this dark and twisted path. The great lure of a murder mystery is to piece together the puzzle ourselves, right? To come up with our own hypotheses and perhaps swap theories around – or in my case, watch documentary after documentary with a pen, a notepad and a bag of chocolate chip bikkies beside me. But I cannot help feeling sorry for the detectives – not just in the Ripper case – but for those in all unsolved/cold cases. I know how I feel in my heart when I want answers that aren't meant to be divulged. Enter: *Fool's Game*. So as much as some readers might be disappointed that not everything is wrapped up in a neat bow, I assure you this was all premeditated – and hey, if you think this is bad, originally I had it that poor Eddy didn't find out who the killer was at all. The reason? I wanted to convey how it would feel to invest time and energy into something and not see the outcome. However, I settled for leaving ropes dangling, allowing you to choose what you will regarding Bill and Ava – like those *Goosebumps: choose your own adventure* books – but isn't that part of the fun? Deducing your own conclusions, with no-one there to tell you you're wrong?

Some say writing a book gets easier, but I am still unsure. What I am certain of, is that writing is not a solo journey, and for that I have a list of folks I'd love to gush over:

First, Enchanted Ink over in the US for making me rethink my ending about leaving it up (as in *way* up) in the air. I'd certainly like to work with your manuscript critique team again. Thank you!

Second, a huge shout-out to my long-time editor, Sally Asnicar of Full Proofreading Services. Sally, I am indebted to you for everything you have done for me thus far, and I cannot wait to collaborate on our next project – yes, check your inbox for book #4.

Third, to my stalwart friends who are always there for me whenever I need advice – especially about IT and how the heck I get my Wi-Fi to work again. You guys are my everything.

Fourth, to Mum. What can I say? You are undoubtedly the best. I love you dearly.

Last, although certainly not least, my late father. Probably the hardest words I'll ever have to write. Edward Raymond May was somewhat the inspiration for my protagonist – not all aspects, yet definitely some. I won't go in-depth about the devastating effects of losing my father last year, but that I based a somewhat heroic character around him speaks of itself. I'll never know another man like my father, and all I can say is I hope every day that I make him as proud as he made me. My life will never be quite as bright without him in it.

Dad, it really was all for you.

Stephanie Louise May is an award-winning international actress-turned-author. After spending years in the acting business, she has turned some of her focus and energy to entertaining people through writing. Stephanie has written novels in genres ranging from romance to horror, and is currently working on a cookbook. Her pastimes include exploring rural Australia, reading Stephen King novels, and cooking Italian or Mexican cuisine while crooning to hits from the '60s and '70s. To keep up to date with her journey, please visit www.stephaniemayofficial.com

 @stephaniemay14

 stephanielouisemay

 stephaniemay_90

 stephanie_may_author